Joyce Mandeville was bo
worked as an interior de
Sussex with her husband a

Also by Joyce Mandeville

CAREFUL MISTAKES

A
TWIST
OF LIGHT

Joyce Mandeville

WARNER BOOKS

A *Warner* Book

First published in Great Britain in 1997
by Little, Brown and Company
Published by Warner Books in 1998

Copyright © Joyce Mandeville 1997

The moral right of the author has been asserted.

A CIP catalogue for this book
is available from the British Library.

ISBN 0 7515 1941 3

Typeset by M Rules in Ehrhardt
Printed and bound in Great Britain by
Clays Ltd, St Ives plc

Warner Books
A Division of
Little, Brown and Company (UK)
Brettenham House
Lancaster Place
London WC2E 7EN

To the husband of my youth,
John Mandeville, who is still the husband
of my heart in the middle years.

To my daughter, Amy Mandeville,
who has taught me to be a mother
and reminds me every day of what it is to be a friend.

ACKNOWLEDGEMENTS

With special thanks to the following:

Imogen Taylor, my wonderful editor at Little, Brown, whose advice and guidance have been invaluable;

Rebecca Kerby, for her careful and insightful reading of the manuscript;

Peta Linley-Munro, for her wisdom, time, and her red pencil;

Barbara Challstrom Van Rozeboom, my beloved sister, who taught me how to fight like a girl;

And Benjamin Mandeville, my ravishing boy, whose appetites, attitudes, and bike tyres force me into reality every afternoon.

PROLOGUE

The new mother moved the sacking away from the tiny red face, marvelling at the perfect mouth and the arc of dark eyebrows of the child she cradled. 'Did you ever see anything so pretty?' She spoke to no one in particular, but addressed her question to the group of women huddled inside the hut. Fashioned from cardboard and corrugated iron, the hut wasn't much bigger than the flatbed of the truck that had brought her here.

'Nothing's quite as pretty as a healthy baby.' The flat vowels marked the midwife's origins in Oklahoma as surely as her faded sunbonnet and her residence in the labour camp. Set up less than two months ago, it already bulged with over five hundred people who'd been blown out of their homes along with rich topsoil. Ida leaned over the midwife's shoulder as she tried to get a better look in the dim lamplight.

'My baby.' The girl's voice was as scratched as an old gramophone record. Harsh from a day and night of screaming and praying and yelling for Hoyt to come and find her. Thinking maybe he would finally be coming back to claim her and his child. If the stories were true the work was out there. California was a place a man could find a job if he just knew where to look.

'Ida, move back. I can't see if you keep blocking the light with your big butt.' Teeth gone, the midwife's nose almost met her chin as she grimaced at the other woman. She'd tired of Ida's hanging around like a vulture hours ago. 'Should have slowed down some by now.' She kneaded the palm of her hand into the spongy white belly of the girl, hoping to make the weary organ contract and stop bleeding. 'Somebody see if there's any ice around here.'

'Nearest ice would be down to the store. Should we send for some?' Ida watched the old woman shove more sacking under the girl. In the flickering light the blood seemed to spread like slick, black oil.

'Wont be time and probably wouldn't change things.' She moved her attention to the girl's face and lifted one of the half-lowered lids with a blood-streaked finger. 'See how her pupil is getting cloudy? This child is going to Jesus.'

Jesus came quickly, sweeping into the tent and carrying the bloodied girl with him to his Pentecostal heaven. The newborn was handed over to Ida, whose baby had been stillborn a week before. Gratefully she put the tiny mouth to her milk-engorged breast, relieved to feel the pressure abate as the infant suckled. She'd named her little blue boy Lee, after Robert E., before letting him be buried in the rich California dirt. 'Lorilee. I'll call you Lorilee so's I don't forget my real child.' She watched her other breast, now working as it should, as it pumped milk across Lorilee's foot.

Cotherstone, West Sussex, January 22nd

Dearest Mary,

Wonderful to talk to you yesterday, darling. I'm going to do the shop later today and I will be sure to buy your Marmite (gag). One thing that will always set me apart from the rest of you is my loathing of that glop. I rue the day your grandmother handed you your first piece of Marmite-slathered toast.

It sounds as though you're having a wonderful time. In spite of it being my home state, I'm afraid I never saw much of California. The aunts weren't great travellers and I never even saw San Francisco or Los Angeles until I was in my late teens. By the time you return in July you will be our resident expert on things 'Golden Stateish'.

As to your thoughts on taking a sentimental journey to my hometown, I'm really pretty neutral. There is nothing much to see and I'm afraid you'd be disappointed. My clan didn't leave much of a dent on the landscape. We simply passed through. Apart from that, Clifford doesn't have a thing to recommend itself. Local wags used to refer to it as the 'armpit of the West'.

One of the reasons (albeit minor) I married your father (instead of Prince Charles or Paul McCartney) is all the bits that surrounded him, all those things which give him roots. Things like the trunks at your gran's place, his going to the same school as his grandfather, his uncle's watch, even this house. I found it all terribly exotic and at the same time wonderfully reassuring. Rock solid, your father.

I know I've always been rather vague about my early days. To me they've become the junk at the bottom of the wardrobe. I think of those times as the things you aren't going to throw away, but you know you'll never use or even look at again. Now, having written that, I find myself taking a new look. I must tell you that some terrible things happened, but there were some wonderful things as well. Memory is a funny thing, it's so hard to know how much it can be trusted.

I'd better close now and get my day started. Daddy and Chaz send their love. Let me sift through my past a little more before I dish it up. I want to make sure I've truly separated fact from fiction.

Love and God bless

Mummy

PS See if you can find a few of those sachets of dried sourdough starters to send me. After all these years, I still maintain it's the best bread in the whole wide world. XXXOOO

CHAPTER ONE

Liz took the letter from her printer and reread it before putting the pages in an envelope. She glanced at her watch and ran down the stairs to put the letter in the slot before the postman was due. She knew she'd committed herself now and didn't want to give herself the out of not sending the letter.

'"Rather vague" – my shiny blue bottom! I've been "rather vague".' The small black dog wagged his tail enthusiastically at her words. He ran to the front hall and grabbed a leather lead from a hook by the door.

'What are you trying to tell me, Patch?' He circled the hall with the lead in his mouth. 'OK, we'll go for a walk. Maybe I'll be able to figure out how to make my mother sound like someone our girl wouldn't mind having for a grandmother.' She shrugged into her duffel coat and grabbed his lead. 'Come on, Patch.'

While the dog snuffled at the backside of an elderly poodle, Liz watched the water crashing against the shingle. The winds were high and a few flakes of snow scuttled through the cold air. She lifted her chin and squinted, trying to see France as she had the first time she'd stood on the beach. Of course France remained invisible, but the thought of that country always reminded her of her mother. Until she was almost thirty her mother told her daughters that she intended to die in Paris. Liz thought the woman came across this idea about the same time she fashioned herself from Lorilee Shook into Laura Sinclair. She had often wondered if the worst of the drinking had started after her mother turned thirty because by then she knew she'd end up dying less than ten miles from where she'd been born.

Clifford, California, July 1962

'See if she's breathing, Lizzy. I don't want to have to touch her.' Ellie turned her face away and ran her hands through her dark hair.

'I know she's dead, Ellie. Her colours are all gone.' The girl wrapped her thin arms across her chest and rocked slightly. She could feel the tears inside her brain, but didn't want them to come out, not yet. She smelled vomit and recognized the scent of the heavy fortified wine her mother loved. A sugar wasp, having already found its way through the torn window screen, sat on the collar of the body's stained bathrobe.

'I told you not to talk about that. Makes you sound even

crazier than you are.' The girl put her hand to her mouth and made a retching sound. 'I think I'm going to be sick.'

'It's not crazy and I know what I see.' Ever since Lizzy could remember she'd seen bands of colours bobbing and waving around people. Her mother was the only one who hadn't thought it was strange.

'What do you think we should do?'

'I guess we'd better go down the road and call somebody.' Months before, their mother had decided her limited funds were better spent on bottles of wine than telephone bills. There was a telephone booth in front of the corner store, about a quarter of a mile away. Typical of their mother, she'd decided they didn't need a phone about the same time she decided she didn't need to drive any more.

'I don't know who to call.' Shorter than her younger sister, Ellie's full figure and heavy eye make-up made her look like a tired twenty-year-old who'd just spent three days on a Greyhound bus. Fourteen years old, she had been the *de facto* head of the family for over six months. Their mother hadn't left the house since New Year's Day. 'Help me think of something, Lizzy. You're the one who's supposed to be the genius in the family.'

'Near genius.' Lizzy liked to be specific. She'd spent her twelve years seeing what happened when people weren't specific. She felt most of her mother's problems stemmed from lack of specificity. Her mother had always reminded her of the fuzzy stuff that flew out of milkweed pods. Never clear about what she really wanted or needed, she'd seemed content to let herself and her daughters be blown around by her changing circumstances and love of wine.

Lizzy had allowed her older sister to take over most of her mother's job, but they all knew Lizzy was better at making decisions, as well as possessing a flair for long-term planning. Their mother didn't seem to mind the shift in responsibility and Ellie had enjoyed the illusion of power and status. Lizzy thought of it as the brains and brawn solution to their problems.

'Near genius or near moron, more like it. You've got to help me figure something out. I don't know what to do.' The black eyeliner was already beginning to move down her cheeks. 'I don't know what to do.'

It looked as though Laura Sinclair had tried to get a glass of water in the bathroom to top off the three bottles of Thunderbird wine she had enjoyed for brunch. (Normally she would have had a bottle for breakfast and another bottle for lunch. Perhaps she'd been celebrating, or feeling especially flush since the cheque from the Welfare Department had arrived the day before.) Things had apparently gone wrong, as she had fallen on her back and choked on her own vomit.

'Let's cover her face. I don't think she would want us to look at her.' Lizzy knew she didn't want to look at that face any more. She could remember when her mother was the most beautiful woman in the world. She made Audrey Hepburn and Jackie Kennedy look like ugly old bags of bones. She knew this wasn't a nice thing to think about the First Lady, but their mother had been the most beautiful thing ever. The air around her seemed to sparkle with bright shafts of colour. It had only been in the last two or three years that all the wine and confusion had caught up with the beauty, bloating and smudging those fine features. Her bright, shimmering colours had faded to the dullness of a Polaroid snapshot left too long in the sun. Lizzy grabbed a ragged pink towel from the hook above the bathtub and placed it over her mother's face, careful not to touch her.

'This is your idea of a solution, cover her face? Why don't I feel this has helped?'

'Give me a break, Ellie. I'm thinking as fast as I can! You can't spring something like this on an impressionable child.' Lizzy needed to use the toilet. She'd noticed before that you needed to go the most when it was the least convenient.

She scratched the bridge of her nose, then slowly peeled a piece of sunburned skin off. She hated summers. Forced away from school for almost three months, Lizzy spent as much time as she could down at the river. Not only was it cooler than the little house, but down there she could pretend things were the way she knew they really should be. Down at the river she would spend the day swimming and writing stories about how she'd been tricked into the wrong life.

'Stop picking at your nose and think. Darn thing's going to fall off if you keep doing that.' Ellie gave her hand a light slap.

The younger girl ignored her sister's slap and worried another bit of skin on her nose. 'We bury her someplace, it doesn't matter where, and then we leave town. If we're all three of us gone nobody will think anything about it.' Lizzy had been wanting to leave town for some time. The only interesting place in the whole town was the library and even there she couldn't see the really good books because she was only twelve. 'If they know she's dead they'll put us in different foster homes and split us up.' That's the way it had happened to her friend Candy Johnson. Her dad was gone and her mother had been killed in an accident at the cannery last fall. All three kids had gone in different directions. Nobody would take all three. 'We're gonna have to take care of each other, El.' Lizzy glanced at her sister, knowing she'd have her work cut out. At fourteen, Ellie had already acquired a taste for boys and cigarettes.

'What do we do for money? We need to get the cheque and the commodities. What do we do about that? What happens when one of the Welfare people wants to talk to her?' Eleanor pointed at the body as though Lizzy wouldn't be able to figure out which 'her' she was referring to.

Since Laura had been fired from the Safeway, the family had been living on the cheque and the box. Lizzy had especially enjoyed the box stuffed with surplus commodities. She loved knowing, according to the Department of Agriculture, that the huge cans of peanut butter, the bags of powdered milk and the fat sacks of cornmeal met virtually all of her nutritional needs. Ellie hated it, of course. She hated being on welfare and she loathed coming home on the bus with the big box stamped

'USDA Commodities'. Lizzy knew someday she'd be an artist or a writer and that she was going to have to be poor, at least until she was really rich and famous. She figured she was just getting it out of the way before it mattered all that much.

'Let me think for a minute, will you? I can't think if you keep talking.' Lizzy glared at her sister, but knew Ellie's keeping quiet wasn't going to make much of a difference in her planning ability. She looked down at her mother, amazed at just how empty a dead body looked.

'Well, I'll tell you what we're going to do.' Ellie sniffed and wiped at her cheeks before smiling at her sister. 'We'll make money, the way people are supposed to. The way Mom did before she was so drunk all the time. Remember what the President said? "Ask not what your country can do for you, ask what you can do for your country." Well, we are going to take care of ourselves, for ourselves and for the country.' Lizzy watched her sister's spine straighten as she spoke the words. By the time she'd finished her little speech, Ellie was standing up tall and thrusting her round breasts out, as if Lizzy was a parade of soldiers going off to war and the bumps under her blouse were the last sweet things they were going to see for a long time.

'First thing we do, Lizzy, is get out of here. You're right about that, we have to get away from Clifford. We have the car. We can steal some gas from Mrs Kirby's and get as far as Nevada. We'll give ourselves new names and I can get a job there, easy.' By now Ellie seemed pretty sure they could do anything.

'You don't know how to drive and that car hasn't been started in over six months.' Her mother had parked the car at the back of the house and tossed the keys on the kitchen table the day she lost her job at the Safeway. Somebody had found a few empty bottles of Thunderbird wine in the ladies' toilet. The manager didn't have to look any further than Laura, with her hiccupping and her inability to balance her cash drawer, to figure out who the culprit was.

'It's an automatic, I only have to point it. I know it works because sometimes Steve drives it.'

Steve was Ellie's current boyfriend. He reminded Lizzy of a pimply wolf with his pinched face and gnarly teeth. He had black half-moons under his nails and stank of car parts and Clearasil. She didn't know how Ellie could stand those dirty hands all over the body parts she was so proud of. They'd met at one of those dances the Lions Club held every summer to show they cared about young people and what happened to them. Lizzy thought having a dance where girls could meet boys like Steve was a stupid way to show public spirit and concern for American youth.

'We still need money. We need money until we can make some.' Lizzy glanced down as she chewed thoughtfully on a cuticle. 'We also have to bury Mom. We'd better do it pretty fast because it's supposed to be over a hundred degrees today.' She remembered the time they'd left a package of meat in the Ford by mistake. The car still smelled like you were going by the county dump even when you were miles away from it.

'Right, right. OK, get something to wrap her in. Her bed-spread should do the trick.' Ellie looked at her Timex. 'We'll wrap her up, but we won't bury her until after dark.'

'Where are we going to bury her?' Lizzy was amazed that Ellie could plan this as though she was sorting out how to pay the light bill. Most mornings her sister couldn't figure out what to wear or what to eat for breakfast. Usually, if she had more than two things to think about, she couldn't decide whether to wind her butt or scratch her watch.

'Same place we steal the gas – Mrs Kirby's. There's bound to be some soft ground around the vines where she's been irrigat-ing.' Mrs Kirby lived by herself on a small farm, down the road from their house. The girls figured she was at least a thousand years old. She only had about twenty acres of grape vines, which she tended herself with the help of one of the seasonal crews that travelled up and down the Valley during the season.

The next crew wouldn't be needed until early September.

'And what are we going to do for money? We still need money.' As the family's near genius, Lizzy wasn't sure she could trust Ellie's plans. She didn't have any ideas herself, but felt duty-bound to keep a sarcastic tone in her voice. It wouldn't do either of them much good to mess with Lizzy's brains and brawn solution. Not now, not when they wouldn't even have the Welfare cheque or the sacks of cornmeal.

'We can get everything we need at Mrs Kirby's. One-stop shopping, just like the Quik-Stop. Between the money she gets from her grapes and Social Security, I bet she's loaded. Now shut up and get the bedspread.' Ellie glanced in the cracked mirror above the basin and wiped at the make-up smeared under her eyes. 'Look at me. With all this blubbering I look like a raccoon.'

'I don't believe I'm hearing this, Ellie.' Lizzy ignored the raccoon remark. Typical of her sister to go from discussing robbery to her smudged eye make-up. Ellie's mind wandered around like the Incredible Blob thing she'd seen at the movies once. Gulp, spit, gulp, spit; that was the way her mind worked, when it worked. Lizzy took a deep breath, then blew it out through her teeth. Just keeping Ellie's mind going in a straight line was like trying to dig a ditch with a teaspoon. 'What happened to working for money and President Kennedy?' She almost smiled, was actually pleased to have found some problem with her sister's plans. Not that she'd ever thought she could rely on Ellie's reasoning ability. Nobody who knew Steve would give Ellie high marks for smarts or objective thinking.

Stealing gas wasn't so bad. It was bad, but not so bad, because all the farms had a big tank or two around the back for the tractors and other equipment. Gas was cheap and nobody would notice or miss the few gallons a car would take. Burying Mom wasn't a problem either. It made a lot of sense. Funerals were really expensive and this way they could keep it private. Sort of exclusive. Their mother would have liked the idea of something exclusive. Probably only really, really rich or famous people had private funerals.

The money was different. Money was really stealing. Money wasn't like gas or funerals. Stealing money meant going to jail and living in disgrace, and probably going to Hell. Especially stealing from Jolena Kirby. She was a washed-in-the-blood Baptist. Lizzy figured she could send you to Hell just by pointing at you. Lizzy was firmly convinced about Hell because so much had been written about it. Nobody would waste time writing about a place that was made up. There were only a few books about places like Oz or Narnia, but millions about Hell. Lizzy imagined Hell would be like the USSR, only hotter, much hotter. It would be awful to have your hair catching on fire and knowing you weren't even protected by the US constitution or the FBI.

'Fine, Elizabeth Ann Sinclair. I'll do it all, and I will leave you here. I'll send you postcards from Las Vegas and you can show them to all your new friends at the foster home. I think with my training as a junior lettergirl it shouldn't be too hard to get a job as a dancer or something.' Ellie folded her arms under her breasts as though she was displaying her courage.

'But Mrs Kirby? She's an old, old lady. What if she sees us and calls the police? She knows who we are! What if we scare her to death?' She could see the old woman staring at her. Right now, at three in the afternoon, she was probably sitting in front of her Amana air-conditioner, sipping Lipton iced tea and knowing what they were planning.

'She lives alone and, little sister, she doesn't hear very well. She also doesn't keep a dog, which is pretty stupid if you ask me. As soon as we get a new house you'd better believe we are going to have a dog.' Ellie flipped her dark hair off her shoulder. 'Two girls living alone will need a dog for protection.'

'We can have a dog?' Laura had never let them have pets. Said it was trashy to have pets all over the place. Lizzy had tried to tell her about the Queen of England having those stubby-looking little dogs, but she didn't seem to hear. Laura, especially during the last few months, had exhibited the ability to hear only what she wanted to hear.

'We can have a dog and anything else we want. We can have a house where we are the bosses. Nobody can come in who we don't like. We can leave all the doors inside open, and no hairy old men are going to hang around because the dog will run them off if they even get on the sidewalk in front of our house. We'll take care of each other better than she ever did.'

Lizzy looked down. She had tried never to think about the men. Ugly, stinking men who visited their mother and sometimes said awful things, especially to Ellie. They always kept a chair wedged against their bedroom doorknob in case one of the hairy men got confused in the night. They always made sure the door was wedged tight, but they never talked about why. The men were like ghosts neither girl could quite admit to seeing. 'I just wish we didn't have to steal. It seems so wrong.'

'I wish we didn't have to either, but we do. We do it once, that's all.'

'Promise?'

'I promise, Liz.'

'Cross your heart and hope to die? Stick ten needles in your eye? Think about your answer, El, because I'm going to hold you to it.' Lizzy stared into her sister's eyes to gauge whether or not she was telling the truth. She decided she couldn't tell a thing by looking in her eyes so she moved her focus just above Ellie's head, staring until the bands of colour revealed themselves.

'Listen to me, Lizzy. Everything is different now, but it's going to be better. I promise.'

'I hope you're right, Ellie.' Lizzy hoped, but her sister's colours were in the wrong place and she didn't know if that was something she needed to worry about or not.

'What's that?' Ellie was straightening the bedspread over their mother's body. The bedspread was a white 'George Washington' one her mother had saved months to buy. When she bought it during a J.C. Penney White Sale for almost half-price she'd been as happy as a child on Christmas morning. She'd told her daughters it had a timeless style and would become a family heirloom. Lizzy thought Laura must have bought the bedspread about three years ago when she was so sure she was about to be made a senior cashier at the Safeway.

'A mason jar. I put Mom's name and life history on a piece of paper and stuck it in the jar. We put it in her hands and if she's ever dug up they'll know who she is, or was, and that she didn't die of foul play.' Lizzy was a little disappointed that she hadn't been able to think of a whole lot for the life history. It was mostly about how she'd been real pretty once before some lousy decisions, mostly about wine and men, caught up with her.

'Where did you ever get such a stupid idea?' Ellie kept arranging the George Washington bedspread around her mother as if she could make it look more like a family heirloom if she got it just right.

'*The Grapes of Wrath*. The ladies at the library thought I might like to read it. I went in there one day after that stuck-up Leslie Rawnsley had been calling me an Okie. Anyway, that's what they did in the book when an old lady died. They buried her with a mason jar that had her life history in it. I figured since Mom was born an Okie it would be kind of nice. A tradition.' Lizzy shrugged her shoulders, knowing it wasn't much as far as traditions go.

'I don't think our mother would have been pleased to be buried with an Okie tradition.' Laura usually said her folks were from Kansas, a place of origin more kindly regarded by most Californians than Oklahoma.

'Well, I guess the other option would be a Viking funeral, but that doesn't seem practical.'

'What's that?' Ellie tugged the makeshift shroud smooth over her mother's shoulder.

'The Vikings were warriors in Scandinavia about a thousand years ago.'

'I know that, Lizzy. I saw the movie, Kirk Douglas and Tony Curtis. You always make it sound like you're the only one who knows anything.'

'Then you should know the Vikings put their dead bodies in a burning boat and set it out to drift and burn away. That's if it was somebody important who they really liked. Sometimes if they didn't like someone they would just stake them out at low tide and let the crabs nibble on them until they drowned. Of course I was thinking about the burning boat for Mom. I think they used the crabs mostly when they wanted to get rid of Irish priests because those guys made Odin mad. Odin was their main god, but they had a whole bunch of gods just like the Greeks and Romans.'

She paused and took a deep breath, sensing she'd wandered from her original plan. 'Anyway, I got the Viking idea because I looked up "Sinclair" once and it was originally a Viking name. They ended up in Scotland, but they were Vikings. Since we don't live by the ocean, I thought the mason jar would be simpler.' She didn't mention reading that 'Sinclair' might have been French once and really been St Claire because she thought Ellie might get all excited about being French. She'd think it was kind of sexy and probably start saying 'ooh la la' all the time.

'That's a wonderful story, Lizzy. Have you heard the one about the tooth fairy?'

'What do you mean?' Lizzy was rethinking the idea of sending a flaming boat down the Kings River. There was a pretty wide stretch about a mile below where the kids usually went swimming and it wouldn't be that hard to steal a boat from the bait and tackle shop. The man who owned it was too busy smelling bad and looking stupid to even tie his little boats up most of the time.

'Our mother's name was not Sinclair. Her name was Shook,

Lorilee Shook. She changed her name to Laura Sinclair because she liked the sound of it.'

'Liar. It was her married name. Our father's name was Sinclair.' Lizzy wished she could run down to the river and throw herself into the cool shadows. Down at the river she wouldn't have to listen to Ellie go on and on. Ellie wouldn't follow her there because she couldn't swim and never wanted to even get wet because she hated to mess up her stupid hair.

'If she had a husband, where is he? Where's his family?'

'He died in Korea. You know that, Ellie. He didn't have any family, he was an orphan. The pictures and the marriage certificate burned in a fire when we were little. She told us all that about a million times.'

'If you say so. Give me that jar.' She peeled back the bedspread and placed the jar in her mother's slack fingers. 'Let's get her wrapped up again and put her in the car.'

'He died in Korea and his name was Sinclair.'

'Come on, Liz. Let's just get this over with.'

'Problem.' Anxious to get control of the situation, Lizzy threw the word out before she'd formulated the problem. She was pleased about the jar even though Ellie insisted on forgetting their family history. She was surprised she didn't feel worse about her mother, but she couldn't even remember the last time her mother had touched her. It almost seemed that Laura had pulled a bedspread over her face some time ago.

'What now, Lizzy?' Ellie turned and gave her sister her 'I'm going to kill you and this time I mean it' look.

'Three things. First thing is you better make sure that car starts before we put anything in it.' She felt a little bad about calling her mother an 'anything'. 'Second, it's four in the afternoon, and we can't bury her until after dark, which will be almost nine tonight. It's too hot to leave her sitting in the back seat. The third thing is dead bodies get really, really stiff. It's called rigor mortis. I don't know how fast it happens, but it happens.'

'What do you want me to do? We have to bury her. We can't very well leave her here. If they find her they'll come looking for us right away.' Ellie started waving her hands around as if she could hide behind them and nobody would notice a girl with big bosoms sitting next to a dead body holding a mason jar. 'They might even think we killed her and send us to jail.'

'Don't go stupid on me now, Eleanor. You've been doing just fine. What we need to do is take this step by step. First I want you to go make sure the car can start and check how much gas we've got. I'll wrap up Mom while you do that.'

'OK. I'll be right back.' Ellie scurried out the bathroom door, clearly pleased to be leaving, if only for a minute or two.

Lizzy knelt next to her mother and rolled the body on its side. She pushed the George Washington bedspread across the woman's back and gently rolled her on to her other side. She remembered watching the nurses rolling her mother in the hospital after the time she'd run her car into the ditch. Laura couldn't get out of bed for a week, but the nurses were able to move her all over the bed with just a little rolling. She finished and sat back on her heels.

'Remember the hospital, Mom? Everybody taking care of you and you just lapping it up? I think that's about the time you decided to let us take over and be the grown-ups. You switched things around so we had to do all the work and you could be a spoiled old baby. It's still going on, too. Even when you're dead we're still looking out for you.'

Cotherstone, West Sussex, January 26th

Dearest Mary,

We have a touch of snow today. Patch had a terrible time deciding whether or not he really needed to go out this morning. Finally your father kicked him out and gave him a lecture about soldiering through. Patch didn't seem awfully impressed as he demonstrated by ignoring your father as the poor man was reading the newspaper. Although your father tried to make up, Patch insisted on staring out of the window rather than assuming his usual station at your father's feet. I think he misses you. (Patch that is. I hope you realize that Daddy definitely misses you!) I keep finding him (Patch) sleeping on your bed.

Daddy leaves for Brussels today and will be gone a week or so. I thought about joining him, but decided it would be too complicated. Once Chaz is away for A levels I'll have lots of trips. I can't believe my youngest heads off next year. I'd like to stretch this mothering business out more, but you and your brother seem determined to grow up.

Yes, I am feeling all broody. Do you realize lots of women my age are still having babies? No, no, I'm not contemplating anything quite so dramatic or rash. My baby days are a thing of the past, but I am thinking about getting another dog to keep Patch company. With you and Chaz no longer available as playmates on any kind of regular basis I'm afraid he'll get awfully lonely. Of course, not only would a puppy keep him young, but it would satisfy my broodiness a little less radically than a change-of-life baby.

I'm very glad you're finding friends. I knew it wouldn't be a problem, but I know you were a little concerned. Americans are mad about an English accent and of course, you are such a delight, even without the accent. I can say that because I am completely objective about my children.

As promised, I've been sifting through the grey matter to give you an overview of the distaff side of your family tree. As you know, your grandmother was called Laura Sinclair, though I believe her real name was Lorilee Shook. I'm not even sure why I know about the Lorilee Shook business, but my sister, at least, was convinced this was her real name. As the oldest child I suppose she had some information I wasn't privy to when we were children.

I do know that she was born in a farm labour camp in Fresno County around 1935. Her mother was still in her teens and probably unmarried. My grandmother had left Oklahoma after poor farming practices had blown all the topsoil out of the state. I don't know who fathered the baby, or if she had any other family, but I do know she died in childbirth or shortly after. Her baby, my mother, was given to a woman who'd lost a baby. Apparently she was never allowed to forget that she was the cuckoo in the nest. She left this woman and her family when she was about fourteen or fifteen.

She always told us she had been married to a man, our father, who died in Korea during the war. I doubt this was true. If a soldier had died, leaving a wife and children, there would have been some sort of death benefits or pension. She once told me she'd never gotten around to applying for the benefits, but that seems terribly unlikely since we lived on public funds for the last year or so of her life. Even if she'd never gotten around to claiming benefits it seems likely that the Welfare Department would have done so to defray some of their costs. She also told us the marriage certificate, pictures and everything else had been lost in a fire, but neither Eleanor nor I remembered a fire.

I recall some very odd conversations with her. I remember telling her I saw little 'things', not bugs or animals, just little 'things' scurrying under leaves and in the weeds. I don't remember seeing them, I just remember telling her about them. She seemed to believe me and accepted it as normal. I also used to see bands of colours around people's heads and bodies. I know it sounds bizarre, but I remember it so vividly. I could, or at least I thought I could, tell quite a bit about people this way. My mother assured me she had been able to do the same thing until she was about sixteen. Interestingly enough, sixteen was about the age my 'colours' stopped.

I know this sounds terribly 'New Age' and Stonehenge-on-Midsummer's-Eve-ish, but it's true. I haven't seen anything odd since I was about sixteen or seventeen, by the way. I questioned you, gently of course, when you were small, and this little 'trick of the light' seems to have passed over you. I do know the Okies were southerners, mostly of Celtic and English stock, who had been displaced by the American Civil War. That region was known to have very strong folk traditions which included ghosts, mysterious lights, love charms, and all that rot. Odd, don't you think? Well, there are more things in heaven and hell and all that.

My mother was an alcoholic. I have little snips of memory in which she was beautiful. She had dark hair and eyes and long, slim hands. She was a little above average in height, slim, but curvy at the same time. Sadly, you're going to have to take my word on this since I have no pictures of her. My sister looked a little like her, but I must take after my mysterious father.

She never left the house the last six or seven months of her life. Ellie and I, I realize now, were typical children of an alcoholic. We covered for her and shielded her as much as we could. Even the social worker who called every few weeks had no idea how bad things really were. We were fairly expert liars in those days.

Even cheap wine can be expensive if you drink enough or if you're poor enough. Men would bring my mother wine. Ghastly fortified stuff made especially for drunks. It cost less than a dollar a bottle and it worked fast. If the men brought wine they got to stay around for a little while. I suppose you'd have to call it prostitution.

One day she passed out in the bathroom and suffocated on her own vomit, or so I thought at the time. It's very strange, but I don't remember being devastated by her death. I was afraid of what might happen to us, but I wasn't really sorry she was dead. In so many ways she'd been dead to me for months. Of course, children perceive things in a different way. At the age of twelve I'm sure I didn't fully comprehend how her death was going to affect us. I think for both of us our survival instincts went into full gear. I suppose we didn't have the luxury of grief just then.

Darling, I'm not going to send this letter today. I'm going to leave it in my drawer and read it tomorrow. I'm not sure I should be telling you all this. I'm also not sure I should be hiding it any longer.

Even on a beautiful snowy morning in Sussex I can still smell a summer in the Valley. It would get so hot the road shimmered. It was over a hundred degrees almost every day between May and October. Fruit of all kinds grew there, no doubt it still does. Clifford had several processing plants where half the people worked during the harvest season. The other half worked in the fields or ran the few little businesses in town. During the summer the air was thick with the sugary smell of fruit and the rotted smell of the processor's by-products. Underlying all was a dry dust smell. I've never smelled dust quite like that of the Valley. If you go there I think you'll smell what I mean.

I love you and I miss you. Write soon and remember to lock your doors. Never forget there are over two hundred million unregistered guns in that country! You are not in England. (Write this on the back of your hand and refer to it often.) Yes, I know you're a big girl, and yes, I'm done nagging.

Love and God bless

Mummy

CHAPTER TWO

Liz chewed on her lower lip as she reread the letter she'd just written. She'd left the computer on in case she decided to delete most of what she'd written about her mother. She was reaching for the thesaurus to find a different word for 'prostitution' when the phone rang.

'Morning.' She settled the book on her lap and let her fingers play along the half-moon indentations denoting various sections.

'Good morning, Liz. How are you doing with all this snow?' Her mother-in-law always began her calls with comments about the weather. Liz thought the woman might ask if it felt like rain in the middle of an atomic blast.

'I'm doing fine with the snow, India, but we've only got a light dusting. How much do you have this morning?' She smiled and looked out of the window towards her mother-in-law's house, which was about two hundred yards down the lane.

'I have more than a dusting, but I do live in the colder part of town, as you know. I don't suppose you had the good sense to go to Sainsbury's yesterday, did you?'

'No, I haven't been for three or four days. I'll probably go this morning and I'd love to have some company if you want to come along.' Liz smiled, knowing the older woman refused to drive in anything wetter than light dew. Since she lived on the south coast of England she rarely drove and was something of an expert at finding lifts with various friends and relatives.

'I want to go early, around nine, shall we say?'

'That would be fine for me. I can pick you up in about fifteen minutes. I'm just reading a letter I wrote to Mary this morning.' She put the thesaurus aside without opening it. If she sent the letter the word would stay. If it had to be done, 'prostitution' would be better than '*demi-monde*' or 'soiled dove'.

'Good. I need some stamps, so when you take that to the post office we can get my stamps at the same time.'

'We can stop at the post office, but I'm not going to mail this until tomorrow. I've been writing to Mary about my mother and I want to sit on it for a day or so before I send it to her.' She tried to make it sound like light domestic chatter, but knew the older woman would take it as the confession it was.

'Is what you wrote the truth?' India's voice took on the same tone she used with shop girls who offered poor goods or sloppy service.

'Of course it is.'

'Then send it, Liz. You have nothing to be ashamed of, and neither do your children.'

'India, I just don't want to upset her. I'm not at all sure it's wise to dump all this on her when she's so far away.'

'Give the girl a little credit, Liz. After all, she's my grand-daughter, isn't she?'

'She certainly is, India.' India Randall had a very high opinion of her progeny.

'End of discussion as far as I'm concerned. She will see it as an interesting piece of her family history. She knows it really isn't about her, or even you, for that matter. You'll post the letter this morning and then I'll buy you a lovely cup of cappuccino and you can have a good cry about things.'

'Who said I wanted to have a good cry?' She closed her eyes and realized it was exactly what she wanted to do. She wanted to talk about Laura Sinclair and cry because there was so little to say about the woman.

'I'll be waiting in fifteen minutes. Don't bother to come to the door, just honk.'

'Thanks, India.'

'You'd better get off the phone or you'll be late, and I hate to get to the shop later than nine.'

'See you in a few.' After hanging up the phone she put the letter in an envelope and addressed it to Mary.

Clifford, California, July 1962

'I got it started, Lizzy.' Ellie stood at the bathroom door, pink with the heat and her success.

'Good. How much gas do we have?'

'Enough to get us to Mrs Kirby's.'

'How much gas do we have, Ellie? I want to know what the gauge says.' Lizzy knew that Ellie, like their mother, had a problem being specific. She suspected her sister liked to keep things vague because it gave her less to remember.

'Maybe a quarter of a tank.' Ellie shrugged her shoulders.

'Good. You're stronger, so you take her shoulders. I'll take her feet.' Lizzy leaned over her mother's legs.

'I thought we were waiting until dark to bury her. Mrs Kirby might see us if we do it during the day. She's always walking around checking on things.' Ellie put her hand to her mouth and coughed. 'It smells awful in here.'

'Were taking her down to the river. We'll bury her down there and come back here to pack our things up. We can go to Mrs Kirby's after dark.'

'I don't like the idea of doing this during the day.' Ellie looked as if she was going to start waving those hands again.

'I don't like the idea of doing this at all, Ellie. The sooner we get rid of her the sooner we get out of here. Have you thought about what might happen if one of those men comes around here tonight?' Lizzy felt a shiver go up her spine in spite of the heat. 'I don't know if they would go to the police, but I don't want to find out. Another thing, if they've come looking for you-know-what, they won't want to be disappointed. I don't think they'll be looking at my skinny self, Miss B-52.' Only vaguely aware of sexual activity, she found 'you-know-what' to be a most convenient term. She was pretty sure Ellie had more information about 'you-know-what' than she'd been willing to share. Sometimes Lizzy felt as if everybody in the world had more information about 'you-know-what' than she did.

'Stop trying to scare me, Lizzy. I just don't think we should risk taking her out during the day.' Ellie bent her shoulders forward as though to conceal her chest just in case any of their mother's men might be looking through the windows.

'Pick up her shoulders, Ellie. Were taking her into the kitchen and then out the back door. You know as well as I do, nobody notices what kids do.' Lizzy had been practising being invisible since she was five. Although she feared she was losing the knack, she felt certain she could make it work again if she really needed to. Of course, that would leave somebody watching Ellie carrying a corpse to the car by the shoulders while the feet hung in mid-air, so she decided she'd better not use what she'd learned about being invisible just then.

'They'd notice if they saw two girls burying a body. Besides, I can't drive during the day. Everybody knows I'm only fourteen.'

'That is the dumbest thing you have said this month. Do you really think the whole town is watching to see if you're driving? Do you think anybody even knows who you are?' Lizzy figured a few people knew who *she* was: the ladies at the library, the judges in the 'Why I'm Proud to be an American' essay contest – people like that, but she was pretty sure nobody knew or cared much about Ellie.

'I have friends in this town. Don't forget I'm going to be a junior lettergirl this fall.' Lettergirls just had to stick out their chests and walk around the football field, but Ellie always made it sound as if it was her ticket to Hollywood or something. The girls would line up to spell 'Clifford'. Ellie was the one who wore the foot-high 'O' on her chest.

'Your friends are too dumb to keep track of themselves, much less you.' Ellie did not seem to attract the best element. Even their mother had commented on that. If a woman who has drunks coming to see her in the middle of the night tells you that you have bad taste in friends, Lizzy knew you should probably worry. Lizzy thought her sister's friends were a bunch of booger-eating mouth-breathers.

'Even you should know you were chosen to be a lettergirl just because you developed early and could make that stupid 'O' stick out farther than anybody else. You didn't have to write an essay or anything like that.' Lizzy brought this up frequently because she had won first prize in the 'Why I'm Proud to be an American' essay contest. Until last year Ellie had to stay at school late on Tuesdays and Thursdays to get extra help with reading. Ellie's grades had been just good enough to be on the squad and Lizzy knew her sister was worried because she was going to have to take algebra in the coming year. In spite of this, Ellie was acknowledged by most of her friends to be the smartest one in her crowd.

'At least I've developed. From the way you look I don't think you are ever going to have anything on the top or the bottom.' Ellie said this to her sister at least once a day.

'Well, let's see if you've developed any muscles in your chest along with those modified sweat glands you're so proud of.' Their mother had bought a set of encyclopaedias at the Safeway, a book a week, a few years ago. By the time she was eight, Lizzy had read every word and was starting on her second reading. Virtually the only books in the house, she'd read them so often she'd amassed a tremendous amount of information. She often looked for ways to slip some of this into her day-to-day conversations. Ellie liked to balance the books on her head to perfect her walk.

'Jealous.' Ellie shot her sister a look meant to terrify and lifted her mother's shoulders off the bathroom floor. 'Come on, Lizzy. I can't do everything by myself.'

Turning her back, Lizzy squatted and grabbed the body's bony, shrouded ankles. She turned her head towards her sister. 'Ready?'

'Just shut up and get going.'

'Are you sure nobody comes here?' Ellie had parked the turquoise and cream Ford Fairlane less than a hundred feet from the riverbank. She'd proven herself an adept driver and confessed to driving lessons from Steve. She hadn't said why Steve had taught her to drive, but Lizzy suspected that 'you-know-what' figured in there somewhere.

'Nobody comes to this part of the river during the day except me. People come here at night because there are beer cans and rubbers all over the place. I'm surprised old Steve has never brought you down here to watch submarine races.' Lizzy was very unsure what submarine races were, and more than a little confused about the role of rubbers. They just looked like little balloons, but the other kids always implied that they were different from the things you got at birthday parties.

'You are disgusting.' Ellie climbed out of the car.

'Well, I'm just asking. Where does he take you when he wants to play a little stink-finger?' Stink-finger was another one of those concepts she was confused about. The other kids whispered about these things and pretended they knew something nobody else did. Lizzy hoped and believed that the kids her age shared her ignorance. Since she was the smartest girl in the sixth grade it didn't seem right for a bunch of booger-eating mouth-breathers to know more than the girl who won the year's most important essay competition.

'You are so vile. It would serve you right to go to some awful foster home. You are talking filthy with our mother dead in the back seat. I don't know why I don't just leave on my own and let them have you.'

'You put up with me the same reason I put up with you: we need each other. You are all I've got, and I'm all you've got. We are just a couple of ditch-bank Okie Viking orphans.' Lizzy decided not to mention that it didn't matter how filthy she talked in front of their dead mother. Ellie seemed to half believe their mother was finally paying some kind of attention to her daughters.

'I'm not a ditch-bank Okie Viking.' Ellie narrowed her eyes and punched her sister in the arm.

'Sure you are.' Her arm hurt where Ellie had punched it, but she wasn't going to let her know it. 'We both are. But it isn't really such a bad thing. The Okies came out of the South after the Civil War and made a new life for themselves. Then they came to California during the Dust Bowl and made another new life for themselves. They must have been really tough and determined. The Vikings were navigators, and poets, and warriors. They travelled farther than anybody else back then. Just like the Okies, they were tough and determined. The way I see it we can be as tough as we need to be.' She bounced slightly on the front seat, pleased at the thought of all that grit and determination coursing through her veins.

'We don't know if we come from the Vikings or not. We don't know where she got the name Sinclair.'

'She probably used the name because she loved somebody named Sinclair. If she loved him, he might be the father of at least one of us. Even if that didn't happen, Kingsburg is full of Swedes and Clovis is full of Norwegians. They came from Vikings and both of those towns are within driving distance of where Mom lived when we were born.' Lizzy was pleased at being able to keep her Viking heritage. 'I figure we have an eighty per cent chance of being Viking, and that's good enough for me.'

'Where do you want to put her?' Ellie turned away from her sister, the Viking, and wiped the unheroic tears off her cheeks.

'Under the cottonwoods over there. The ground is real soft and we can cover the turned dirt with leaves. She'll be safe there.' She liked the idea of her mother being safe and staying out of trouble.

Lizzy threw the last handful of leaves over the soft brown mound. The dark dirt would dry within the hour and become the same bleached tan as the rest of the ground. The area was full of ruts and mounds and one more wouldn't draw anyone's attention. Especially since almost everyone who came here had other things to think about, like beer and rubbers. 'We need to have a funeral now. What do you think we should say?'

'I don't know, I've never been to a funeral, not a real one, anyway. What are we supposed to say? I'm surprised you don't have something all arranged.'

'I would have something written down, but I didn't have a lot of time to plan this thing, Ellie.' Lizzy had written some lovely things for the funerals of dead birds and road kills they had found. Ellie stopped attending these services around three years earlier, about the same time she got interested in boys.

'I'm sure you've thought of something.' Ellie crossed her arms and glared at her sister.

'I do have a few ideas. She didn't go to church, but she always said Jesus was her Saviour. Personally, I think if he was her Saviour, he should have done something for her a few years ago. I think we should just leave Jesus out of this, because I don't think he was all that interested in Mom or us. I think we should talk about her accomplishments.'

'What accomplishments? Mom never accomplished anything.'

'She had two daughters. That's one accomplishment. She could be really funny.' Lizzy realized being funny wasn't really an accomplishment, especially since she had usually been drunk when she was funny. She chewed on the inside of her cheek for a moment before conceding her sister's point. 'You're right, El. We'd better not talk about her accomplishments.'

'Maybe we should just say goodbye. That's all we have to do.' Ellie wiped the dirt from her hands.

'We could sing her favourite song. Songs are always good at funerals.'

'What was her favourite song?'

'"Shrimp Boats Are A-coming".'

'What?'

'You know, "shrimp boats are a-coming, their sails are in sight, shrimp boats are a-comin, they'll be dancin' tonight",'

Lizzy sang in a warbly soprano, and thought it sounded great.

'You can't sing that stupid song at a funeral and I don't know why you think it was her favourite.'

'Do you have any better ideas? If you do, I'm all ears.'

'We will just say goodbye, it's the most dignified thing to do and she'd have liked that.'

'You first.' Lizzy leaned back against a cottonwood and watched her sister, disappointed that her first human funeral was going to be so mundane. Even the cat she'd found flattened by the road had a funeral with singing and interpretative dance.

Ellie folded her hands in front of her waist and faced the mound of earth. 'I love you and I hope you go straight to heaven. I'm going to take good care of Lizzy and make sure she's OK. I'm sorry I used to get so mad at you. I know you tried.' Ellie pulled on the sides of her hair, making a mourning veil across her face. She snuffled softly. 'Goodbye, Mom.' She turned to the younger girl. 'Your turn, Lizzy.'

Lizzy faced the mound but kept her arms stiff at her sides. 'I always wished you could've been like the other mothers. I wish you would have taken me to school and talked to my teachers. I wish you would have let us have a dog. I wish you would have loved us as much as you loved your stupid wine. I want you to know that when I have kids I'm going to love them more than anything. I'm going to take care of them and make sure that they have a father who loves them. I'm never going to let hairy, smelly men wander around my house in the middle of the night scaring my kids half to death. I'm going to keep my kids safe and I'm going to notice if they're near geniuses. I'm not going to be anything like you.' Lizzy grabbed a dead branch from the ground and began to beat the makeshift grave with it. 'I'm not going to be anything like you. Do you hear me? I'll be so different nobody will even guess that we were related. I'll be a wonderful mother, you'll see.' She beat the soft earth with every gasping word.

Ellie pulled the stick away and locked the girl's arms in her own. 'It's OK, Lizzy. It's going to be OK.'

'She shouldn't have been like that, El. She never loved us enough. She never thought about us.' Lizzy's tears splashed in an arc across her sister's shoulder.

'We'll take care of each other from now on.'

'We don't know what we're doing, El. We're just kids.' Lizzy wiped her nose with the back of her hand.

'We can't do much worse than Mom.'

'That's true.' Lizzy took a deep breath as she stifled a sob.

Ellie turned her sister towards the car. 'Come on. We've got some packing to do.'

Lizzy shoved three pairs of worn underpants into a brown-paper grocery sack. 'We have to pack her things, too. We need to make it look like we all left. We don't need to take everything, just the important things somebody would take with them if they were leaving town in a big hurry.' She glanced nervously at the clock and then at her sister. If a man was coming tonight it might be as early as ten. 'We can take her stuff to the Salvation Army barrels in town, but we can't leave it here.'

'You get her clothes and stuff. I'll strip the bed and finish the kitchen.' Ellie began tearing the sheets from the sagging mattress. 'Lizzy, come here.'

'Ellie, we have to get out of here in the next two hours. Just get your part done and leave me to mine.' Typical of Ellie, she thought. Wants an audience to strip a bed and throw a few things in a bag.

'Look here, on the side.' Ellie pointed at a rip in the side of the worn mattress where a canvas bag lay nestled in the grey batting.

'Let's take a look.' Lizzy grabbed the bag and tore the zip open. She looked at her sister and grinned. 'You just found Mom's bank account.' She emptied the bag on to the bed in a small shower of coins and notes.

'Oh my God, Lizzy. Where did she get this? She never told me we had any money. Even when we almost got the electricity cut off, she never told me about this.' Ellie began to separate the hoard into piles of greenbacks and coins.

'She was probably saving it for a rainy day and didn't notice when it started raining cats and dogs around this place.' Lizzy thought it was all too typical of the woman to save money and then forget where she'd put it. She figured they were lucky that old Ellie had such sharp eyes.

'Where did it come from?' Ellie was busy counting the money and making little chirping sounds. She reminded her sister of one of those birds on the nature movies they were always showing at school. Ellie looked like one of those silly birds with twigs in its mouth that didn't seem to know it only had twigs and not gold bars or the Hope Diamond. 'I wonder where she got all this.'

'I guess the hairy men were bringing her more than wine.'

'How can you say that about your own mother?' Ellie stopped her happy chirping and stared at her sister in disbelief.

'Because it must be true, Eleanor. I'm not so mad at her any more, now that I know she was doing something to look after us.' It almost made Laura seem like a good mother. Like one of those animal mothers who would do anything to take care of their children. Maybe it wasn't as noble as throwing yourself in front of an elephant, but maybe she'd tried more than Lizzy realized.

'I know what must have happened. She must have earned this money before she left the Safeway and just forgot where she put it. Or maybe Safeway gave her the money because they felt bad about firing her. I bet she was saving it to move us into a better place. I bet she wanted to surprise us with this.' Ellie nodded at her sister, willing her to agree with the theory.

'Maybe you're right, El. How much is there?' She didn't believe for a minute their mother had received a bonus for being fired from Safeway, but it seemed important to Ellie, so she would play along.

'Just a second.' Ellie counted methodically, with the tip of her tongue sticking out of the side of her mouth. 'Lizzy, we have two hundred and twelve dollars and eighty-seven cents! Oh Lizzy, we're going to be all right!'

'This doesn't really change anything, Ellie. We still have only an hour and a half to get out of here. I'm still twelve and you're only fourteen.'

'But now we've got enough money to live on.'

'Now we know where our next meal is coming from, but we're not exactly Rockefellers. Stick that stuff back in the bag and get the bed stripped.'

'Well, at least we don't have to steal from Mrs Kirby now. We have money and we can buy our own gas. That should make you happy.' Ellie patted the bag as though it were a baby's pink bottom.

'We don't have to steal any money from her, but we'd better help ourselves to some of her gas. We can't have you driving into the Shell in the middle of town and yelling, "fill 'er up!"'

'Why not? I thought you said nobody in town knows who we are anyway.'

'I've given that a second thought. I figure the guys who work down at the Shell are exactly the kind of guys who would know who you are and how old you are. Those guys are the kind who get all stupid whenever the lettergirls and cheerleaders start bouncing around. We leave town with a full tank of gas, but not from the Shell.'

'I guess you're right.' She screwed her mouth into a grin, pleased that her sister had acknowledged her effect on boys. 'Just don't forget that you are not the oldest. You're not the boss.'

'I don't think either of us should be the boss. I think we should be equal partners, like those Sunset Strip detectives on television.' Lizzy admired the way they could solve crimes by looking at broken glasses and crushed flowers. She also admired the way they always got along and cooperated with each other.'

'I'm still the oldest.'

'I can't argue with logic like that, El. Come on, let's run away from home.'

Cotherstone, West Sussex, February 3rd

Dearest Mary,

Thank you so much for the wonderful photographs. They've really inspired your father and brother and all the talk is now about coming out to California for a week or two and then escorting you home. Let us know what you think. Frankly, part of me recoils at visiting California, but the boys seem terribly excited by the idea. That sounds awful. I want to see you, of course, and I want to see where you've been living, but California is a place I've been avoiding for years.

Big news from the place where you think nothing ever happens; your little brother is in love. OK, maybe it's only lust, but it seems to be the strongest attachment he's had since he realized Madonna wasn't saving herself for him. Her name is Sarah and she seems quite nice. Her mother is a tennis partner of Elaine's and Elaine tells me she is a very nice girl, in spite of the nose ring.

I'm not being the least bit judgemental. I mentioned the nose ring last and I didn't say it made her a bad person, did I? She is in fact a very pretty girl and has very nice manners. Hopefully the hole will fill in once she comes to her senses. I've always wondered what happens to one of those rings when someone has a cold. Does it get all snotty and disgusting? And how is it attached? You live in San Francisco, find out for me. While you're at it, find out about that body piercing stuff. Do people really have their nipples and genitals done? Judas Priest, I was almost thirty before

I got up the courage to have my earlobes drilled. Makes me shiver just to think about it.

Anyway, since your brother is so enamoured of the excellent Sarah I've decided to buy the biggest box of condoms I can find and leave them in his bathroom. Your father thinks this will only encourage them, but I maintain Chaz doesn't need any encouragement in this area. I've seen the smouldering looks passing between those two and I'm not ready for my baby to make a baby.

Your father is due in from Brussels tonight. He's stopping in Calais so I have to clear space in the garage for the cases of plonk he'll be dragging home. I told him not to get any chocolate this time because I'm still waddling around with about half a stone from Christmastime. I don't have any willpower these days so I prefer that the lovely stuff never comes through the front door.

Since you seem interested, I'll continue with the sordid story of my childhood. When my mother died, my sister and I decided we would hide her body and leave town. Seen too many movies, I suppose, but we actually thought we could make new lives for ourselves and nobody would be the wiser.

Before we left, we found a small amount of money that my mother had either saved or forgotten. I don't recall how much it was, but I'm sure it wasn't much. Basically we had a used car, a few dollars, the clothes on our backs, and each other.

We buried her in a shallow grave along the banks of the Kings River. We had a little ceremony and I recall pitching a fit because I was just so angry with her for the way she'd lived and died. I've often wondered if her remains ever showed up. I was always very vague when questioned about where we'd put her because I didn't want her to be dug up and stuck in a pauper's grave. I was rather pleased with the arrangements we'd made for her. I hope she's where we left her. I don't know why I care where the bones are, but I do.

I don't know if this is shocking or if you're finding it rather interesting. Daddy's family, lovely as it is, is pretty quiet. They always do the right thing, don't they? The only thing I've ever heard is that your Great-Great-Uncle Basil had a native wife in addition to your Great-Great-Aunt Felicity when they lived in Rangoon. Actually, no small thing that, at least not for poor old Aunt Felicity.

Daddy will be writing to you this week, but don't hold your breath on Chaz taking pen in hand.

Love and God bless

Mummy

PS Your grandmother has decided to sell her car. I never thought it would happen, but India confesses to feeling old.

CHAPTER THREE

Liz poured herself a cup of coffee and emptied the clothes dryer. She shook out her son's denim shirts and decided there was no real point in ironing them. He liked to look rumpled, always had. Big year for Chaz. First passion, and getting to wear something other than the regulation uniform to school.

She paired up his socks, noting that he'd only used three pairs in the whole week. 'Hope Sarah doesn't have a foot fetish or this whole thing will be off, Patch.'

The dog looked up from his rug by the stove and slammed his tail against the floor. He stretched and hurried over to her as though he was eager to have more information about socks and sexual fetishes.

She squatted down and ruffled the fur on the dog's head. 'I think I've become a woman of a certain age, Patch. I hang out around here and talk to a silly dog. Another few years and I'll be a crazy old lady with a bus pass.' A picture slipped into her mind, startling her as she covered her mouth and rose to her feet.

She hadn't thought of her in years. The crazy old lady.

Clifford, California, July 1962

'Turn the lights off, Ellie. Just take it real slow. The gas tanks are behind the tractor barn up on the right.' Lizzy had spent one summer being best friends with Mrs Kirby's granddaughter Sandra. She'd been a little afraid of Mrs Kirby and her rows and rows of preserves and her starched aprons. She kept a daily schedule you could set a clock by, in marked contrast to Laura's casual approach to life and housekeeping. She sometimes questioned Lizzy about Laura, and forbade her granddaughter to spend any time at Lizzy's house.

That hadn't been a problem, because Lizzy never took anyone home anyway and Sandra would have been too snooty to come even if she had been invited. They'd only been best friends for one summer because Lizzy got sick of hearing about Sandra's seven Barbie dolls and her father's big job at the cannery. Sandra always made it sound as if there would never be another canned peach in the whole world if it wasn't for her dad, the night manager at Libby Canning.

'I can't see if I turn the lights off.' Ellie peered around the steering wheel. Laura had bought the car second-hand from some Swedish bachelor farmer over by Kingsburg. She'd been convinced the only decent cars were Lutheran Fords. The worth of Lutheran cars had been one of their mother's few religious convictions.

'There.' Lizzy pushed the headlight button in. 'Give your eyes a minute to adjust if you want. There won't be anything in the way because Mrs Kirby always keeps her car in the tractor barn. This is also the time she reads her Bible, so we don't have to worry about her. Matthew, Mark, Luke and John are keeping her busy tonight.' Lizzy had gone to Vacation Bible School at the Baptist church for two weeks every summer for as long as she could remember. She thought most of what they taught was pretty silly and she was surprised that the teachers didn't laugh when they told some of those stories. Lizzy didn't say anything about the stories being stupid because the snacks were terrific and they always had lots of great crafts to do. Last year when the other kids made the Tower of Babel out of popsicle sticks, she'd made a box for playing cards which the Baptists didn't approve of. Mrs Grafton, the preacher's fat wife, made her sit in the prayer corner for the rest of the morning.

Mrs Grafton would have been surprised to know that Lizzy actually sat in the prayer corner and prayed. Having had doubts about the Baptist view of the world for some time, she decided this was the opportunity she'd been looking for. She shut her eyes tight and explained to God that she was tired of taking everybody else's word for what he was supposed to be like. Mrs Grafton made God sound a lot like her own husband, but that didn't make any sense, Lizzy prayed, because then God would be getting all bug-eyed and sweaty-lipped while he was begging himself for favours. If God would just give her a sign like the ones he'd supposedly given some of those people in the Bible, she'd believe in him and get washed in the Blood of the Lamb, even if that did sound really awful and sticky. She didn't pray for a burning bush or to be swallowed by a whale, but she thought an excellent sign would be for God to make Mrs Grafton skinny. Not only, she prayed, would this prove what God could do, but Mrs Grafton would have to be happier if her knees didn't scrape together with that funny wet sound when she walked.

When she opened her eyes and found the fat Mrs Grafton walking towards her with that funny wet sound she decided it was time to leave Vacation Bible School for good. She wasn't sorry her religious education had come to an end, but she knew she was going to miss the snacks and the crafts. It was only later in the day that she realized she'd left her card box behind.

'I wish you wouldn't say things like that. I think we need to keep God on our side. I'm praying right now as I drive that he will be with us and we will be successful.' Ellie had been going to something every Tuesday night called 'Young Life'. Everybody pretended to pray while they eyed each other and passed notes back and forth. Most of them liked it so much they didn't even care that Big Bob, the teen's pastor, was a smelly creep with greasy hair and a permanent leer on his face. One thing Ellie had learned at Young Life was to talk about anything to do with God in a funny, slow voice that you didn't use any other time.

'I'm not sure you're supposed to pray before you know you're going to rob an old lady. That's even worse than your Big Bob praying before the football game that your team will break the bones of the other team.' Big Bob was married to Mrs Grafton. Sometimes, before the football game, Big Bob and Mrs Grafton would sing a duet of 'Onward Christian Soldiers', which had become the Clifford High School official fight song. Mrs Grafton could also be heard Thursday night at 1300 on your AM dial singing alto with the Salvation Singers. Sometimes, as a special treat, she'd stop singing and witness across the radio waves. She would talk real soft and then she'd start crying. She never said exactly what she'd done before she'd been saved, but she must have been pretty bad since she was still talking about it. How that woman suffered for her faith.

'Just watch your mouth.' Ellie's voice had lost its special religious quality and resonated with a nasal anger. 'I think maybe we should leave right now and just get gas out on the highway. I think we've got plenty in the tank to get out there.'

'I don't think we can take that chance, Ellie. The last thing we need is to run out of gas and have the Highway Patrol come and help us out.' Laura had taught her girls the poor person's fear of the law. Policemen were large, nosy men intent on separating children from their mothers. They bothered people who were just trying to get by as best they could when they should be out catching real criminals.

'OK. I can see a little now.' Ellie eased the car towards the tractor barn.

'You're doing fine, El. Just a few more yards. Turn left here. Stop now.' She patted Ellie's arm. 'See, that wasn't such a big deal.' Ellie's arm felt damp and sticky and Lizzy could smell her sister's sweat over the scent of Palmolive soap.

'Let's just get this over with.' Ellie stepped out of the car and removed the gas cap. Lizzy ran around the back of the car and pulled the gas nozzle from the tank.

'Don't move or you're dead.' A bright light shone on the girls. 'Put your hands up and keep them up. I've got a gun and I'm not afraid to use it.' The light shook in rhythm with a war-bling voice.

'Don't shoot, Mrs Kirby! It's me, Lizzy Sinclair, Sandra's friend.' Lizzy was hoping Mrs Kirby really liked her a whole lot, but had just been afraid to show it. She knew some people weren't very good at showing their emotions.

'What are you doing back here?' The light still jerked in their direction.

'We were looking for our cat. We thought she might have come over here and we didn't want to bother you.' Ellie's voice squeaked as she answered.

'You were looking for a cat in my gas tank? What kind of cat is in a gas tank? You two were trying to steal my gas.'

'We weren't going to steal anything, Mrs Kirby. We were going to leave the money right on top of the tank for you. Lizzy told me this was the time of night you did your Bible study so we didn't want to interrupt you. It's just that we were almost out of gas and didn't think we could get into town before we were dry.' Lizzy recognized the panic in her sister's voice and tried to signal her to be quiet. Once Ellie started talking she sometimes had trouble shutting back up.

'Who are you? Who sent you out here? How many of you are there? The flashlight's beam swung across the back seat of the car. 'What's this mess you have in the car? You girls been robbing other people blind?'

'It's just some stuff from our house, ma'am.' Lizzy had never used the term before, but thought it might appeal to an old lady. Kids in the movies always seemed to say 'sir' or 'ma'am' when they were trying to convince some old person just what nice young people they really were.

'Who is that with you, Lizzy Sinclair?' From the tone of the old woman's voice, Lizzy now knew that Mrs Kirby hadn't been harbouring kind thoughts about her, nor was she impressed with the form of address. She said Lizzy's name the way somebody might say 'Adolf Hitler' or 'dog shit'.

'It's my sister. I think you've met her before, ma'am. Her name is Eleanor and she is a junior lettergirl.' Lizzy thought the old lady might have heard that you needed fine personality attributes, as well as nice breasts, to be a lettergirl. This could make her feel more kindly towards them than she apparently did just then.

'You girls are running away from home. You have stolen your mama's car and looks like half of everything she owns. I don't suppose you've given a thought to how your mama's going to feel when she finds out what you've done. Your mama's not much, but even she deserves better than this. I think you two had better goosestep in front of me to my house. We'll call your mama and let her know what her two little darlings are up to.'

'We don't have a phone, ma'am.' Lizzy felt good about telling the complete truth. No house, no phone.

'Then I'll just call the Sheriff and he can stop by and see your mama. Now get going.'

Eleanor looked at Lizzy and made a sound like a mouse caught up by an owl. Lizzy stepped forward and stood less than a yard from the old woman. 'We don't have a mother either, Mrs Kirby. Not any more, at least.'

'What kind of nonsense do you think I will believe? I have known your mother since you were barely able to walk.'

'Our mother died this morning, ma'am. We're leaving town because if we don't, the County is going to put us into foster homes and we might never see each other again.' Lizzy was ashamed at the tears burning down her cheeks. 'Please, Mrs Kirby, don't tell on us. We can take care of ourselves and we don't have anyone else. Can't you just pretend you never saw us? We won't tell anybody we were out here, promise.' At first she tried to stop the tears until she realized they might just be the thing to impress the old woman. She tried to do a huge, heartbroken sob, but it caught at the back of her throat and almost choked her.

Lizzy rubbed the back of her sunburned arm across her eyes. She could hear some frogs down by the irrigation ditches and the scrapings of a few crickets. The old woman still shone the light on them and she felt like one of those gangsters getting the third degree in the movies. She knew she'd cracked way too soon. She turned to Ellie to apologize when the flashlight's beam was turned away from them.

'The Bible teaches us that we do it for Him when we do it for the least. You two'd better come into the house while we figure out what we are going to do.' She turned and started towards the farmhouse. 'Come on. I'm not turning you over to anybody. You have my word on it.' She took several steps and turned towards the girls, who hadn't moved. 'I said you can trust me, and you can.'

Lizzy looked at her sister in the dim light and shrugged. 'She wouldn't lie, I don't think she knows how.'

Ellie put her hand into Lizzy's. 'Worse comes to worse, I guess we can outrun her.'

'Yeah, like some old lady would really want to hold on to the two of us. You think there's some kind of bounty on our heads or something?' She wished there was. If there was a bounty on their heads they'd already be rich and famous.

'Come on, Liz.' Ellie followed the old woman and pulled her sister behind her.

'Mrs Kirby, I think you should know what happened . . .' Ellie leaned against the kitchen table looking pale and tired.

'I don't want to know anything. If anybody asks, I want to say I don't know anything and I want to mean it. I don't tell lies, I never have. I can say I saw you, but I want to say I don't know what happened to your mama, and I want to say I don't know where you've gone. Too many people sticking their noses in everybody's business these days, if you ask me. Most things in this world are best known to God and nobody else.' She stared at the sisters for a moment as though she'd never gotten a good look at girls before. 'When was the last time you two had something to eat?'

Lizzy hadn't seen the woman this close in over a year and was surprised at how old she looked. Not that she'd ever looked young. Of medium height, she was as thin and wiry-looking as a young farmhand. Her skin, deeply lined from a lifetime in the sun, had a yellowish cast, like old bruise. Her hands were twisted and spotted with dark, scaly sores. The front of her cotton dress hung crooked and she held her left arm tight to her side. Lizzy squinted slightly and Mrs Kirby seemed to be surrounded by a smudged sepia colour. The colour deepened around her left side to a deep brown around the hand she kept to her side.

Ellie turned to her sister and shrugged. 'I don't think we've eaten today.' The thought of food was appealing to Lizzy, especially since Mrs Kirby probably had something other than the USDA commodities they were used to eating.

'Sit down there.' She indicated the scrubbed pine kitchen table. 'I'll feed you girls and I'll tell you a story about leaving home. You just might learn a thing or two.'

'I never knew why I ended up there.' The old woman glanced

behind her and narrowed her eyes. 'I'll tell them if I want to. Go away now.' She blinked and looked back at the girls without explaining her outburst. 'I wasn't really an orphan because my father was still alive, but that was true of lots of the kids. Women used to die so easy back then. The mothers would die and the fathers didn't know what to do with the kids. My father had a sister, but she had a bunch of kids of her own. He kept my brother, but I was sent away. He said he was coming back for me when he got things figured out, but I knew I'd seen the last of him. All the kids knew you didn't get put in a place like that if anybody wanted you.'

'Sounds pretty bad, Mrs Kirby.' Lizzy kept looking behind the woman to see if she could figure out who or what Mrs Kirby had been talking to.

'It was bad, but it got a lot worse. Anyway, I lived there for a year or two before they put me on the train. The Orphan Train they called it. The idea was to clear out the orphanages back east and send kids into the farm country where you can never have enough of them. Somebody in New York or Washington decided we'd all be adopted by nice farm families and live in the fresh air and sunshine.'

She picked at the front of her dress and shook her head. 'Maybe some of the kids did end up like that. I hope to Jesus everybody didn't land up in the mess I did, but some probably had it even worse. I ended up with some people in Missouri who had an ugly little farm. The man, I was supposed to call him 'Pa', but I never did, said he was growing dirt. Thought it was a big joke, but that is pretty much all he managed to grow. I was more like some nigger slave than a daughter. I was there for about four years; I left when I was twelve.'

'Why did you leave?' Lizzy wiped the egg salad from her sandwich out of the corner of her mouth.

'I didn't mind the hard work, and I never knew anything but being poor, but I wouldn't put up with his filthy man ways.' She looked at the girls and nodded. She jerked her head, her chin pointing to something behind her. 'Likes to pretend it didn't happen, likes to pretend the world isn't like that, but it happened.' She looked behind her and nodded with satisfaction. 'I know the evil that lurks in the world waiting for God to go to sleep. Just waiting for him to doze off.'

Lizzy had figured out whatever was behind Mrs Kirby was tied up with that brown colour and the bent arm and was best ignored. 'What about his man ways?' She had an idea about these, but she wanted to hear the old woman's version. She'd heard things about men and what they had between their legs. Once she'd seen something really strange when one of the hairy men was visiting her mother, but she didn't like to look at that memory. She'd heard the other kids giggling about where men wanted to put their things, but she didn't see what was so funny about it. It sounded really stupid and she didn't understand why any woman would be dumb enough to let a man come near her with that thing. Jimmy Ficks down by the river said it was what her mother had been doing with the hairy men, but she told him he was dead wrong. She'd knocked him down and kicked him in the chest for saying such ugly things about her mother. She'd kicked him extra hard because she knew Jimmy Ficks was right, and she hated him for that.

'His wife was real sickly and he wanted me to be like a wife to him. It was a terrible sin to even think about it. I was just a kid, but he still tried his man ways on me. I left and I never went back. I was so scared, I can't even begin to tell you how scared I was of him.' The old woman sipped at her ice tea while the girls finished their sandwiches. 'I think he might have been a Mason. I've never trusted Masons. That's some good advice for you girls.' She took another sip from her glass. 'They worship false idols and don't follow Jesus. Say they've been around longer than Jesus, but that's just another lie. Nothing in this world has been around longer than Jesus, but not many people know that.' She glanced behind her and leaned towards the girls. 'They pee on each other.' She nodded her head violently.

'Those men pee on each other before they can join. I've heard some other things too, but I think they're too unnatural, even for the Masons, so I figure some of that is just rumour.'

'Oh, I see.' But she didn't. Lizzy was wondering why the Masons had the biggest building on East Street if they were so bad. Besides, being a wife didn't seem to be such an awful thing, so Mrs Kirby must have meant something else. Lizzy knew that old ladies liked to talk in circles and they didn't like to answer too many questions. She was about to ask some more about wives and Masons when Mrs Kirby started talking again.

'People didn't keep track in those days, not like they do today. It was easy to walk a few days and find yourself a world away from where you'd been. I walked to Kansas and went to the nicest house I could find and asked for a job. I didn't care what I was asked to do as long as it was honest work. I was never afraid of hard work. Things were different then. We didn't have Welfare and Social Security and all those other excuses for not working. We worked or we didn't eat, and that's the way it should still be.'

'Did they give you a job?' Ellie leaned forward across the table. Lizzy knew she was probably thinking about being some kind of fancy social secretary in a big house who spent all day talking on a pink princess telephone like the one Mrs Eisenhower had when she'd been in the White House. Probably thought she'd sit around writing notes with an ostrich feather pen, too.

'No, I had to go to three more houses until I could find work. Looking back, I know it was part of God's plan. I met my husband in that house, the man God had chosen for me.'

'Mr Kirby worked in the house too?' Lizzy had seen the pictures of Mr Kirby, dead over thirty years. A small, bald man, he didn't look like part of God's plan to Lizzy.

'No, he worked in a grocery store. It was his job to deliver the groceries. I knew he was the boy for me as soon as I saw him. 'Course, I had to wait for him to notice me. I don't even think he knew I was alive for the first two years. After that we started keeping company and saving our money. When we were sixteen, we left Kansas and came out here for the cheap land.' She smiled, showing the girls her white dentures. 'We were married almost forty years and had five children. Things weren't always easy, but there was more good than bad. He was a good man who did his best, and he wasn't a Mason. Goes without saying, I wouldn't have anything to do with a Mason.'

'That's a nice story, Mrs Kirby.' Ellie had that soft look on her face and Lizzy could see that she was sitting there thinking of old ratface Steve and how they would grow old together. Lizzy could see them now: sitting on the front porch while he picked the food out of his teeth with one of his black fingernails.

'It's not a nice story. Haven't you been listening to a word I said? I want the two of you to know this isn't going to be easy. Times have changed and folks can't just disappear and start over any more. Government keeps track. They keep track so when the Communists and the Masons take over they'll know just where to find each and every one of us.' She smiled and tapped the side of her head with her finger. 'But I know there's a greater plan than the Communists and the Masons can even dream about. Jesus knows where we are; every last person in the world has a place in Jesus' book, and he's keeping track.' She jumped up in her seat and batted her good hand behind her. 'I did not tell something I shouldn't have. They need to know about Jesus' book.'

'We thought we'd change our names. That should at least fool the government and the Masons.' Lizzy had been experimenting with names for almost two hours. Nothing had quite clicked, although she was leaning towards Mary. She knew she definitely didn't want to be a Gidget or a Gigi.

'I don't know if you're tough enough to do this. You can call the Sheriff right now and tell him your mama is dead. I'm not so sure that they won't try to keep you girls together. It might be the best thing. Not like when I was a girl.'

'No. We stay together, on our own. I've had my fill of welfare and social workers. Besides, Mom hasn't really taken care of us for a long time anyway. We've gotten pretty good at looking after each other.' Ellie played with the crumbs on her plate and stared at her sister, as though willing her to agree.

'Ellie's right, Mrs Kirby. We stay together and we take care of ourselves. If you could do it by yourself, then we can do it together.'

'Then I'll pray for you every night that God gives me. I'll pray that the good Lord keeps you safe. I just hope I don't hear on the TV about them finding the bodies of two young girls. Satan is out there along with the Masons, so promise me you'll be careful.'

'We'll be careful. Nobody is going to find us. We're from pretty tough stuff, our mother always said so.' Lizzy couldn't remember if her mother had said that or not, but she wished that she had.

'Your mother was a fool, but you are still God's children and I will pray for you. I'll also forget you were here. One of the nice things about being old is folks expect you to forget things.'

'You mean you're going to lie for us?' The thought of Mrs Kirby lying for them was rather exciting. Lying was even worse than playing cards for a Baptist. The worst was taking God's name in vain, but Lizzy thought it was silly for someone as important as God to care about something like that.

'I won't remember who you are. I think you'd better go now.'

'Before we go, would you tell us who else you were talking to, besides us, that is?'

'I wasn't talking to anybody else.' She looked at Lizzy with her rheumy eyes. 'What a crazy thing to ask.'

Cotherstone, West Sussex, February 6th

Dearest Mary,

Since we haven't heard from you this week I have to assume you're having a wonderful time. Please give us a call when you receive this. Reverse the charges, I just want to hear your voice. I know you are fine, but you are almost six thousand miles away and you are still my little girl. Silly me – yesterday I pulled out the photo albums and had a good cry looking at your baby pictures. No, I don't miss you a bit.

I checked the condom box this morning and two are gone. I haven't told Daddy because he already worries so much, about everything. Nice for me, I suppose; he does the worrying so I don't have to. Actually I'd be more concerned if at Chaz's age he was still spending all his time playing rugby and video games. As long as they don't use my bed I can live with this.

Your grandmother sold her car yesterday, so we went and bought earrings. There is logic there somewhere. She wanted to spend the proceeds on something that would last, so she bought earrings for you, your cousin Barbara, and me. I love mine, but you have to come home to see yours. They are drop–dead gorgeous!! No, I won't give you even a tiny hint as to what they look like, Miss Sticky Beak.

Were having a little dinner party this Saturday. A man that your father works with and his wife, a couple from St John's, and the new GP and her husband. Yes, finally a lady GP. Just in time for my menopause. Is there no end to my good fortune? I'm going to do that chicken in filo thing that always looks so impressive, but only takes a few minutes.

Since I don't know what you're thinking about my shattered youth I'm not sure if I should continue the tale. You might have read enough, and that's fine if you have. At the end of the day, it's nothing but another story. I'll wait to hear from you.

Stay well and call me as soon as you finish reading this.

Love and God bless

Mummy

PS Patch agrees with me about getting a puppy. Now I only have to convince your father.

Chapter Four

'Mum, can you take me to school today?' He leaned over her head and studied the computer monitor. 'What shattered youth did you have?' His large fingernail tapped at the words on the screen.

'Excuse me, Chaz, this is a private correspondence.' She gave his lean midriff a slight jab with her elbow.

'How come Mary gets to hear everything before I do?' He picked up a half-eaten croissant from a plate on her desk and shoved it in his mouth. 'Dad says you two have an oestrogen curtain that separates you from the rest of the world.' He licked his fingers and shrugged into his backpack.

'An oestrogen curtain?' She looked at her son and smiled,

thinking that he looked even taller than he had last night. Food had always distracted him. Why worry about shattered youth when there were pastries to be had?

'You know; all that girly stuff you two do with the make-up and shopping.' He pushed the brown hair off his forehead and ran his hand across his chin.

'Do you feel left out baby?' She knew the answer, but felt the question was expected.

'Yeah, maybe we can shop for some blue nail varnish on the way to school.' He lifted her car keys from the desk and waved them inches from her nose.

'Nail varnish is a bit tarty at best, and, frankly, blue has never been your colour.'

'I'm crushed.'

'How can I make it up to you, my precious?'

'You could drive me to school.'

'If I drive you to school, I have to also pick you up.'

'Perfect. That will give us more quality time and give you a chance to prove how much you love me.' He grinned and raised his eyebrows at her.

'So my driving you to school is important for your mental health?'

'Exactly.'

'Then do me a favour and run upstairs and grab my beige loafers for me. I'll wait for you in the hall.'

'Thanks, Mum. We need to stop at Toby's, I told him we'd give him a lift.' He tossed the keys in her direction before he loped out of the room.

Clifford, California, July 1962

'I don't know about you, Ellie, but I'm feeling pretty darn good about leaving this town.' Lizzy rolled down the window and breathed in the cool night air. 'Leaving' took on almost a

magical sound and she whispered it under her breath as she
noted buildings and said a silent goodbye.

'We just shoved our mother's clothes in the Salvation Army
barrels and you're feeling pretty darn good? You are one sick
kid, Elizabeth.' Ellie dangled an unlit cigarette from her lips
while she tried to drive and push in the car's lighter at the same
time.

'Here, let me do that.' Lizzy shoved the lighter in and sat
back, waiting for it to pop out, red and glowing. 'Let me know
if you want that done again. I really think it would be better if
you didn't smoke and drive at the same time, at least until you
get the hang of both of them.' Lizzy couldn't help but recall
Ellie not learning to ride a bike until she was almost seven. Even
when she finally got the balance down, she kept running into
things although she clung tight to both handlebars in a white-
knuckled death grip. 'You need to pay extra attention to your
driving and save smoking for another time.'

'It helps my nerves.'

'Bullshit, bullshit, and a bigger pile of bullshit. You've only
been smoking a few weeks and you still don't inhale so I don't
think it does anything for your nerves. You just think it makes
you look like Marilyn Monroe or Natalie Wood.' Lizzy thought
it did make her sister look a little like Natalie Wood, but she
wasn't about to tell her that. Tell a girl like Ellie something like
that and you could practically guarantee she'd never do anything
but sit around trying different expressions in front of the mirror.

'I don't need to listen to this from some snot-nosed kid who
isn't even sorry her mother is dead.' The older girl nodded
towards the lighter. 'See if that thing is hot yet.'

'I can feel sorry she's dead and still feel good about leaving
town, can't I?' She pulled the lighter out and held it for Ellie to
light her cigarette. She'd almost just taken the thing out of
Ellie's mouth and lit it herself, but then she'd have to explain
why she knew how to smoke and she didn't feel like getting into

that while Ellie's nerves were supposedly in a state. 'Ellie, you missed the turn. Go back and make a left.' Lizzy used her most disgusted voice. If Ellie was messing up the driving before they even got out to the highway this was going to be harder than she'd thought. She shook her head at the bad luck which had made her the younger sister. She'd always felt the natural order of things had been disrupted by her being born second.

'I know where the highway is, Lizzy. I have to make one stop before we leave town.' Ellie leaned forward slightly into the steering wheel, her fingers tapping against the metal.

'What stop do you need to make? You didn't tell me about any stops.' Lizzy turned to her and bounced on the car seat. She felt like a general who'd just heard about a mutiny.

'We're stopping at Steve's. This is something I have to do, Lizzy.'

'We can't stop at Steve's! Already Mrs Kirby knows and if you tell Steve, why that's one more person who might start blabbing about us all over town. At this rate the whole place will know what we've done by morning.'

'Stop telling me what to do. Steve wouldn't tell anybody. Besides, I already told him we're leaving.' Ellie glanced at her sister and put the cigarette in the car's ashtray.

'Jesus H. Christ, Ellie!' Lizzy kicked at the car door to avoid kicking her sister and causing a crash. 'What were you thinking of? When did you tell him? Why did you tell him?'

'He's the most important person in my life, that's why I told him. I couldn't just up and leave town, could I?' Ellie used her Jackie Kennedy voice. The words came out like little puffs of cotton. No matter what you said with a voice like that, it sounded sweet and sensible.

'Yes you could, Eleanor. You could leave without telling him a damn thing because I am the most important person in your life now that Mom is dead. Blood is thicker than water and I'm blood. Steve is nothing but old scummy pond water compared to me. He's nothing but a boyfriend and you can get another of those just about anywhere. Look under any good sized rock and you'll find something a lot more interesting than Steve.

'I will never understand you, Ellie. Here we are, running away and you tell the dumbest, smelliest boy I've ever seen or smelled what we are doing. It would serve you right if we got caught except I would get caught too, and I don't deserve that.' She grabbed her sister's cigarette from the ashtray and tossed it out the window.

'Why did you do that? Do you have any idea what those things cost?'

'No I don't, but I guess you can't afford them unless they're free.' Lizzy was glad it was dark, because she was pretty sure she had bright red lights coming out of her eyes that were scaring old Ellie half to death. She was so mad her skin felt hot and cold at the same time.

'You are a know-it-all and a brat. You have no idea about love or loyalty or anything.'

'Cow. Stupid cow!' Lizzy turned her face towards the car door and sent her bright red-eye lights into the dark.

'Get into the back, Lizzy.' Ellie was trying to sound like she thought a mother would.

'Why should I get in back? I have to figure out where we're going.' They were parked outside the entrance to the trailer park where Steve lived with his aunt and uncle. Lizzy didn't know where his parents were, but she had suggested to Ellie, just the week before, that they had left because of the smell. Ellie had just gone off in a huff, so Lizzy thought she'd probably hit pretty close to the truth.

A brightly lit sign declared Trail's End to be a mobile home park of distinction. The sign didn't give any clue as to what made Trail's End distinctive. Even by Clifford's standards, Trail's End was considered to be seedy. There were more trailers than mobile homes, and the predominant colour of most was rust brown. It appeared that some attempt at landscaping had taken place as evidenced by several truck tyres which had been painted white, their centres filled with dirt. Either they'd never been planted or tall grassy weeds had been deemed acceptable to whoever had come up with the tyre-planter idea. The park did feature a swimming pool, but the pump broke years ago, leaving five feet of green water as a haven for countless frogs, who fed on the mosquitoes and horse flies which bred in the thick, mossy sludge.

Ellie let out a long, whistling sigh. 'You need to get into the back so that Steve can sit in the front. That's why we stopped at the Salvation Army barrels right after we left Mrs Kirby's. I needed to make sure there was enough room for you before we picked up Steve.' She spoke slowly as though she was explaining herself to a dull toddler.

'He's not coming with us? He is not coming with us!' Lizzy shouted and grabbed at her sister's arm.

'Shut up before somebody hears us,' Ellie whispered and nodded to encourage her sister to do the same.

'You planned this, you stupid, stupid cow. The two of you planned this and never even asked me about it. Did you think I might like to know what you had in mind? Did you think about me at all, even for a second? Why is he coming with us, anyway? We don't need him or anybody else, for that matter.' Lizzy's voice had dropped to a whisper to match her sister's.

'They're just terrible to him here. He's been planning to run away for a while, anyway. He's coming with us to do the driving and take care of the car. Besides, this way we have protection.'

'Protection? Protection from a juvenile delinquent? We will be lucky if he doesn't slit our throats and eat our livers.' Lizzy had recently come across a copy of a particularly lurid crime magazine. She'd read the article on cannibal killers twice in case she ever got into a situation where she might need to know about such people. She hadn't expected to need the information so soon. 'I don't trust him, El. He's got round dark balls, like empty spaces where other people have nice colours. I don't know what it means, but it's too ugly to be something good.' She'd dreamed a few nights before about those empty black places she saw on Steve. She woke up sweating and had been afraid to go back to sleep.

'Would you just shut up about those colours?' Ellie turned away and looked out of the dark windows towards the Trail's End sign.

'I don't care if you believe in the colours or not, but even you should be able to see he's a juvenile delinquent.'

'He's not a juvenile delinquent. He got in trouble once, but it really wasn't his fault. He was just sitting in the car.' Ellie sat up a little straighter as she defended her man.

'He was driving the car while his friend robbed a liquor store with a gun. If he hadn't been only fourteen he'd be in Folsam Prison right now, looking forward to a tasty meal of bread and water.' Lizzy wished he was in Folsam right now. She wished he was in Folsam and she wished that the guards had forgotten to give him his bread and water. His throat would get too dry to ask for anything and he'd just shrivel up and blow away like the piece of poo he was.

'He made a mistake and spent three months in Juvee. He's paid his debt to society and it doesn't even go on his record if he stays out of trouble until he's eighteen. He's got that all behind him.' Ellie shivered slightly at the thought of her beloved in the infamous Juvenile Hall. Juvee was right across the street from the Welfare office in Fresno. Kids would scurry by and give it furtive looks. Lizzy had always made a point to hold her breath when she walked by Juvee in case criminal behaviour was some sort of airborne germ.

'I don't think three months in Juvee puts anything behind anybody. Rosa Martinez' sister Carla was there for four months and all she did was make poodle dolls out of coat hangers and those plastic bags they put over dry cleaning. She gave one to Rosa and it was the tackiest thing I'd ever seen.' Lizzy warmed to her thoughts on the penal system. 'And don't pretend that you didn't know that Carla was pregnant just a few months after she'd been making all those poodle dolls. As soon as she got out of there she started doing that baby making thing. That's probably what she learned to do in Juvee.' Whatever you did to get pregnant was a crime before eighteen or marriage, so Lizzy figured it would be something those at Juvee would be familiar with.

'Carla is pregnant? I thought she was living with her aunt in Concord. She told us her aunt was lonely and she was going to keep her company.' Ellie's voice lost her whisper in the excitement of hearing a scrap of gossip. Most gossip was interesting, but anything that involved pregnancy was enough to grind everything else to a sudden halt.

'Carla is living in her bedroom just the same as always. Her mother is so fat, she's telling everybody she's going to have a baby, and when the baby is born everybody will say it's Carla and Rosa's little brother or sister.' Lizzy was fairly puffed up with this scoop. Most kids only knew the gossip about their own grade. She didn't consider herself to be a gossip, but she did have a knack for acquiring information. She was the first one to know that Mrs Lindstrom, the school nurse, was getting a divorce. 'Rosa says Carla's belly button sticks out and it's all brown. Her boobies have gotten even bigger than yours. She must look like a big old cow.' The 'big' jumped from her mouth as she spread her arms wide to describe this new bovine aspect of her friend's sister.

'My gosh.' Ellie put her hand across her flat belly. 'I hadn't heard anything about it.'

'I think it happens more than we know. I think it's interesting that only girls ever get mononucleosis so bad that they have to leave town for a few months. The boys and the nice girls are only out of school for a few days, a week or two at most.'

'What about Linda Dorsey and Pam Thorpe?' Ellie was clearly trying to remember every lengthy absence in the last few months.

'I can't say for sure, but Linda's boyfriend definitely has been in Juvee.' Lizzy sat back, satisfied that she had made her point. 'Pam's a different story because she's always had those icky rashes inside her elbows, so she might really have been sick.' She felt she'd needed to come to Pam's defence because the fat girl with the runny nose and bad skin had always seemed like a fellow outsider to Lizzy.

'I think you're right about Pam, because she's too ugly to get pregnant, but just because Linda's boyfriend had some trouble doesn't mean she's knocked up.' Ellie pouted her lips and turned away.

'It means we shouldn't take a convicted criminal with us. You learn things at Juvee that can turn you bad. I think you could put the best kid in school in Juvee and they'd turn rotten. Even you have to admit Steve is not the best kid in town.' She watched her sister's reaction in the dim light hoping her well presented arguments would make a dent in the stupid ideas Ellie had about Steve. She remembered a commercial on TV where people had a hard, invisible wall go up in front of them as soon as they brushed their teeth. Ellie seemed to have that same kind of wall around her only hers wasn't stopping cavities.

'Someday you'll understand, Lizzy.'

'I think I'd rather burn in hell with Mrs Kirby's Masons than understand what you see in Mr Steve Ratface.' Lizzy closed her eyes and could almost hear her mother talking about this man or that man and how some day the girls would understand why she put up with the things she did and why they had to put up with her stupid men and her smelly wine.

'His name is Steve Ratcliff. I don't want you calling him Ratface.'

'Ratface suits him better.'

'Shut that window, Lizzy. It's getting cold up here.' Ellie pushed slightly away from her snuggling up to the driving Steve.

'I have to keep the window open so I don't suffocate from the smell of car grease and Old Spice.' Lizzy shivered in the back seat, but didn't want to cooperate with the young lovers any more than necessary. Steve hadn't even glanced in her direction when he got in the car back at Trail's End. He only seemed to notice Ellie and her big, overstuffed shirt.

'No wonder you're cold. Pull yourself a little closer and I'll keep you warm as toast.' Steve chuckled and reached his arm across Ellie's back and ran his hand down the front of her shirt. 'Something's sticking out inside your shirt, Ellie. Here, let me brush those toast crumbs away.' Ellie squealed and said something Lizzy couldn't hear.

'I'm closing my window. You can sit on your own side now, Ellie.' Lizzy was annoyed when her sister stayed sitting practically in Steve's lap. 'Ellie, I said I closed the window. You shouldn't be cold now.' She raised her voice until she was almost shouting.

'Shut up, Lizzy.' Ellie didn't even bother to turn around.

'Just shut up and go to sleep, sister. Time you wake up I'll have you in the Sierra Nevadas.' Steve's voice cracked slightly higher, skipping above the Southern drawl he affected.

'Have you ever driven in the mountains? You don't drive in the mountains the same way you do in the valleys, you know.' Her mother had always refused to drive into the mountains, although on clear days they could be seen from their house. The girls had seen snow all their lives, but had yet to touch it. Laura had instilled in her daughters a certainty about the difficulty of mountain driving. She thought highway driving was also fraught with risk unless you possessed exquisite eyesight and lightning fast reflexes. Unlike most drunks, she knew she was a lousy driver. Many times she'd driven five or more miles out of her way to avoid the dread highways with their invitation of speed and grisly deaths.

'I've been driving since I was twelve, sister. Mountain driving is just a little steeper and curvier. Long as you watch the road, you're OK.' Steve glanced over his shoulder, looking at Lizzy for the first time.

'Watch where you're going.' Lizzy gave his head a push for good measure, her hand coming away coated with a film of hair oil. 'You haven't been driving as long as our mother and she never would drive into the mountains. I think we should have taken the desert route. It would have been easier.' There didn't seem any reason to try to talk sense into Ellie directly. Two against one, that was what it was. Anything Steve Ratface said, Ellie would agree with before you could say jack shit. Ever since she'd met him Ellie had lost whatever decision-making capacity she'd had. It was always: 'Yes, Steve, whatever you say, Steve.'

'I told you before, yes, it would be easier to go into the desert, but this is smarter. If we went through the desert we would be easier to spot. If we break down we'd be stuck in the middle of open road where anybody could see us. Besides, anybody looking for us will figure we'll head for the desert.' Steve stretched his long pimply neck until it made a cracking sound. 'Light me one, Ellie.'

'They'll think we went through the desert because it's the way we should have gone. It was the smart way to go. The problem is, once somebody figures out Steve is with us they'll start thinking we wouldn't do things the smart way. If we did things the smart way we wouldn't have old Ratface with us,' Lizzy muttered, hoping Ellie would hear her, but Steve wouldn't. She watched in disgust as Ellie scrambled to light a cigarette as quickly as possible. She usually moved as if she was practising for underwater ballet. Funny how much energy she seemed to have whenever Steve wanted something.

'There are lots of little towns in the mountains where we can buy supplies. Lots of cabins and side roads, too. I figure we head for one of the ski resorts and find a cabin that nobody uses this time of year. We can stay there until we work out what we're going to do.' Steve glanced towards the back seat again.

'We don't need to go to some stupid cabin to work out what

we're going to do. Ellie and I are going to take this car to Nevada. Once we get there we give ourselves new names and make up some good stories about where we're from. After that we get jobs and get ourselves back in school. Everything is figured out as much as we can figure things out.' Lizzy wanted to get Steve out of long-range planning as quickly as possible. She could see them leaving him in the men's room at a Bob's Big Boy and driving to Nevada, where they'd be safe and happy. She could be Mary Charles and Ellie could be Victoria Charles. They'd still be named after queens of England, so they'd be less likely to forget their new names.

Steve's voice startled her because she'd placed him so carefully in the men's room at Bob's Big Boy. 'Trust me, sister. I know what I'm doing.'

'Trust you?' Her voice rose to a squeak. 'I don't trust juvenile delinquents. And I'm not your sister, in case you hadn't noticed.'

'Shut up, Lizzy. Steve needs to concentrate.'

'Steve doesn't need to concentrate. Concentration requires some kind of brain, and his head is as empty as a coconut. Steve is dumber than dirt and we all know it! Ellie, what is wrong with you? This was supposed to be just the two of us, and then you bring this creepy, ratfaced thing along. You are letting this smelly boy decide where and how we live the rest of our lives.'

The car swerved to the side of the road and screeched to a halt. Steve reached across, into the back, and grabbed Lizzy by the hair. 'Shut up, brat!' He slapped her across the left side of her face. 'Do you hear me? Answer me!' He shook her head back and forth.

'Let me go!' Lizzy clawed at his arms and tried to kick the back of his seat.

'Stop that!' He slapped her again, harder this time. He grabbed the hair at the back of her neck tighter, twisting it in his hands until she couldn't move.

Lizzy sat as still as she could. Her cheeks burned as her chest heaved with the effort to stifle a sob. She wanted to scratch his face off, but the smallest movement hurt.

'I'm driving and I decide where we go and why. I'm sick of you and if it was up to me I'd leave you on the side of the road right now. Do you hear me?'

Lizzy tried to nod, but heard the hairs in his hand breaking with her efforts. 'Yes, I hear you.' She spoke as softly as she could because it wouldn't count if nobody heard the words.

'Let her go, Steve, she's just a kid.' Ellie patted Steve's arm as he released his grip on the younger girl.

'I don't like it when people try to shove me around. Just keep her and her smart mouth away from me.' He pulled a strand of Lizzy's hair from between his fingers and looked at it as though he couldn't figure out how it got there. 'Make her behave, Ellie. This is our chance and I won't let her or anybody else ruin it for the two of us.'

'She'll be good, won't you, Lizzy?' She turned to Lizzy and lowered her voice. 'Lizzy, you need to be good. Stop being so fresh and just cooperate. Please, please don't mess this up for us. This is our big chance.'

Lizzy turned away and stared out of the car window into the black night.

Cotherstone, West Sussex, February 12th

Dearest Mary,

I didn't realize how I missed you until I heard your sweet voice yesterday! Your touch of an accent was something of a shock, I must admit. Of course you come by it honestly. In spite of Mrs Harper's best efforts to eradicate it in my youth, I've managed to hang on to a bit of that old valley twang. Kidding aside, you have just a hint of California in the vowels and it sounds very nice. Shocking, but nice.

I didn't want you to think I was putting you off on the phone, I just am much more comfortable writing to you about what happened so long ago. It has taken me years to even think about all of it. Sounds quite mad, I know, but I really shoved those memories very deep. I'd forgotten some of the worst parts until you were about the age I was when everything happened. I went to a counsellor for a year or so and that helped some. I suppose by writing to you and putting things on paper in dribs and drabs I can view it as just another story. It gives me some distance and even after all these years, I still need that.

You said yesterday how surprised you were about your grandmother and what a terrible mother she must have been. I like to think that under different circumstances she would have been a fine mother. Raising children is not a one-person job, and she was trying to raise the two of us by herself. Her own childhood had been difficult and disruptive. Shuttled around in labour camps and always being reminded that you didn't really belong in the family

*must have been ghastly. Don't forget that parenting is something
that is taught, and she probably had some pretty lousy teachers. I
don't want to think what my mothering skills would have been like
if my 'fairy godmothers' and your gran hadn't shown me the way.*

*To compound her problems my mother's education was very
limited, though she was a keen observer of those around her. She
did try to reinvent herself as Laura Sinclair. Of course it would
have taken a great deal more than a mere name change to become
a new and improved model. Her naming her daughters Eleanor
and Elizabeth is very odd. She loved to tell us we had been named
after the two greatest queens in English history. I don't know
where she got this information. I don't remember her being much
of a reader and I don't recall any other interest in history. I've
always thought it curious that a little Okie girl would name her
daughters after queens. I can only assume she hoped we would take
on the qualities she thought the 'QEs' had. Maybe some morning
I'll wake up with a burning desire to wear a ruff and a red wig.*

*My mother always made us aware of 'trashy' behaviour and
did her best to keep us away from 'trashy' people. Of course, most
people would have regarded the three of us as trashy. I think what
she did in many respects was to isolate us so that we were neither
fish nor fowl. We were taught that we were better than the kids
who lived in similar circumstances to our own, but the children she
would have chosen for our friends wouldn't have much to do with
us because of her. The middle-class mothers were put off the idea
of their children spending much time with the offspring of an
alcoholic prostitute. Can't say in retrospect that I blame them.*

*She really wanted to give us more of everything, and not just in
the material sense either. She tried to instil in us that we were
better than our lives indicated. She wanted us to have some sense
of middle-class values, but she was terribly unclear, in her own
mind, what those values were. Having no real role models, she
simply pasted together what she could glean from the world around
her; that terrible, narrow, poverty-stricken world she'd been
born to.*

Deep down, I believe she was an intelligent, beautiful woman who suffered from a horrible, fatal disease. I have to think about what she could have been if she'd found some of the love and stability that I've been given in my life.

Try to step back and don't judge her by your standards. A woman's options were much more limited back then. These past thirty, forty years have been nothing short of revolutionary for women and society. I think she tried, but eventually drowned herself in wine because she fell so short of her own standards.

I know this is a lot to swallow and I can stop at any time. If you prefer I can write it all down and you can look at it when you feel ready. The choice is yours. At the end of the day we can do nothing about the past, but we can change the future. Yes, I do believe I shall needlepoint that on a cushion!

It's two days to Valentine's Day, but I don't think Daddy and I will do anything special. He has a miserable cold he can't seem to shake. I'm trying to get him to go to the doctor, but you know how he is. He's always self-diagnosing and has decided that he can't be helped by anything the doctor could do. He's probably right, but I wish he would get it checked out. He sounds horrible and neither of us can sleep with his nocturnal snortings and hackings. I'd sleep in the guest room, but creature of habit that I am, I love my familiar bit of bed.

I think Chaz has something special planned for the lovely Sarah. He's quite smitten and I suppose that's how first love is supposed to be. They are always pawing and snogging in front of us, which I find more than a little disconcerting. I'm sure they're like rabbits when we're not around, but I really don't like having it shoved in my face. Oh well, I suppose that's Chaz. Remember how long it took us to convince him that his willy was a toy for private and not public play?

I forgot to mention to you that I've decided against getting another animal, at least for now. I stopped by the Wentworths' the other day and they have just bought the loveliest Lab puppy I have ever seen. It has a coat that looks like brown velvet.

Gorgeous, but it piddled twice and pooped once in the span of time it took to drink two cups of coffee. I'd forgotten about the down side of babies in the house. I suppose I'll just have to stay a bit broody until summer, when I can keep the little monster outside until it's fit for the house. I guess I could get a kitten, but they always turn into lazy cats. I want something that will follow me around and adore me. Is it too late for me to be elected Queen of the Universe?

Well, child of mine, since we filled the coffers of BT yesterday, I don't have a great deal more to write. I'm going to close now and walk Patch in this green and pleasant land which is presently grey and gloomy.

Love and God bless

Mummy

PS Could you look into a friendly fax? Since your answerphone is always having fits and some of your housemates seem preverbal, I worry about not getting in touch with you in an emergency. No, I don't anticipate an emergency. XXXOOO

CHAPTER FIVE

They'd laugh when they got home in the evening. One of the family jokes, her need to augment every holiday by changing the display on the mantel. Liz opened the box marked 'Valentine's Day' and lifted out a small clear plastic container which held old greetings cards her mother-in-law had come across when she was clearing out the worldly goods of one of her many dead relatives.

She set it aside and pulled out a crêpe paper garland of red and pink hearts she'd found in London last year.

She arranged the garland so that the hearts hung over the edge of the mantel and moved with the slightest movement. She'd have a fire going when they came home and the hearts would be dancing gaily to dispel the midwinter gloom of an early sunset.

Liz stepped back to admire the garland and dipped her hand into the box without looking. The brush of feathers made her glance down and her gaze was met by a kewpie doll in a miniature red feather boa. 'I'd forgotten all about you.' She pulled the doll out and blew on the tiny boa to refresh the feathers, which had been flattened by a year's storage.

She put the doll on the mantel, its flat feet buried in bright pink and red hearts. She stepped back, but the round-bellied, sway-backed doll now looked like an obscenely grinning pregnant child. She took the doll down and tossed it back into the box.

The Sierras, California, July 1962

Steve had been right. When she woke they were in the mountains. In the dawn light she watched the trees change from cottonwood and scrub oak to pine and fir. The road wrapped itself around the mountains like a smokey grey ribbon. Great slabs of white granite seemed pressed into the mountains, while others looked to have slid into deep gullies and narrow valleys where slivers of water cut through the stone. The air was cool and sharp with the smell of pine.

Ellie was curled up asleep against the car door, while Steve was driving and smoking with his left elbow out the car's window. Lizzy was pleased to note an angry red pustule on the back of his neck that had to hurt something fierce. She hoped it would get infected and spread. Maybe it would get so bad his whole head would fall off and she could kick it away like a rotten apple. That was about how big his head should be, considering how dumb he was and how tiny his brain must be. Maybe his head would be nasty and smelly like a carved pumpkin a few days after Hallowe'en. It would be all black and mouldy inside and tiny little flies would buzz around it. She smiled as she thought about the maggots chewing up the soft pulp of Steve's head.

Steve glanced into the rear-view mirror and saw her staring at his reflection in the small glass. 'I was wondering when you would wake up.' He smiled his wolfish smile as she looked away and covered her mouth.

'About what happened earlier; I don't see any reason it should happen again. Just be careful and it won't.' He ran his hand through his hair as he took another look in the mirror.

'It shouldn't have happened the first time.' She decided she would never speak to him again. Just didn't seem worth the effort. She would find a way to get the car and Ellie away from him and break the spell he had on her. Before last night she'd thought 'crazy in love' was just a stupid expression.

'Won't do you any good to pout and pull faces. We're in this together. I know Ellie wants you two to stay together, and she knows I'm the one the two of you need. How far do you think you would have got today on your own?' He waited a moment for an answer that didn't come. 'We're already three counties away. You two would still be trying to get out of town. Like it or not, I got you out of Clifford and out of a hell of a lot of trouble.'

There were about a million things she could have said to him, but she wasn't about to give him the satisfaction of a conversation. It would be like having a discussion with a worm or a cockroach. She softly kicked at the back of her sister's seat in hopes of awakening her so she'd have someone to talk to who wasn't a worm or a cockroach.

'What time is it?' Ellie sat up and rubbed her eyes. She

turned and looked at the back of her seat with a slightly confused expression.

'About time to take a pee. I'm just waiting for a road or something where I can turn off. Think you can keep an eye on the kid while I take a leak?' Steve reached over and stroked the top of Ellie's head as he pulled the car in the direction of a side road. He climbed out and walked towards a small grove of trees.

'What about it, Lizzy?' She turned around and gave her sister a bright smile, marred slightly by the dark patches of smeared make-up under her eyes.

'What about what?' She didn't look at Ellie. She was as much, maybe more, at fault as Steve for his being with them. Lizzy didn't see why her life should be ruined just because Ellie was in 'love' again.

'Come on, Lizzy. Don't be like that.' Ellie was still wearing her lettergirl's smile as Steve walked away from the car. It was the same smile she'd practised for a week when she found out the photographer from the *Clifford Clarion* was coming out to take pictures of the new squad of lettergirls. Ellie had been smiling so much to practise that she kept getting little spastic attacks in her cheeks. Made her look as if she was trying to hide a mouse in her mouth half the time. Ellie adjusted the rear-view mirror and rubbed at the dark smudges under her eyes.

'I can be any way I want, Ellie! My mother is dead and my sister is crazy about a moron who thinks he can hit me whenever he wants.' Lizzy began to cry in great gasping sobs. 'I want my mother. I want my mother and I want to go home.' Laura before the bad times. The beautiful, sweet-smelling Laura who sang silly songs and made her laugh. The Laura who would draw a few lines on her fist and make her fist say stupid things that would make you laugh so hard it almost hurt. 'Mrs Kirby said they wouldn't break us up and I think she was right. We should go back and tell somebody what happened. We should turn around right now while he's peeing. This whole thing has gotten way out of hand.'

'Not now, Lizzy. We can't go back now.' Ellie turned away from her sister, her lettergirl's smile gone.

'But Mrs Kirby said . . .'

'Mrs Kirby is crazy, in case you didn't notice.'

'I still think . . .'

'Hush. He's coming back and I don't want him getting mad at you again.'

'You shouldn't have given him any money.' Lizzy had watched in disbelief as Ellie had handed Steve money from the bag.

'We have to have groceries, don't we? Groceries cost money here the same as they do at home.' Steve had parked the car around the back of a small general store. Ellie had been instructed to keep an eye on her sister.

'We have to take care of each other. You told me we would have a dog and locks on our doors. You said we wouldn't have hairy men crawling around and bothering us and then you go and invite him along like this is some kind of school dance and you don't want to be without a date. I think you are crazy. No, I take that back. I know you're crazy. You're crazier than Mrs Kirby, and even you said she was crazy.' Lizzy stared out the window, refusing to look at the older girl.

'Lizzy, listen to me. I knew we couldn't do it on our own. I barely know how to drive and I don't know anything about how a car works. Steve loves me and he'll make sure that nothing bad happens to us.'

'He'll make sure nothing bad happens? What do you think about what he did to me? That wasn't bad? Was that a good thing? You never even asked me if he could come along. What kind of boy hits little girls, anyway?' Lizzy hadn't described herself as a little girl since she was five, but she felt in this case it strengthened her position.

'He didn't hurt you, Lizzy. Besides, you said some awful things about him. He's not dumb and he doesn't smell bad. All guys smell like that. I think it's their glands or something. You were just trying to get his goat and you know it. If you're nice to him I'm sure he'll be nice to you. Just try sweetening up a little. I know you can do it.' Ellie turned the rear-view mirror in her direction and started combing her long dark hair. Lizzy watched her making flirty little faces to herself in the mirror.

'I'll tell you right now, Eleanor, I'm never going to be stupid about boys. I think they are very dangerous.' She paused for a moment. 'And he is dumb and he *does* smell very bad. Maybe you can pretend, but I can't. He's just going to be around until he gets bored with you. Mom said boys are like that, and for once, I think she was probably right. You've always had lots of boyfriends and they either get another girlfriend, start playing football, or they just get bored with you. Steve is too creepy to get another girlfriend and he's too skinny to play football, so he's definitely going to get bored with you. Better check your watch so you can look back on this moment and remember the exact time you heard the truth.'

'You are such an expert, aren't you? You don't have the slightest idea about anything.'

'You don't have to be an expert to figure this one out, El. Any moron could tell you nice people don't hit kids and nice people don't rob liquor stores.' She took a deep breath before speaking. 'Take a sniff, Ellie. That's rat you're smelling, even if you're too dumb to know it.'

'He is not a rat, and I've told you before about that stupid robbery; he just drove the car.'

'Yeah, he just drove the car because he's so ugly the other guy was ashamed to be seen with him. Even a funny face like you should be able to do better than old ratface.'

'Sometimes I really hate you.' Ellie stuck her tongue out at her sister.

'Then it shouldn't bother you to find out that right now the feeling is mutual, and I expect this feeling to last quite a long time.'

'Why don't you just shut up?'

'Because I enjoy intelligent conversation and if I shut up I won't hear anything worth listening to.' Lizzy jerked open the car door and stepped out.

'Lizzy, get back in the car. Get back in the car, now!' Ellie spoke through clenched teeth and pointed towards the back seat.

'I just want to stretch my legs, if that's all right, Queen of the World. I believe that's still one of my rights as an American citizen.' She turned away from the car and saw a young man in a forest ranger's uniform approaching.

'Hi, girls. You're up bright and early this morning.' He leaned against the passenger side of the Ford and grinned at Ellie. 'Where you staying?'

'Up the road a little.' Lizzy smiled at him, surprised that her voice didn't shake. He was very tall, but didn't look as if he was old enough to be out of high school.

'You camping?' He grinned at Ellie again, ignoring Lizzy although she was standing right next to him.

'That's right.' Ellie flashed a smile and sat up a little straighter.

'I'm here with the fire patrol for the next three weeks, unless they send us somewhere else, that is. Between the government and the fires we never really know where we're at from one day to the next.' He glanced appreciatively at Ellie's chest. 'How long are you going to be up here?'

'We won't be very long. We're just passing through, sort of.' Lizzy looked towards the general store for a sign of Steve.

'Which camp are you staying in?' He adjusted his hat, revealing the dark stubble of a crew cut.

'Which camp are we staying in?' Ellie looked at Lizzy and shrugged her shoulders.

'We're staying at the big one.' Lizzy nodded and hoped that there was a big one. A forest ranger was just a campfire story and a nature hike away from a cop. Wouldn't do to have a him sniffing around and asking questions.

'So you're staying at Granite?'

'That's right, Granite. We're staying at Granite. I think I'd forget my head if it wasn't grown on.' Ellie giggled and moved her head back and forth to demonstrate how securely it was attached.

'Maybe I'll see you over there tonight. The younger guys usually go over for the campfire. Have you been to one of the campfires yet?'

'No, but maybe I'll go tonight.' Ellie gave him one of her newspaper smiles.

'Good. Real good. Glad I ran into you.' He nodded his head and stepped away from the car. 'What's your name, by the way?'

Ellie blinked and opened her mouth. 'I'm . . .'

'She's Victoria and I'm Mary. Lizzy glanced at her sister and shook her head slightly. Victoria and Mary Charles. We're from San Diego. Our brother is in the store and our parents are back at Granite. Our grandfather is with us too.'

'See you later.' He waved and walked towards the front of the store. Halfway there he turned and gave Ellie another little wave, which she returned with enthusiasm.

'Nice one, Eleanor. I'm surprised you didn't jump out and do the shimmy for him.'

'What are you talking about?'

'The last thing we need is some dumb ranger chasing us around. We shouldn't be drawing attention to ourselves.'

'I didn't do anything.'

'You just grinned and flirted and practically stuck those big old things in his face.'

'I was just being nice.'

'Fine time for you to start being nice. Never been nice a day in your life and all of a sudden, the one time I'd like you to be lousy, you turn all sweet and lovely.'

'I thought you were the one who wanted to turn around and give ourselves up. Why didn't you just spill the beans and get it over with? You missed your big chance.'

'I kept my mouth shut because we're partners. Unlike you,

when I make a deal I stick with it. We both have to agree what we're going to do next.'

'You mean all three of us have to agree.'

'You are pathetic, Eleanor.'

'You two stay right here while I go take a look at that cabin over there.' Steve pointed to a small peaked roof a few hundred yards off the unpaved logging road they'd been travelling on. 'I'll be back in a minute, so just sit tight.' He climbed out of the car and swaggered off like the Marlboro Man.

'Ellie, tell me again how breaking and entering is going to make our lives better.' Lizzy had watched enough police shows to know this was a seriously bad idea.

'Steve thinks we should stay off the road for two or three days, in case somebody is looking for us. All we want to do is find an empty cabin where we can hide for a few days.'

'That's another thing, Ellie. If he hadn't come along, I don't think anybody would be looking for us. We made things look like we left with Mom in the middle of the night. That was the plan. Remember, the plan we agreed on? But you and the creep had to ruin that. Now his aunt and uncle are going to tell somebody he's missing too. Even his stupid family will put two and two together once they hear we're gone.'

'It will be a while before anybody knows the two of us are gone.'

'It's going to be a pretty short while if you think about it. You don't show up for lettergirl practice and I don't go down to the river. Neither one of us goes to the store or empties the mailbox. The rent doesn't get paid this week and Mom's hairy men find an empty house. That's seven lettergirls, one faculty adviser, Mr Lopez at the store, the mailman, Mr Carlson the landlord, about twenty kids at the river, and Mom's hairy men. Add that to Steve's aunt and uncle plus his friends, if he's got any, which I doubt. You don't have to be good at math to know that's an awful lot of people to get suspicious.'

'People will just figure we're on a trip or something.' Ellie shrugged her shoulders and looked at her fingernails.

'People would have thought Mom and her two daughters ran out of town. Jesus H. Christ, we sure had enough reasons to pull out in the middle of the night. Nobody would have thought it was even a little weird, but once they figure out that Steve is with us, they'll start looking.'

'Why?'

'Because they'll know a woman who leaves town in the middle of the night with her two daughters does not, I repeat, does not drag a fourteen-year-old criminal along for the thrill of it all. Mom may have had her problems, but she wouldn't have been stupid enough to bring him along with us just because her boy-crazy daughter had a crush on him. She thought he was trash. She told me that more than once.' Laura had never mentioned Steve, but Lizzy felt that was an oversight she would have corrected if she'd realized she was about to die.

'She wouldn't have felt that way if she'd gotten to know him.'

'She *thought* he was trash because she didn't know him. If she'd gotten to know him she would have *known* beyond a shadow of a doubt that he was trash.' Lizzy gave the back of her sister's car seat a kick in frustration.

'And just what do you think we are? Who the hell do you think you are? You go on about this one being trashy and that one being trashy, but you never stop and think how people see us. Our mother was a drunk and we are just a couple of Okie kids. We don't even know who our father was. We don't even know if we had the same father. On top of everything else we are bastards. Lizzy, the two of us are just about as trashy as you can get without having your address read "Number Five, City Dump".'

'It doesn't matter what other people think of us, Ellie. What matters is how we feel about ourselves. I'm smart and I'm tough. That's what I think matters.' She spoke quickly, eager to reassure her sister, and herself.

'You won't feel that way when you're older. You won't feel that way when you start wanting nice clothes and you want to live in a nice house. We *are* trash and so is Steve, but we aren't going to stay this way. Steve and I are going to work hard and make some money. We've got plans and dreams and I'm not going to let you or anybody else stop us.'

'I'm glad you've got dreams, Ellie.' Lizzy closed her eyes and saw her mother motionless on the bathroom floor. She watched her lying there with the flies buzzing all around her and climbing on her sick-stained face. *How long did you plan this, Ellie? How long did you and Steve plan to kill her?* She'd choked on her own vomit. She could see Ellie and Steve holding her on her back while she choked. Maybe they drugged her. It would have been easy enough to do. *Did she stare at you, Ellie? Did she stare at you with those bloodshot eyes? Did she know what was happening?*

'The dreams are for you too, Lizzy. You're real smart and you can do anything you want. We'll all take care of each other, you'll see.'

Lizzy didn't answer, but swore at herself for not paying more attention when Steve was driving.

Cotherstone, West Sussex, February 19th

Dearest Mary,

Another day in paradise. There is about an inch of slushy snow on the ground and it has started to rain. The water heater is acting up again and the bloody thing is only three months old. I snapped at the poor woman whose husband comes over and stares at it every two weeks. He is such an incompetent, but he is the authorized dealer so I have no choice in the matter. I try to be a nice person, but, well, you of all people know what a bitch I can be.

Your father is still feeling horrid. Of course he's keeping the same hours and even drove up to Leeds yesterday. I am convinced if he would simply sit in a shellsuit and sip hot lemonade for three days he would be a new man. If he would even stay home for one day and drink hot lemonade it would do him a world of good. If I ever neglected myself the way he does I would be nagged into the next county. Oh well, that's life, what are you going to do? Answer: not a hell of a lot.

I think I may be suffering from that SAD business. You know, that thing where you don't get enough gamma rays or something into your brain because of lousy weather, combined with the fact that the only shoes in the shops right now are stupid-looking. I know I'd feel better if I could find a pair of really great shoes. I know, I know, terribly post-feminist.

Chaz is fine. Apparently he and the lovely Sarah have cooled things down for now. I think I heard some rumblings about a Claire person who is new on the scene. I haven't met her, may not, but I would like to know if she has any sort of metal or pierced bits on her face.

Patch's skin is acting up again and I had to give him one of those foul-smelling medicated shampoos. In protest he peed in our bed. Stupid twit. I told him I was going to replace him with a basket of kittens. He was unimpressed.

Your grandmother is doing just fine sans her car. Although I've told her I will make myself available she insists on walking to do her shopping. She says she feels better for the exercise and doesn't want to bother me. The interesting thing is, before she sold her car I was driving her to the shops all the time! I told her it was my pleasure, but you know how stubborn she can be. Your father comes by his stubbornness honestly.

I saw your friend Alice Glenn on Sunday. She looks absolutely splendid in her seventh month of pregnancy and sends her love. She and her husband are building a house on William Close and hope to be moved in by the time the baby is born. They seem very happy, but I still think she is awfully young to be so settled. I'm delighted you are footloose and fancy-free. You still are, aren't you? The ties that bind come soon enough.

Silly coming from me, I suppose. After all, I was married at eighteen to a man several years my senior. Although I'm glad you didn't marry so young, I have no regrets that I did. I can't imagine what my life would have been like without your father. That sounds pitiful and that's not what I intend. I'm sure I would have had a fine life, yet I'm also sure it's a great deal finer with your father. I still think it's a bit of a fairy tale, but you already know that story.

On to the story you don't know. Actually this is still about your father. I remember thinking, shortly after I met him, that this, our relationship, was the end of the curse. I thought of the women in my family as being cursed by men, or with men. My grandmother had died giving birth as a teenager with no man in sight; my mother, well, you know about that; and then there was Ellie and her Steve. Steve Ratcliff aka Steve Ratface, the joyriding boyfriend. That sounds so flip: the joyriding boyfriend. To this day I have problems being civil to men with the name Steve.

I didn't know until we started out that first night that Steve was coming with us. I tried to talk Ellie out of it, but she was in love. I still don't understand how a girl who lived in the same house as me could not have seen Steve for what he was. I always felt that one thing I learned at my mother's knee was how to spot one of his kind a mile away. God knows, Ellie and I had seen enough of them walking into our mother's room.

The original plan had been for us to travel to Nevada, via the desert, but Steve wanted to stay in California and go into the Sierra Nevada Mountains. I wanted to stick with the original plan, but Steve roughed me up to get his point across. Steve won.

I think it must have been the first time either of us had been that far from home. Of course, by then I realized the only real home we had was each other. That was the most frightening thing of all, since Ellie hardly seemed to know I was alive any longer.

Enough for now. I'm starting to think a Cadbury's Dairy Milk would make it all better, and that is a very bad sign. I went through enough with Steve without gaining weight from his memory. More next time, stay tuned.

This letter sounds so black and depressing. I'm definitely going shopping for some wonderful shoes. Send us some more pictures, we loved the last lot.

Love and God bless

Mummy

CHAPTER SIX

'India? India?' After ringing the bell to no avail, she'd used the key her mother-in-law kept hidden inside a pair of wellies by the front door. The front hall was dark and the curtains were still closed in spite of it being after ten in the morning. 'India, it's Liz.' She raised her voice, afraid it wouldn't be answered. She sniffed the air, but could smell nothing. The house should smell of eggs and coffee by this time. India always had a plate of eggs and a pot of coffee in the morning.

She hurried up the stairs and knocked on the woman's bedroom door. 'India, it's Liz.' She pushed the door open and saw her mother-in-law sitting up in bed. 'India, you scared me half to death!'

'Sorry, it's my throat.' The old woman put her hand on her neck and winced.

'I bet you've caught that thing your son has.' She laid the back of her hand gently on the woman's cheeks. 'I think you're running a fever. Have you called the doctor?'

India shook her head and pointed to a bedside chair. 'Don't get so close. I don't want you to catch this too.'

'I'm not worried about that, India. I've been sleeping next to my husband and his disease for over a week. If I'm going to get it, I'm going to get it.' She sat in the bedside chair and a large black and white cat jumped into her lap. 'Morning, Mugs.' She patted the cat's head and he immediately began to purr and butt his head against her hand.

'Mugs hasn't been fed this morning. I was going to get up, but I went back to sleep. I didn't wake up until I heard the doorbell.'

'Well, let me take care of the cat's brekky and then I'll get something organized for you. I'll give the doctor a call and see if we can get something to make you a little more comfortable.'

'The doctor can't do anything. These things just have to run their course.'

'Like mother, like son.' She smiled and pushed the cat off her lap as she stood. 'I've been trying to get your son to the doctor for a week and he's been telling me the same thing.'

'He's right.'

'Maybe he is and maybe he isn't. Bottom line, young lady, you are going to have the doctor come around.'

'These things . . .'

'These things can go into pneumonia. I won't hear another word about this. Your son won't listen to me, but you're going to.'

'You sound like me. When did you get so bossy?' The older woman smiled up affectionately.

'I learned at the feet of a master.' She bent over in something similar to a Regency bow.

'Good girl. I'm glad somebody pays attention.' She pointed back to the bedside chair. 'Sit down for a minute; Mugs and I can wait. There's something I want to tell you.'

'What is it, India?' She sat quickly and folded her hands in her lap so she wouldn't fidget. India hated fidgeting.

'I've been lying here thinking how I don't have that much longer to live, and I just want you to know how much you've given to this family.'

'India . . .'

She held her hand up to silence the younger woman. 'You probably think I'm being morbid, but I'm not at all. I know I'm not going to die from this thing, but I am over eighty, and one of these days some silly thing is going to kill me. I don't want to have my last thoughts about things I didn't say.'

'That seems reasonable enough.'

'I just want you to know how much I've enjoyed having you in the family. You've been a wonderful wife and your children are my favourite grandchildren. You have consistently been a credit to the Randall family.'

'Thank you, India. I want *you* to know that you have been wonderful to me through the years and I have loved being part of the family.' She smiled and reached over to touch the older woman's hand. 'This means a great deal to me, it really does.'

'I have a favour to ask of you and I hope you'll give it some consideration.'

'Ask away.' She began chewing on the inside of her cheek. India's sense of drama often made tiny requests seem like million-pound loan applications, but she had a funny feeling about this one. She wondered if her mother-in-law had purposely staged this to be something akin to a dying wish, but dismissed the thought as unworthy.

'I want you to see what you can do about mending things between my sons. It all happened so long ago, and I think if you said something to them it might make a difference.'

'India.' She wanted to say so much that she had never said. Old anger and passion threatened and begged to be announced. 'I'll think about it, but I'm not sure it would make a bit of difference to either of them.' She stood and pulled her cardigan closed. 'Now I'm going to make you some breakfast and call the doctor.'

Blue Creek, California, July 1962

'Don't take those down, Steve. Just take down the ones around the back.' Lizzy put a hand on Steve's arm to stop him from removing the wooden shutter from the front of the cabin. A logger's cabin, it hadn't even had a lock on the door, just shutters to protect the windows from the high snows that fell in winter. The structure was built on concrete blocks, about two feet above the ground. The unpainted walls blended into the woods as though it had sprung up after a heavy rainfall.

'I have to get them down or we won't have enough light inside.' He held a tyre iron he'd found in the trunk of Laura's Ford.

'If somebody drives this way we don't want them to see that we're here, do we? If you leave the shutters up and park the car behind those trees, nobody will see us.' She'd decided a few things since her conversation with Ellie. First, old Ellie was under some kind of spell. Lizzy had read about the Czarina in Russia and the way she had gone crazy for Rasputin in spite of the fact that he was old and smelly and her husband, the Czar, was really handsome and probably a lot cleaner than the mad monk. Steve didn't seem to have hypnotic vision or anything like that, but he did make Ellie do crazy things. If bringing him along wasn't crazy, Lizzy wanted to look in a dictionary and check the definition of the word.

She had also realized she'd better not do anything else to make Steve mad at her or Ellie. Giving him the silent treatment was almost guaranteed to make him mad, so she'd have to talk to him, and talk nice, at that. He reminded her of a dog that lived down the road from what had been their home. An old Dobermann, it usually just barked, but once, it broke its chain, got out and almost killed a full-grown bull on the next property. She was pretty sure Steve was capable of a lot more than barking.

He cocked his head and looked at her. 'Good thinking little sister.' He dug in his pockets and pulled out the car keys. 'Give these to Ellie and tell her where to park the car.' He tossed the keys and Lizzy caught them with one hand.

She ran into the cabin without looking back. Ellie was in the rudimentary kitchen, spreading butter on slices of bread and humming. Her hips swayed gently to her own music and her hair moved like a soft black cloud across her back. Ellie buttered and swayed for a minute or two before she noticed she had an audience. 'What are you looking at?' She hadn't spoken to Lizzy since they'd arrived.

'Steve wants you to move the car back into the trees. I'll show you where he said he wants it to go.' She smiled at her sister and opened her hand to show her the keys. A peace offering.

Peace was important until she could figure out how to fight the war.

'Well, I'm glad you two are talking. He really is the sweetest guy once you get to know him.' Ellie glanced around the cabin as though it were a four-bedroom, three-and-a-half bathroom model home with wall-to-wall carpet and a sunburst clock over the flagstone fireplace. 'I think this is going to work out fine.'

'Do you feel OK, Ellie? Your colours have a lot of light pink I've never seen before.' Lizzy saw an extra layer of opalescent pink light which seemed to divide like shards of crystal around her sister's trunk.

'Lizzy.' Ellie looked at her sister in exasperation. 'Please don't start that again.'

'I just thought you should know. I don't know what it means, I just know it means something.' As far as she knew, her mother was the only person in the world besides Lizzy who'd ever seen the colours. Laura didn't know what they meant, but Lizzy knew they had to mean something. Only Steve Ratface and one of the hairy men who used to come to see their mother had the black balls of space where colours should have been, but she'd seen Mrs Kirby's sepia light around sick people before.

'Maybe it just means I'm in a good mood.' Ellie giggled and went back to her sandwich-making.

'Have you thought about where everybody is going to sleep?' The cabin had two rooms and six iron cots covered with old mattresses.

'Steve and I will sleep in the other room and you can sleep out here. You can have any bed out here you want.'

'Ellie, you can't sleep in the same room with Steve. You'd be sleeping together and that's not right.' Unsure of what it meant, she knew it was considered to be a bad idea.

'So what? It wouldn't be the first time we've done it.' She flipped her hair aside with a fourteen-year-old's impression of sophistication.

'It's wrong to sleep together unless you're married. That's

how you get babies and end up like Carla Martinez. What would we do if you had a baby?'

'Lizzy, you are entirely too young to understand. You don't get a baby every time you do it. Besides, there are things you can do so that it doesn't happen at all.'

'It's still wrong. You've told me that yourself, lots of times. Last year you even signed the pledge at Young Life that you wouldn't sleep with a boy until your wedding night. What about your pledge? You gave your solemn word and signed your name.' Last year, when Ellie had talked about the pledge, Lizzy had tried to get her to explain about sleeping together and why it was so bad when a man and woman did it before they were married. She and Ellie had slept together all their lives and it was usually pretty boring. Sometimes they would get the giggles or Ellie would snore when she had a cold, but it was still pretty boring.

'I changed my mind about the pledge. It wasn't all that solemn anyway. I just signed it because they made you feel like you were fast or something if you didn't.'

'Maybe you are fast, Eleanor Sinclair.'

'I am not fast and you don't know what you're talking about. Do you have any idea about what men and women do together?'

'Duh, do I look stupid, Miss Barely-Has-a-C-Average? I know all about what happens. I probably know more than you because I've seen the special shelf in the library that has all those books.' It was true, she had seen the shelf, but only from the other side of the librarian's counter.

'You are such a bad liar. You are a bad liar and a little snot-nosed kid.' Ellie put her hands on her hips and looked at her sister with satisfaction. 'I bet you'd like me to tell you. Want to know what we do together?' Ellie dangled the information like a bright trinket.

'I don't care. You can tell me if you want, but I don't really care because I can't imagine you knowing anything I'd want to hear.' She tried not to look excited. Lizzy knew a lot of things would start making sense once she had this whole sleeping-together thing figured out.

'If you don't care I guess I won't tell you after all. I'll finish making these sandwiches and then I'll move the car. I just hope we don't make so much noise at night that it scares you.'

'What noise? Why would you make any noise?' The words were out before she could stop herself. She'd played right into Ellie's hands. That was one of the problems with being the youngest. The oldest always had a chance to figure you out before you realized there was anything that needed to be figured.

'You little pervert! I knew you wanted to know.' Her voice crowed with triumph.

'Of course I want to know. There's nothing in the encyclopaedia and the librarians don't let anybody look at those books until they're twenty-one.'

'I'll tell you, but it's going to cost you.'

'Cost me what?' Ellie could drive a pretty hard bargain. Once Lizzy had had to do her chores for three weeks or Ellie would have told their mother about the black eye she'd given that sissy Bobby Steven. Her mother used to really care about things like that when they were younger.

'You have to finish making these sandwiches and not call Steve Stupid or Ratface for the next forty-eight hours.'

'I don't mind making the sandwiches and I suppose I can keep the truth to myself for two days.' She tried to sound reluctant. No harm in not telling Ellie she'd already decided to be nice to Steve until she could figure out how to escape and save their lives.

'First off, you know what your own body, the part between your legs, looks like, right?' The girls sat facing each other on one of the thin mattresses. Ellie had her ankles daintily crossed and off to one side. Lizzy sat Indian-style and leaned forward, her chin resting on her hands.

'Sure. I've seen the pictures on the Kotex box.' No need to tell Ellie that she'd taken a mirror and studied herself to see if she matched the drawing on the box. She'd been concerned because she seemed to have some extra flappy things that weren't on the drawing. She'd thought the whole place to be pretty unattractive and was relieved it wasn't something you had on the top of your head where everybody could see it.

'OK. It's really pretty simple. The man puts his thing in your hole.'

'What thing?' More evidence that a lack of specificity was an inherited trait. Ellie always talked 'things' and 'whatsits' when she could have used a proper word.

'His penis, silly. Have you ever seen a penis?'

'Once. I saw a boy's penis down at the river.' A little wormy white thing. Some of the girls took turns touching it. It would move a little when they touched it and the girls were all running around screaming and making real fools of themselves. Lizzy hadn't touched it and couldn't figure out why anyone would want to.

'Well, a man's penis isn't the same as a boy's penis. A man's penis is bigger, and when he gets horny it gets even bigger and really stiff. It gets to be like a zucchini or a banana. That's when he knows he's ready to put it in the hole.'

'That's it? He sticks his zucchini inside you? That just sounds stupid and embarrassing.' She shivered at the thought of Steve Ratface and his zucchini. 'I think this is really disgusting and I can't see why everybody thinks it's such a big deal.'

'It is kind of disgusting. Steve says it gets better, but I still don't like it much.' Ellie pushed her hair off her face. 'He likes to do some other stuff, too.'

'What kind of stuff?'

'After he puts it in he moves it in and out a couple of times until some stuff comes out the end of his penis.'

'He pees inside of you?' Lizzy wouldn't have put it past Steve to pee in Ellie's ear. 'Ellie, I can't believe this is normal.

This couldn't be something that married people do. Can you imagine Mrs Grafton doing something that nasty with Big Bob? I can see him doing it, but not her.' She thought for a moment. 'I sure can't imagine people like the President and Mrs Kennedy doing anything like that.'

'Those people have kids, so they've done it even if they don't do it any more. That stuff that comes out isn't really pee. Steve calls it 'jizzum' or 'come'. It's the part that has the sperm in it. If one of those sperm gets too far inside you, wham, you're pregnant. That's why I know it's normal because it's the way you get pregnant. If nobody was doing it there wouldn't be any people.' Her voice lowered to a whisper. 'He also likes to put his hands on my boobies and rub his finger around inside my underpants.'

'Why do you let him do that to you? It sounds awful. Why would he want to do it anyway? It's got to be embarrassing for him, too.'

'He thinks it's great. I guess all men do. That's why those hairy men would come to see Mom. I know she let them do those things to her.' Her voice got very faint and Lizzy had to lean forward to hear her. 'I guess I'm just like Mama, but I hope she liked it at least.'

'But she didn't have any babies after me. If she was doing that stuff with men, how come I was the last baby?'

'There are things you can do so that you don't get that way. You just have to keep the sperm from getting too far inside you.'

'How do you do that?'

'Well, you can buy rubbers, but they're real expensive.'

'What does a rubber do?' Lizzy thought of the soiled rubbers littering the riverbank after bright summer nights.

'The guy puts it on his thing before he goes inside of you. It keeps the jizzum from getting in you.'

'Ugh. We used to fill them from the river and use them for water balloons.' Lizzy shivered and stuck her tongue out. 'How do you keep the jizzum out if you don't have rubbers?'

'Either the guy pulls out real fast or you stand up right away so it doesn't get stuck inside of you.'

'I'm never going to let any man do those things to me. I think it's awful. I'm not going to marry anybody unless he agrees to never try that stuff on me.' She wondered if this all had something to do with how Steve had brainwashed Ellie and turned her into a maybe mother-murderer.

'You'll change your mind. I really hated it at first, mostly because it's pretty weird, but once you get used to it it's not so bad. Best of all, Steve is real sweet when he wants to do it. I figure it's the best way to get them to do what we want.'

'I don't think I'd ever want anything that much.'

'I do. I don't want to be alone like Mom. I want somebody to love me and I want to love somebody back. Steve loves me. I know you don't like him, but we love each other. He loves me more than Mom ever did and if I have to do some things I don't really like to prove I love him, then I'll do them.'

'You can do what you want, but you're wrong about Mom. She loved us as much as she could.'

Ellie shook her head. 'It wasn't enough, was it? I know that now that somebody really loves me.'

'But what about me, Ellie? I really love you, I always have.'

'You don't get it, do you? It's like that song: "You're Nobody Till Somebody Loves You". I'm somebody now.' Ellie took another look around the cabin and turned to her sister with a beatific smile. 'You'll see someday.'

Cotherstone, West Sussex, February 25th

Dearest Mary,

Received your lovely letter this morning. Oliver sounds like quite the fellow, but did you really have to go all the way to California to meet someone from Sussex? Small world, I guess. Actually, if you're going to get all misty about someone, I suppose it's best that he be a Brit rather than some Californian. I'd be awfully sad if you settled out there and we only saw you once a year or so. Then of course I'd feel really stupid and guilty about being petty and not putting your happiness first. I might have a terrible time of it, have to go on Prozac or become a Baptist. Good choice, a Sussex man. I can recommend them highly.

Your father finally seems to be on the mend. He's sleeping better at night and no longer goes through a box of tissues a day. He sends his love. He also says to tell Oliver that he has a violent temper and you are still his little girl. I hope Oliver will be duly impressed, as none of your other beaux have been. It would please your father no end to have some swain terrified of his greying self.

Sarah is back in our lives. Not sure what happened to Claire, but Sarah has removed the nose ring and looks quite demure without it. She's really very sweet and offers to help me in the kitchen. Brighter than I originally thought, Sarah is that shy sort who takes a while to warm up. I just hope she's not too sweet. Chaz is used to the women in his life being tough broads and I'm not sure if he can handle sweet. On the other hand, the fact that she is sweet and shy must have a certain novelty value that he might find appealing. Time will tell.

Your grandmother now has the upper respiratory rot that your father is finally shaking. Yesterday we went to her house and removed her to the spare room here. As you can imagine it was under protest, but she's really in no shape to be on her own when she's this ill. The other option was for me to move in with her for a few days, but this seemed too disruptive to the three of us. I've been going over there for a few hours every day for the last few days, but she really needs someone to be around all the time right now. Anyway, after we got her tucked in with a hot-water bottle and a cup of tea she admitted she was relieved to have someone to look after her.

Once this health crisis is over we're going to broach the subject of her moving here permanently. You know how she prides herself on her independence, but she is increasingly frail. She is still sharp as a tack and good company and I for one would love to see more of her. It will be an adjustment, of course, but life is about adjusting. Yes, that is my thought for the day. Profound, don't you think?

Of course, since Gran is here, Mugs is also in residence. Patch was delighted at first until Mugs opened the poor dog's nose with one of her stiletto-like claws. Typical cat, she keeps jumping up, just above his range. It's making him quite mad, poor baby. He can't sleep a wink.

I believe in my last letter I started to write about Steve. This is rather slippery, since you have to know what I knew about men to understand what I thought of Steve.

I knew nothing. I know it sounds odd. It is odd – bizarre actually. I was the child of a woman who was a prostitute, at least occasionally, but I had virtually no knowledge of men or sex. I suppose I ignored a lot of what went on around me, or perhaps my mother was more careful around her daughters than I recall. I was well and truly gobsmacked, not to mention completely repulsed, when my sister filled me in on her version of the way of a man with a maid. I suppose I hoped she was making it all up to torture me. (Although in truth, I was the one of us who used words as weapons. Made Ellie crazy when I'd throw around my fifty-cent words and snippets of information I'd gleaned from the encyclopaedia.)

I wonder when I hear or read about very young girls having sex. I can't help but wonder if it is their idea at all. I certainly don't remember any sort of sexual stirring until I was about sixteen. Of course, considering my background, it might be odd that I ever became interested in men and their bizarre nocturnal habits. All that to say I suspect a huge number of young girls are being coerced into behaviour they're not really interested in. Since you're much nearer to being a young girl than moi, I'd love to hear your thoughts.

In retrospect, part of the reason for my ignorance and naïvety was the lack of media bombardment. Sex wasn't blasted across every billboard or screen in those days. People on TV never went to bed together, even if they were married. I know around this time there was a great uproar when a sitcom couple were shown to have a double bed rather than two singles in their bedroom. It didn't make a bit of difference that the couple were married in real life. Romance was the order of the day and nothing was ever viewed beyond a sweet kiss. Even a really juicy snog was rarely seen. In the movies sexual passion was dealt with by showing ocean waves crashing to the shore. All pretty silly when you think about it. Although this was the early sixties, nothing had started swinging yet.

Be that as it may, my sister Ellie was having sex with the odious rat-faced Steve. She wasn't enjoying it, but she had figured out that this was the easiest way to control him. Looking back on our discussions of the subject, I know now that Ellie was almost as ignorant about sex as I was. She thought she had gained some sort of hold over Steve, but in truth, I suspect it was the other way around. I think she was something of a victim of the old 'urge to merge'. Whether or not her mind enjoyed the act, her body was in charge.

I know that having sex outside of marriage doesn't seem like a very big deal to you. Remember, though, this was before the 'sexual revolution' and such things simply weren't done. Oh, of course they were done, but they weren't admitted to. An out-of-wedlock pregnancy was a terrible disgrace, even to a couple of little bastards such as ourselves. No doubt because of her own history, our mother had done everything possible to make us as prudish as she could. She kept us in ignorance about our bodies to the point that I can recall thinking sanitary towels were large bandages for the knee until Ellie set me straight. My mother's plan worked pretty well for me, but failed miserably with old El.

As disgusted as I was with my sister and her penis-impaired boyfriend, I knew that the balance had shifted away from me. I knew they held all the cards and I was going to have to play along with them. They were a couple and I was now the outsider. Apart from my worries about their relationship to each other, and its exclusion of me, I had another concern. By this time I had started thinking that the two of them had murdered my mother. A pragmatist then as now, I was upset by the idea, but I was terrified that I would be next.

Looking back I'm appalled at my reaction. I would certainly hope if I died in the bathroom you and Chaz would react differently, wouldn't you? Don't tell me if you think there's any possibility of your just getting on with your lives. Poor Laura Sinclair. Lousy mother, silly woman that she was, she deserved a better deal than she got. Of course, I suppose we can say that about most of the people in the world.

Oh well, enough stirring of this old pot. Patch just brought me his lead along with a sunny grin. This little tyrant is more trouble than a two-year-old. I'd better close. After a quick walk I have to get Gran down to the GP to make sure her lungs are still clear. The doctor offered to come out to the house, but your Gran told her she should save her home visits for the 'old and infirm'.

Frankly, I think she's a member of that club and worthy of all its rights and privileges.

Well, my love, stay well and happy. Write soon.

Love and God bless

Mummy

Chapter Seven

'She's a lovely girl, my granddaughter.' India folded the letter they'd received in the morning's post and handed it back to Liz.

'I'm a little surprised at how much I miss her. She hasn't lived at home for over four years, but I always knew she was just an hour or so away. I do wish she was a little closer to home.' Liz busied herself with tidying the small white room usually reserved for guests.

'Would you feel the same way if she'd chosen to go to Canada instead of California?'

'You know I wasn't thrilled with the idea of her being in San Francisco, but the choice was hers.' She began to pick a few dead blossoms from a small vase of flowers.

'Oh, for heaven's sake, Lizzy, stop fussing with those flowers and sit down and talk to me! You're like a cat on a hot tin roof today. What's the matter?' India patted a spot on the bed next to her. 'And don't tell me you're worried about me, because you know I'll be fine.'

Lizzy sat down and took the older woman's hand. 'I think I'm finally becoming just a little homesick.'

'Homesick? You know there's nothing left there for you, don't you?'

'It's totally irrational, I know. I think because Mary is there the place has been on my mind. Funny, when I first came over and decided to stay, I felt as if I really belonged. I felt that this was my home, my real, always had been waiting for me, home.'

'You don't feel that way now? How can you not consider this your home? You are marked in every square foot of this house. I can feel you in it even when you're not here.'

'Really?' Lizzy smiled and looked at the small fireplace. When she was pregnant with Mary she'd become convinced there was an earlier fireplace behind the ugly contemporary tile one which had squatted at the end of the room. Five days before giving birth, she'd taken a pickaxe and uncovered the delicate Victorian structure which now adorned the room. Ever since, she'd thought of it as Mary's fireplace.

'You're as much a part of this family and this place as any of us. This is your home, Liz.'

'It's my home now and will be for the rest of my life, but sometimes, sometimes I feel like such a stranger. I think there's a part of my brain which is always having to adjust to being a foreigner. I will always be a foreigner, India. Do you know what I'm saying?'

'Of course I know what you're saying. Don't forget I was born in Madras. I don't remember much because we left when I was four, but this is still my home. I can't imagine being homesick for Madras.'

Liz squeezed her lips together for a moment to keep from laughing. 'You may have been born in Madras, but you were always *of* here.'

'Of course I was, as are you. You are as much a part of this place as me.' She smiled and patted Liz on the hand. 'Homesick. What a silly thing to even think about.'

Liz gently withdrew her hand from the older woman's and stood up. 'I think we'd better get you ready to go to the doctor. Have you thought about what you want to wear?' She went to the wardrobe and opened the doors, turning her back on the old woman. A hot tear fell down her cheek. 'I'll be back in a minute, India. I think I left something on the stove.'

Stepping out of the room, she pressed her face against the cool wall in the hallway as a few more tears joined the first.

Blue Creek, California, July 1962

'How long are we planning to stay up here?' They had been at the logger's cabin almost a week, and Steve and Ellie still seemed content to play house. Lizzy had watched Steve for three days, observing his secret dark places and studying his moods, before she broached the subject of leaving. The dark, empty balls never left, but they would fade slightly and sometimes grow smaller when Ellie was close. They became denser when he looked at Lizzy, larger if she approached him.

'We need to stay up here until they stop looking for us.' He sat against a tree, a cigarette in his hand. 'You know, rich people spend shitloads of money to send their kids places like this. Just pretend this is your summer camp and think of all the fun you're having.' Steve worried a black hangnail on his thumb while he spoke.

Lizzy thought that black, greasy hangnail probably tasted pretty bad, but Steve didn't seem to mind. 'I think summer camp has a few more activities. Besides, I think it's probably all right by now. We've been gone a week. I bet lots more interesting things are going on to keep the police busy.' Lizzy looked for signs of temper before she added, 'We were only supposed to stay up here a day or two, that's what Ellie told me. I think we need to get to Nevada.' She breathed more easily as he kept smoking and hangnail-worrying without the black, empty spaces changing.

Steve looked up and squinted at the sun behind Lizzy. 'Well, I don't think we're in any kind of hurry.'

'We may not be in a hurry to leave, although maybe if you

don't think we are you might want to think about that a little more.' She grinned and hoped he wouldn't start making horrible ratface looks at her. 'Something we do need to hurry about is some food. I've been thinking that if you go down the hill to the store somebody might remember you from last time. Little stores like that don't get a lot of customers. They'd notice somebody like you.' Lizzy figured they'd remember him because he was such a greasy-looking creep. Although she and Ellie bathed in the creek every day, she doubted that Steve had been down there more than once. She wouldn't have been surprised to see bugs or maggots climbing through his oily brown hair.

'Unless you know how to cook pine cones, I'm going to have to buy groceries. Besides, you don't have to sit around worrying about anything. I'll let you know when you need to worry.' He flicked his cigarette butt several feet away into the pine needles covering the dry ground.

Lizzy promptly ground the butt out with the sole of her shoe, just like she'd seen Smokey the Bear do in all the television announcements about preventing forest fires. She glanced over at him and decided it wasn't the right time to lecture him on fire safety. 'I do worry. It's what I do. Even when Mom was alive I figured it was a big part of my job to worry, since nobody else seemed to do much of it.' Lizzy smiled what she imagined to be a winning smile while she studied his face, searching for a reaction to the mention of her mother. 'I have a better idea. Why don't you let me and Ellie do the shopping and get what we need? Nobody will know we're with you.'

'I don't think Ellie drives well enough to get down to the store and back. She's never driven up here before and I don't think she could do it.'

'Maybe you could drive us almost all the way down. Then we could drop you off and Ellie could drive to the store from there. After the shopping we can pick you up and you can drive us back up here.' Lizzy hoped a little time away from the cabin and Steve would focus Ellie's thinking and start the un-brainwashing that would need to take place before she was going to be much help with their escape. Even though her sister seemed cheerful enough, Lizzy figured she'd have to be sick of those things she said Steve liked to do to her.

'You are a planner, aren't you? I guess it would work OK if you girls went ahead and did the shopping.' He smiled and his upper lip curled slightly. 'Looks better for girls to do the shopping anyway. More normal. Just make sure you don't talk to nobody. I don't want anybody messing around with either of my girls.'

Lizzy wanted to grab a rock and drive it into his skull. She wanted to pick up a stick and shove it through his eye socket until it came out of the back of his head with the eyeball still stuck on it. 'You don't have anything to worry about, Steve. I don't think anybody would want to mess with us.'

'I don't know about that, little sister. Ellie is real pretty and you aren't so bad yourself. Give you a few months and you'll fill out just fine.'

Something in his voice made her want to hide her face behind her hands, and she felt her cheeks grow warm and red. 'I don't think I'm going to fill out at all. Some people get brains and some people get beauty. I've got the brains so I don't need the beauty.' She'd said this so many times she almost believed it, even though she hoped it wasn't true. Much as she hated Steve, she felt a guilty excitement at the thought of beauty and curves. It wouldn't be completely horrible to have boys making fools of themselves over her, as long as they weren't boys like Steve. Being pretty didn't have to make you stupid just because it worked that way on Ellie. Fact was, Ellie had been stupid even before she got the pouty lips and the big breasts the boys always looked at.

'You'll fill out, Lizzy. You've got those icy blue eyes that make some boys crazy. I'll be beating them off with a stick in a few months.' He stuck his thumbs into his belt loops. His fingers hung down, framing the front of his jeans. 'My uncle snuck me into one of those Swedish movies last year for my birthday. It was about all these girls who went to a nudist place on their vacation and all the shit they got up to. You might end up looking just like those girls. They had blue eyes and most of them were tow-heads just like you. They were built like you too, long and kind of bony. That was one wild movie.'

'I'd better go see what Ellie's doing.' Lizzy turned to walk towards the cabin. She didn't want to know any more about a bunch of stupid girls who were too dumb to keep their clothes on when they didn't even know who might be watching that movie. She'd heard Swedes were supposed to be sexy, but she couldn't see why, since the only Swedes she knew about were the farmers who sat around all winter drinking coffee in the café in Kingsburg. They didn't seem very sexy, with pot bellies and permanently sunburned necks.

Steve reached out and pulled her back to him by the tail of her shirt. 'Let's just see what's going on here.' He wrapped his arm around the front of her waist, pinning her arms and holding her back to his chest. His free hand went under her shirt and felt at her hard, small nipples. 'Not much more than bee stings, but more than a mouthful is a waste.' He started to push his hand down the front of her shorts, ripping at the thin cotton fabric.

Lizzy raised her foot and shoved it down on his with all her weight.

'Bitch!' His hands fell away as he hopped on one foot, bellowing and raising little motes of dust with each hop. 'Fucking little bitch cunt!'

'Don't you ever touch me again! Do you hear me? I won't let anybody touch me like that, not ever. Not in a million years!' She fought for breath and backed away from him, judging the distance until she would be safe to turn and run.

'Don't give me that crap. You're just like your mama and your sister. Another month or two and you'll be the same as Ellie. You'll be begging me for it just like she does. Won't be able to keep your hands off me, little sister.'

'I'm not like anybody in the whole world, you'll see. You stay away from me or you'll be so sorry you'll wish you'd never been born.' She moved her hand across her front where he'd touched her, expecting to feel something filthy she could brush or scratch away. 'Leave me alone.'

'I'll leave you alone.' He approached, step for step, as she backed away. 'I'll leave you alone. You don't have anything very interesting yet. Nothing that would keep a man happy.' He smiled and rubbed at his crotch.

'You're disgusting.' She watched in horror as the black balls seemed to spread and swirl around him. 'You're disgusting and I'm going to tell Ellie what you tried to do to me.'

'You're going to keep that pretty little mouth of yours closed for once.'

'Try and make me. You can't stop me from saying what I want.'

'I won't have to try very hard, little sister. You keep your mouth shut or I'll make you wish you had.'

'I'm not afraid of you.' Her mouth was dry and she could feel her heart jumping in her chest like a rubber ball.

'Then you're not so smart after all.'

'I'm smart enough to tell Ellie. If Ellie knew what you just pulled she'd be madder than hell and you know it.' She started taking larger steps as she backed away.

'And just what is it you think Ellie is going to do to me? Why should I be afraid of you or Ellie?'

'You should be afraid of both of us. We're tough and we're strong and there's two of us. We're blood and you're just a crappy boyfriend!' Lizzy stumbled against an outcropping of rock and fell to the ground.

'I'm shaking, Lizzy. I'm scared to death of one skinny kid and a lettergirl.' He leaned back and kicked a spray of dirt into her face. 'Did you taste that, Lizzy? Did you feel that?'

Lizzy wiped at her face, her eyes stinging with tears and dirt. She nodded, not taking her gaze away from him.

'That's what the dirt feels like when you're in the grave. That's what your mama feels on her face. Do you want to be in the grave?' He leaned over her, his face less than a foot from hers. Streamers of black seemed to dance around his face, moved by a breeze of their own making.

She shook her head slowly from side to side.

'Good. Now, if you want to get out of here, you cooperate. If you want to see thirteen, you cooperate. Do we understand each other?'

She looked away and nodded.

'Say it, Lizzy.' His words left a fine spray of spittle across her cheek.

'Yes,' she whispered, hoping the word didn't count if it couldn't be heard.

'I can't hear you. Say it louder.'

'Yes.' She raised her voice a fraction.

'Say it louder, bitch cunt.'

'Yes, yes, yes!' She shouted so loud she thought her ears might start bleeding.

'Better. Now you can get up.'

Lizzy scrambled to her feet as he grabbed her arm.

'Remember: shut the fuck up or you'll be tasting dirt forever.' He released her arm and she bolted for the creek.

Cotherstone, West Sussex, March 3rd

Dearest Mary,

Daddy just called me and read me your fax which was waiting for him at the office. Because of the time difference I won't call you and wake you up. Good news can always wait until morning, so I will make sure this gets faxed first thing.

Gran is going to be just fine. She doesn't have pneumonia and all her vitals seem to be in amazingly good order. She's feeling quite smug because her self-diagnosis was spot on. Tea and sympathy will be dispensed as needed until she's up and about. She must be feeling better already because she's begun to complain about the way I had the roses pruned. I also bought the wrong kind of oatmeal, but to balance things out she told me I make lovely coffee.

All indications are that you have inherited my propensity for worry. This isn't something I'm thrilled to see, much less take credit for. I've always envied those golden people who swim through life absolutely knowing that everything is going to work out splendidly. Strangely enough, those people are usually right. I've often wondered if they swim through because of attitude or because they inherently know things are going to be fine for them. Perhaps they're simply too stupid to know about the monsters under the bed and the beasts that lurk just on the other side of the dustbins. People like that probably don't have a clue about every tin of food being a potential source of botulism and they'd certainly be unaware about the recent research concerning the elusive fresh-water sharks known to be in even small lakes.

Now that I've put some of my concerns down on paper I realize that we are right to be worried. Besides, if I didn't worry about things like this I'd have huge gaps in my day which I'd probably fill in some less creative manner.

Our blokes are fine and send their love. Chaz has a game this weekend which should be really wonderful since we have had rain all week. The pitch is going to be like mushy peas. I'd love to stay home and read the Sunday papers, but I always feel like a BAD MOTHER when I don't stand there in wellies and wax, freezing my bottom off. I was hoping that Chaz would ban me from games because I cringe every time he's in one of those pile-ups that they're all so fond of, but it doesn't really bother him. The other mothers don't seem to mind, but perhaps they all grew up with thick-necked rugby-playing brothers. I appear to be the only one who dwells on ripped ears and broken noses.

Patch is not fine, I'm sorry to report. Poor lamb feels as though the deck has been reshuffled and he has been dealt a losing hand. Yesterday, after an honest morning's work of cat-pestering, Mugs turned on him, jumped on his back and rode him clear around the sitting room. If it had been within the cat's capacity I'm sure he would have worn a stetson and yelled 'yippee yiyeah'. Patch was well and truly mortified, partly, I'm sure, because I couldn't stop laughing. Down at the mouth as he may be, he's giving Mugs a wide berth. I'm glad he's backing down because I had visions of him walking around with indigestion and a mouth full of cat fur. It wouldn't be good for Gran's recovery to have her darling Mugs eaten by a spaniel cross.

Now that he knows Gran is all right, Daddy is off to Belfast tomorrow. He'll just be gone two days and then I believe he's home for two weeks. He doesn't know it, but he's spending most of this weekend sharpening knives, servicing the lawnmower, etc, etc. I can't win for losing on this one. He hates to do all those piddly little things, but he doesn't like me to do them because I always do them 'wrong', and God forbid I spend good money paying someone to do something he can do. Male ego, I suppose, they all like to think they should be good with their hands. Yes, yes, I know I shouldn't play along with this mighty hammer guy thing, but I realized a long time ago that I had married a very traditional man and I would have to work around him since he was not likely to change. I'm actually quite comfortable about the arrangement, but I still like to whine a bit.

Now as to your response to my last letter. I am not a Victorian about sex! Not, not, not. Even if I had realized that you felt that way about my views, I wouldn't have told you about my background any sooner. I don't think it's the sort of thing a young girl needs to know. Besides, every child thinks their parent is Victorian about sex. I'm not the least bit strait-laced, anyway. I'm certainly a firm believer in monogamy for myself, but I'm not terribly judgemental of other people. OK, I am judgemental, but only if I find them annoying or I dislike them for some other reason. And I thought I was quite wonderful when you wanted to go on the pill at sixteen, and let's not forget the two years' supply of condoms I've squirrelled away in your brother's bathroom.

Now that I have established that I am indeed the most wonderful and liberal of mothers we can move off this because it makes me a bit uncomfortable thinking about you having sex at sixteen. (I'm wonderful and liberal, but I do acknowledge that I'm just a little neurotic.)

I'm glad you like the idea of our coming out this summer for a little holiday. I would love to see San Francisco again. I'd also like to take Highway One south along the coast for a hundred miles or so. I'd love to show our chaps what a proper ocean looks like. I'm not interested in seeing the mountains this trip. I think it would be too hot and there is always a terrible risk of fire up there in the summer.

Well, darling, I'd better close. Love you and miss you.

Love and God bless

Mummy

Chapter Eight

'Oh, Liz, I've been hoping to see you.' The square little woman barrelled towards her, a clipboard clutched to her chest. 'I'm doing the rota for the next month and I see you haven't done any kitchen or bar duty for the whole season.'

'No, I don't think I have.'

Carrie Clipboard had three square little sons who looked just like her. She was always bustling around the club making bacon sandwiches and handing out packets of crisps to the under-twelves. 'Normally I'd ask you to double up on shifts, but we've got some new mothers who are awfully keen. Why don't I just put you down for the kitchen for the next two weeks? I know the smoke bothers you in the bar and I can't quite see you pulling pints.' She put her clipboard down on the table in front of Liz and started to fill her name in.

'No, not this season.' Liz glanced towards the changing room doors, willing Chaz to come out and rescue her from Carrie Clipboard, who smelled of bacon and enthusiasm. The husbands were at the bar earnestly discussing the morning's games, or perhaps the amount of time it took them to get to London.

'But you've always worked in the kitchen.'

'Carrie, I'm taking a break from a few things this season.' She glanced around the room, wondering how Carrie had missed all those articles about reading body language that seemed to be stuck in every magazine and Sunday supplement whenever the editors ran out of more interesting things to print.

'Now, Liz, you know many hands make light work. If we all do a little bit, nobody has to do a lot.'

'Carrie, I've been doing my little bit in that greasy kitchen since Chaz was seven years old. I think it's time for those new mothers who are so keen to take over.'

Carrie sat down across from Liz and peered at her through a fringe of mousy hair. 'What's wrong?'

'Nothing is wrong, Carrie. I'm just tired of the rugby club kitchen.'

'Your whole family has always supported the club. Chaz has always played and your husband has been on the board two or three times. What's going on?'

'If I'm sick of rugby, something must be wrong?' Liz grinned and ran her hand through her hair. 'I'm sorry, Carrie. The truth is my mother-in-law has been ill and I've moved her in with us. Mary is so far away, and I'm just feeling, I don't know.'

'It sounds like you've got a lot on your plate right now. Listen, Liz, I couldn't help noticing that you've been acting rather odd this morning.'

'Because I didn't want to work in the kitchen?'

'Before that. I've been watching you and you haven't been talking to anyone, you've been staring into space.'

'I think I'm just anxious for spring. It's been such a long winter and March is always an awful month.' *I'm also not terribly fond of being stared at as though I were a photograph at an exhibition.*

'It was probably an awful month last year as well, Liz. Did you stare into space and snap at people then?'

'I'm sorry I snapped at you, Carrie. Go ahead and put me down for the next two Sundays.' It wouldn't be so bad. At least it was warm in the kitchen and she wouldn't have to watch while some fourteen-stone man-child tried to kill Chaz all in the name of good, wholesome fun.

'That's the spirit. You'll feel better keeping busy.' She picked up her clipboard and launched herself out of her chair. 'I have to go and talk to Bob Pierce about the bar rota. Thanks for everything, Liz.'

'My pleasure, Carrie.' She caught a glimpse of Chaz coming through the changing room door and glanced at her watch. With any luck, he'd be ready to go home after half an hour of manly camaraderie. She took a deep breath and looked down at her hands. It had been years, but maybe she could learn to make herself invisible again.

Blue Creek, California, July 1962

This time she watched carefully as they drove down the mountain towards the general store. She studied the way he placed his hands on the wheel, and how he shifted his right foot from one pedal to the other. She experimented with the placement of her own foot and decided driving was pretty easy.

To her surprise, Steve hadn't changed his mind about the girls doing the grocery shopping while he waited up the hill. Lizzy knew he was convinced she was too afraid of him to say anything to Ellie. She hadn't decided if he was right or not, but she suspected he wasn't too far wrong. She had to fight a feeling of panic whenever she thought of the sharp grains of dirt that had found their way into her mouth. The taste of the grave.

She studied the two of them. He gave no clues to what had happened. He still fondled Ellie, but he made a show of ignoring Lizzy. Twice she caught him looking at her, but she refused to meet his eyes, although she couldn't block out the horrible swirls of black that seemed to rise ten or twelve feet above his head.

Ellie had changed, she was sure of that. The strange pink shards of light seemed to be aligning themselves on her body like bits of iron clinging to a magnet. The lively whips of her long dark hair had been replaced with sweet nods of cooperation whenever Steve talked to her. Her buoyant stride had slowed to the careful, mincing step of someone walking on a rocky beach.

Lizzy tried to remember what she'd read about brain washing. She was certain that it took more than a few days to accomplish. Besides, Steve was dumber than dirt. He wasn't wily and inscrutable like the Communist Chinese or Koreans.

They probably came by brainwashing naturally because they were Communists and didn't value life and free will the way Americans did. They didn't care who they starved so they'd get much faster results than Steve ever could. Besides, clearly Steve was not depriving Ellie of food or water. If anything, she was looking fatter than ever.

'Lizzy, pay attention, will you? Steve asked you a question.' Ellie talked just like some of her friends' mothers did when they wanted to impress their husbands with what firm parents they could be.

'What?' She didn't care what Steve had to say. She'd heard enough from him to last her a lifetime. She hadn't spoken to him since he got so ugly and nasty with her. She'd felt something poking at her bottom when he'd held her and she knew it must have been that swollen zucchini Ellie had talked about. She shook her head slightly to get rid of the idea of that thing.

'I said you won't get any smart ideas while you're in the store, will you? You keep your mouth shut tight and don't you try to pull any crap.'

'Why don't you tell me what a smart idea might be, Steve? I'd love to know what you consider a smart idea to be.' The words were out of her mouth, bouncing against his eardrum, before she realized she had said them. She watched with fear while his shoulders tightened and the cords on his neck popped up.

'Ellie, you shut that little cunt up or I will. I've had it with her and her mouth.'

'Steve, she doesn't mean anything by it.' Ellie turned to Lizzy in the back seat and frowned. 'She's got a fresh mouth, but she doesn't mean it. Do you, Lizzy?'

'Sorry, Steve.' Lizzy thought she might vomit because she'd used her mouth to apologize to Ratface. She stared at the back of his neck and imagined a spray of vomit across the rash of angry pimples she could see above his grey T-shirt.

'I'm telling you right now, Lizzy, if I hear that you said one word inside that store, I will beat you to within an inch of your life. Do you hear me?'

Lizzy closed her eyes and tried to remember how she used to make herself invisible. She'd been able to walk through rooms and nobody would see her. She could sit in corners and people would swear the room was empty.

'Do you hear me? Answer me, you little bitch!'

'Please, Steve, she's just daydreaming. She's always going off in her own world like that.' Ellie reached over and began to stroke Steve's arm, but he jerked away.

'I've got half a mind to stop this car, pull her out and show her I mean business. The little bitch has been begging for it and it's about time somebody set her straight.'

Lizzy thought of the zucchini pressing against her shorts and choked back sobs. Her stomach lurched and she swallowed hard. Sweat formed little pearls on her forehead as she smelled the rising damp of her own fear.

'Answer me!'

Lizzy groaned and vomited a spray across the back of the seat, just missing Steve's neck.

'Why are you being like this? You shouldn't be making him angry. We need him, can't you see that?' Ellie had taken her sister away from the car to clean the vomit off the girl.

'We don't need him. He's horrible and he wants to hurt me, you heard him.' Lizzy grabbed her sister's shoulders. 'I know you don't want to believe me, but he doesn't really care about you either. He hates me and he's used you. He's used both of us to get out of Clifford and away from his aunt and uncle. I know you want so much from him, but it's not going to happen. Believe me, El, it's not going to happen.'

'Stop it! Stop talking like that. Everything would be fine if you didn't try to make him so mad. Would it hurt you so much to be a little nice for a change? I don't know why you do it. You were fine for a few days. Why can't you be like that all the time?' She daubed at her sister's face with the greasy rag she'd found under the front seat of the car.

'Ellie, listen to me. After we drop him off we can just keep driving. We can go down the hill for a mile or two then turn around and drive back to the cabin and get our stuff. We can drive right past him and watch the dumb expression on his face when he knows what we've done.'

'I'm not going to do that and you know it. Besides, if we did something like that he'd tell on us. He'd tell the police where to find us and then I know we'd be separated.'

'We don't know that, Ellie. I think maybe they'd do every-thing they could to keep us together. I bet they could find a nice foster home that would take both of us.'

'They wouldn't let us stay together. They wouldn't want me to be around you. They'd send me away and they'd probably never let us see each other again.'

'No, Ellie. We're sisters and even if we couldn't live in the same foster home, they'd at least have us close enough that we could see each other.'

'I'm what they call a bad influence. They would make sure we weren't together any more. I've heard about what happens. I know what I'm talking about.'

'You are not a bad influence. Your grades are all right and you're a lettergirl.' Much as Lizzy hated to admit it, even to her-self, lettergirls did have to be nice girls with decent grades. In spite of the cigarettes and the boys, there were about twenty girls in school who were a lot rougher than Ellie. The head cheerleader, Janine Simpson, who was much more important than a junior let-tergirl, had been arrested for drunk driving in May. Cheryl Parker, last year's Almond Blossom Princess, wasn't even allowed into the Mode O'Day shop because she was a known shoplifter.

'I'm not a lettergirl any more, Lizzy.'

'You will be if we go back. We've only been gone a few days and you've hardly missed any practice. We can probably be put in a foster home right in town.'

'Lizzy, I can't ever go back and I can never be a lettergirl. I can't even be a girl any more. Everything is changed and I can't change it back. We can never go back to how it was.'

'Why not?' She pushed aside the rag in her sister's hand and held her shoulders. 'OK, we ran away after burying a dead body which happened to belong to our mother, but other people have done things too. How about Janine Simpson and Cheryl Parker? Janine is still head cheerleader and Cheryl even got to crown the new princess at this year's Almond Blossom Festival. There isn't all that much talent in Clifford. It's not like every other girl in town would be able to march around the field with a letter on her chest. The squad will take you back because they need you. You haven't even missed any games yet.'

'Lizzy, listen to me and try to understand. Remember that stuff I told you about making babies and how you can stop them?' Ellie pulled a long strand of hair through her teeth with a slight sucking sound as she looked at her sister.

'Sure.'

'We didn't really know about those things when we first started doing it.'

'Ellie, what are you saying? Please don't be telling me what I think you're telling me!' Lizzy pulled the hair out of Ellie's mouth and put her face an inch or two from her sister's. 'Don't tell me one of those sperm things got stuck inside of you.' She thought of Winnie the Pooh and how he looked with his big butt sticking out of Rabbit's hole.

'I'm going to have a baby.'

Lizzy stepped away and smiled as she thought of the way Ellie got things wrong more often than not. 'Come on, El. You just think you're going to have a baby because you're afraid you'll go to Hell for breaking the Young Life pledge. You're not going to have a baby.'

'I haven't had a period in three months and my boobs are really sore. Sometimes I feel sick in the morning too.'

Lizzy exhaled slowly and chewed on her bottom lip for a moment. 'Does Steve know what he's done?'

'I told him about it two or three weeks ago.'

'How long have you known?'

'Hush. Here comes Steve and I promised him I wouldn't tell you yet.'

Steve ran his fingers down Ellie's back before he kissed her. 'Be careful on the road. Take it slow and don't talk to anybody.' He kissed her again and opened the car door for her.

'We won't be long, Steve. Promise you won't run off?' Ellie smiled and blinked at him.

'You can't get rid of me that easily, Ellie.' He leaned into the open window of the car and gave her breast a squeeze.

'Stop that, Steve!'

'You liked it plenty last night.'

'See you in a little bit.' Ellie smiled as she turned the key in the ignition.

"Don't forget the Fritos.' He thumped his knuckles on the front fender as they pulled out.

'Our mother is dead, you're going to have a baby and he's thinking about his stomach.' Lizzy didn't look at him as they drove away because she knew she'd probably make a terrible face if she did.

'We've got to eat, don't we? That's the whole idea of going to the store, isn't it?'

'Maybe the whole idea of going to the store is for us to turn this car around, get our stuff, go down the mountain and turn ourselves in.'

'I don't want to talk about any of this.'

'Well, that's too damn bad, because we *have* to talk about it! You need to see a doctor and we have to figure out what we're going to do with a baby. And what about Steve? He should go to jail for getting you pregnant.' She gasped as a new thought occurred to her. 'I could be an accessory to the crime. I knew what you two were doing, so now I'm an accessory. I think this may be a lot more serious than anything Cheryl or Janine did.'

'I told you I didn't want to talk about any of this. I don't have anything to say. Can't you just shut up for once? The more you talk the worse you make things. When you're older you'll know everything can't be solved by talking. Look, there's the store just up ahead. Remember what Steve said: just keep quiet.' She made a sharp left into the parking lot.

'How long have you known?' Lizzy reached for a box of crackers as she whispered to her sister.

'Maybe a month, maybe a little longer. Now please just shut your face.'

'You should have told Mom, she would have understood.'

'Will you shut up? We can talk when we get back in the car.' Ellie turned and began looking at cereal boxes. She grabbed a carton of milk and a bag of Fritos before pointing her sister towards the front of the store.

'That will be five dollars and seventeen cents.' The man in the dark green apron stacked the groceries into two paper sacks.

'Here you go.' Ellie smiled and handed the man a five-dollar bill and two dimes.

'Thank you, miss. That's three cents change and don't spend it all in one place.' He smiled at Lizzy as he handed the change to Ellie. 'I think somebody was in here yesterday looking for the two of you.'

'I don't think so. Nobody knows we're here.' Ellie shoved the pennies in her jeans. She pushed one of the bags at Lizzy and grabbed the second one as she turned towards the door.

'Who was looking for us?' Lizzy tried to catch Ellie's eye. Maybe Ellie would come to her senses if she knew the police were after them.

'This was one of the boys from the fire crew. He said he was looking for a real pretty girl with dark hair in a turquoise Ford.

I saw you pull in and thought you must be the girl. He said you might have a younger girl with you.'

'Oh yeah, we did meet him.' Ellie glanced at Lizzy and frowned. 'If he comes in again, tell him we're leaving today.'

'You should call the police and tell them we're being held captive by a crazy boy up at Blue Creek.' Lizzy's ears roared as she said the words. The excitement of such daring made her feel as if electricity was shooting through her body.

Ellie turned pale and then started giggling. 'OK, you win.' She turned to the man behind the counter and shrugged her shoulders. 'We made this stupid bet on the way down. She said she'd say something crazy and I bet her that she wouldn't have the nerve. Now I have to do her chores for two days.' She smiled her best lettergirl's smile at the man. 'Sorry to pull such a silly stunt.'

'You girls have a safe trip back.' He shook his head and turned to a woman behind them with two small children and a sack of charcoal.

'But its true!' Lizzy turned to the other woman and started to speak as Ellie grabbed her arm.

'Sorry. You know what twelve-year-olds can be like. Come on, sis.' She yanked on Lizzy and pulled her out of the front door.

Lizzy glanced back and thought about yelling to the people in the store, but she could see through the window that the man and the woman with the kids and the charcoal were smiling and laughing, probably at her. She allowed herself to be led to the car, crushing Steve's bag of Fritos as they walked.

'Are you out of your mind? What made you do that?' Ellie slammed the car door shut and turned to her sister.

'It was a test.'

'A test? A test of what?'

'It was a test of you, Ellie. I thought maybe when I said that you'd come to your senses. I'm sorry to tell you you've gotten a big fat "F" on the test.'

'Do you know what you almost did back there?'

'I almost got us away from Steve. I was trying to save our lives.'

'Our lives are just fine.'

'Our lives are worse than maggot lives right now, Ellie, and you know it.' She looked out of the window and watched the woman leaving with her kids and her bag of charcoal. She didn't even glance towards their car because she was too caught up with thinking about her stupid barbecue. The man in the store was probably busy cutting bologna or filling the freezer with ice cream. 'Are you going to tell Steve? He might kill me if you tell him.' Kill her or make her wish she was dead.

'I'm not going to tell Steve, but don't pull something that stupid again. Do something like that again and you'll wish Steve had got hold of you first.'

'Good. You passed your second test with flying colours. The way you've been acting, I wasn't sure if we were still sisters or not.' She ignored Ellie's threat. They'd been threatening each other with bodily harm as long as Lizzy could remember. 'You've been acting really weird around me.'

'I've just been so scared, Lizzy.' Ellie's voice was little more than a change in her breathing. 'I've been so scared for weeks. Steve is the only person I thought I could talk to.'

'I still don't see why you didn't tell Mom. Maybe she could have done something to help you. I know she would have understood.' Lizzy could never recall her mother actually being angry with her daughters. Laura had been a very good-natured drunk.

'I didn't want to be another little Okie girl with a bun in the oven. Mom lied about us and I was going to have to start lying about this baby. I didn't want to be like Mom, but that's what was happening. I just couldn't stand it.' Ellie sat with her hands on the steering wheel. She stared out at the tiny parking lot behind the general store. 'All my life I've known we were better than that. All of us, even Mom.'

'There's nothing wrong with either one of us. We're as good as anybody else.' Lizzy could almost hear her mother's voice ringing in her ears. The lullaby she'd sung to her daughters. When they were little she would tell them about queens and cavaliers. She said everyone in the whole world was descended from queens and cavaliers if you looked back far enough.

'That's easy for you to say, Lizzy. You're smart and you always have ploughed ahead, no matter what. It never bothered you that we had such lousy clothes and lived in a house worse than most Mexicans live in. As long as you have school and your precious library you're happier than a pig in shit.' Ellie pushed the hair off her face and gave it a hard twist before shoving it behind her ear. 'But I care. I've always cared. I like nice clothes and pretty houses. I'm not like you. I want something more.'

'You sound like Mom now. She always made it sound like a new dress would change her life.' Laura used to stand in front of the Mode O'Day shop and twist and turn until her reflection in the glass fitted itself into the dresses in the shop window. She would never go into the shop to try anything on, but would study the changes to the window display with a connoisseur's eye. Laura prided herself on knowing which dresses had real style, and why.

'Maybe a new dress would have changed her life. Maybe if she'd had a few nice things and a few nice friends she wouldn't have ended up the way she did.'

'Did you help him do it, Ellie? Did you help him kill Mom?' She took her sister's hand in her own. 'I think I could understand if you did do something like that. It would have speeded things up since Mom was drinking herself to death anyway. Last month or so she was passed out so much, she was more dead than alive.'

'I don't know what you're talking about. You're talking crazy again.' Ellie's voice was low, her lips barely moving.

'You know what I'm saying. If Steve or somebody didn't kill her outright, I bet nobody did anything to help her either.'

'She was dead when I found her.'

'What about Steve? Where was he?'

'He was around. He came over a few minutes after you left. I was in the kitchen.'

'And he told you he found her?' She'd watched Perry Mason enough to know she was on to something. Once the witness got real sad and whispery they were about to spill the beans.

'No, he told me she'd been in the bathroom a long time and maybe I should check on her.'

'Can't you see, Ellie? He pushed her down and made her vomit. He got rid of her so he wouldn't get into trouble for making you pregnant.' Lizzy leaned towards her sister and mimicked the older girl's whisper. 'We have to get away from him before he kills me and maybe you too.'

'He wouldn't do that, I know him. He wouldn't have hurt Mom either.'

Lizzy decided to ignore Ellie's opinion. She knew the Czarina thought Rasputin was a swell guy, so Ellie's good opinion of Steve was just another symptom of brainwashing. 'Promise me you won't tell him what I said. I think he'd try to kill me right away if he knew I'd figured the case out.'

'Lizzy, sometimes I think Steve is right about you. You are one crazy kid.' She took her sister's face in her hands and looked at her. 'Things have changed for us. We're not going to end up like Mom. We're going to have a new life. The three of us are going to have a new life.'

'Ellie, listen to me. There's something you don't know about Steve.'

'You're the one who doesn't know something about Steve. Steve loves me and he's happy I'm going to have his baby. Having a baby proves we're grown up enough to be doing what we're doing; leaving home and all.'

'Will you just listen to me, Ellie?'

'No, I won't listen to you. Steve is right and has been all along. He's been warning me that you might get jealous about the two of us. He warned me and you just proved him right.'

'Jealous? Why would I be jealous?'

'You're jealous that I've found somebody who loves me. You're jealous because I almost have a husband and you're a skinny kid who's about five years from having a boyfriend.'

'Steve isn't almost a husband and I'm not jealous of you. If Steve was my boyfriend he'd want to do those disgusting things to me and it would make me sick. I wouldn't do those things to save my life.' She looked at her sister and narrowed her eyes before she spoke. 'What I'm going to say is going to make you very mad, but you need to know what Steve did. He tried to do it to me. He put his hands on my chest and tried to put his hand down my pants. I could feel his thing pressing into my bottom. He wanted to do it to me, too. Ellie, are you listening to me? Do you know what I'm saying?'

'How can you say things like that? How can you sit there and lie to me?'

'Ellie . . .'

'Don't "Ellie" me! Did you really think for a minute I would believe that Steve would touch you when he could have me?' She spread her hands as though she were displaying items of rare beauty in a Persian bazaar. 'Look at us, Liz. Why would he want anything to do with you?'

'How should I know? I just know he didn't want to tickle me and take me to the movies. He wanted to hurt me with his thing.' Lizzy shivered at the memory of his hands on her.

'I'm not listening to this one second longer, Elizabeth.' Ellie turned the key in the ignition and the engine roared to life. 'I don't want to hear another word about this shit.'

'You'll see.' Lizzy folded her arms across her chest and stared straight ahead as they pulled out of the parking lot.

Cotherstone, West Sussex, March 12th

Dearest Mary,

We're delighted with your list of gender jokes from the States. Actually, Gran and I were delighted. Your father and brother got a bit huffy about some of them, but oh well.

In answer to your query: I haven't written anything about my work lately because there has been precious little of it. I have to get back on my schedule of three hours each morning. The problem is I don't have anything or anyone that's terribly motivating right now. If I found out tomorrow that we needed a new roof I'm sure I would have a synopsis and three chapters to my agent in forty-eight hours. I'm afraid I'm like Mugs. If I'm being fed I'm content to sleep away the day. You see, it's all your father's fault. He keeps me too well. Just kidding. He does keep us well, but I still want to win the Booker some day.

Of course, that's another thing. I'm not feeling very inspired right now. I've got about a hundred pages of something in my computer, but I can't seem to fall in love with it. I don't really give a fig what happens to the characters, so, obviously, neither will anyone else. I know I can slap together a book, but deep down I want to do so much more. I want to write something that will make the angels weep. I want the reader to sit in appreciative silence for an hour after they're done reading. I want to be one of the greats and I don't think I ever will be.

If you wrote something like that to me I would tell you that you could be one of the greats. I would tell you to keep striving and keep your eye on the goal. Damned good advice. I should keep it in mind.

We are going out tonight with a group from Daddy's office. I think we are celebrating two birthdays and one wedding anniversary. We are going to the Windmill and your father has been talking about the Stilton-stuffed steak all week long. Bless him, he deserves the occasional cholesterol binge. He seldom whimpers any more about the grains and veg I'm always shoving at him.

Since your grandmother is feeling better, she's going to have a bit of a hen night this evening. While we are out, Mabs, Helen and Sue are coming in to play bridge with her. It will be awfully nice for her. I'm sure she's tired of having us as her primary social outlet.

Spending all this time with your gran has made me wonder what my mother would have looked like had she not died so young. She would have been sixty-seven this year. I look at myself in the mirror and wonder what I'll look like at that age. I have no idea what an old woman in my family looks like.

I don't know if I'm prone to heart disease, osteoporosis, or, God forbid, Alzheimers. When I had my bout with cancer I was so frustrated by the lack of genetic information. I realize knowing what has happened with your family's health isn't a clear indicator of your own destiny, but it is information I'd like to have.

We need the generation before for so many reasons. They are our road maps. You and Chaz are so fortunate to be able to track at least one side of your family back to Noah and the Ark. How I envy you being able to look at old photographs and recognize your features on someone else's face. Of course, you also have the family stories, the books, the jewellery, all those weird and wonderful things that members of your family hung on to. I hope you realize just what a lucky duck you are!

Enough said. Perhaps now as I'm getting older I'm really

starting to understand the value of the process of ageing. Watching Gran makes me look forward to growing old; if I can do it as well as she does, that is. The lady has always had a knack for relishing whatever life has presented to her. Ageing doesn't seem to have bothered her at all. I want to be just like her when I grow up.

Although I never mentioned her a great deal, I've never stopped thinking about Ellie. Eleanor. El. I miss her. I can't begin to tell you how I've missed her through the years. Our relationship was a volatile one, but I loved her so much. She would be forty-eight this September. Wonder what she would have looked like. I didn't understand some things about Ellie until I started reading about birth order and what it does to us. Firstborns are the more conventional. They want to please and succeed. Sound like anyone you know, darling? Secondborns are much more inclined to be unconventional; who gives a flying fuck what anyone else thinks? Yes, my jewel, even I use that proud Anglo-Saxon word when I can't think of something better.

My sister wanted what she saw on television. She wanted us to live in a neat white house with a border of petunias growing in the front garden. She wanted clothes that matched and shoes that weren't scuffed. Life with our mother was much harder for her. I didn't give a fig (or a fuck) about clothes, houses or petunias. All I cared about was reliable access to books and the time to daydream. Obviously some things change. As you know, I love wonderful clothes and have become houseproud in the extreme. The irony is not lost on me that I ended up with my sister's dream.

Because of the books and my ability to daydream I was always able to 'check out' of whatever was going on around me. Life with my mother wasn't as much of a problem for me because I wasn't really there. I was on desert islands, in Tibetan villages, Tudor manor houses, wherever I wanted to be. Poor Ellie couldn't do that. Her head simply wasn't wired like mine. I think if I hadn't had my alternative reality I would have gone quite mad.

I actually remember being rather an observer of what was going on around me, but somehow I didn't see any of it as having a great deal to do with who or what I was. Does that make any sense at all? Part of me could always, or almost always, step aside and look at things from the outside. Poor El was always sitting right in the middle of it.

Our mother had been dead about a week when Ellie told me she was pregnant by the loathsome Steve. Needless to say, I was shocked and horrified. This was about the worst thing that could happen to an unmarried girl in those days. In truth it's just about the worst thing that can happen to a fourteen-year-old girl today.

I didn't understand at the time why Ellie hadn't told our mother she was pregnant. I felt that no one could have understood better. Ellie didn't see it that way. I suppose she felt that our mother would have been perfectly useless and she was probably right. I think Ellie was afraid the pregnancy was simply confirmation that she was just another bit of Okie trash. Of course this happened across the social spectrum, but Ellie's view was so narrow she assumed only little Okie girls became pregnant without benefit of marriage.

To her hormone-screwed mind, Steve was the protector. I suppose this would make sense to a Desmond Morris, but the logic still eludes me. She sincerely believed he wasn't merely her protector, but mine as well. Creepy, rat-faced beast was her James Dean, Cary Grant and Paul Newman all rolled into one fingernail-chewing boy.

I suppose Steve was my first sexual encounter. He grabbed me and made his intentions known. Fortunately I had the presence of mind to kick him hard enough to discourage his base inclinations. Lower than pond scum. Of course I told El about this, but she refused to believe me. I had never heard of rape, but I knew he wanted to hurt me and I could guess his weapon of choice.

God, this all sounds so twisted and bleak. Sometimes I wonder if that time was just a bad dream, but it shaped me too much to be a dream. It also makes me terribly grateful for the life I have today. As cavalier as I tend to be about God, I thank her every day that my children haven't repeated my history. I'm so glad the *two of you were born into a warm, loving family where you could grow into the lovely creatures you have become. Yes, I'm embarrassing myself with this maudlin prose.*

Patch sends his love, even though the poor lamb has a wound on his back. I just hope I don't have to take him to the vet for cat scratch fever. How humiliating.

We love you and miss you. Write, fax, soon.

Love and God bless

Mummy

CHAPTER NINE

'Bearing up, Liz?' Her neighbour Alison McQuinn leaned across the table after moving a bottle of wine out of the way.

'Better than I would have thought.' She thought of Mary and the huge expanse of earth that separated them.

'Mike's father spent a month with us last autumn and I thought I would lose my mind. No more aged relatives for me.' She wrinkled her nose as she lifted a triangle of toast to examine the pâté on her plate.

'Oh, I didn't realize you were talking about India staying with us. I thought you were asking me how I was doing without Mary.' She took a sip of her wine and glanced at her own pâté, wondering if she should be as concerned as Alison seemed to be with the neat block of pinkish paste. 'India's fine to have around. My mother's been dead since I was quite young, so India's rather more than a mother-in-law to me.'

'I envy you. Mike's mother died a year or so ago, but if she hadn't died when she did I probably would have strangled her myself. Ghastly woman.'

'I have to admit she wasn't a favourite of mine. She always made me feel as if my hem was falling out or I had spinach in my teeth. I half expected her to inspect my fingernails.'

'Slap your knuckles with a ruler, more likely. She never quite understood that she had retired from teaching.'

'I suppose it's hard to undo the habits of a lifetime.' Liz spread some pâté on a piece of toast, marvelling that Alison didn't realize that most people thought Alison's husband had married a carbon copy of his mother.

'How is Mary doing? I think you were very brave to let her go off by herself like that.'

'She's gone to San Francisco to take a couple of graduate classes. It's not as though she's taken off by herself on the Hippie Trail.' Alison didn't have any children of her own, and studied the offspring of her friends as though they were exotic but dangerous animals.

'I always forget that you're from California. I suppose you have family there who can keep an eye on her?'

'I was orphaned as a child and my only sister died years ago.'

'How grim. Although having said that, families aren't always all they're cracked up to be. Mike has a sister . . .'

Liz breathed a sigh of relief as her husband put a hand on Alison's arm. 'Forgive me for interrupting, Alison, but we need Liz to settle a point.' He winked at his wife as Alison turned to the person next to her.

'No problem, darling, what do you want to know?'

'Thanks for stopping Alison tonight. She does go on sometimes.' She sat at the foot of the bed and brushed her hair.

He took off his reading glasses and put them, along with the book he'd been reading, on the bedside table. 'I had been eavesdropping and you sounded as if you needed some help.'

'I didn't, you know.' She patted his legs, which were buried under the winter-weight duvet. 'I can handle Alison and anyone else. I'm all grown up now.'

'I don't mean to sound paternal, Liz.'

'I know, but you do.'

'I just want to protect you, I always have.'

'And you've done it very well, but I can take care of myself.'

'It flatters an old man to think he's still capable of defending his lady fair, even if it's from the neighbourhood bore.'

'Your "lady fair", my ass.'

'And a lovely ass it is.'

'I thought you were the one who was so tired.'

'An excuse to get you to myself. Did I tell you how lovely you looked tonight?'

'Yes, but you can tell me again.' She put down her hairbrush and climbed under the duvet with him.

Blue Creek, California, July 1962

She'd worked out her plan in the car after they'd picked Steve up. It was simple enough, so not much could go wrong if she was careful and kept her wits about her. All she had to do was wait until they went to bed.

One thing she could be sure of was their going to bed early. Steve would start talking about going before it was even halfway dark. He'd start rubbing against Ellie while she was still making the dinner sandwiches. His colours would change and the black balls would start to close up and the tiny red bands around him would widen and grow.

That night he looked at Lizzy and winked, as if she was now a part of the big man-woman secret. The big secret that everybody probably kept secret because it was just too stupid to even think about. After he winked, she looked back at him and experimented with burning holes in his flesh by staring hard enough. It didn't work, but he did turn away.

Lizzy knew she'd probably never be able to burn him up with thought control, but it made her feel a little better to think about his flesh turning black and curling up at the edges like a piece of barbecued meat. She also thought about how his emaciated corpse would look, hanging down from the big pine tree next to the cabin. Eagles could swoop down and snack on him until there was nothing left but a wind chime of bones strung together with gristle and sinew. Any man seeing that would think twice about bothering her or Ellie.

Lizzy waited until the familiar sounds began in the next room. Ellie would start giggling, and pretty soon Steve would say something she couldn't hear, in a funny, low voice he only used in that room.

She listened to the sounds the way a hunter listened to its prey. She gauged their mood and movements and bided her time. As soon as she heard the squeaking of the rusty bedsprings, she took the car keys from the nail by the door. She slowly turned the doorknob and waited for another squeak from the bed before she opened the door. The rusty hinges groaned, but she was hoping Steve and Ellie would be too busy to notice the sound.

Steve had backed the car into the pines about fifty feet from the cabin. Lizzy figured it would take him at least ten seconds to hear the car, decide there was a problem and get out of the cabin. Another five seconds would probably bring him to the car, but by then she could be headed for the main road. She'd already decided she would run him over if she needed to. Lizzy rehearsed it in her mind and she knew she wouldn't be afraid to run the car right over him. She would enjoy the crunching and squishing noises his body would make as the wheels ground him against the trees and over the pine-covered granite outcroppings. His screams would be music to her ears.

The car door opened smoothly and she quickly sat in the driver's seat. She hadn't sat on the driver's side since she was a little kid pretending to drive. Fumbling with the keys, she finally slid the right one into the ignition. Her foot found the gas pedal and she pushed down slightly and let it come back up. Lizzy closed her eyes and took a deep breath. She decided on a quick prayer, just in case Big Bob and Mrs Grafton hadn't been completely full of hot air. She started to pray to herself before deciding it might be more effective to whisper her prayer reverently, like they always did in the movies when things were really bad. Lizzy climbed out and knelt in front of the car, the Fords grille forming an altar of sorts.

'Dear God, I know I don't have any right to ask you for anything because I probably don't believe in you. At least I don't believe in you if you're the way they say you are at Vacation Bible School. They always make you sound like a really grumpy old man who's really, really rich and can do favours for you if he likes you enough. I guess I don't believe that because I've never known any man who ever did me favours. I've never known anybody rich either, but if I did I bet they wouldn't have done me any favours either. The only people who've ever done anything nice for me have been ladies, but in all fairness I have to admit I haven't really known any men very well, but of course you already know that; if you're there, that is.

'Anyway, if you're really you, you know we're in a lot of trouble. I need to get out of here so that I can go get the police and rescue Ellie. I don't need to tell you what Steve is like. By the way, I hope you aren't going to make any more Steves because it would be a very bad plan. In fact, I think the world would be a better place if you made better people. I don't mind the stuff like the earthquakes or the tornadoes, but some of the people are just awful.

'So now you know what I need, please help me. I also think it would be a big help if Ellie would stop being pregnant. If there is a way you can stop her from having a baby it would make things much simpler for the two of us. If you do that I promise I'll keep an eye on her so that it doesn't happen again.

In fact, if you get us out of here and stop her from being pregnant, I'll basically do anything you want me to for the rest of my life. I think that's a pretty good deal and I hope you will agree. Amen and goodbye.' Lizzy rose and brushed the dirt off her knees before kneeling in front of the Ford once again.

'I was just thinking about stopping Ellie from being pregnant. I wouldn't want the baby to die because of what I've asked you for. It's only a baby, even if Steve is part of it. Maybe you could take the baby from Ellie and stick it inside some woman who's been wanting a baby and can't have one? In fact, if you look around I bet there are other girls like Ellie who don't need to be pregnant. Think about it. Amen, again.' She stood and climbed back in the car.

She turned the key and heard the engine trying to come to life. The effort of the engine seemed to bounce against the trees, magnified fivefold. It heaved and stuttered, but wouldn't turn over, wouldn't start. She muttered, then begged, but the engine and God refused to listen.

The cabin door slammed open and she felt a hand on her neck through the open window before she had time to slide to the other side of the car. She tried to pry his fingers off, but he was too strong and his fingernails were sunk in her flesh like talons.

'I told Ellie you would pull something like this. You little bitch! Where the hell did you think you were going?'

His free hand slapped her ear, shoving her face into the steering wheel. 'Answer me!'

'I was going to get help. I was going to get so far away you would never be able to touch me again!' Lizzy didn't see any point in lying. Her ear felt as if it might explode and its ringing made her feel she was swimming in the deep end of the diving pool. She could feel something trickling down her neck and knew it was her blood from where his filthy nails were digging into her skin.

The door opened and he dragged Lizzy out, pinning her

arms behind her back, shoving her face against the hood of the car. 'I'll teach you a lesson, bitch.' She could feel his breath, hot against her neck, and she tried to twist away from his heat and his smell.

'Let me go, please let me go.' Her hands were wedged between them and she could feel his chest, hot and slick with sweat and anger. She curled her hands into tight fists to avoid touching him.

'I'll let you go after I beat your brains out, bitch!' He grabbed her hair and pulled her head back. 'Your pretty little face is going to look like a pizza by the time I'm through with you. You're going to wish you were in that hole with your mama the whore.' He ground himself against her back with a groan.

'Don't! Just let me go!' She gasped as her hands felt the tangle of flesh and wiry hair behind her. Something trembled to life against her wrist, forcing itself against her fingers.

'Put your fingers around it,' he growled in her ear as it danced by her hand.

'No. I can't do that.' She shook and felt a splash of tears fall around her mouth. 'Let me go.'

'You make nice to me, girlie, or I'll shove it in your mouth before I kill you.'

She curled her fingers around his penis and it jumped and grew as he groaned and bit into her shoulder.

'Move your hand, Lizzy.' He mumbled the words wetly against her shoulder. 'Feels so fucking good.'

'Steve! Steve, what's going on? Let her go!' Ellie ran towards them, buttoning a shirt across her naked breasts.

'Stay out of this! She was trying to run away. She was going to get us thrown in jail. Is that what you want?' He clung to the younger girl, shoving her between himself and Ellie.

Ellie pulled at his arm and he released Lizzy. He shoved Ellie to the ground and began to kick her as she pulled into a ball, protecting her belly and her breasts.

'Don't you ever do that again! I told you we shouldn't have

let her come. I knew something like this would happen. This is your fault, all your fault!' As he pulled his foot back to deliver another kick, Lizzy grabbed his foot, forcing him to the ground as his leg was twisted away from him.

'Run, Ellie! Get out of here!' She felt herself being pulled to the ground as her sister scuttled away. She kicked as hard as she could, but she missed her mark and fell back against the hard earth.

'I warned you. I fucking warned you. I kept telling you not to make any trouble, but you wouldn't listen.' He stood over Lizzy in the dim moonlight, leaned over and picked something off the ground. He lifted a rock over his head.

'Ellie, stop him!' Lizzy rose on her arms and began to scuttle backwards. Her sister's dark form rose behind Steve.

'Bitch!' Steve positioned the rock over Lizzy's face.

'No!' Ellie grabbed him from behind, her hands tearing at his face.

'I told you to stay out of this!' He swung around and grabbed her head, bringing it down as he raised his knee, which he smashed against her forehead with a cracking sound. As she crumbled, he shoved her aside and turned to Lizzy.

'You wouldn't listen, would you?'

'Ellie? Ellie?' Her panic increased with the silence.

'Shut up and don't move.' Lizzy crawled across the ground towards the fallen girl.

'I said, don't move!' She felt his hands on her waist, flipping her on her back. He grabbed the hair at the back of her neck and straddled her. He leaned down and bit her breast until she screamed in pain. 'Move again and I'll bite the damn thing off!'

'Get off me!' She struggled, but he tightened his grip on her hair as he tugged at the elastic on her cotton shorts. 'Stop it!'

'I'll stop when I'm done with you.' He shifted his weight to pull off her shorts. 'I'll show you. You're a whore, just like your mama.'

'Get off me!' Lizzy balled her fist and chunked it into his

groin. He fell to the side with a sharp intake of air. She tried to stand, but his leg lay heavily over hers.

He rose to his knees, taking a rock in his hand. 'Bitch.'

'No!' The night exploded with stars.

Cotherstone, West Sussex, March 17th

Dearest Mary,

Good to hear your voice this weekend. I'm glad you've found a shop that sells Ribena and Hobnobs. Being a Yank by birth, I don't think Hobnobs have a thing on Oreos, but I suppose there is no accounting for taste. All that to say, when I first came over here I would have killed for a bag of Fritos, so I do know how you, or your taste buds, are feeling.

After we spoke to you we had a long talk with Gran. She's decided to close up her house and move in with us, just until she feels better, of course. She insists we all view this as a temporary arrangement. Just until she's back on her pins. Whatever makes her happy.

The truth is she is really feeling her age and I wouldn't be shocked to find out she's suffered some small strokes. She's easily confused and you know that's not like her at all. The sad thing is she seems to have lost her curiosity. She's always been, dare I say, almost nosy. Now, if it doesn't involve something she eats or wants to see on telly, she simply isn't interested. I'm going to call her doctor about it today. He'll probably tell me she's getting old, but I still want to check it out.

Daddy and I are going up to London tomorrow for his annual replacement. Lets just hope and pray the shop hasn't done something insane like changing the same stock they've carried since

King Arthur was a boy. Your father is still reeling from the duvet cover I bought four years ago.

Oh well, as your father likes to remind me, he never has to be embarrassed by a thirty-year-old picture of himself in a Nehru jacket. Actually, I'm secretly delighted with his lack of a bold fashion sense. I always feel a little sorry for women who are married to dandies; I like to be the pretty half of the couple. I can't imagine being married to a man with a ponytail or one of those baggy Armani suits. Jesus, I've become a Brit. Next thing I know I'll be declaring crooked teeth give a face character.

Chaz is leaving this morning for his school trip to Germany. He's awfully excited about being able to drink buckets of beer. I don't envy the teachers who are taking that lot.

I think I'm going to take this opportunity to at least air his room out. Actually, I'd like to take a blowtorch to it and be done with the whole thing. I suspect there are several new species of mould growing in that room and I'm not anxious to see any of them.

By the way, I'm not writing to you about all this family stuff so that you can be upset about my childhood. Please don't waste your emotional energy doing that. It's over, done, not to be repeated. My existence gives proof to the expression 'life goes on'. I'm proud that some very positive things in my life are a result of that time. For instance, my complete disavowal of violence comes from then. You benefited from this directly because I refused to so much as slap your hand or allow anyone else to discipline you or Chaz physically. Gran and I had our only real arguments over this. She is from the 'spare the rod, spoil the child' school. I'm forever grateful to you and your brother for not becoming mass murderers because I didn't spank you when you were two.

I also found out how terribly fragile life can be. I remember reading some novel, some thriller sort of thing, and the author was going on about how difficult it is to actually kill someone. In truth, it is fairly easy to die. A bit of bad luck and some bad timing is all it really takes.

Sorry. Must be the air pressure today. I think I'll go breathe

*the air in Chaz's room and clear my head. Nothing like the smell
of dirty socks and adolescent boy to wipe the cobwebs from the
brain. Do you suppose that's what women used to carry in those
little phials of 'smelling salts'? Perhaps what those phials held were
scrapings from their sons' rooms. Nothing like that smell to remind
one of the need to carry on and finish the task at hand.*

*I'd better close now. I need to get your brother down to the
station. It has been such an effort to get him packed, I'm debating
whether or not to stop at the station or merely slow down and
chuck him out of the door!*

Hugs and kisses. Stay well and write soon.

Love and God bless

Mummy

CHAPTER TEN

'Liz, I think we should talk about what's been bothering you the
last few weeks.' He put his napkin aside and leaned back in his
chair. Around them, the lunchtime crowd was thinning as the
restaurant's smartly dressed patrons paid with their company
credit cards and returned to their offices.

'You know it has nothing to do with you, don't you?' He'd
brought this up before, but she'd always slid around it, offering
quick explanations and easy smiles.

'I don't know what it's about because just now was the first
time you've admitted to me that anything was wrong.'

'Nothing is wrong. We have a wonderful life and I'm very
happy.' Their life was wonderful. A Sunday supplement life that
most people could only dream about. Even the pots and pans

matched, fitting beautifully into the custom-fitted kitchen. Doting husband heading the family business. Two handsome children and a cheeky dog. More than enough for anyone.

'If you're so happy, why do I feel as though there's a black cloud over the house I can see from a mile away? You've been sad and distracted and it makes everything and everyone around you a bit low. Even Patch seems to have lost some of his good humour.' He spoke gently, trained by years of living with her past and present.

'I'm sorry, darling.'

'Lizzy, I don't want you to be sorry. If there's a problem I want to help you with it.' He took her hand in his. 'I know it's been difficult with Mother moving in, but if need be we can get some help for you.'

'India is fine. I like having her around, you know that.' She fought the urge to pull her hand away from his. He loved to solve problems and felt everything had a point of resolution waiting to be reached.

'Is it me? Have you finally got tired of living with an old man who's set in his ways and buys exactly four white shirts every year?'

'You know that's ridiculous.' She saw a mixture of pain and relief in his face and regretted her dismissive tone. 'You're not the problem. You've been my anchor. Everything good has been built around you, around us. I don't even have words to describe how I feel about you because love doesn't really touch it. It's so much more.'

'I believe you, I want to believe you, but I have to wonder when you ignore me as you have lately.'

'Have I been ignoring you?'

'You've been ignoring your life. You're preoccupied. I feel as though you're going through the motions, skimming the surface.'

She drew the fork through her largely untouched meal and then looked at him. 'I thought it was gone. I thought it was all

over, but it never will be. I keep slipping back and it seems like
yesterday. I just wanted to answer Mary's questions, but instead
it's like these horrible archives have opened up and I can't shut
the door.'

'Lizzy, it all happened so long ago. It is over.'

'Not for me. I feel as if the dead are right behind me, waiting for me.' She saw he was about to speak and put her finger
to his lips. 'Please don't tell me it's ridiculous because I already
know it is.'

'I was just going to say you might find it worthwhile to talk
to someone about this. It helped before.'

'It didn't really help, it just buried it for a while.'

Blue Creek, California, July 1962

'Lizzy, can you hear me?' Ellie dabbed at her sister's head with
a damp undershirt. The bleeding had almost stopped, but a flap
of skin hung worryingly from Lizzy's scalp. The girl pressed at
it gingerly as though she was hanging a stubborn bit of wallpaper. 'Talk to me, Lizzy.'

'Yeah, yeah, I hear you.' Lizzy tried to open her eyes and
groaned with the effort. The inside of her skull felt as if it had
been sunburned and filled with gravel. A day at the beach in
hell.

'What were you trying to do, Lizzy? What did you think you
were doing?' Ellie sat back, pulling a soiled sheet around her
chest after wiping her nose and eyes on the fabric.

'I was going to get help.' Lizzy licked her lips and tasted the
salt and iron of her blood. Her stomach started to heave and
roll, but she swallowed hard and took a deep breath. 'I thought
I could fix things.'

'Why? You've made him so angry. I thought he was going
to kill us.' Ellie stuck a wad of the sheet into her mouth to stifle
a sob.

'We've got to get away, Ellie. He killed Mom and he's going to kill us.' Lizzy opened her eyes and stared at the ceiling.

'No, he wouldn't hurt me if you hadn't tried to run. He's just scared and angry. He couldn't have you running off like that. Besides, you could have got yourself killed. You don't know how to drive.'

'I could have learned real fast. It can't be that hard.' Lizzy closed her eyes slowly, hoping to draw the curtain on the bad dream. 'He sure was angry, El. You got that right.'

'Stay awake, Lizzy. I was so scared when I couldn't wake you up. I thought you were dying.' She shook the younger girl gently and dabbed once again at her sister's head. The wallpaper wound seemed to be staying in place.

At Ellie's insistence, Lizzy gingerly opened her eyes, forcing them to focus on the small brightness available. 'What time is it? It's light now.' Slivers of light came in through the nailed shutter. The last thing she remembered was Steve holding the rock over her head.

'Morning, maybe late morning.'

Lizzy blinked her eyes and turned towards her sister in the dim light. 'He got you, too. Are you OK?' She reached for Ellie's face and touched it briefly, her fingers brushing against a swollen eye and darkened cheek.

'Sore, mostly.' Ellie turned her cheek away and pulled the sheet higher across her chest to hide the angry welts which rose towards her shoulders.

'What happened to your clothes?' She remembered a shirt Ellie had been wearing.

'He took them. He's got all the clothes.'

'We have to get away, Ellie. If we stay here he's going to kill us both. You know that, don't you?'

Ellie kept her face turned, refusing to meet her sister's gaze.

Lizzy winced as she pulled herself up and reached for the older girl's arm. 'You know that, don't you? He's going to kill us if we don't get away. We have to leave tonight after he falls asleep. We'll stay off the road and go through the woods.' She leaned back into the thin mattress.

'He's locked us in. He's done something to the latch or shoved something against the door. I tried, but I couldn't get it open.' Ellie began to sob.

'Well, one good thing about all this.'

'What's good about any of this?'

'I bet you don't think he's real sweet any more.' Lizzy closed her eyes and tried to ignore the gravel rolling around inside her skull.

'Do you know where he is?' Lizzy tried to lift the latch. Her legs felt rubbery and she leaned against the door. She took a deep breath and tried the latch a second time, but it still wouldn't lift. She tried moving it from side to side without success.

'No. I think he's outside because I heard him leave and I didn't hear him come back. He must be someplace close because I didn't hear the car start.' Ellie sat hunched on the bed, staring at her feet.

'Maybe you should try talking to him. See if you can get him to open the door.'

'He said he never wanted to see me again. He said I could rot before he'd open the door, and I think he meant every word of it.' Ellie touched her swollen cheek.

'Maybe you could promise to do some of that sex stuff for him. You said it was the way to get him to do what you want.' As disgusting as it seemed to Lizzy, she felt her sister should give it a try. She'd been doing it with Steve for weeks anyway. What was one more time?

'I don't want him touching me. I don't even want to be in the same room with him.' Ellie looked at her sister in disgust. 'I don't know how you could think I'd do such a thing.'

'This is not the time to get all high and mighty on me, Ellie. Besides, you don't really have to do anything with him, just promise to do stuff. Get him all happy and then we can tie him up or bash him over the head.' Lizzy tried to put some enthusiasm in her voice. She wanted to tap into some of that junior varsity lettergirl spirit which she knew Ellie still had.

'Then where do we go? What do we do?' Ellie's voice sounded older than Mrs Kirby's. It even had a crackle like an old wedding bouquet inside a bell jar.

'We go to the police.'

'We can't go to the police, you know that.'

'We have to, Ellie, everything has changed now. You're going to have a baby and we can't take care of a baby by ourselves.' She decided against mentioning the prayer. She didn't want Ellie to start thinking they had some kind of holy advantage. If she started thinking that, she might decide God and Jesus would take care of everything without any kind of effort on their part. Ellie might want to just wait around until some of that manna from heaven that Mrs Grafton told them about rained down and solved their problems. 'We need the police whether we like it or not. We need protection from Steve and we need somebody to take care of us. The pretending is over and it's time to admit we're just kids.'

'They'll break us up. I know they will. They'll take away my baby and they'll break us up.'

'Maybe they should take away that baby and give it to somebody who can take care of it. We can't look after it, and what if it ends up just like its father? Do you want a kid like Steve around for the rest of your life?' Lizzy started feeling a little guilty about the second part of her prayer. She hadn't thought that her sister might seriously want to have a baby.

'That's a terrible thing to say! How can you say that?'

'Because it's true. It's going to be another little bastard, just like me and you. You're the one who hates welfare and being poor so much. If you keep this baby you'll always be poor and trashy and so will the baby. You'll be like all those other mothers sitting down at the Welfare office with their snotty-nosed little kids. You'll be wearing flip-flops and house dresses from Woolworth the rest of your life if you keep this baby.

'Give yourself a break, El. Give the baby away and we can both start fresh. Maybe you can go to a new school after the baby is born and be a lettergirl again. After that you could even go to college with me some day. You could work a little harder and bring your grades up, I know you could.' Lizzy warmed to the idea of Ellie at college. 'You'd meet better guys there.'

'Mothers aren't supposed to give their babies away. Mom could have given us away, but she didn't.'

'My point exactly.'

'What do you mean?'

'I mean, if she had put us up for adoption we probably would have had a better life and so would she. Maybe if she had been on her own she wouldn't have drunk so much. Maybe she wouldn't have ended up buried by a riverbank holding a mason jar. If she'd given us up we certainly wouldn't be sitting here, locked up by your crazy boyfriend.'

'We wouldn't have each other for sisters, either.'

'Yeah, I guess every cloud has a silver lining.'

'Do you mean that, Lizzy?'

'What I mean is you should give that baby to some nice rich people so that you both have some kind of chance.'

'I mean, are you really glad that we're sisters?'

'Are you?'

'I asked first.'

Lizzy shrugged as she decided to confess. 'You've always been the most important person in my life.'

'I know what you mean. At least I know that now. When I saw Steve hurting you I knew.' Ellie turned her face away from her sister. 'I'm sorry I got you into this.'

'It's OK, Ellie. I think Mom was the one who really got us into this mess anyway.' She put her arms around her sister and pulled her close.

'He's back.' Lizzy pressed her ear to the wall adjoining the other room.

'What's he doing?' Ellie whispered as softly as she could.

'I don't know, I can't tell. Try talking to him.'

'No. Maybe he'll just leave. He's got the money and the car, so maybe he'll just leave us alone.'

'The money! You gave him the money?'

'I didn't give it to him, he took it.'

'Eleanor, sometimes I don't think you're worth the flesh you are printed on.'

'Go to hell, Lizzy!' Her whisper turned to a hiss.

'Thanks to you, I'm spending my summer vacation in hell.' Lizzy cocked her head towards the door. 'Listen.' Something heavy was being scraped across the floor towards their door.

'What's he doing?' Ellie stood rigid, her arms at her sides.

'He's shoving the bed against the door. Even if we could get the door unlatched we wouldn't be able to open it, at least not right away.'

'Why's he doing that?'

'Because he doesn't want us to get out of here, that's why.'

'We can climb out of the window.'

'No we can't. The shutters are still nailed on.' Lizzy didn't admit that leaving the shutters in place had been her idea.

'He can't do that. He can't just lock us up like this.'

'He just did, El.' Lizzy thought she might throw up again.

'What are we going to do?'

'I don't know, let me think.' She looked around the room, then walked slowly around the floor with a soft, bouncing step. She stopped in a corner and dropped to her knees. 'This just might work.'

'What?'

'The cabin is built on blocks. If we tear out part of the floor we can crawl out.'

'How do we tear out the floor? We don't have any tools.'

'We've got something better.' Lizzy pushed her fingers against the wood. 'We've got dry rot. The next time Steve leaves we tear apart one of the beds and make a hole in the floor. We should be able to get out of here in about half an hour.' She grinned up at the older girl.

'Are you sure it will work?'

'How bad do you want to get out of here, Ellie?'

'What's that supposed to mean?'

'I mean, it will work if we really want it to work. We'll make it work because it has to; our lives depend on it.'

Lizzy liked the way that sounded. She felt like one of those really beautiful actresses in a Second World War movie. She could almost feel the slim-fitting serge uniform hugging her form as she inspired a bunch of soldiers who all looked something like Ronald Colman.

'What do you want me to do?' Ellie squatted down next to the patch of rotting floorboards.

'I want you to believe with your whole heart that we can get out of here.' She decided she would write a long letter to President Kennedy about this as soon as they were safe. He would probably invite her to the White House and have her speak at a press conference. Kids all over the country would be told to be more like Elizabeth Sinclair. She would tell everyone they could do anything they wanted as long as they believed in themselves. *Life* magazine would have a picture of her playing on the front lawn of the White House with Caroline and her pony Macaroni.

Cotherstone, West Sussex, March 26th

Dearest Mary,

I'm afraid this isn't going to be one of those chirpy letters from home. I received a call last night that Karen Linley died yesterday. Remember her? She had two boys, Gavin and Phillip? I knew she'd had surgery, but the last time I spoke to her she said she was in remission and feeling wonderful. I think that was about four months ago. I feel so awful that I didn't know she had become ill again. Perhaps I could have done something to make things a little easier for her. I'm taking some food over to them later today. At least I can do that.

I suppose this is the slide into the second half of life. When contemporaries start dying of illness, rather than mishap and mayhem, one knows one's number has slipped into the slot.

I am not feeling sorry for myself in spite of how this reads. I'm simply stating that I have clearly arrived at that point. Poor Karen. We used to see each other at the park when you and her boys were little things. Well, enough of that. I suppose Karen is the last one who would want gnashing of teeth and rending of garments.

Apart from the above, we are all fine. Gran seems more herself these days. The weather is brightening and that always cheers her, gardening buff that she is. I've asked her to take our garden over and redesign a few things. I introduced her to Dave, the fellow

*who's been helping me in the garden, and they got on like a house
on fire, so I don't think he'll mind taking directions from her.*

*I don't think you've met Dave. He's very old-time Sussex. He's
about thirty-five, has long hair and wears his beard in a braid. He
keeps some animals, makes charcoal, and tends to a few gardens.
He wears antiquated clothing, most of which appears to be
handmade. Since he's usually covered in grass clippings he has a
greenish tinge and makes me think of those sculptures of the Green
Man we saw in Glastonbury. I suspect he was born in this century
by mistake.*

*Your father and I had a nice trip to London to take care of his
shopping. Thank God, everything he needed was available. We
had a lovely lunch and had a chance to catch up, just the two of
us. It would have been nice to spend the night and see a show, but
we don't feel we can leave your gran for any length of time.*

I'd better close now. Stay well and happy.

Love and God bless

Mummy

*PS I tried to find my blue pullover that you like so much
yesterday. Did you take it with you, you cheeky thing? If you did,
please remember that it needs to be dry-cleaned.*

CHAPTER ELEVEN

'Good morning, Liz.' Alison turned around in the pew and
spoke to her in a whisper.

'Morning, Alison. How are you today?' She glanced around
St Mary's and nodded at a friend across the room. She debated

moving to get away from the woman. Social though they were, she didn't like to socialize at funerals. Through the years she'd come to hate the tea party atmosphere that seemed to invade even the most tragic of deaths.

'I'm fine, but I still can't believe how fast Karen went. I saw her just two months ago and she was the picture of health.'

'It's terribly sad. I stopped by yesterday and her family is taking it awfully hard. I feel so sorry for her sons.'

'I was thinking how awful this must be for you, Liz.'

'Why?' She knew what Alison meant, but she didn't feel like letting her off easily. If the woman insisted on sticking her foot in her mouth every time she spoke, Liz wasn't about to be the one to help her out. 'Why should it be awful for me?'

'Well, you've had your own health problems.'

'I haven't had health problems, Alison, I've had breast cancer.' Healthy as a horse, if the truth be told. Probably why the cancer chose her. Why settle for second best when looking for a host?

'That's what I mean, darling. You and Karen had the same disease. Thank God you were cured. Poor Karen.'

'I won't consider myself cured until I hit the five-year mark, and that's two years away.' She'd never really consider herself cured. She'd always know there was an errant cell or two waiting to take over.

'It seems so many of my friends have had problems lately. Breast, skin, ovarian, all kinds of cancers.'

'Maybe it's one of those cancer clusters you read about, Alison. Let's hope you're not next.'

'Oh, Liz stop being so brittle. I'm just making conversation, for heaven's sake.'

'I'm not being brittle, Alison. Don't you recognize dry wit when you hear it?'

'Good grief, Liz. You of all people should know that cancer isn't a dirty word and it's something that can be publicly discussed.'

'I don't mind discussing cancer. I just feel it would be better to discuss Karen's life rather than her death. She was a lovely woman and I would like to remember her that way, as I'm sure would her family.'

'You're right about that, Liz. She was a lovely woman and will be sorely missed. Tragic to die so young. I don't think she was much older than me.'

'Oh my dear, she was much younger than you. She was just a year or two older than me.' Liz smiled and looked towards the front of the church. 'I must say, the flowers are lovely.'

Blue Creek, California, July 1962

'Can you hear him?' Ellie whispered to her sister.

'Yeah, he's still in the other room. I can't tell what he's doing. I don't want to do anything to the floor until he's gone from the cabin.' Lizzy stood with her ear pressed against the door.

'What if he doesn't leave?'

'He's got to leave sometime to pee.' She realized peeing wouldn't take up much time at all, especially for a boy. Thirty, forty seconds tops. 'Come here, I've got an idea.' Lizzy grabbed her sister's hand and drew her to the middle of the room. 'Let's take off our sheets and make a tent so that we can talk. We need to make a plan.'

'I don't want to take my sheet off. It's too cold.'

'It's not cold, stupid, and besides, our body heat will keep us warm. Eskimos are usually naked inside their igloos. The guys who go to the North Pole always sleep naked. You just don't want me to look at you and I promise you I won't. It's almost black in here and I don't want to look at your stupid body anyway.' She knew her sister went through elaborate machinations to avoid showers after gym class. She was always covering herself and squealing if anybody caught a glimpse of her underwear.

'OK, but remember, no looking.'

'Too bad you didn't worry a little earlier about who saw you naked, Eleanor.'

'When this is over I'm really going to hate you.'

'Sure you are.'

'I mean it. I'm going to hate you so much.'

'Ellie, if we ever get out of this you are going to love me more than you ever thought you could love anybody.' She would take Ellie to Washington DC with her. If nothing else it would provide a moral lesson to the nation. People would look at Ellie and see how much prettier she was, but they would know that Lizzy was the real heroine. Ellie probably wouldn't even notice Lizzy getting the attention as long as one or two of those marine guards made eyes at her. Of course, they wouldn't be making eyes at her if God didn't answer the prayer about the baby. If she was still pregnant. Mrs Kennedy would probably want to keep Ellie in the background because she'd had so many problems having babies herself. Maybe Mrs Kennedy could just arrange some kind of sightseeing tour for Ellie during the press conference and when the photographers from *Life* magazine were around.

'If? What do you mean, "if"?' Ellie's mouth was an almost perfect 'O' shape.

'Shut up and get your sheet off.'

Ellie stood staring at her sister as though she hadn't heard a word she'd said.

'Now. Get your sheet off right now and help me make a tent so we can talk.'

'What do you mean, "if", Lizzy? Don't you think we can get away from Steve?' The girls had climbed under the sheet, their mouths three inches apart in the dark.

'Ellie, I mean *if*. Steve has locked us in a cabin a million miles from nowhere. He's got our money and he's got our car. We have no food and no water. We can go for a long time without food, but we can't go more than four days without water. If we don't make something change, we die.'

'But the floor, Lizzy. We can dig through the floor.'

'Yeah, we can dig through the floor, but not while he's around. Unless— That could work. That could work.' Lizzy giggled with relief. To her own surprise she grabbed Ellie and hugged her until the older girl pushed her away.

'Stop that, Lizzy. Tell me what could work.'

'You've seen it work on TV about a million times before. It's the oldest trick in the book. One of us starts ripping up the floor. It doesn't matter how much noise we make, the more the better. The other one hides behind the door and cracks his head open as soon as he walks in to see what all the racket is about. Once he's knocked out, we just step over him and start running down the hill.'

'We'd have to get some clothes first.'

'Duh, Ellie. That goes without saying. I don't think either one of us wants to run down a hill with our rosy red bottoms showing.'

'Do you think it will work?'

'It sure beats waiting around to die of thirst.'

'I want to be the one to hit him over the head.' Ellie wriggled slightly with excitement.

'No, Ellie. We only have one chance to make this work. I'm afraid you might not hit him hard enough. You might get all mushy at the last second. I hate him with more hate than I thought there was in the whole world. I wouldn't mind eating his eyeballs for a snack or picking my teeth with his pinkie bone.'

'You're disgusting.'

'I think it must be my Viking blood. I want to hang him up and strip the skin off his body. There's nothing I could do to him that would be bad enough. I don't even care if they send me to prison until I'm older than Mrs Kirby. He's going to pay for what he's done to us.'

'Tell me what you think we should do.'

'First off, let's take apart one of the beds to make tools. We'll worry the wood a little bit to get it softened up. It's real spongy, so if we twist it some it should poke right through once you have a chance to make some real jabs at it.'

'Why do we need to do that? After you knock his block off he can't hurt us.'

'I want that hole to be big enough for you to fit through by the time he's in the room. That way, even if I mess up and only slow him down, you can still be into the woods before he figures out what's going on.'

'But then you might not get away. I can't let you do that.'

'It's better that one of us gets away than both of us die here.' Lizzy had read President Kennedy's book *Profiles in Courage* and knew this was exactly the kind of thing the man would want to hear when she met him. 'Besides, if I don't get away you can send help back.'

'I can't believe you'd do that for me.'

'Ellie, I'd do anything for you, just like you'd do anything for me.'

'Then if you can't stop him, I'll jump on him too. He's not as strong as he pretends to be and I know we could take him. If we surprise him, we can take him.'

'OK, Ellie. Can you promise you won't get all mushy and think about what a good kisser he is?'

'He's not a very good kisser.'

'Then why did you let him put his thing in you?' Lizzy thought the kissing part, at least, might be fun.

'Because he was something just for me. He wasn't a part of you or Mom. He was just mine, for me. I don't think I've ever had anything I didn't have to share.' She was quiet for a moment. 'I guess he wasn't the best choice.'

'The best choice?' Lizzy whooped and began to laugh. 'I hope I never see your bad choice.'

'There you go again. Stop making me out to be the fool all

the time!' Ellie threw back the sheet as her voice rose. 'I'm sick of you laughing at me and thinking you're so much better and smarter than me!'

The door burst open with a reverberating thud that shook the whole cabin. 'Stop it!' Steve stood in the doorway, the sun streaming behind him. 'What are you doing?'

'We were just talking, Steve.' Ellie grabbed the sheet and backed away from him as she tried to cover herself.

'I don't want the two of you talking about me.' He walked over and grabbed Ellie's shoulder. 'Do you understand?'

'Get your hands off my sister! Don't you ever touch her again.' Lizzy grabbed for his leg and tried to pull him down.

He kicked her away, striking her in the face with the side of his foot. He reached for Ellie and threw her off the bed on to the floor. He stood over them, his breath coming in rasping gulps.

'This is the way it's going to be? I came in here to give you another chance and this is what I get? Bitches.' He backed out of the door and slammed it shut. They could hear the bed being shoved back against the door.

Ellie began to shake. 'Now he won't come in again. What are we going to do, Lizzy? We're going to die in here. He's going to let us die in here!' She wrapped her arms around her chest and began to rock herself back and forth.

'We start working on the floor, Ellie. It doesn't matter how much noise we make any more. We dig up the floor and if he tries to stop us we kill him with the tools we make from the bed. I'd love to stick something through his brains.' Lizzy's hands twitched at the thought.

'It won't work. It won't work and we're going to die.' Ellie was trying to curl herself into a ball on the bed.

'It won't work if we don't get started and it won't work if you're going to lie there like you're already dead. Get your fat butt up and show some spirit, Ellie!' She watched with satisfaction as the Ellie-ball unrolled and found that it still had legs.

'Before we try the floor, I think we should see if we could use this thing like a crowbar on the shutters.' Using a discarded spoon as a screwdriver, Lizzy had been able to free the side bars from one of the beds.

'What do you mean?' Ellie sat on the floor where she had been watching her sister work. Dark half-moons had formed under her eyes.

'I mean maybe we can undo the shutters and get out through the window. It would be a lot easier and faster than the floor, if it works.' She looked at her sister briefly and then looked closer. 'Are you OK? Do you feel sick? You're putting off some funny colours.' Ellie's soft pink lights had shards of brown digging into the space around them.

'I'm just tired and I want to get this over with. Show me what to do.' Ellie stood and looked at the side bars for the first time.

'We need to get these in the little space between the frame and the shutters. Then I think if we move them back and forth a little, we might get somewhere.' Lizzy worked the side bar against the wood. 'It's moving, Ellie, it's moving.' She glanced towards the door. 'Stand over there and let me know if you hear anything.'

Ellie crept to the door and held her ear against the wood. She looked at her sister and shook her head. Lizzy signalled her back.

'Take this and work on this side of the shutter. Try not to make any noise. It will be easier if we can get out of here without a fight.'

The girls worked without speaking, but the wood creaked and groaned. The rusty nails could be heard scraping out of the old pine shutters. Within minutes they could see light entering the room and glimpsed the ground under the window. Ellie gave a final shove and the shutter swung free. Steve stood under the window, a box of matches in his hand.

'I told you I wasn't going to take any more shit off of you two. I tried to warn you, but you wouldn't listen.' He kicked a pile of dry pine needles and twigs next to the cabin. 'Do you know it hasn't rained for four months up here? Middle of fire season, so nobody's gonna think nothing about one more fire. It'll get so hot your bones won't even be left.' He lit a match and passed his finger through the flame as he grinned. 'Just wanted to make sure it worked.' He tossed the match on the pile.

A puff of greasy black smoke arose, then orange flames shot a foot above the pile, and began to lick up the side of the cabin as Steve used a stick to spread the fire under the building.

Lizzy grabbed her sister and pushed her towards the window. 'We've got to jump now, Ellie!'

'Oh Jesus, I'm scared!' Ellie stared at the flames.

'Now, Ellie, now! Put your knee on the sill and throw yourself out!' Lizzy pushed her sister's knee up and gave her a shove.

Ellie launched herself above the flames and rolled clear, scrambling to her feet. 'Jump, Lizzy! Come on!'

Lizzy hesitated and threw the side bars out of the window towards Ellie. The flames crackled at the ledge and smoke rose in swirls. She felt a searing pain when she tried to put her knee on the windowsill. She closed her eyes and dived out of the window as though she was once again diving into the river. She fell to the ground, her mouth filled with fine, powdery dirt. Spitting, she jumped to her feet and watched as Ellie picked up one of the side bars.

'You're right, Steve. Not even bones will be left.' She pushed the side bar towards his face and he backed away from her, stumbling, then falling on his back. He lifted his head and started to speak. Ellie raised the side bar and hit him across the right cheekbone. He fell back, his head making a thudding sound against the hard ground.

Lizzy stared at the boy and poked his side with her bare foot. He let out a low groan. 'Give me the bar, Ellie. I'll finish him off.' She reached for the piece of iron.

'No. I'm going to do this.' Ellie raised the side bar and drove it through Steve's left eye. His body shuddered for a moment, then lay still.

Cotherstone, West Sussex, April 3rd

Dearest Mary,

Today it feels as though spring has finally sprung. I could lie and tell you I've seen a thrush, but it at least seems like I should have seen a thrush.

We are all doing fine. Chaz arrived home from Germany, no worse for wear. Had a wonderful time, loved the beer, all that sort of thing. Came back talking about some Selene person. According to all reports, she's quite the dish. Apparently she'll be over here next year for a week, and he's already counting the days. I think I shall start keeping a bucket of cold water by his door for hormonal emergencies. I've read about spontaneous combustion and I suspect it happens to young men like Chaz with some frequency.

Gran is going out to lunch today with two of her friends. It will be nice for her and I must admit I'm looking forward to having the house to myself for an hour or two. She's a dear, but I am used to having a bit more time to myself.

I'm doing a book signing this weekend in Brighton. I hope someone comes! These are wonderful for the ego, but only as long as people turn up and tell me my work made them cry. I love to leave tears and misery in my wake.

Your father is fine, but he's not looking forward to the next two weeks. He's having new computers and new telephones installed at the same time. I'm going to buy earplugs so I don't have to listen to a litany of the unnatural and unlikely acts committed by aforementioned equipment.

Since you still seem interested, I will continue with my story. Do you remember when you were small, I told you the scars on my legs were from a car accident? I told everyone that, as a matter of fact. I've said it so many times, I almost believe it myself. I couldn't bear to recall or relate the truth, so a car accident was convenient. We can all relate to car accidents.

The truth is Steve tried to burn us alive. We were holed up in a little cabin while we were in the mountains. He set fire to the cabin after locking us in, but we managed to jump out while there was still time. Ellie jumped first. Actually I shoved her and then I jumped. The flames were pretty high by the time I got out so I am left with these souvenirs.

I've had my share of minor burns since then. They always hurt like hell and leave me feeling very sorry for myself. The odd thing was on that day, I didn't even realize I'd been burned. I suppose it was a combination of panic and adrenaline. Funny stuff, that whole mind–body connection.

I recall having vivid daydreams all that week about killing Steve. Kid's stuff, but I had told Ellie I was going to poke his eyes out, eat his eyeballs, beat his brains out, all that sort of thing. I never found out if I could have done any of those things because Ellie did it for me. With one stroke she drove the side bar of an iron bed into his eye and through his brain. She'd knocked him out first, by the way. Too bad about that.

Before she knocked him out he didn't put up much of a fight. I think he, like me, was so shocked that Ellie, of all people, was capable of violence. Ellie was usually so compliant, so passive with him. I am sorry I never got to test my own mettle against Steve. He died instantly and I think that was a shame. My sense of justice was offended because he should have suffered more. Perhaps I really am a bit of a Viking.

Do you remember seeing that famous picture out of Vietnam with the very young girl running away from a napalm attack?

That was the two of us. Running through the woods away from a fire and the horror that had become our young lives.

I read about the girl a few years ago. She was sent to the US and was enrolled in university. She had some scars, but she was building a good life for herself. I was very proud of her and very happy for her. I know Ellie would have felt the same way.

All sorts of images come to mind when I write about this time: trial by fire, the cleansing fire, the phoenix. I try to look at it in a metaphorical sense to keep it in some kind of perspective. If I think about it too long my lungs fill with black smoke once again and the flames lap at my knees.

I think I'd better close now. I'll take Patch down to the beach and throw a ball for him until he gives up. I could use a few lungfuls of sea air today.

Stay well and happy.

Love and God bless

Mummy

CHAPTER TWELVE

She found out during drinks. They'd been invited to a reception at Brighton's Royal Pavilion by the company's bankers. Drinks in the kitchen.

Fires had been lit and the security guards almost looked like the guests. You had to peer closely to see that all of the Duke of Wellington's copper pots were wired to alarms. She looked up and noted that the room's supports were topped with plaster greenery to make them look somewhat like palm trees. The guests milled around the plaster pig carcasses and stuffed game birds which allowed the tourists a glimpse into the world that fed George IV.

She turned away from the solicitor's wife who bred Dalmatians to have her glass filled by the po-faced young waiter. Her elbow caught the woman's arm and a small wave of champagne crashed against Liz's dress, turning the pale blue silk a few shades darker.

'Whoops!' The woman grimaced and handed Liz a napkin. 'I'm so sorry.'

'My fault entirely. I did slam into you after all. Too eager for another drink, I suppose.' Liz smiled at the woman and dabbed at the wet spot with the napkin. She glanced down to see the result and handed the napkin to the waiter. 'Excuse me. I think I'd better put a little water on this.'

She wove her way through the group, ignoring several people she'd met earlier. She hurried down the stairs to the loos, but didn't bother to go into the door marked 'Ladies'. She slipped into an alcove and closed her eyes for a moment, feeling the damp silk, cool against her reconstructed right breast. Finally she opened her eyes and looked down.

She hadn't been mistaken. Not as intense as when she was a child. Hardly noticeable. A touch of colour in the air. The sepia colour of disease.

Blue Creek, California, July 1962

'Is he dead?' Lizzy ran over to look at the boy lying in the dirt.

'He's dead.' Ellie gazed at Lizzy in disbelief. 'I killed him. I can't believe I killed him.'

Lizzy pulled the side bar from the body and shoved it into the undamaged eye socket. 'I killed him too.' She examined the blood with satisfaction before turning away. 'I think I'm going to throw up.' She looked at the burning cabin behind them. 'I think I'd better wait to be sick. We've got to get out of here, fast.'

The flames were jumping and running through the dry pines above the cabin. Like Chinese fireworks, the brush around the building was exploding with bright snapping sounds. Birds, squirrels and chipmunks were abandoning the trees while their shrieks of protest added to the cacophony.

'We've got to get the car keys. See if he's got them in his pocket, Ellie.' Lizzy backed away from the body, disgusted with the gore still pouring from the face.

'It won't do any good. He'd taken the distributor cap off the engine in case you tried to get away. He did that a couple of days ago. That's why you couldn't start the car.'

'Where is it, Ellie? Where did he put it?'

'He didn't tell me.'

'Come on.' Lizzy grabbed her sister's hand.

'What are you doing?'

'We have to get out of here.' She could feel the heat of the fire across her bare back and bottom.

'We've got to get some clothes first.' Ellie had to yell above the roar that seemed to surround them.

'No time! We have to get out of here, now! Would you rather be naked or dead?' She grabbed the older girl's hand and began to run downhill towards the road. The air felt cool and clean as they raced away from the flames and the body. She listened to a loud crackling sound and thought it might be the fire licking its chops over what was left of Steve.

'I've got to stop a second, Lizzy. I need to rest.' Ellie leaned forward, her hands on her knees, her sides heaving.

'We can stop for a minute, but only a minute. There should be fire trucks pretty soon. They keep lookouts all over the mountains for smoke. We'll be OK once the fire trucks get here. They'll have food and water and we'll be safe.' Lizzy couldn't remember the last time she'd tasted water or felt safe.

'It's all over, isn't it? All this and I'll end up in Juvee and you'll go to some foster home. All this for nothing.' Ellie gulped for air and wiped her grimy face with the back of her hand.

'You're not going to Juvee and neither am I. We tell them that Steve stole the car and kidnapped us. Even if they find him and figure out how he died it's OK because you can kill somebody if they kidnap you.' Lizzy thought for a moment. 'I'm almost positive.'

'They're going to see us naked. I wish we'd kept our sheets.'

'If we'd kept our sheets we'd be dead now. The sheets would have caught fire and we'd be a couple of dead Okies.'

'Liz, I feel really awful. My stomach hurts and I can't catch my breath.' Ellie put her hand on the soft bulge above her pubic bone and gasped.

'Smoke inhalation. You've got too much smoke in your lungs and then we started running and you've never been very good at running. The firemen will have oxygen and stuff. They'll know what to do.' Lizzy looked behind her. 'We've got to get out of here.' The cloud of smoke was growing closer.

'I'll try.' Ellie straightened her back and made squeaking sounds as she tried to suck enough air into her lungs.

'You'd better do more than try, El.' Lizzy started down the dirt road at a slower trot to accommodate the older girl. 'Come on, El. Just a little farther. The trucks are probably on their way. We'll hear the sirens any second now.'

Ellie's face was covered with cold sweat. The skin around her lips was tinged with blue and the strange brown shards of light were all round her belly now. The pink cloud she'd worn was almost completely gone. Lizzy could hear the fire trucks coming up the road and tried to pull her sister off to the side.

'Come on, El. Wake up, Ellie!' She shouted in her sister's ear and pinched the fleshy part of her cheek as hard as she could.

'I can't breathe. It hurts and I can't breathe.' Her eyes fluttered and closed again. 'Jesus, this hurts.' She groaned, then gasped, grabbing Lizzy's arm with such ferocity her nails dug into the younger girl's flesh, leaving four angry-looking welts.

'I'll take care of you, Ellie. I'll always take care of you.' She kissed her sister on the lips and ran down the road towards the sound of the approaching sirens.

They wrapped her in a fireman's heavy vinyl jacket and pretended that none of them had seen her without her clothes on. They gave her some water, called for two ambulances and told her they'd take good care of Ellie. She was fine until the tall boy who'd flirted with Ellie at the general store put his arm around her shoulder and told her she was a good girl. She started crying and thought she'd probably never stop.

Dry Creek Hospital, July 1962

'Did you know that your sister was going to have a baby?' The man leaned towards her, putting his face close to hers.

Lizzy nodded. He said he was Ellie's doctor, but he looked more like a cowboy. He had on boots and a big belt buckle. His face was sunburned and little lines shot away from his eyes and his mouth. His breath smelled of cigarettes and coffee. 'She told me.' She knew this might make her an accessory to a crime, but that didn't really matter any more. The doctor didn't seem to be mad at Ellie.

'Your sister is sick because of where the baby was growing. It should have been down in her womb, but it got stuck in one of her Fallopian tubes. It was in the wrong place, but it kept on growing and getting bigger. The problem is the tube broke and your sister started bleeding from the inside. She's lost a lot of blood.'

'Is the baby dead?'

'I'm afraid it is.'

'Good. Ellie doesn't need a baby right now. She needs to get back to school.' Lizzy was flooded with relief knowing she didn't have to worry about the baby any more. 'A baby would have ruined her life. I told her that just the other day.' It had happened right away: both her prayers had been answered. God must have been in a pretty good mood that night she prayed, because she had said some pretty sassy, rude things to Him. She made a mental note to be nicer the next time she prayed.

'I don't know your sister, but you might be right. Now, Ellie is a very sick little girl.' The little lines around his eyes deepened.

'But she's going to be all right. We've only got each other so she's got to be all right.' Lizzy sat straighter in the bed they had assigned to her after bandaging the burns on her legs and arms. 'She has to be all right.' She said it with as much conviction as she could.

'We're working on it, sweetheart. We're working on it.'

'But that isn't enough. Maybe if I talk to her. Ellie needs me to talk to her.' As she tried to swing her legs off the bed, she winced with pain. 'This really hurts. I didn't start hurting until they started wrapping me up.' She looked at the doctor accusingly.

'The body does that. Things don't hurt sometimes until your brain tells your body it can relax and take it a little easy. You need to stay in bed and rest so those burns can heal.'

'How long is it going to hurt like this?' She tried to bend her bandage-encased knees.

'Lucky for you, the burns didn't go very deep. You're not going to need skin grafts. You'll be uncomfortable for a few days, but when you think about what could have happened, I think you'll see you got off pretty easy.'

'I don't feel lucky and I don't feel like I got off easy.'

'I know, sweetheart. I just mean you could have been in a lot worse shape. You're going to have some scars and your legs are going to hurt for two or three weeks. Burns hurt worse than just about anything, but the nurses are giving you something to help with that.'

'What's this for?' Lizzy held up her hand where a needle and a tube were taped.

'That's where we can drip in extra fluids and some antibiotics. After a burn we have to make sure you don't lose too much water out of your body.'

'You mean dehydration.'

'That's right.' He smiled at her. 'Have you been in the hospital before?'

'No, but I heard the word on *Dr Kildare* and looked it up. I just like the sound of it.'

'In that case, you're going to hear a lot of words you like the sound of over the next two or three weeks.'

'I wonder what happens after two or three weeks.'

'I don't think you need to worry about that.'

'Wouldn't you worry about it if you didn't know what was going to happen to you in a few days?'

'I guess I would, sweetheart. I know that Fresno County has been contacted and the social workers will figure something out for you.'

'For me and Ellie, you mean.' She didn't like the way he'd dropped Ellie's name from the social worker's agenda. 'Ellie and I are a team.'

'I'm sure they'll get something figured out for both of you.'

'Do they call you Liz or Elizabeth?' The Sheriff smiled all the way up to his eyes. His shiny pink face was round above his brown uniform shirt.

'I like to be called Lizzy.' She pulled the bed sheet up to her chin. 'Are you here to arrest me?'

'Where did you get an idea like that, honey?'

'I just want to know if you're going to arrest me, because if you are, I have lots of reasons why you shouldn't.'

'I'd like to know everything that happened, but I guarantee I'm not going to arrest you and neither is anybody else. You have my word on that, Lizzy.'

'How about Ellie? Are you going to arrest her?'

'Lizzy, there is no way either of you girls is going to be

arrested. You just tell me exactly what happened so as I can file my report. Once you've told me about it, you don't ever have to talk about it again if you don't want to. How's that sound?'

'Which part do you want to hear first?'

'How about the beginning?'

'OK, but it's going to take a while. You'd better sit down and get comfortable.'

'So Ellie shoved it through his eye and he was dead. I did it to him too, just because I wanted to know I could. After that we ran down the hill, and you know the rest.' She looked at the man and waited for a response.

'I think you're a very brave girl and I hope this is the last bad thing that ever happens to you.'

'So we can leave when we get better? We won't be going to Juvee?'

'Definitely not Juvee, Lizzy. We've already called Fresno County and somebody down there is making arrangements for you, honey.'

'And for Ellie.'

'Yeah, we're going to have to make arrangements for her too.'

She heard the whispering outside her door and she knew as soon as she saw his face. She started trembling as he sat down by her bed and took her hand.

'How are you feeling, Lizzy?' He smiled, but the smile stopped short of his eyes. The little lines on his face stayed in place.

'Ellie's worse, isn't she?' She pulled her hand away from his and held it with her other hand.

'I'm sorry, Lizzy. Maybe if we'd been able to treat her sooner, we could have done something. I want you to know she died without waking up and she didn't know what was going on. I don't believe she suffered.'

'I think there's been some kind of mistake. I read about this once. Sometimes they open graves and find the body upside down. They weren't really dead. You'd better go look at her again.' She grabbed his arm and shook it. 'You've made a terrible mistake! She's still alive, I know she is!'

'I wish that were true, Lizzy. She died about an hour ago.'

'No she didn't! She can't be dead, she can't be!' She threw aside her bedclothes and tried to climb out. 'I'll prove to you she's still alive. I'll see her colours and I'll know.'

The man stood and lifted the sides of her bed, surrounding her with iron bars. 'I'm going to send one of the nurses in. She'll give you something to help you sleep and I'll make sure somebody stays with you so you're not alone.'

'Lizzy, I'm sorry, but we can't let you see her. It would only upset you more and it wouldn't do any good.' The nurse held a tiny paper cup with a pill inside. 'The doctor wants you to take this so you can get some sleep.'

'I don't need to sleep! I need to see my sister. I need to see. I can't just take somebody else's word for it that she's dead.' Her voice was raw with shouting at nurses, and with unspilled tears. 'Not when I know she's still alive.'

'Lizzy, I've already told you this is something you don't need to see. If you're not going to swallow this pill, I'm going to have to give you an injection.'

'And I've told you a hundred times that I've seen two dead bodies already. I need to see her because I know what dead looks like and I know she's not dead. I need to tell her some things. There are things she needs to know even if she is dead.' Angry at herself for admitting the possibility, she shoved the nurses hand away and watched the little pill skid across the floor. 'If even a part of her brain is alive, she'll be able to hear me.'

'Put her in a wheelchair. I'll take her down there.' The doctor leaned against the door frame.

'I don't think it's a good idea.' Older than the man, the nurse spoke through gritted teeth.

'I think it's a lousy idea. I think it's the last thing this kid needs, but I think I'd feel the same way in her shoes. Let's give her a little credit and let her do what she wants.'

'You're just feeling guilty because you let her die.' Lizzy looked away from the doctor. She fell back into her pillows. Now she'd have to see for herself that Ellie was dead. She'd known it all along.

'I don't feel guilty, Lizzy, I just feel sad.'

Somebody had put a sheet over her head. Lizzy lowered the sheet and stroked Ellie's hair back, flat against her head. She hardly looked like Ellie at all, with her colours all gone. There were little bits of gum from the adhesive tape that had held tubes in her mouth and nose. Lizzy picked those off as best she could.

'You were right, Ellie. It was all for nothing. Everybody is trying to be real nice to me, but it was still all for nothing. They've sent to Fresno County to tell a social worker to come and get me in a few days. I told the Sheriff about Steve and he just said we were really brave little girls.

'I told him that Steve killed Mom and made us bury her in the riverbank. That was kind of a lie, but it was just a little one and he believed me. He said I'd have to show the police where she's buried, but I think I'm going to forget where we put her. I wish they would let me bury you at the riverbank, but they'll probably bury you in Potter's Field.

'That reminds me; the Potter's Field thing. I want you to know what I've figured out about God. I thought of it because of Potter's Field. Since you're going there I think you should know why they call it that. After Judas got the money for telling on Jesus, he gave it back to the Romans. They didn't know what to do with it so they went and bought some land where the potters lived. They used the land to bury Judas and other poor people. I can't remember where I heard that but if you can still hear me I thought you might like to know that. Of course, that

Potter's Field wasn't the same one you'll be going to, but it will still be called Potter's Field.

'Anyway, what I wanted to tell you is I've found out that God answers prayers, but whatever you do, don't pray. I don't know if you can pray any more, but if you can, don't. I prayed that we would get away from Steve and you wouldn't be pregnant any more. You know how all that turned out. I was praying for things that should have been good, but it went all wrong. I don't feel bad about Steve being dead, but you should be alive and so should all those trees that burned down. I imagine there were some animals that got stuck in there too.

'You need to know I will always love you. I wasn't very good about loving you when you were alive, but I'll never, ever forget to love you now.

'The doctor said the baby died a day or so ago. I figure the baby died about the same time Steve did. I kind of like to think the baby is with you and doesn't look a thing like Steve. I know you didn't really mind the idea of a baby. I hope that Pastor Bob is right and you'll go to heaven. I know you won't go to hell because deep down you were always a good person.' Lizzy leaned over and kissed her sister on the lips before she pulled the sheet up, over her head. 'I will love you forever, Eleanor Sinclair.'

Dearest Mary,

We all enjoyed your last letter very much. I am a bit concerned about the hours you seem to be keeping. I know, I know; you've never needed a great deal of sleep. You started that the day we brought you home from the hospital.

We are all fine, with one exception. I had my three-year check last week and things aren't quite as good as they could have been. I don't want you to be overly concerned and I certainly don't want you to cut your trip short. Worst case is I might have to have another round of chemo. Well, obviously that isn't the worst case, but I really feel just fine. I'm keeping a very positive view and I think that is more than half the battle. I go in to the hospital at the end of this week for a few days of tests and then we should have a clearer picture of what's in store. It's going to take quite a bit more than a few random cells to knock me out of the running.

Good news!! My editor has queried me about doing a sequel to The Red Door. *I'm very pleased and have finished the first two chapters. I always loved those characters and it is a joy to be fooling around with them once again. Just what the doctor ordered. I'm so pleased I invested in the laptop. I can work on the manuscript even while the hospital staff are draining me of vital fluids.*

In answer to your question about Ellie: no, she didn't die from burns. Ellie's pregnancy was an ectopic one. The foetus had implanted itself in her Fallopian tube, rather than her uterus. Had there been some pre-natal care this would have been detected and dealt with. Of course there wasn't, so the foetus continued to develop until the size of it ruptured the tube. By the time she got medical attention, peritonitis had set in as a result of the internal bleeding. She was given antibiotics as well as transfusions, but apparently it was too late. From what I have read since, it must have been horrifically painful. Her doctor told me she hadn't been in pain, but I'm sure that was a white lie to spare me. I don't know where she got the strength to run down the hill with me.

I've tried to see some sense in what happened to Ellie, but I don't believe there is any. Struck down at fourteen because of a pregnancy which was caused by that hideous boy. There is nothing good that can be taken from that.

For many years I mourned Ellie as a sister. The last few years I've mourned her as a third child. My wild child who was taken from me much too soon. There are times I can almost glimpse her out of the corner of my eye. Of course, I know she's not there, but for me she still walks just out of my path of vision.

Well, darling, I'd better go have my health-packed lunch and get back to work. Please don't be overly concerned about my news. I'm sure it's nothing that can't be fixed. Stay well and happy.

Love and God bless

Mummy

CHAPTER THIRTEEN

'Hello, Liz. How are you today?' Gillian Cramer's voice scratched its way out of the telephone lines.

'I'm fine, but you sound horrible.'

'I am a mess. Awful cold and I'm going to leave the office at lunch and go home to work. Oh, hold on.' An explosive sneeze and a muffled cough could be heard above taped chamber music. 'Sorry, I've been doing that all morning.'

'Gillian, you sound as if you're going to infect the whole damn office. Why don't you just go home now and save a few lives?'

'Sweetie, I'd love to leave now, but I've got to get a few ducks in a row first. Actually, you're one of my ducks this morning.'

'Quack, quack.'

'Just wanted you to know I have your chapters and I'm going to read them this afternoon.'

'Good. I'll look forward to hearing what you think.' Gillian had acquired Liz when her previous editor had left the publishing house to write erotic bodice-rippers.

'I just wanted to know if you have any sort of time line on this book. Helps us all if we can have a publication date in mind.'

'My plan is certainly sooner rather than later. I've got everything plotted out, so it's just a matter of writing it down.'

'Good girl. So are you saying three months, six months?'

'Three to four months, I should think.' Surely three or four months wouldn't be asking for too much. Three or four months to write a little light fiction, put her affairs in order, say her goodbyes.

'Wonderful. If something changes and you need more time, that's fine too. Just keep me posted.' Liz heard another muffled sneeze. 'Oh God, I feel awful. Tell you what, sweetie; I'll call you next week when my nose is functioning and my lungs can once again hold air, and we'll have a good chat then. I'll have read the chapters and you'll probably have more for me to see. How does that sound?'

'Fine, Gillian. If you want to reach me next week you need to call me at St Luke's in Chichester. I'm spending a few days in hospital next week. If you'll hold on a minute, I'll find the number for you.'

'Why are you going to hospital?'

'I'm having some tests done.'

'I don't mean to pry, Liz, but one isn't usually admitted to hospital for tests.'

'I had breast cancer about three years ago. There are some indications it's back.' 'Indications' sounded so much more hopeful than she knew she had a right to be. She hadn't been wrong about the colours. Whatever they were, they didn't lie, then or now.

'Well, I'm sure you'll be fine. You're the picture of health and there are so many wonderful things they're doing these days.'

'All those wonderful things were done to me last time, Gillian. I'm pretty sure I've pulled the short straw on this one.' The first time she'd said it out loud. She'd told everyone else it was a silly thing to get out of the way. Brave and noble, full of life. An inspiration to us all. That's what they'd say when she was gone.

'Liz, don't say things like that! You're going to be fine. You have to believe that.'

'I really hate that whole thing, Gillian. Where the hell did that kind of thinking come from anyway? People used to get sick and they died and nobody blamed them. Now, if you get cancer, if you don't "beat it", you're considered to be lacking in pluck and courage. Pluck and courage and the will to live have nothing to do with this. I am also so sick of seeing pictures of some child who's being kept alive on machines and having some damned presenter talking about what a "fighter" the kid is. The kid isn't a fighter and disease isn't something that's overcome with a cheerful outlook. You try being full of courage and hope when you've already got one fake breast and every indication is that the disease has wandered into your lymph system as well as your bones. I'm going to die in a great deal of pain and the sooner I deal with that fact the better off I'll be.' She pulled the telephone's handset away from her mouth and looked at it with horror. The words had tumbled out before she could stop them.

'Liz, I'm so sorry. I didn't mean . . .'

'No, I'm the one who should apologize. I need to wait for the test results and find out what my options are. I'm sorry, Gillian, you just got in the way of a very bad time.'

'Liz, if there's anything I can do, you know you just have to ask.'

'You can forget everything I just said and get over your lousy cold. I have to run and I'll talk to you in a few days.' She hung up the telephone and went out in the spring rain without a coat or an umbrella.

She opened up her jewellery box and lifted off the ring tray. She reached to the back and pulled out a tiny envelope which had been wrapped in a double layer of cling film. She weighed the packet in her hand, knowing they were all still there. She'd carefully saved them up the last time. Just in case it got to be too much. Just in case she couldn't stand a minute more. She buried the packet under the assortment of trinkets, some precious, most not.

Dry Creek Hospital, July 1962

She spent that first day crying. She rocked back and forth in her bed, keening an ancient tune. She closed her eyes and listened to the dirge she had composed. She sang it in a language all could understand.

He dropped an ugly, brindle-coated pup on her bed. 'She's a Queensland Heeler. We use them to drive cattle around here.' The doctor sat in the chair next to her bed, stretched his long legs out and stuck his hands behind his head.

'They're as ugly as sin and they make the world's worst family pets. I usually get fifty dollars for one of these, but I can't seem to get rid of this one.' The puppy tried to hide under Lizzy's blankets.

'This one is more chicken than dog. She's afraid of the other dogs, and piddles and cries whenever I get too close to her.' Almost as if on cue, a dark, wet circle grew under the puppy.

'Want to know why they are such lousy family pets?

Lizzy tried to ignore the pup, but it found her hand and nuzzled it. She looked away from the doctor, but nodded her head.

'They can only love one person, ever. They are the most loyal, pig-headed animals in the world. They can't live with a family, at least not very well.' He put out his hand and the pup climbed towards Lizzy's chest with a squeak.

'See what I mean? She's decided she's your dog and good riddance to her.' He turned to walk away.

'Get her out of here. I don't want any ugly dog.'

'It speaks.' He smiled and turned back towards her bed. 'Every kid wants a puppy. It's written in the constitution of the United States. Besides, this ugly little spud seems to like you. She hasn't liked anyone else, so I guess you're stuck with her whether you like it or not.'

'I guess you forgot that I'm going to some foster home and they sure aren't going to let me take a dog with me. Especially a dog that hates everybody. Take her away.' She picked the pup up and shoved it in the direction of the man. To her surprise and embarrassment, she felt the tears erupting again and she turned her face away from him.

'That's not the real reason, is it, Liz?' He took the puppy and put it back on the girl's bed, where it scrambled up to her face.

'It's reason enough.' She pushed the animal away and stared out of the window, where the pines trembled in the light wind.

'You reckon if you love something it's going to die. You've been lying here thinking this is all your fault, and I want you to know that just isn't so. You did everything you knew how to do. You saved yourself.'

'I saved myself, but Ellie is dead. Ellie and her baby and my mother are dead. There isn't a person in this world who loves me any more. I'm just wondering when I'm going to die and why I haven't died yet. I tried holding my breath to speed things up, but it didn't work. I've tried to keep the blood from moving in my veins, but I can't do that either.

'I've always thought you could die from a broken heart, but I don't believe that any more. My heart is broken, but I'm still here and they're not. It's just more of the grown-up garbage you're supposed to believe. I want to die. If I die right now maybe I can still find Ellie and Mom before they get too far away.' She turned back towards the man. 'You're a doctor and I know you could give me something to die. It would be a lot easier for a lot of people if I were dead.'

'Lizzy, honey, I know this has been real bad, but . . .'

'Real bad? You don't know what real bad is! You with your hospital, and your boots, and your dogs. I don't have anything or anyone. You come in here and try to cheer me up with a stupid dog nobody else wants. Do you honestly think I could care about a stupid dog after everything that's happened? I'm not a little kid. I'm a lot more grown up than you think I am.'

'You're a lot more grown up than you need to be.'

'That's awfully easy for you to say. It's easy to say things and make it sound like you understand how I feel, but that doesn't make it so. I wish that Steve had killed me. I wish I was the first one who died. Now I'm nothing but a problem for social workers.'

He squatted down by her bed. 'Listen to me, Lizzy. We're all trying to fix things so that you can be a kid again. I've been talking to the social worker and we're trying to find a place where you can be a kid, a kid with her own dog.'

'You still don't get it, do you? I can't be a kid again. Maybe I'm not a grown up yet, but I'm sure not a kid again.'

'You can be a kid again. We'll put you some place where you'll be protected and loved and you'll be a kid again.'

'Just like that? Why are you doing this? Your job is being the doctor, not the social worker.'

'Right now, I'm responsible for you. You were admitted to my care and I'm responsible for you as long as you're in this hospital. I'm talking to the social worker, but I told her I thought you might be happier talking to me than somebody you don't know.'

'I don't know you, not very well.'

'You know me well enough to know that I care about you and I listen to you.'

'You say you do.'

'You know I do, so let's cut the crap and talk like friends.'

'OK.'

'First thing I need to know is about your family.'

'It was just the three of us.'

'How about your father?'

'I don't know anything real about my father. Mom always said he died in Korea, but that was probably a lie. She just wanted us to feel like normal kids, I guess. Mom always had trouble with men. I wouldn't be surprised if even she didn't know who he really was.' She thought of the hairy men and knew that one of them could have been her father. She might have been running into him in the hallway for years, but she hoped not.

'It's OK that you don't know who he is. You'd be surprised at how many women have trouble with men. Lots of men have trouble with women, for that matter.' He grinned at her and settled into the chair by her bed.

'Well, I think she had more trouble than most.' She began to stroke the warm, loose skin of the pup. 'Mom tried, but she always got things wrong. I think Ellie was a lot like her. After watching my mother and sister I've pretty much decided I'll avoid men as much as possible.'

'I think that's a pretty good policy for you, at least for now. Now we've taken father off the list, how about any grown-up friends you'd like to live with? Anybody you're close to? Somebody in the church, the neighbourhood?'

'I don't go to church. If God is what he's supposed to be, I wouldn't be here, would I? The only time I ever really prayed I got what I asked for, but it was all messed up and things just got worse and worse. I think all the religious stuff is a lot more dangerous than anybody realizes. You take a look at history and you'll see what I mean.'

'What about history?'

'Stuff like the Crusades and things like that. People get all wound up about God and they forget about people. It's like God hogs all the attention. People get so worried about what they think God wants them to do, they forget about taking care of each other. Maybe He doesn't want things to be that way, but that's the way things are.'

'I'm not going to argue religion with you, Lizzy. Truth be told, I'm not much of a churchgoer either. Is there anybody in your neighbourhood you might like to live with?'

'It wasn't really a neighbourhood, not like the ones you see on television. We kept pretty much to ourselves, anyway.' On television everybody lived in a two-storey house with shutters on the outside, and every house had a front path bordered with neat little rose trees. The mothers in the houses all wore pearl necklaces while they did the housework, and the fathers didn't seem to do anything but walk around with the newspapers in their hands while they solved everybody's stupid little problems. All the fathers she knew worked at the packing sheds, drank too much beer, and went down to Sanger for the cockfights when their wives weren't looking.

'Nobody at all?'

'How about you? You're sort of a friend.' He didn't seem like the sort of man who would go to the cockfights, and he definitely didn't work in a packing shed.

'I'm afraid I'm one of those men who has a lot of trouble with women. My wife decided a few months ago I wasn't quite what she needed any more. You need somebody who can do a better job than a bachelor like me who works eighteen hours a day.'

'Well, that's great.' She felt tears gathering in the back of her throat. She'd just about decided that was where the whole conversation was leading. He would take her to live on his ranch. Things had gone so badly, she didn't think President and Mrs Kennedy would be that pleased to see her at the White House, either. They might let her take a tour with a lot of other people, but there wouldn't be any press conference now. Nobody would be telling their kids to be more like Lizzy Sinclair.

'Sorry, Lizzy. You wouldn't have liked my wife anyway. I sure didn't. Now lets think on this. Anybody else?'

'There are two ladies at the library who like me a whole lot. They let me help out sometimes, and they always remember my birthday.' Miss Harper and Miss Johnson shared a neat bungalow down the street from the library. They'd been running the library since way before Lizzy had been born. Once they'd let her keep a book a month overdue just because they knew how much she loved it.

'Good. That's a place to start.'

'I said they like me. Liking somebody is a whole lot different than having them live with you. In case you haven't noticed, little girls are a dime a dozen.'

'People are a dime a dozen, Lizzy. That doesn't stop them from caring about each other. We just thought it might be nicer for you to go with people you already know.'

'They are not going to want me and they certainly aren't going to want a dog. They live in a really nice house with Miss Harper's mother. She's about a million years old. It's not a kid's kind of place.' Lizzy closed her eyes and could almost smell the clean smells of beeswax and flowers that filled their house. It overflowed with books, and Miss Harper had a big hi-fi she was always playing records on. The house seemed to vibrate with music, ideas and good smells.

'You just said you weren't a kid any more. Maybe they'd like to have a grown up around who's only twelve. Let me ask them.'

'You can ask, but they're going to say no.' The tears started again as the picture of the pretty bungalow faded from her mind.

'It's going to get better, Lizzy. I'll make sure of that.' He gently shook her shoulder. 'Do you hear me?'

By wiggling her jaw slightly, she could plug her ears from the inside. She took deep breaths and the sound filled her head until she couldn't hear anything but her own windy cave noises. After a few minutes he took the pup and left the room, closing the door behind him.

The long silence started that day. She had tried to be invisible, but it didn't work. The nurses still fussed around her, happy to care for a passive, cooperative patient. The silence had been an accident that first day. Lizzy discovered that her silence caused the nurses to back away, respecting the quiet she spun around herself like a web.

It defeated the earnest young priest from the town. He tried to pray with her for three days and finally made do with a perfunctory sign of the cross on her forehead. On the fourth day he merely raised his hand in blessing as he passed her door. By the fifth day he didn't even glance in her room.

The doctor stopped by twice a day, but she ignored him. He didn't bring the dog back.

Cotherstone, West Sussex, April 17th

Dearest Mary,

It was wonderful to talk to you last night. I just want to reiterate what I said on the phone: don't come home. There is nothing you can do. I feel quite confident that this is merely a blip in my recovery. I feel just fine and I certainly don't have a sense of impending disaster. Your half-year abroad is something you've been looking forward to for the longest time. I'd never forgive myself if you cut the time short because of me. I have every intention of living forever.

I realize you think I'm trying to downplay everything, but it isn't that at all. If my childhood prepared me for anything it prepared me for disaster. The only thing to do is to keep one's wits about oneself. Not that I see this present situation as a disaster, mind you. I simply don't see it as the occasion for great dramatics.

One of the nicest things about being a 'woman of a certain age' is that you've learned to cope with things. You've acquired a few tools through the years that get you through the rough patches. When I was a child, especially after my sister died, I felt like a brine shrimp in a whale's mouth. Today I feel that I'm the whale and the disease is the brine shrimp. All in all a much better position to be in.

I think Gran is almost excited about my being away for a few days. She's been busy planning menus and she's promising the boys all sorts of old-fashioned cooking. I think she's planning a steak and kidney pudding for tomorrow night. I hope Chaz can manage to keep it down. I told him the trick is to swallow the kidneys whole, avoiding choking, of course.

Patch is going to the office with Daddy during the day while I'm in hospital. We felt that was wiser than having Gran try to keep an eye on him. He can be awfully demanding about walks and such, as you know. I hope he isn't such a bother at the office that he has to go into kennels. Oh well, that's your father's worry.

I've sent the first few chapters off to my editor and she seems pretty pleased. This is the first time in years I've written something I know I'm going to get paid for. My fingers are flying. I now understand why the big-name writers can sit at their keyboards for ten hours at a time. Much easier to do when you know it's not a complete gamble.

I'm buying new curtains for the sitting room this afternoon. I think I'll also order new soft covers and really spruce things up. Of course, this is a wee bit dangerous. The new things will make the walls look dingy, so I'll have to have the decorators in. The fresh walls will make the carpet look tatty and so on and so on. Oh well, it's only money, as I keep telling your poor grey-haired father. If work is going to tie me to the house this spring, I want things to look great.

I'd better close now. I need to pack for hospital before the lady from the curtain shop comes by. I also need to do some last-minute grocery shopping. I want to make sure Gran has lots of kidneys and suet in the house.

Stay well and stop worrying.

Love and God bless

Mummy

CHAPTER FOURTEEN

'You're late.' She'd tucked herself into a corner booth , so she could watch him before he saw her.

'Sorry, Liz. Traffic, you know.' He leaned over and kissed her cheek before sliding into the seat across from her.

'What are we doing here?' She studied the specials on the blackboard beside the bar as she spoke. The less she looked at him the better, she knew that from experience.

'I've been so worried about you. Mother said you were due to go into hospital this week.'

'Tomorrow morning.'

'Mother was vague, but she said something about tests.'

'Tests, scans, prodding fingers. Hours of fun. I think I'll have the bream.'

'For Christ's sake, Lizzy, tell me what's going on.'

'It's back. The cancer is back.'

'Are you sure?'

'I'm absolutely positive. The tests are for the doctors.'

'I'm sure there are things that can be done. You did so well before.' He took her hand, turned the palm up and kissed her wrist.

'I did so well last time for about three years. I know that it's back and I know it's back with a vengeance. It's started travelling.' She let her finger brush lightly against his temple where the hair had begun to turn silver.

'How can you be sure?'

'I can feel the changes. It's as though the sand has shifted under my feet. It's almost like when I knew I was pregnant, even before I'd missed a period. I just know.' She winced, recalling that he hadn't believed her then, not at first.

'I'm going to be there for you.'

'You can't very well be there for me, now can you?'

'I can if you'll let me. He'll do anything you ask, you know that.'

'I'm not going to ask my husband to welcome you to my sick-room.'

'I should think if you can forgive me, my own brother can do the same.'

'What makes you think I've forgiven you?'

'Haven't you?'

'Not completely, never completely.'

Dry Creek Hospital, August 1962

'Hello, Lizzy. My name is Sheila Borden.' The woman held her hand out for Lizzy to shake.

Lizzy looked at the hand, thinking the woman looked just like a schoolteacher, only duller, in her beige shirtwaist with the wet circles under the arms. She tucked her own hands under her sheets, protecting them from the intrusion.

'Lizzy, I can't help you if you won't cooperate with me. Everyone here is just trying to help you.' She sat down next to Lizzy's bed and opened a manila envelope. 'I can put you in a home where people will care about you. I can make sure you have a safe place to live and good food to eat.' She reached her hand out to touch the girl, but Lizzy pulled away.

She closed her eyes and pulled the sheet up under her chin. She could see her mother's body in its makeshift shroud. She could see Ellie stumbling, naked, on the dirt path, the sky behind lit with fire. She knew she'd never be safe, not really. She shut her ears and let the windy cave noises take over. The only sounds she could hear were the ones of her own making.

Spring Valley Juvenile Facility, September 1962

Miss Borden had taken her there. She chattered at Lizzy, but Lizzy leaned back into the seat and soon fell asleep. When she woke, Miss Borden was still rattling on, but Lizzy didn't hear her. She rarely had to use the windy cave any more. Everyone spoke a foreign language which she couldn't understand unless she chose to translate, which she rarely did. When she left the hospital the doctor had spoken to her as she got into the car, but she had had no idea what he'd said.

She didn't know exactly where it was. It was in a valley, but she didn't recognize anything else. It smelled of disinfectant and urine. The walls were tiled in dull green with cheerful posters stuck on with masking tape. The posters extolled the virtues of staying in school and brushing your teeth after each meal. She was assigned to the junior girls' unit where the feeling seemed to be that mental health could be achieved by learning to make a dirndl skirt.

Not that she minded. The girls were allowed access to the library once the sewing class was over and they had checked their chores on the duty roster. She was quick with her hands and Ellie had taught her to make a dirndl skirt two years before. Some of the girls had a terrible time with the zippers, and the girl with red hair wasn't allowed to use the scissors because she always jabbed herself and smeared the blood on her face. One of the other girls stuck pins in her hands and made tattoos with black ink. She wasn't very artistic and hadn't managed much more than a cross with little points coming off of it.

The chores were simple and no one really seemed to notice or mind her silence. The screamers and shouters and swearers tended to absorb the staff's time, so Lizzy was relatively free within the confines of the walls and exercise yard.

A man with his glasses taped together spoke to her once a week. He asked pointless questions, but didn't seem very disappointed when she didn't answer. He told her she needed to be in 'group', so twice a week she had to sit in a circle with other twelve-year-olds. Most of the time a boy named Kevin talked about his penis while one of the staff tried to shut him up and another one of the staff said he needed to discuss his feelings.

Lizzy just closed her eyes and talked to Ellie, although Ellie never talked back.

Sometimes Ellie would leave, but she would always come back to sit by her bed while she went to sleep. Lizzy couldn't have fallen asleep if her sister wasn't there, and Ellie seemed to know that.

Nights were bad because of the noises that would echo against the tiled walls. Sometimes even the quiet girls would scream at night. The staff would walk around shushing and snapping, but that would just scare the jumpy ones and set them off. The girl with the sores on her arms would hoot like an owl all night long. During the day, the same girl would dig her fingers into her arms and hiss if anyone came near.

On the day Lizzy found the blood on her underpants she gave the offending garment to the next staff member she saw. The man blushed and handed her over to one of the young women who staffed the girls dormitory. She gave Lizzy a box of pads and a thick white elastic belt to hold the pads snug against her body.

She told Lizzy about being a young woman now, and something about the wonder of being a woman. Lizzy translated her words, but wanted to tell her the wonder could go all wrong. She wanted to tell her those little parts could break and bleed and kill you. She drew her feet up to the chair seat. Clasping her arms around her knees, she rocked herself until the young woman stopped talking and left.

Spring Valley Juvenile Facility, October 1962

Miss Johnson started crying when Lizzy walked into the visitors' lounge. Miss Harper just kept shoving at the man with the tape on his glasses. Miss Harper wasn't very tall, but she was powerfully built.

'Look at this child. Look at her! What kind of a snakepit are you running here?' She shoved her stubby finger into his chest. 'This time I don't leave without Lizzy in the back of my car.'

'Lizzy, my dear Lizzy. We have been so worried about you. You were only supposed to be here for three weeks and then we don't know what happened. It's been some kind of awful mix-up.' Miss Johnson pulled the girl towards her chest. 'They wouldn't even let us see you. You must have thought we'd forgotten all about you, but that's just not so. We've been worried sick.'

'Miss Johnson, Miss Harper, we've been through all this.' He gingerly pushed Miss Harper's finger away from his chest. 'We couldn't release a child who was traumatized to the point of being mute. Surely you understand that?'

'I understand that a child can't live, much less get well, in a place like this. I wouldn't talk either if I'd been through what she has, and neither would you. She needs a home and people who care about her.'

'You have to understand our position . . .'

'You have to understand that I mean business. I will sue the state, this institution, and you personally, if this child isn't released to us today. We have already spoken to her case worker. The home study was done on us over two months ago and we are now a certified foster home.'

'I have spent the last fifteen years taking care of mentally ill children. How long have you done that? What are your qualifications? You two are what, a couple of librarians? Isn't that what Miss Borden told me?' He raised his voice to match Miss Harper's.

'I have spent the last thirty years working with normal, well-adjusted kids, and I know one when I see one. I've known Lizzy since she was three years old. She was the youngest kid we ever gave a library card to, as a matter of fact. The last time we saw her she was a happy, intelligent kid, in spite of a home life that would make most people crazy. She's been through hell, and the last thing she needs is to be in this hell-hole. She's not mentally ill and never has been. She's coming with us today, or by God you're going to wish she had.'

'I can't go against the County's wishes on this. These decisions are made at County, and Fresno County says that Elizabeth Sinclair, Minor and Ward of the Court, is to be kept in here until further notice.' He again pushed Miss Harper's finger away from his chest.

'The order says she is to be let into protective care. I had my attorney make some calls and we've got a family court judge who's waiting by the phone if you need any information. If we make sure she attends school and receives appropriate medical care we will meet the criteria for protective custody.'

'That's the problem, right there; she can't attend school. She refuses to speak, maybe she can't speak, but she certainly can't attend school.'

'My mother lives with us. She taught school from the time she was twenty-one until she retired last year. She has agreed to instruct Lizzy at home until she's fit to return to the classroom.'

'Fine. I'm going to release her to you, but promise me you'll return her if you can't take it. This is going to be an impossible task for the three of you. She's suffering from a serious personality disorder and there's no way of predicting what she might do.'

'That may be true, but I know Lizzy's never going to get better here.' Miss Harper pulled an old-fashioned fountain pen from her pocket. 'Sign this release and we're gone.'

'Remember what I said: I want her back here at the first sign of trouble. She needs professional guidance and care.' He signed, a small black scrawl.

'She needs to be treated like a human being, and you've seen the last of her.'

The car pulled out of the driveway with a still angry Miss Harper behind the wheel. She glanced in the rear-view mirror at

Miss Johnson and Lizzy in the back seat. Lizzy stared out of the side window as she clung to Miss Johnson's hand. Miss Harper reached over the back of the seat and patted Miss Johnson on the knee. 'How are you two girls doing back there?'

'Rose, you were a force of nature. I'm just sorry you didn't hit that awful man.' Miss Johnson paused, pushing fine, pale hair behind her ear before she continued. 'Imagine keeping Lizzy in a place like that when we had told them as soon as we heard what happened that she was meant to live with us.'

'We'll make it right for her, Beryl. She'll be all right now.' She tried to catch the girl's reflection in the mirror. 'How are you doing back there, Liz? Good to be out of there?'

Lizzy nodded briefly and closed her eyes. She tried to find Ellie, but she wasn't there. Tears of sorrow and relief escaped down her face.

Cotherstone, West Sussex, April 25th

Dearest Mary,

Sorry I missed your phone call last night. I was awfully tired and decided to make it an early evening. I should have the test results in three days and I promise to call you immediately. I'm going to fax this so you receive it before we talk. It is so anticlimactic when I've talked to you the day before a letter arrives. I suppose I don't need to write at all, but I'm afraid if I don't write letters once a week I'll break my best habit.

Patch apparently was a wonderful office dog. Daddy says the staff would like him back any time. Of course, they would have to say that, wouldn't they? I imagine the staff will be finding his red rubber balls under the desks for weeks to come. By all reports, lunch was a bit of a problem. As you know, he feels a meal isn't a meal until it's shared. Word has it he developed a taste for anything with cress and pickle. Little bugger would sit there with his paw on whoever's knee until they handed over his 'due'.

The boys survived Gran's cooking and she was happier than anyone to see me back. Says she'd forgotten what a lot of work a family could be. I was a bit surprised, since cooking for our two didn't seem like much compared to the lot she took care of for years. I suppose those thirty or forty intervening years have something to do with that. Hospital wasn't too bad and I'm so glad I was able to go private. NHS and private may have the same level of medical care, but the rooms and food are so much nicer at the private hospital. I was even able to get quite a bit of work done, thanks to my rather posh room and, of course, my wonderful new laptop.

Amazing little tool, the laptop. I know you don't find it mind-boggling, but I'm of the generation which was gobsmacked by the little silver ball on the electric typewriters. And let's not even discuss self-correcting ribbon. Even today I still think that's magic.

In addition to work, I got caught up on all those little grooming things you nag me about. Not only did I give myself a manicure, but I plucked my eyebrows, and even shaved my legs, twice! I look a vision.

Being in hospital always reminds me of Aunt Beryl. She loved to visit people in hospital. She didn't need more than a nodding acquaintance to be at someone's bedside. I think she would have gone into nursing had she not fallen in love with Aunt Rose. Since Aunt Rose was going to be a librarian, Aunt Beryl was more than happy to memorize the Dewey Decimal System and start stamping books.

She wasn't really submissive, but she was fairly typical of an American wife in the early sixties. She was a wonderful cook and very proud of her home. She liked Rose to be in charge and generally deferred to her. They were quite happy together. I don't remember any rows, just an occasional disagreement. In many respects they had one of the best marriages I've ever seen. I don't know if theirs was typical of a lesbian marriage or not. Perhaps being the same sex makes it easier to live together.

I've often wondered what they would have thought of all the gay pride things going on now. I'm not completely sure they would have thought of themselves as gay. There were certainly no mutterings about them in our little town. Of course in those innocent times, two women could live together their whole adult lives without men and nobody would raise an eyebrow. Their fostering of me was evidence of that. Only people of high moral character were allowed to be foster parents. Of course, their moral character was above reproach, but had they been 'out' to the town, there would have been a great hue and cry.

They were angels. I don't think it's an exaggeration to say that they, and Mrs Harper, saved my life. Events had almost destroyed me, but they took me in and loved me without reservation. They gave me stability and a grounding that allowed me to heal and grow. Extraordinary women in every respect. I feel myself getting weepy just thinking of them and what they did for me.

I'd better close now. I need to top off the groceries and see to the laundry, which is threatening to take over the house. I think I need a wife!

Stay well and happy.

Love and God bless

Mummy

PS Better to find out now about Oliver. There's lots more talent out there, and here, for that matter. XXOO

PS II I read a magazine last week with an article about hair colour. I'm thinking about adding some pale gold highlights. What do you think? The crowning glory has been looking a little drab the last few years. Mentally chew on this and we'll hash it over when I call you. I so miss having your advice on this sort of thing. I'm looking forward to having lots of girlie time again.

CHAPTER FIFTEEN

'Liz? What are you doing?' He stood in the doorway, peering into the darkened bedroom.

'Nothing. I was just sitting here thinking.'

'I want you to put tomorrow's meeting with the doctor out of your mind. I'm going to be there with you and you're going to be fine.' He turned on a small lamp by the bed and she could see his reassuring smile. 'I know you're going to be fine.'

'I saw the doctor today.'

'I don't understand.'

'I told you it was tomorrow, but the appointment was today. I knew what the results were going to be and I needed to hear them on my own.'

'Lizzy?'

'There isn't a lot of good to be said. It's in my bones and my pancreas. He's recommending a course of chemo, but it was fairly clear that he doesn't expect too much success.'

She watched as his face lengthened and aged. 'One man's opinion. We'll find another doctor. Maybe one in the States or Canada. I'm not going to let this happen to you.' He sat heavily on the bed and took her hand.

She squeezed his hand and tried to smile, but her lip began to tremble. 'You saved me once, darling. Perhaps there's some sort of cosmic rule about one to a customer.'

'You were the one who saved me. You gave me your youth, your beauty, the children.' He pulled her to his chest and cradled her like a small child. 'You're my life, Lizzy.'

'I know,' she whispered against his shirt, which was already wet with her tears.

'Please don't leave me.'

'I'll stay as long as I can. I promise.' She thought of the pills in the jewellery box and knew she'd have to throw them away.

Clifford, California, October 1962

The first thing she recognized was the nightclub with the World War Two bomber sticking out of the roof. It was one of the more distinctive landmarks along Highway 99. She'd been disappointed five years before to be told that the plane had been built into the roof and hadn't been the result of a crash. In a landscape of orchards, vineyards, truckstops, and juice bars shaped into fifteen-foot-high stucco oranges, it had provided the most food for thought.

Every time her mother drove past the nightclub, Lizzy would imagine the uniformed airmen, and their girls in bias-cut dresses. They would be sipping martinis and looking at each other with smouldering glances. The women would have their hair piled and twisted into gleaming rolls, with maybe a flower tucked into the side.

They would dance and sway to the music of the band, and clap for the girl singer who everybody knew had a fiancé who had been shot down over the English Channel. She was the bravest thing and her singing just seemed the sweeter because of her bravery and longing.

Sometimes in Lizzy's story the girl was the only one left untouched when the plane lost its way in the thick fog and crashed into the roof of the nightclub. She would sing to the others to keep up their spirits while they waited for the ambulances. Lives were saved that night because she gave them hope and the will to live. The girl singer looked quite a bit like Lizzy.

As the car approached the edge of town, she knew the fastest route to the women's bungalow would take them right by the house she'd shared with Ellie and Laura. She wasn't surprised when Miss Harper went about two miles out of her way so that they didn't even come close to the old house. She sat up and squinted, hoping to get a glimpse of the ramshackle building. She couldn't see it, but she could see the clump of tall poplars and pines that surrounded Mrs Kirby's clean white farmhouse. She looked to the right and stared at the air above where she knew the house would be.

Miss Harper's mother was sitting on the front porch when the car pulled up. The late October sunshine made it almost eighty degrees, but the old woman wore a woollen cardigan buttoned over her ample chest. She got out of the chair and started waving and smiling, but stopped when Lizzy finally got out of the car.

'What did they do to you? What have they done to this child?' she called to the trio, and shook her head in disbelief. She put her hands on her wide hips and looked around the yard as though the culprit would climb from behind a hedge and submit to her discipline.

'Nothing some decent food and a good home can't take care of; isn't that right, Lizzy?' Miss Johnson placed her thin arm across Lizzy's back and gave her a little hug. 'We're going to have a good bath and a little rest before dinner. That sounds like just the thing, doesn't it, Lizzy?'

'Well, I wish to hell we could have taken every last one of those kids. Disgusting. Our tax dollars are paying for that damn place. Jesus H. Christ, it was straight out of Dickens.' Miss Harper slammed the car door for emphasis and turned to her mother. 'Made me nuts to be in there for half an hour, and I went in perfectly normal. The kid has already been to hell and back and I don't . . .'

'Rose, dear, watch your language, for pity's sake. It's over now and Lizzy will be fine. The only thing that matters now is Lizzy getting strong and happy again.' Miss Johnson pushed a strand of hair off Lizzy's face. 'I want to show you your room, sweetheart. We've been working on it ever since we knew you'd be coming. We weren't sure about your taste, so I hope you approve.' She took the girl's hand and led her up the grey-painted steps.

The room still smelled of paint. The walls were washed with pale pink and the single bed was covered with a pastel quilt that appeared to be faded with great age. A stack of paper and a box of pens and pencils were carefully laid on a maple desk. Lizzy ran her hand over the books in the bookshelf, recognizing many of the titles. She tried to smile at the women, but the lower part of her face wouldn't move. She shrugged her shoulders and nodded.

'Do you like it, dear? We just didn't know, but we've really tried to make it a room you'd like.' Miss Johnson clasped her hands together and nodded towards the bed. 'I wanted to tell you about the quilt. My great-grandmother made it. She was a pioneer who came to California in a covered wagon all the way from Missouri. I had it on my bed when I was about your age. I know it's old, but I thought it would be nice for you to have something really special and unusual. If you don't like it I can always get you something else.'

'Of course she likes it, Beryl. Don't be silly.' Miss Harper still sounded annoyed, but she was smiling. 'The desk and some of the books were saved from when I was a girl. We wanted you to have some of the things we've cared about.'

Once again Lizzy tried to smile, but the tears fell before a smile could form. She put her fist to her mouth to stifle a sob of relief and surrender. Her knees were weak and she could feel slight tremors running through her arms.

Miss Johnson put her arm around Lizzy's shoulder to steady her. 'The first thing we need to do is get you cleaned up. I'll help you, and when we've done that you can have a little rest in your new room. How does that sound?'

'I'll leave you girls to it.' Miss Harper hurried out of the room.

'I've never had children, but of course you know that, I suppose. When I was a girl I always thought I would have lots and lots of children. Just never met the right man, I guess you could say.' She poured more warm water over Lizzy's head.

'When we heard what happened to you, I told Rose this was our chance to have a child. And what a wonderful child. I said, imagine Lizzy Sinclair as a daughter. If I had a daughter I know she'd be just like you. She'd be smart and funny, and she'd love books and stories as much as I do. Now, let's get you out before you turn into a pink prune.' She placed a hand under Lizzy's elbow and gave a small grunt as she helped her out of the water.

She wrapped a thick white towel around the girl's hair and used another to dry her thin body. 'I don't want you to worry about not talking, sweetheart. Rose says sometimes she wishes I wouldn't talk quite so much, but of course she's just teasing, I think. Anyway, when you start talking I would love it if you would call me Aunt Beryl. You can call Miss Harper Aunt Rose, and I guess you can call Mrs Harper Mrs Harper. Would you like to do that, Lizzy?' She nodded at the girl as though Lizzy might have forgotten what a nod entailed.

Lizzy closed her eyes and nodded.

She could hear them in the other room. Aunt Beryl's high trill bounced around the room like a small bird. Lizzy imagined it was like a well-loved canary, allowed the run of the house. Bright and clear, it seemed to fly above the other voices. Aunt Rose's voice was a low rumble that played along the floor, while Mrs Harper's voice was sharp and precise from decades in the classroom. She heard her name batted back and forth; the shuttlecock of their thoughts.

Atop her bed, a grey Persian cat began to purr and knead at the covers. Lizzy petted her, grateful that the doctor's dog had not found its way to her. A dog was something she would have had if they'd made it to Nevada. They would have had a house with a dog.

They would have had pillow fights and eaten candy every day. Ellie would have become a dancer in a nightclub until she was discovered, to be a movie star. They would probably have kept a house in Hollywood where they would stay when Ellie was making movies. Lizzy would have written a book that became really famous and she would have taken singing lessons so she could be a famous singer as well as a famous writer.

President and Mrs Kennedy would have offered to adopt her, but she would have turned them down because she and Ellie were doing great all on their own.

Lizzy wasn't surprised that Ellie wasn't by her bed. She hadn't been in the car either. She guessed that Ellie hadn't been interested in coming back to Clifford. The girl pulled her knees to her chest and fell asleep.

Cotherstone, West Sussex, May 2nd

My darling Mary,

Obviously the test results aren't what any of us hoped for. I will undergo the chemotherapy because even a slim chance is a chance. In the meantime I'm going to treat each day as a gift. By the way, in case you think I'm sounding terribly controlled, I've been up most of the night crying and railing against fate. This morning the anger is gone and I'm busy making plans.

First off: go ahead and come home if you want. I know I insisted you stay, but in the clear light of day I think you should do what feels right for you. I feel I have a great deal of time left, but if you want to be here, then this is where you should be.

Secondly, I'm hiring a housekeeper. I don't want to worry about a messy house and thrown-together meals. I also don't want anyone else in the family, especially Gran, to worry about them either.

Thirdly, I'm rewriting my will. I've already spoken to Daddy and he thinks it's quite sensible. I'm going to make you and Chaz my sole heirs. Presently your father and I have the standard husband-and-wife sort of will and I think some changes make sense.

I came into our marriage with very little money and two suitcases of clothes, and I have often felt it wasn't the best way to start a relationship. I wish I'd been a little more careful of my 'single funds', but I'd never had any experience with money. Of course, your father has always been more than generous, but one shouldn't have to depend on generosity. Just as my writing was at least promising to earn me some money, that part of my life was put on hold for motherhood.

I've figured up what I've earned since our marriage and Daddy has agreed that this amount will be passed on to you and Chaz equally. I also received small inheritances when Rose and Beryl died. This too will go to the two of you. I want you to start your lives with some funds of your own. Of course the pair of you will also receive whatever royalties come through in the future.

As you know, I also have my wedding ring and some other good pieces that your father has given me through the years. In addition, I have a wonderful cameo that belonged to Beryl and a string of pearls that belonged to Mrs Harper. (Good old Rose was entirely too 'butch' for such things, but she did leave me some first editions of Twain and Jack London which I'm bequeathing to your father.) Everything else in my jewellery box came from Daddy's side of the family. I'm going to have each piece valued and then I want you to choose the things you like best and whatever else will bring the total to approximately half. I'd like you to keep the rest of it for Chaz's daughters or granddaughters. Unlike Gran, I don't believe in giving family pieces to wives, at least not in this day of frequent divorce.

Fourthly, I have every intention of finishing this book, and hopefully more. Hemingway said something about writing being easy; you simply sit down at a typewriter and open a vein. This recent episode should make me a better writer. Two pluses: better writing and I'll finally lose some weight. I know that last bit was in terrible taste.

Fifth, I'm going to squeeze every drop of goodness that I can out of this and I expect all of you to do the same. I want us to be honest with each other. I want us to say what we feel. I don't want to waste months or minutes in denial. This thing could become the dead elephant in the room that everyone is afraid to mention.

*I simply won't have it. If I am truly dying I want to die
knowing that everything was said that needed to be said. I want
all of you to know how rich and full you have made my life. If I
am going to die I'm going to do it properly and in order.*

*If it comes to that, I'm going to need your full cooperation,
Mary. Men are lousy at this kind of thing. The three of us, I'm
including Gran, will negotiate these rocky shoals together.*

I love you and I always will.

Love and God bless

Mummy

CHAPTER SIXTEEN

Liz pulled the chairs out to the middle of the lawn and
inspected them carefully. For once, the mice seemed to have
stayed out of the garden shed, or at least they hadn't shredded
the canvas for their nests. The wooden frames looked pale and
bleached, but she'd bought a can of teak oil last week, knowing
all the garden furniture would need a quick brush-up.

As the day promised to be a fine one, she decided to spend
the morning getting the garden ready for her daughter's return.
Spruced-up furniture on the lawn, bird feeders full, baskets
planted, all as it should be for Mary's homecoming.

The bleached wood gave off a golden glow as soon as the oil
touched it. She worked quickly, delighted with the transforma-
tion and enjoying the feel of sun on her head and arms. She
looked up when she saw the shadow blocking the sunlight.

'Come to help?' She smiled at India, who stood over her with
an enormous golf umbrella.

'I am helping. I'm saving you from a terrible sunburn. What are you doing out here without even a hat?' She handed Liz a broad-brimmed straw hat which had seen many years of service.

'Mad dogs and Englishwomen?' She dutifully put the hat on her head to save an argument. It could always be removed when India tired of the garden and returned to her chair and her television.

'You're still an American, and a blonde to boot. You know as well as I do what the sun can do to skin like yours.'

'I know, but it feels wonderful and I want things to look just right for Mary. I've only got five more days as it is.'

'That's fine, but the gardener could do most of this, and you shouldn't be working out here like a coolie.'

'I'm almost done with the furniture and then I want to get the baskets planted. I bought the plants this morning. Go take a look at them, why don't you?' She indicated the potting bench with a nod of her head, and was relieved to see India head in that direction. She watched the old woman carefully make her way to the bottom of the garden and knew it was probably the last May either of them would see. She splashed the last of the oil on with renewed vigour as she wondered if it was warm enough to clean the fishpond as well.

Clifford, California, January 1963

'You're afraid you'll have to go back to school, aren't you?' They sat at the dining room table, going over the day's lessons. The old woman put her finger on the girl's jaw, forcing the gaze in her direction. 'You don't have to worry about me, Lizzy. I know how to keep secrets.'

Lizzy shook her head and started to work on an algebra problem. She glanced at the watch on her wrist and was glad to see the appointed time for the lesson was almost over. Mrs Harper insisted on keeping regular times for her lessons. Lizzy enjoyed the work, but didn't like the woman's questions, not today at least.

'Lizzy, look at me.' She waited until the girl looked up. 'I heard you singing yesterday. You were behind the garage and you were singing. If you can sing you can talk.'

Lizzy wrote quickly on the pad she always kept at hand: 'Somebody else.' Ever since Ellie had disappeared from the back of her brain, Lizzy had trouble conjuring up her image. Once Ellie had decided to leave, she'd even taken her memory with her. Lizzy found that singing about the shrimp boats coming into harbour reminded her of Ellie. When she sang she could see Ellie standing by the river with her arms crossed over her lettergirl's chest. The sun was still shining hot on Ellie's head as long as the song lasted.

'It wasn't somebody else, it was you. Do you think I don't know a few things about children after teaching more than two-thirds of my life? I know you don't want to go back to school, and you don't have to. You can stay right here and work with me.'

Lizzy's eyes narrowed to slits as she looked at the woman before she turned away.

'It's true, Liz. I don't want you to go to school if you don't want to, and neither do Rose or Beryl. In just the three months you've been working with me you've grown too far beyond your class to get anything out of it anyway. If we sent you back today, I'm not sure the school would know what to do with you.'

'Truth?' She wrote the word quickly, underlining the question mark.

'Truth, Lizzy. You have one of the best young minds I've ever taught. The school system wouldn't know what to do with you if we sent you back, but I do.' She patted Lizzy on the hand. The old woman's hand seemed edged in strong greens and glowing yellows. Her papery old skin felt hot. 'I wouldn't know what to do with myself if you went back to school. You've made my retirement much more interesting than I thought it was going to be. I've started thinking of you as a gift for my old age. There's no chance of this old brain getting rusty when I have to keep it sharp to teach you everything you need to know.'

Lizzy smiled at the woman, but stood quickly and walked into her room, closing the door behind the woman's feverish expectations and vivid enthusiasms. She had watched for weeks how the colours around Mrs Harper would grow richer and brighter as they pored over her work together. The little woman appeared to grow larger with each success, seeming to gorge on the results of their efforts.

Lizzy rested her elbows on the maple bureau and leaned her face into the mirror until her nose was two inches from the glass. She remembered the girls at school talking about it. If you stared into your own eyes long enough you would see your true self. She stared, trying not to blink at her own image. She studied her face until she'd memorized the desert landscapes of her irises.

'Must have wasted all my magic on being invisible,' she whispered, as softly as she could, enjoying the feel of the words hissing against the back of her teeth. She was relieved that her true self hadn't appeared in the mirror. She didn't think she was quite ready to see who she really was. Julie Wingdorf had seen her true self and she said it had been really scary.

Julie Wingdorf also said she had a chant, which when said to the Devil could make someone as stiff as a board, so Lizzy wasn't surprised the mirror trick hadn't worked. If the mirror trick had worked then she might have to start believing in the Devil. She didn't want to believe in the Devil because he seemed every bit as pointless as God. Just another spoiled man who wanted everything to go his own selfish way. A foul-tempered child with an ant farm.

She waited. Her silence with herself broken, she knew she'd lost whatever that coin had bought her. A matter of time, but a time she could choose and savour.

Mrs Harper didn't mention it again. The old woman seemed to know there was a process to be observed which was beyond her control. She once hummed a song about shrimp boats in front of the girl, but didn't seem surprised when Lizzy looked at her with disinterested eyes.

Lizzy started to speak to Mrs Harper several times, words lining up inside her throat. The words would play along her tonsils until she swallowed them back and grabbed for her notepad, relieved that they remained unspoken.

Weeks later, she found Mrs Harper alone in the kitchen. The room smelled of last night's stew and the morning's toast. Lizzy tapped her on the shoulder to take her attention away from cleaning the sink.

'Truth?' Lizzy spoke, the word ringing in her ears. 'I won't have to go back to school?' She covered her mouth to prevent more words from spilling out and fouling the air with thoughts and feelings, long hidden from others.

'Oh, my dear.' She leaned over and kissed Lizzy's cheek.

'I'll only talk if you let me stay. I never want to leave here. Promise me I won't have to leave. Not ever.' She lowered her voice, frightened by the anxious whining she knew to be her own.

'You don't have to leave until you want to go. I promise: you don't have to leave until you are ready.'

'Good.' Lizzy nodded her head and looked away. 'I'll never want to leave.'

'Of course you feel that way now. Someday this house will seem awfully small and you'll want a lot more than we can give you.'

Lizzy thought of her room and the lessons at the dining room table. She thought of how Aunt Rose was rude to social workers and how Aunt Beryl would braid her hair with ribbons. 'I've got everything I want here.'

'We're fine for now, Lizzy, but when you're a grown woman

you'll want to have your own family. You'll find a nice man and have children of your own.'

'No. No, I don't think so. I had a family and I lost it. I wouldn't want to have something like that again because I don't want to lose it again.' She shivered and thought she might see Ellie again. The Ellie with the blue lips who was lying naked on the dirt road. She rocked herself slightly to get the picture out of her head before it made the words get stopped in her throat again.

'The only way to be sure that you don't lose something is never to have anything to start with.'

'Then it's better to have nothing. That way you don't have to worry. I've worried enough.'

'It's too late, Lizzy. You already have something: you have us and we have you.'

'It's not the same. You're not my real family. The County pays you to take care of me. It's not the same as blood.'

'Lizzy, do you think we take care of you because of the money?' She put her arms around the girl and held her until the trembling in the young body stopped. 'You're the same as blood to us. You're a part of our family now. A very important part. Like it or not you've got a family.'

'Truth?'

'Very much so.'

It was hard to be outside. The sky went on endlessly, providing no comfort, no canopy of protection. Even the porches were suspect, their tiny roofs hinting at security that wasn't there.

She would scurry into Mrs Harper's Chevrolet for trips to the library. Agreeing to go only during the times she could be assured the other children were at school, she was allowed entry to all the stacks, all the secrets of the adult world. She was surprised at how disappointing the restricted books were. Clearly if there were secrets to the universe, they weren't stored at the Clifford Public Library.

As stores were outside her realm of safety, Aunt Beryl carefully acquired her clothes from the big stores in Fresno. Armed with the girl's measurements, she prowled the 'Young Miss' sections while Rose sat in the front seat of the car, smoking cigarettes and reading Ayn Rand, Liz curled into the back seat writing responses to the questions Mrs Harper assigned each day.

Beryl would hurry to the car with each pastel shirtwaist dress, each dyed-to-match skirt and sweater set she thought might be 'perfect' for Lizzy. Rose would look up and grunt, and Lizzy either nodded or shook her head. Beryl would hold the garment up towards the sun to check the colour, offerings to some god of fashion, before she would return to the store to buy or reject it.

Months were spent rushing through lessons, gorging on information served up by Mrs Harper and an occasional science teacher from the high school. Imagining her mind to be a cup, Lizzy filled it as quickly as she could, anxious for the memories of Ellie and her mother to slop over the top, to drop down and disappear.

'Take a look at this, girls.' Winking at Lizzy, Mrs Harper tossed a small stack of papers between the women.

'What's all this?' Rose blew her cigarette smoke away from the table.

'Is this Lizzy's work?' Beryl, a non-smoker, made a show of shoving smoke out of her face.

'That's right. She's just completed her first university course.'

'We wanted to keep it a secret.' Lizzy leaned forward, unable to conceal her excitement. 'I got a ninety-two. That's the same as an A minus.'

'What school? How did you manage this, Mother?' Rose looked to the older woman.

'Carlisle. They offer almost half their curriculum as

correspondence courses. It's fully accredited, by the way. And don't worry about the cost. When I wrote to them about our girl they were able to arrange scholarship funds.'

'This is wonderful, Lizzy. I'm so proud of you.' Rose thumbed quickly through the papers. 'Why English history?'

'Mrs Harper is always talking about being born in England and visiting her cousin there, and of course, I was named after a queen of England.' Laura began to surface, but Lizzy raced on, leaving her behind. 'Also it sounded like it would be pretty easy. I thought it would be nice to start with something easy.'

'Lizzy? Is real knowledge easy?' The older woman looked at the girl over the top of her glasses.

'Facts are easy, but real knowledge comes with real effort.' She repeated the words in a singsong voice as she moved her head back and forth like a mechanical doll.

'You can always tell who grew up in Clifford. They know that real knowledge comes with real effort,' Rose pretended to whisper to Beryl, who giggled. Her mother had drilled the words into generations of her students, most of whom went on to become farm workers and fruit packers.

'Mock if you must; it is true.' Mrs Harper pushed her glasses up the bridge of her nose.

'What happens after the correspondence courses? She's barely thirteen.' Beryl put the papers back on the table and gave Lizzy a hug.

'Age has nothing to do with it, Beryl. When she finishes what she can do at home I'm sure we can find a place for her at the state university. She can take the bus and still live with us.'

'But the university is huge. Everyone would be at least four or five years older than Lizzy. What kind of life is that for a child?' Beryl looked to Rose for confirmation.

'Mrs Harper has already talked to me about all of this. I've thought about it and I've decided I stopped being a kid when Ellie died. I really want to do this.'

'Oh, Lizzy, you can't just stop being a child. There are going to be parties and dances you'll want to go to. You'll want to be with young people your own age; boys as well as girls.'

Lizzy shook her head. 'It's too late for that, Aunt Beryl.'

'Don't be silly, darling. Why you're only thirteen.'

'Not any more, Aunt Beryl. Too much has happened for me to be thirteen. I've seen what happens to fourteen and I know I don't want that.' There she was again, only this time white and still, with bits of adhesive around her mouth. 'I've been watching other kids, and as far as I can see, being a teenager is stupid, not to mention dangerous. I'm just going to skip all that and do things my own way.'

'Beryl's right, kiddo. You can't just skip over five years of your life. There are things you need to do, things you need to experience at this age. Don't be in such a rush. The advanced courses are great, but don't forget how old you really are.'

'I haven't forgotten and I'm not in a rush. I just don't think I'll feel really safe until I'm a grown up.'

'Speaking of safety, I'm concerned about you being on the campus of such a large school. You really haven't been outside the house and library since you came to live with us.' Beryl leaned towards the girl. 'How do you think you'll manage?'

'I'll manage fine, I know I will. It's at least a year away and there's nothing there I need to be afraid of.'

'But how can you be sure?' Beryl persisted.

Lizzy sighed, hating to state the obvious. 'Nobody will notice me. I'll be so quiet I'll just blend in and nobody will notice me. People will think I'm just another kid.' She was relieved to know she didn't need to explain to them that she was so much more.

Cotherstone, West Sussex, May 10th

Dear Oliver,

I miss you. I still think you're a bit of a turd, but I do miss you. I told my family I'm no longer interested in you, so you'd better stay out of dear old Sussex until I get you well and truly out of my system. How long do you have left on your visa?

Silly Sussex. You're not missing a thing; except me, of course. I had to run an errand yesterday and ended up ploughing through a sea of Zimmer frames in front of the post office. Didn't mind. After all, they did fight the war for me, or so they all say.

Well, I've survived the first two days of family fun. It really hasn't been so bad, but Mother went into hospital this morning for chemo. Everyone is trying to be terribly up and brave about it, but it all feels wrong.

Mum and Dad picked me up at Heathrow and if I hadn't been told, I think I would have known as soon as I saw her. She has a funny, almost wild look in her eyes. It is not my imagination, so don't even suggest it.

I suppose in reaction to the illness, she's gone into some kind of hyper-drive. The house looks wonderful, but even so she's ordered all kinds of new stuff which has yet to be delivered. Two days before I came home she planted about a dozen hanging baskets in addition to putting a coat of oil on all the wooden garden furniture. As if that isn't enough, she seems to have memorized the last three Delia Smith collections. There is a new deep-freeze in the kitchen which is stuffed with lots of gorgeous goodies cooked by her own beringed hands.

Bless her cotton socks, I suppose she thinks the Grim Reaper can't catch her if she doesn't stand still.

Oh God, that last sounded despicable and I didn't intend it to, not at all. You of all people know how I feel about my mother and how I reacted when I found out she was seriously ill. I guess the thing that bothers me is all this damned activity. I want to sit down and have a good cry with her, but we're all so busy putting on our best faces.

I'd better close. I told her I would spend the afternoon with her watching as the poison is dripped into her veins. Maybe we can have a good chat, since she won't be able to fly into the garden or whip up a lemon soufflé.

Stay well. If for no other reason than I have enough to think about.

Love

Mary

PS Some woman who claims to be your mother called and invited me out to lunch. I think I agreed to go, although I'm certainly not at the 'meet the parent' stage. We are tentatively scheduled for this Friday, which gives me time to back out if I decide you're not worth the trouble.

PS II The dog insists on sleeping with me, but at least he doesn't hog the duvet like some I could mention.

PS III Had a dream about you last night. Wicked boy!

Chapter Seventeen

St Luke's Hospital, West Sussex, May 13

'These are really wonderful, darling.' Liz sat cross-legged on her bed and sniffed appreciatively at the arrangement of blooms.

'I tried to cut something from the garden, but as you know, things seem to be a little late this year.'

'Never mind, these are gorgeous. Sit down and tell me how everything is going at home.' It was day three of the chemo and she was feeling worse than she was willing to admit.

'First tell me how you feel.'

'Like a pincushion, but just fine apart from that.' She'd found that she kept nodding off, but told herself it was just the result of inactivity. She'd resigned herself to death, not to malaise.

'You look good. Still have all your curls.' Mary fluffed the hair around her mother's face, which was as straight as it had always been.

'Hopefully I won't lose any of it this time. I suppose I can always wear a wig, but even the conservative ones make me feel like Dolly Parton or Lily Savage.'

'I don't think you have quite the same fashion sense as those two.'

'Enough about hair. Tell me how things are going at home.'

'Chaz seems a little withdrawn, but maybe that's just his age. It's so odd because he looks like such a man, but he's still this goofy little kid most of the time.'

'I think, rather I know, boys don't grow up as quickly as girls. In many ways Chaz is still my little boy, even though he's coming up to six feet. I suppose I've encouraged that.'

'I don't recall being encouraged to exhibit infantile behaviour.' Mary looked at her mother with mock severity.

'You weren't. Chaz was my last baby so I wanted to keep him that way as long as I could. I suppose I couldn't wait for you to grow up because I was so anxious to see how you'd turn out. Of course you both have grown at just the right rate, in spite of my meddling.'

'Speaking of meddling, Gran and the housekeeper are getting on like a house on fire. They both love to nag and pry and are having a field day. Oliver called yesterday and I swear one of them was on the extension for at least part of the call.'

'You're kidding?' She laughed, thinking of India and Connie scrambling for the extension.

'God's truth.'

'Which one do you suppose it was?'

'Either or both. They're both terrible gossips and are having such fun together.'

'What do you think of Connie, except for her curiosity, that is?' She'd hired her because she seemed quiet, clean and not terribly lovable. She didn't want the affection due her to go elsewhere.

'She seems efficient, clean, cheerful, all that good stuff.'

'And she seems to get along well with everyone?'

'I think we're all on our best behaviour still. After all, you've only been gone three days. I, for one, am looking forward to things getting back to normal.'

Liz glanced around the hospital room before smiling at her daughter. 'Yes, normal would be nice, wouldn't it?'

'Normal would be wonderful. Normal will be wonderful.' She glanced out of the window, away from her mother.

'It looks like a beautiful day. I'm being allowed out to the sun deck later and I can hardly wait.' Ever since admission to hospital Lizzy had been feeling she could get well if she could just feel the sun on her head.

'Enjoy it while you can. Said on the news this morning that it would start raining again tonight.'

'You must be missing the lovely California weather by now.'

'Oliver always said we were living in San Francisco, not California. San Francisco has worse weather than Sussex most of the time.'

'So you're still in contact with him?'

'Who?'

'Very funny. Oliver, of course.'

'I'm conflicted, as they say.'

'Which means you're mad about him even though he's making you crazy?'

'Something like that.' She turned back to her mother and grinned. 'Is this what happens when you have too much time on your hands? You start speculating on romance?'

'I'm not speculating on romance, I'm speculating on my daughter.'

'As you've said before, my love life is never simple. I envy you and Daddy. Find the right person, settle down and get married. Easy peasy.'

'We were just lucky, I suppose.'

'Was he the only man you ever dated?'

'More or less.' She rubbed the top of her hand where the needle was taped. 'Why don't we play some backgammon or something?'

Valley State University, California, January 1966

Her favourite place was the student union. Just four years old, it rose, a block of concrete and glass, above the older Spanish-style buildings. It housed a cafeteria and dozens of upholstered chairs and sofas, spread randomly across the second floor. She sat in the cavernous room watching the students mill in and out. Several she studied with special interest, creating lives for them she thought would suit their appearance and movement.

A week before her first day on the campus she'd finally consented to go shopping with Aunt Beryl. To the woman's distress, she insisted on buying nothing but black and grey clothes, explaining that they would make her seem older, allow her to blend in. She begged for, and received, tortoiseshell glasses fitted with clear lenses. She felt safe behind the round frames and liked the way the light glinted against the glass, obscuring her eyes when she looked in the mirror under bright lights. Removing the ribbons and barrettes, she worked her hair into a single plait which ended halfway down her back.

Aunt Rose told her she looked like a beatnik, and Lizzy said that was the whole idea. Better to be disguised as a beatnik than be revealed as a child.

'Can I sit here?' He nodded towards the empty side of the sofa.

'Go ahead.' She glanced up and quickly pulled her book closer to her face.

She'd noticed him before. It was hard not to; he stood apart in his sharply creased chinos and his pressed madras shirts. His light brown hair was trimmed with surgical precision and his face was tight and shiny, as though he had scrubbed it until it shrank. Ever since the protests had started they had been easier to spot. The hated ROTCees.

Formed years before as an alternative to the military academies, the Reserved Officers Training Corp had allowed young men to finance their educations and graduate with an officer's commission. Until Vietnam the ROTCees had been no more distinctive than the fraternity boys or the football players. Within a few months their trim looks began to put them apart from the denim and tie-dye which quickly became the campus uniform.

Even the beautiful sorority girls, with their perfect teeth and shining hair, began to wear sandals and bare their midriffs. Just the year before they had practised smoking cigarettes in a ladylike fashion, but now they showed each other how to roll marijuana into slim sticks. They went to the student health centre and got their six-month supply of birth control pills without even pretending that the tablets were needed to regulate their monthly flowings. They stopped wearing girdles and discarded their bras, provided their breasts were the right shape.

Vigils were held every day by the fountain. Usually silent, but sometimes with speeches, songs and abuse hurled at the ROTCees as they marched by in ever-decreasing numbers. Some draft cards were burned, and sweet-faced women of forty drove in from town to stand next to the students. Another mother for peace.

'You must be a freshman.' He leaned towards her.

'Junior.' She shifted slightly to create more space between them.

'Could have fooled me. I thought you were about eighteen.'

'I'm sixteen. Yes, that's very young. Yes, it's a long story.' She'd developed a pat response months before and rarely deviated in its recital. 'No, I'm not a genius, and yes, I have work to do.' She added the last when she noticed him grinning at her. To her dismay, she found herself blushing. She turned away and held her book inches from her face.

'You must have got up on the wrong side of the bed this morning.'

'Why don't you just leave me alone?' She glanced up and tried to see his colours without staring, but he grinned at her scrutiny.

'I suppose you don't talk to guys in the ROTC? Girls only say yes to the boys who say no and all that?'

'I don't say yes to anyone, although that's none of your business. I'm a goddamn nun, if you must know.' Liz began to gather her books into a satchel. She'd always been able to get rid of boys through a combination of bad manners and the truth about her age.

'I'm sorry. That was a rude thing to say and I didn't mean . . .'

'What did you mean? If a girl doesn't want to talk to you it must be because she's sleeping with every asshole who has a peace symbol painted on his forehead?' She almost looked around to see if anyone had heard her. 'I don't care if you are ROTC or SDS. The only men I'm interested in all died at least a hundred years ago.' Not true, but she found the boys on campus to be terrifying. She ignored them, and so far, in the main, they had ignored her. Sometimes she felt she had truly regained the ability to make herself invisible.

'Listen, I'm sorry, I truly am. It's hard to find a friendly face on this campus any more.'

'I'm not surprised if this has been an example of your typical behaviour.' She stood up. 'I really don't know where you get off talking to me that way.' She looked at him again and still couldn't see any bright bands of colour.

'Let me make it up to you. Let me buy you a cup of coffee or something.'

'I don't want coffee and I have to catch my bus.' She walked towards the door.

'Don't you drive?' He followed a half-step behind her.

'I take my test next week.' She'd been practising with Aunt Rose for three months. Aunt Beryl had taken her out once before it became Rose's job. Sometimes Aunt Beryl revealed a nervous disposition.

'Good luck with it.'

'Thanks.'

'Can I give you a lift to wherever you're going?' He held the door open for her.

'No, I told you I'm taking the bus.' Liz could feel his sleeve brushing against hers. She moved slightly to avoid contact.

'Then let me walk you to the bus stop. It's the least I can do.'

'You don't have to do anything except leave me alone.' She squinted in the thin winter sunshine and shoved the glasses to the top of her head to cut the glare.

'My name is Jim Wolters. Biology major, graduating in June.'

'Then you're going to Vietnam?' The ROTCees were almost always sent immediately into action. She considered herself to be apolitical, but the war and the propaganda from both sides was impossible to ignore.

'I won't know for sure until June. What's your major?'

'History with an English minor.'

'Planning on teaching?'

'Probably not, haven't really decided. What about you?' she asked, in spite of herself.

'After the service, I'll decide. Maybe med school, if I'm not too old.'

'Or too dead.' The ROTCees entered the service as second lieutenants. Second lieutenants had a very short life span in the rice paddies of South-East Asia. Liz had read an article in the campus newspaper just the week before.

'Sounds more like you're majoring in brutal frankness. For what it's worth, I'm planning to stay alive.'

'That's what everyone thinks. Nobody really believes they're going to die.' She almost caught a glimpse of Ellie out of the corner of her eye.

'Everybody around here thinks they're experts. The people in the military want this war less than anybody. The military are the ones who fight and die in this. I bet you've never even seen a dead body.'

'Don't be so sure about that, Jim Wolters.'

'You remembered my name.' He grinned at her.

'Of course I remembered your name. I have that kind of memory. When I was a little kid I used to read the encyelopaedias for fun.'

'My folks would have loved having a kid like you. I was always out climbing trees when I should have been studying.' His sleeve was touching hers once again. 'Do you live with your parents?'

'No, I don't.'

'The dorms? You don't look like a sorority girl.'

'Why don't I look like a sorority girl? Because I'm not pretty or because I look poor?' The sorority girls always seemed to be cut from the same mould. There was a definite sameness in their perfect teeth and pert noses.

'You're pretty, very pretty, in fact. You just don't look like one of the sorority girls. That's a compliment, by the way.'

'What, that I'm pretty or don't look like a sorority girl?' Only Aunt Beryl had ever suggested she was pretty.

'Both. You're very pretty and you don't look like a sorority girl. You don't dress like everybody else and that's a nice change. Most of the people around here have more of a uniform than the ROTCees.'

'I know what you mean. When I first saw the campus two years ago, most of the guys looked like you. Now you stand out like a sore thumb.' She smiled at him, half hoping he was offended. It would be much easier if he would just stop talking and walk away.

'Yeah, I know what you mean. Whoever thought hair would be a political statement? Now back to my question: where do you live?' He put his hand lightly on her shoulder.

She stopped walking and turned towards him as his hand fell away. 'I live with my guardians. My mother died when I was twelve and I never knew my father. Are you done with the third degree?' She could still feel where his hand had been so briefly.

'Just one more thing.'

'What is it?'

'What's your name?'

'Elizabeth Sinclair. Liz.'

'One more thing.'

'You're pushing it.' She bit her upper lip to keep from smiling.

'Will you go out with me tonight?'

'No. I don't date.'

'Never?'

'Never. I told you: I'm a goddamn nun.' She turned and hurried towards the bus stop.

'Liz, wait!'

She lifted her hand and waved without looking back. Relieved that the bus was waiting, she hopped on and found a seat. Looking out of the window, she wasn't surprised to see Jim Wolters watching her. She squinted and turned her head, but the colours still eluded her.

Cotherstone, West Sussex, May 16th

Dear Oliver,

How are you and all that sort of thing? I keep reaching for the phone to call you and then I realize the time difference and, oh well. I think about you all the time. How's that?

I've reread your letter and you're right, of course. Whenever I feel stressed I go for the snappy response. I'm sorry about that and I promise to work on not being so sharp. I know I don't have to be clever with you.

I am glad we've got a few months or weeks of separation coming up and I won't apologize for feeling that way. I do miss you terribly, but I have to give this time to my family, just my family. Writing the weekly letter to you will be my one indulgence.

To really understand the situation with my mother you would have to understand her bizarre upbringing. I think she's just now coming to grips with it herself. I suppose it's one of those now-or-never situations for all of us. She's slowly telling me everything and I suppose it will be my job to tell my brother.

The short version is she was orphaned at twelve by her alcoholic mother, her only sister died, and then she was adopted by two lesbian librarians. (One of the lesbian librarians was my second cousin once removed, I think.) I suppose because of all that she's spent the last two and a half decades creating the perfect family. The funny thing is, we almost are. We have our warts, of course, but no addicts, no kleptomaniacs, no sexual deviation. (Of course,

I'm not counting my second cousin once removed or my brother the wanker.)

I suppose I'm here because we are so nearly perfect. As the almost perfect daughter to the almost perfect mother, I need to be here with as few distractions as possible. Too bad that our near perfection doesn't extend to my mother's health.

I need to be here for my little brother. He's the baby of the family and I think he's more than a little gobsmacked right now. Chaz loves his comforts and he knows things are going to get very uncomfortable. He's a darling, you'll like him, even I do. I'd like to make this easier for him as well. He's just enough younger than me that I've always felt vaguely maternal about him. I keep thinking he's much too young to lose his mother and then I have to remind myself that I'm only a few years older myself.

I frankly don't know what to think about Daddy. I don't know if it's all just show, but he pretends that Mummy is getting better every day. He's quite a bit older than her, so maybe he can't believe this is happening. If he mentions the 'will to live' one more time, I'm going to scream. They've always appeared to have a very good marriage, but I suspect the intensity and passion are mostly on his side. He always says he adored her from the first time he set eyes on her. I suppose his 'will to live' comments are his way of coping.

I would have thought I could have at least relied on my grandmother, but she's acting a bit odd herself. Her idea of support is to bring around her chums who have had cancer so they can tell my mother their war stories. God, they've got a mountain of them too. If her friends haven't had cancer their husbands have. One of them yesterday was chirping on about how her husband weighed less than seven stone when he finally kicked it. I wanted to throttle the old cow, but Mummy sat there with an interested smile on her face.

Tag; I'm it!! I want to do this for her. I adore her and I want to make this as easy as possible for her, but I'm so scared. She's dying and I've never seen anyone die, I've never even seen a dead body, and now I know I might be the one to pull a sheet over my own mother's face. Not only that, I know she'll never see my children's faces, and that breaks my heart. She would have been a wonderful grandmother. I always assumed she would be around as long as I needed her.

You'll probably never meet her, and that makes me terribly, terribly sad. I'm tempted to ask you to fly over for a few days to meet her, but I'm afraid of that happening. I'm afraid the dying will drive you away because you'll think of death whenever you think of me. I'm afraid you would distract me from her and her needs. I'm afraid that your being here would open me up to all the emotions I'm keeping packed away and I would be totally useless to everyone if I gave way right now. This all sounds ridiculous, I know, but it's the way I feel.

Darling, I am so scared. If you know anybody who's not an atheist, please have them pray for my mother. I tried to do it the other day, but I just got all weepy and I didn't want her to see that. Fuck it! I'm getting weepy just writing to you.

Love to all. Please call Karen and remind her to forward my mail. I left her a sheet of stamps and envelopes, but you know Karen.

Love

Mary

PS I know this is such a depressing letter, but I'm not having a very good time.

PS II I miss you so much I could spit. For what it's worth, I only think of you when I masturbate. I used to think of Daniel Day-Lewis (as he appeared in The Last of the Mohicans), but you've replaced him.

CHAPTER EIGHTEEN

'I don't think I've seen these before.' She took the photographs from her mother's desk. Drained of colour, the old snapshots showed two middle-aged women at a lake. The heavy one held a fishing rod while the slim one carried a picnic hamper.

'I didn't remember them either. I can't recall seeing them for years. Amazing what one finds in the back of desks. Shame that the colour has faded so much.' One of her goals was to clean out every drawer and cupboard. She didn't want to leave a mess.

'When do you think these were taken?'

'Hard to say, but I suppose sometime when I was a teenager. See Beryl's dress? I think it must have been around nineteen sixty-five.' She ran her finger lightly across the print. What a pair they were. Beryl held up the picnic hamper, an offering to the photographer and future unknown viewers.

'I don't really remember them.'

'I'm sorry to hear that. My aunts were one in a million.'

'Do you still think of them that way, as your aunts?'

'Definitely. Except for a matter of blood, they were family. All in all, they were a much bigger and more positive influence in my life than my own kin ever were.'

'Tell me about them.'

'I've told you about them before.' Liz smiled at her daughter, aware that the girl seemed anxious to keep words flowing, perhaps to still the inevitable thoughts that never left.

'You told me about them when I was a kid. You didn't say anything about them being lesbians or what effect that had on you.'

'You want the grown-up version of my childhood memories?'

'Exactly.' Mary plopped on her mother's bed and watched as Liz sorted the pictures on her desk.

'Let's see, first of all, Aunt Rose wore the pants in the family.

She was like one of those men who is happiest when some lady down the street has a burst pipe. She loved to jump into an emergency and save the day. Thank God for that particular trait. In many ways, at least at first, I was another burst pipe or flat tyre for her to fix.'

'She looks pretty butch in those pictures.'

'"Butch" is one word that would fit. Whenever I read debates about nature versus nurture being the cause of homosexuality I think of Rose and Beryl.' Liz stood and held her hands about a foot from either side of her body and forced her head down until she'd created a double chin. 'Rose was built like this, like a man. Her shoulders and neck were thick and she carried all her weight in her belly. Didn't have even the suggestion of a waist. I don't recall her having much in the way of breasts and she had that flat butt that so many stout men develop. Her mother, Mrs Harper, wasn't built like that at all. She was quite curvy, in an old lady sort of way. I suppose today Rose would probably have an operation, change her name to Ron, and marry Sheila, who used to be Stan. She smiled at her daughter as she sat and picked up another picture of the women. 'Just kidding, Mary. The love of Rose's life was Beryl. She loved her to distraction with the kind of intensity only a man can muster. Definitely nature.'

'How about Beryl?'

'Beryl was an altogether different story. She was as "girlie" as anyone I've ever known. She kept dolls on their bed until the day she died. She loved pink and practically bathed in White Shoulders cologne. Much to her embarrassment she subscribed to movie magazines and followed Hollywood gossip. Oddly enough, she wasn't interested in the Joan Crawfords or the Marlene Dietrichs. She would get terrific crushes on the John Waynes and Errol Flynns. Beryl would go on about this one or that one being a dreamboat.'

'Dreamboat? What, pray tell, does one do with a dreamboat?'

'I never asked, but it does conjure an image, doesn't it?

Whether she was gay or bi I couldn't tell you, and I doubt if she could have herself. Maybe she just fell in love with a sweet teddy bear of a man who had the wrong bits. I vote for nurture and true love in Beryl's case.'

'Did you know they were gay?'

'Nobody ever told me, if that's what you mean. I knew they shared a bed and I knew I had to keep quiet about it.'

'Was that hard, keeping it quiet?'

'Not really. I was the child of an alcoholic. I was used to keeping secrets. Besides, I kept to myself until I started university.'

'Did you start making friends then?'

'Just one.' She put the photographs in a pile. 'I didn't become much of a social butterfly until after I married your father.'

Clifford, California, February 1966

'Hi, Liz. Did you have a good day?' Rose stood at the sink, inexpertly peeling potatoes.

'Yeah, it was fine. How did you get stuck in here?' Liz reached for a glass. 'I thought after your last attempt it was agreed you'd never touch unprepared food again.' Several weeks before, Rose had made a tuna casserole that even the cat refused to eat.

'Very funny. Just for that you can make a salad.'

'Where's Aunt Beryl?' Liz took a head of lettuce from the counter and began to strip the leaves off.

'She's going to be a bit late tonight. One of our little old ladies from the library, a Mrs Kirby, went into a nursing home last night. Beryl's gone over to take her a few books and see how she's settling in.'

'I wonder if that's my Mrs Kirby. Does she live on a farm by my old house?'

'Did live on a farm. I guess she finally had to give it up. I think she had a heart attack two or three weeks ago. She's been in the hospital, but according to Beryl, there's no way she can go back home.'

'That's too bad, She's a nice lady.'

'Do you think so? I always thought she was a sanctimonious old biddy. She's told me more than once I should throw out half the books in the library because they're not suitable for a Christian community.'

'I don't doubt it for a minute. That sounds just like her.'

'Then why do you think she's nice?'

'The night my mother died, Ellie and I stole some gas from her. She could have turned us in, but she didn't.'

'I'm surprised she never said anything about it. She knows you've been living here with us.'

'She promised us she wouldn't. She told us she would forget she ever saw us.'

'How odd. I would have thought she would have held you at gunpoint and called the Sheriff.'

'She did hold a gun on us, but she didn't call the Sheriff. She was an orphan, sort of, herself. I guess she felt sorry for us.'

'Well, I suppose I'll have to start thinking more kindly of her. Would you like to go see her? She's over at Oakview.'

'I think I will. I'll go tomorrow after class.' Liz tore the leaves into a bowl. 'Would you like me to make dinner?'

'Thought you'd never ask.' Rose tossed a half-peeled potato into the sink. 'I wish Beryl would find a new hobby. I hate it when dinner is late.'

'Do I know you?' Mrs Kirby peered over her blankets at Liz. The old woman's eyes were pale and cloudy with cataracts.

'You used to know me, Mrs Kirby. I'm Liz, Lizzy Sinclair. My family used to live down the road from you.'

'Come closer. I don't see much any more. Doctors say they can't do anything about your eyes once you get this old.'

'Can you see me now?' Liz stood next to the bed and leaned her face two feet from the woman's.

'You've changed. I don't think I would have known you.' She turned her head slightly and talked towards the wall. 'Don't you think she looks different?'

'It's been four years, Mrs Kirby.' Suddenly it seemed much longer.

'You didn't get very far, did you, Lizzy?'

'No, I guess not. I ended up back in Clifford, but it turned out all right, at least for me.'

'I heard about your sister dying. It surprised me, because I'd been praying for both of you.' She cocked her head and frowned. 'Well, if prayers don't work then I don't know what does.' She muttered this last as though it had been said many times before.

'It was horrible, she was only fourteen.' Liz said it almost in wonder. When Ellie had died, fourteen hadn't seemed so young. Now that Liz was sixteen, she was already two years older than her sister would ever be.

'Age doesn't mean anything. It doesn't matter when you die. The Lord keeps us here as long as we need to be here and not a minute longer. Your sister didn't need to be here very long. You should rejoice and sing praises that she is in the bosom of Christ.'

'I suppose that's one way to look at it.' She recalled what Rose had said earlier about the old woman being a sanctimonious old biddy.

'It's the only way to look at it. Read your Bible and you'll find out everything you need to know.' She batted at the air, pushing something aside. 'Won't tell her that. Won't tell her her future.'

'My Aunt Beryl, Beryl Johnson from the library, said you were pretty well settled here.' Liz hoped they could move off the Lord and her future. She checked her watch and calculated that she could politely leave in ten minutes.

'She came by to see me yesterday. She's a sweet woman, but I didn't know she was your aunt.'

'She isn't really, but that's what I call her. She and Miss Harper are my guardians.'

'I don't much like that Miss Harper or her mother. Mrs Harper taught two of mine and she was always filling their heads with stuff I didn't feel too good about. Always going on about the Greeks and the Chinamen and what they had to say about everything. I told her, just like I told you, the Bible is where you find the answers.' The old woman plucked at her covers and seemed lost in thought for a moment. 'Always thought she was better. Been to college and thought she knew more than me. Wasn't even a bible college, but she always set great store by her information. Never thought she knew as much as she made out she did.'

'I came by today because I wanted to see how you were feeling, and I wanted to thank you for what you did for us, for me and Ellie.'

'What did I do? Who are you, anyway?' She looked up at Liz and squinted.

'I'm Lizzy Sinclair, Mrs Kirby. You fed us, you didn't turn us in when you had the chance.'

'That's right. I think I should have turned you in. I think God wanted to take your sister, but maybe He wouldn't have been in such a hurry if I'd turned you in. I wonder if I didn't change God's plan. Got in the way of what He wanted.'

'I think my sister would have died anyway.' Liz swallowed hard, thinking about Ellie's blue lips and dead baby. 'You gave us a chance to get away. It didn't work, but you tried and I appreciate that.'

'Have you found somebody else to love?'

'I've got Beryl and Rose, and Mrs Harper. They've been wonderful and I feel like I'm part of the family.'

'No, I mean somebody for you, somebody you've chosen.'

'No, nothing like that.'

'Everyone needs that. Everyone needs someone just for them. Especially us that lose our families when we're young. I stopped being an orphan when I met Mr Kirby. I started to belong. I was really part of something then. That's God's plan: man and woman making a life.' She licked her lips and stared into the corner of the room. 'He loved me as much as a man could love anything.'

'Some people get along fine without that, and I think I might be one of those.'

'Some people get along, but they aren't fine, and besides, you aren't one of them. I remember when you came to see me with your sister. You knew what you wanted and would have done anything to stay together. You are someone who's not made to be alone. You find yourself your man and start belonging to something bigger than yourself. Stop being an orphan, Lizzy Sinclair.'

'I'll think about it, Mrs Kirby.' Lizzy giggled with discomfort in spite of herself.

'You can laugh, but it won't be long before you know what I mean. You take a look at your heart and you'll find a spot that's empty and needs to be filled. It needs to be filled with a husband and a family. I know because I had one of those empty places myself. I needed a family of my own, just like you do.'

'I think I'd better be going. They're expecting me at home.'

'You go along, Lizzy Sinclair. I'm glad you came by. You're going to be fine and I praise God for that.'

'Yes, Mrs Kirby, I'm fine now.' Liz was relieved to be getting away from the old woman and reminders of what God had done for her.

'You're not fine yet, but you will be.' She turned away and hissed to her unseen companion, 'I'm not going to tell her about that. None of her business.'

Cotherstone, West Sussex, May 23rd

Dear Oliver,

I'm sorry I was out last night when you called. I went to dinner at my friend Mike's house. I think I've told you about Mike. Remember the story about playing doctor and getting caught on the beach? That's Mike. Not to worry, darling, I had dinner at his house to meet the beauteous and frightfully exotic new girlfriend.

I felt such a mouse! This girl's father is Irish and her mother is Somalian, of all things. She's at least six feet tall and incredibly gorgeous. Mike is cute, in kind of a funny-looking ginger sort of way, so they are something of an odd couple. Anyway, there was this incredible sexual sparking between the two of them all night; I felt like a voyeur. A short, rather washed-out voyeur. Had a nice time, missed you.

Things are settling down around here. Connie, the housekeeper, seems to have got into a rhythm and we're all getting used to each other. It no longer feels so weird to have a non-family member in the house all day.

My mother appears to be holding her own, but I see a gradual weakening. She's still doing some work every day, but I suspect her last book has been written.

Daddy has been in Norway for the past few days, but is coming home tonight. Tomorrow everyone, except yours truly, is going to some big cricket thing at Arundel Castle. As luck would have it, tomorrow is also Connie's day off. For the first time since I've been home I'll have the entire house to myself. About bloody time.

I have to close in a minute. Gran and the 'girls' are going to London to see a matinée of The Mousetrap. *Very avant-garde, don't you know. I promised to take them as far as Brighton station because Louisa, a girl of eighty-one, doesn't like Worthing station. Don't ask. I did and my head is still spinning.*

I still haven't heard from Karen, or anyone else for that matter. Give them a call and tell them I'm desperate for news.

I love you and miss you.

Mary

PS Teila, Mike's girlfriend, has an inside leg measurement on her trousers of thirty-six inches!!

CHAPTER NINETEEN

'You look tired. How about a cup of tea or some cocoa?' Mary stood in the doorway and watched as her mother adjusted the belt of a dressing gown around her waist.

'No thanks, darling. We were eating and drinking all day.' She tied a bow in the soft belt, pulling the fabric closer than she had even two days before.

'What did you have to eat?'

'Oh, goodness, they had everything, salmon, roast chicken, wonderful puddings.'

'Sounds very nice, but what did *you* eat?'

'I had a bit of everything.' She'd weighed herself before getting dressed in the morning. Over half a stone gone just since Mary had been home.

'You've got to do better, Mummy. You don't eat enough.'

'I don't have any sort of appetite.'

'You still need to eat.'

'Mary, I need you to do something for me.' Liz turned to her daughter and felt the telltale ache of tears building behind her eyes.

'I'd do anything, you know that.'

'Then for the love of God stop nagging me about eating and getting well! Stop making me feel like a loser and a quitter because of what's happening to my body.' She turned away and wiped the moisture from her cheeks.

'That's not what I meant, Mummy.'

'It's how it sounded. You all watch every bite I take. Every move is monitored and judged. I feel like a bloody lab rat. Just let me be.'

'I'm only trying to help. I'm only trying to make things easier for you.' Mary stepped back towards the door.

'Then stop making me feel guilty for dying. Stop reminding me that I'm deserting you just like my mother deserted me.'

'I don't feel like you're deserting us. None of us feels that way.'

'I feel that way. I feel like a horrible person. I feel like I'm no better than my useless mother. I feel as worthless and pointless as she was.'

'Oh, Mum.' Mary stepped forward and pulled her mother to her. 'I don't know what to say to you. I don't have the words to tell you how I feel.'

'That makes two of us.' She leaned against her daughter and sobbed.

Valley State University, California, March 1966

'I live with my mother and younger brother. I was planning to get a place with some of my buddies, but my brother started acting up and I thought I should stick around and help my mom with him.' Jim took a sip of his coffee and glanced around the student union cafeteria.

'How about your dad?' Liz stirred more sugar into her coffee. Since she had accepted an invitation for coffee she thought it best to try and drink it. She would have preferred a soda or a glass of milk.

'Honest Jack Wolters. Your friend on the freeway.'

'You've got to be kidding.' Honest Jack was a regular on late-night television. He owned a string of used car lots up and down the Valley. Honest Jack wore gold lamé cowboy shirts and snakeskin boots. He offered easy payments and seemed singularly pleased to have a bilingual sales force. According to the ads, Honest Jack's was the Happiest Place on the Highway.

'Believe me, I wish I was kidding. Honest Jack left Mom about ten years ago. He married somebody else and has two little girls.'

'Why are you in ROTC if your dad is Honest Jack?' ROTC was a path usually taken for financial reasons.

'Unlike you, I'm no scholarship material. My grades were just good enough to get me into school.'

'But Honest Jack must make millions.'

'I don't know if he does or not. He's pretty much forgotten about us, anyway. When he left Mom he found the smartest son-of-a-bitch lawyer he could.'

'She didn't get anything?'

'Next thing to it. She ended up with a ratty little house and a big mortgage.'

'That's rotten.'

'That's life.'

'No, I mean it's really rotten. It's one thing when your parents are dead or don't know about you, but to have to see the guy on TV almost every night; that's really awful.'

Jim smiled and leaned back in his chair. 'It's for the best. Knowing what I know, I figure we don't need him in our lives.

Besides, if I'd grown up with him I'd be wearing shiny cowboy shirts and selling used cars.'

'Instead you're going to Vietnam.'

'Instead I'm going to college and drinking coffee with a pretty girl.'

'I don't think I'm that pretty.' She'd thought about it a lot since he'd mentioned it that first day they'd met. She had decided she *was* pretty, just not *that* pretty.

'That's one of the things that makes you so pretty. You don't seem to put too much stock in how you look.' He gazed at her and she lowered her eyes. She'd left her glasses at home because she thought she might see him. 'What about you? You said you live with guardians?'

'It's a long story. I don't like to talk about it.' She looked at her cup on the table and wiggled it back and forth in the saucer. An oily black ocean, not a shrimp boat in sight.

'Who do you live with now? Are they relatives or something?'

'Not really.' She thought of the women and wondered what they would think of her denial. 'But they're sort of my family anyway.'

'What's the big deal?'

'It's not a big deal. I just don't like to talk about my life or the people I live with.'

'I'm sorry. I didn't mean to pry. I just wanted to get to know you a little bit. I think we could be friends.'

'It's all right, I'm the one who should apologize. I'm not used to . . . I have a very odd background, to say the least. You are actually the only person close to my age I know.' Liz shrugged her shoulders, hoping the gesture would either make him understand or stop him from asking more questions.

'How's that possible? What about the people in your classes, in your department?'

'I keep to myself. People don't usually notice you unless you want to be noticed. I found that out a long time ago. When I was little I was convinced I could make myself invisible. The weird thing is in some ways it worked.' She looked across the table at him. She almost told him about seeing the colours, but thought better of it. He'd want to know what his were and she still couldn't see any. She could see the colours of others in the room, but not his. 'In some ways I can still make myself invisible.'

'I don't understand why you don't want to be seen. People do all kinds of things just so they will be noticed.'

'People also do lots of things so they *won't* be noticed.'

'You're trying to change the subject, Liz.'

'Some things happened when I was twelve and I just shut down. I didn't even talk for a while.' She took a sip of the coffee and stirred it again with the spoon.

'What happened? You said your mother was dead; is that part of what happened?'

'That was part of it. Everything changed so fast, I guess my brain didn't have a chance to adjust. My sister died, this guy died, there was a horrible fire.' Liz rubbed her hand against her mouth, sorry she'd revealed as much as she had. 'I'd better be going. I've got to check on some things at the library.' She rose and pulled her books against her chest, creating a little fence, a little space between them.

'Can I have your number? I'd like to give you a call.'

'It's in the book; Rose Harper in Clifford.' As an afterthought she smiled at him. 'Thanks for the coffee.'

'Hi, Liz.' Aunt Rose was sprawled across the living room sofa with the evening papers. 'Have a good day at school?'

'Pretty good. How was your day?' She dropped her books on the coffee table.

'Just fine. Someone called for you a few minutes ago; a Jim Wolters.' She smiled at Lizzy over the top of her half-glasses.

'Did he say what he wanted?' She sat heavily on the arm of the sofa, her legs crossed in front of her.

'I didn't ask. I figured it was pretty clear why a young man would be calling you.'

'Well, if he calls back, I'm not here.'

'Why? Has he done something to upset you?' Rose sat up.

'No, not really. He bought me coffee today and started asking me lots of questions about my family and us.'

'Us?'

'You know: who I live with; how we are related. That kind of thing.'

'Those are reasonable questions when you want to get to know someone.'

'I don't like getting the third degree.'

'Are you afraid to tell him about me and Beryl; is that it?'

'No.'

'Well, just in case that is the reason, I want you to know you can tell him whatever you want. We aren't exactly mom, dad, two-point-four kids and a dog, but we are your family. I'm not ashamed and I hope you aren't either.'

'I'm not ashamed, Aunt Rose. I just don't want to get to know him and I don't want him to get to know me. As it is, I started blabbing about Mom and Ellie. I wish I'd never talked to him.'

'What's wrong with him?'

'Nothing is wrong with him. He's nice and he's cute and all that.'

'But?'

'But he's in ROTC. He's going to Vietnam right after graduation.'

'Thousands of boys are going to Vietnam. I think the war is horrible, but I'd hate to think that nobody will talk to some poor kid because he's going to go overseas.'

'Don't you see? This isn't about the stupid war, not really. Well, maybe it is, partly. I do have to wonder about somebody who's willing to go, but it's more than that. He's going to die over there. Let some girl who hasn't watched her family die talk to him and go out with him. I can't do it. I have a new life now. Even thinking about where he's going brings it all back to me.'

'So that's what this is all about. I've been sitting here thinking you were ashamed of us.' Rose shook her head back and forth. 'I was afraid you didn't know how to explain about us.'

'That's crazy, Aunt Rose. I would never be ashamed of you and Aunt Beryl.' She leaned over and kissed the woman on the cheek. 'I just don't want to know anyone, get close to anyone, who is going to die. I started to tell him what had happened and I just knew I couldn't go through that again.' Ellie cool and white on the hospital bed. Their sails in sight.

'Then you have to avoid everyone, Lizzy. Everyone is going to die. My mother is almost eighty and has a bad heart. You're close to her and she's going to die. She might die tonight. Does that mean you won't kiss her goodnight, because she might die?'

'Of course not. I already love Mrs Harper. I don't even know Jim, much less love him.'

'Lizzy, listen to me. You can't spend your whole life with us and our friends. You need more. You need people closer to your own age. You need Jim or someone like him.'

'Even Mrs Kirby said that, but I don't want to lose anybody else. She said orphans needed to make their own families, settle down and have babies and all of that.'

'Far be it from me to agree with Mrs Kirby, and God knows I think you can be happy without babies, but there might be a grain of truth in what she had to say. You do need to open yourself up to other people. You have to learn to be in the world again.'

'I wish Ellie was here. I wasn't afraid when Ellie was around.' Eighteen now. She would have calmed down and gotten her wits about her, developed better taste in boys, at least.

'I do too, Lizzy, but she's not. She's dead, but you are very much alive. You are young and alive and so is this young man. Please don't decide he's doomed and put him in the grave before he's dead.'

'I hadn't thought of it that way.'

'Well, start thinking about it. The other thing for you to consider is the fact that most of the boys come back. You sound like he's going to the electric chair instead of Vietnam.'

'He's going over as a second lieutenant. If you ask me that's just the same as the electric chair.'

'How do you figure that?'

'They die. They get picked off like flies. The Vietcong look for the second lieutenants and kill them first.' Liz leaned against the older woman for comfort. 'At least with the electric chair you get to choose your last meal.'

'Maybe you're right and it's not the best position to be in. The fact is, second lieutenants come back too. I bet a lot more come back than die.' She put her arm around the girl and kissed the top of her head. 'What does he say about it? What's he feeling right now?'

'I don't know him well enough to ask. What am I supposed to say? How do you feel about the prospect of becoming worm food? How do you feel about getting blown to bits or dying slowly in some tiger cage off the Ho Chi Min Trail? I can't ask him things like that.'

'Get to know him. Find out what he thinks. Ask him how he feels about going to war. Ask him how he feels about fried fish or black watchbands. This may be one of the most interesting human beings who's ever walked the face of the earth. What if you don't get to know him and thirty years from now he wins the Nobel Prize? What if he ends up the next Mick Jagger? You'll be kicking yourself, won't you? Take a chance and get to know him. Living well is all about taking chances.'

'Fried fish and black watchbands?'

'Exactly. The most interesting things about people are the little things. What's the expression, "God is in the details"? Find out what he's all about before you make a decision about him. Find out about the person inside the skin.'

'I'll think about it.'

'I know what that means, Lizzy.'

'What?'

'It means you are trying to pacify me, put me off. Thinking about it means you've already thought about it and come up with a big fat no.'

'Not necessarily.' She sat up, uncomfortable with Rose's intuition.

'Almost certainly. I can read you like a book, young lady. What I want is for you to promise me that you will look at this man with fresh and honest eyes. I want you to find out who he is before you make a decision about him.'

'I'll think about it.' She looked at Rose and saw her open her mouth in protest. 'I mean I'll really think about it, the way you want me to.'

'Good; that's all I'm asking.' Rose rattled her paper and shoved her glasses up the bridge of her nose. 'Now, will you go ask Beryl when dinner is ready? And Liz?'

'Hmm?'

'Beryl's got a slab of cod sitting in the kitchen. Remind her I hate it when she fries the fish.'

Cotherstone, West Sussex, June 1st

Dearest O,

Things have been getting rougher around here. My mother is angry with herself for 'abandoning' us. I've tried to assure her we don't blame her, but she seems to have the whole thing tied up with her own mother's death and her feelings as a child. She's incredibly angry with herself and, by extension, she's having a hard time not being angry with the rest of us. I think I'm the only one who's really aware of it. She's terribly good at hiding things.

I've been doing some reading and apparently her response is fairly standard. She's started pulling away from people. Last week she could listen to Gran's friends, but this week she pretends to be resting if they're around.

I hate myself for it, but I find myself resenting her right now. I know none of this is her fault, but I can't help but resent her for what we're all going through. I get upset with her if she feels sorry for herself and I get upset with her if she starts being noble and brave. She can't win for losing. And the thing that really fries me is I can't tell her I'm mad! We've always been fairly honest with each other and now I'm tiptoeing around and I really hate that.

Well, I feel better now. I needed to get that out of my system, I suppose.

On to other things. I've been doing a lot of novel reading. Haven't done much of that for the last three years and am enjoying it thoroughly. Let me know if your time frees up because I'm putting together a reading list for you.

To help me get through today, I am beginning to think about tomorrow. I still haven't decided what I'm going to do when Mum dies. I have definitely decided that I'm not going to stay here and be the dutiful daughter. I had a long talk with Daddy last night and he agrees that would be a mistake. (A bit of a neat freak, I think my slovenly ways get on his nerves.) He told me he is planning to keep the housekeeper and everyone will adjust as best they can.

My friend Amanda Cooper has a flat in South Ken and she's asked me to share it. Since these things take time, I'm sending out my CV to museums and libraries now. Daddy has told me that he will pay half my rent for the first year, which is awfully sweet of him, especially considering how much my California time cost him.

I am concerned about how he will cope emotionally. I'll be leaving and my brother is planning to board in September when he starts his A levels. That leaves Daddy here with Gran and a part-time housekeeper. He assures me that's not my concern, but I can't help being worried. That being said, I wouldn't be shocked if Chaz decided to stay home. He's a bit of a mama's boy (he denies it) and I don't know how he'll react when reality hits.

On the plus side, the dog is happier than a pig in shit. He's got people around all day and I make sure he gets to the beach every afternoon. I really missed having a dog when I was in SF. Remember that row we had about my giving money to every panhandler with a dog? Anyway, Patch says hello. I've told him you're a keen ball-player and he's anxious to meet you.

I've got to run. I need to go to do the shopping and run approximately one thousand errands. I need a wife!

Love

Mary

PS I'm faxing this to you, but for God's sake, if you're going to fax me something please remember that you're sending it to my father's fax machine. I don't think the words 'personal and confidential' are a guarantee that half his office won't read it.

CHAPTER TWENTY

'Mary, I'm really touched that you saved these.' She spread the letters on the dining room table like a game of solitaire. To her surprise, she felt relaxed, almost happy. The day had a sense of normality about it. A morning that smelled of coffee, toast and laundry powder.

'I couldn't throw them away. Sometimes when I would get homesick out there I read them all at one go.'

'You, homesick? Even with the excellent Oliver to keep you occupied?' She fished whenever possible, although Mary was unusually quiet on the subject of the man.

'Stop gloating.'

'I'm not gloating, I'm just feeling pleased that you're such a sentimental girl.'

'I come by it honestly. I bet you saved my letters home, didn't you?'

'Of course. Sometimes when I missed you I'd read them all in one go.' She grinned and put her hand over her daughter's. It felt warm and plump under her own.

'Let's put them in a scrapbook.'

'I think that's a wonderful idea. It can be a memento of your trip and a little capsule view of our relationship. I like the idea of my grandchildren reading it.'

'I'm going to tell them about you. I'm going to make sure that all your grandchildren know you.'

'How many do you suppose there will be? "All" sounds like

a large number.' She tried to look forward, to feel a fierce love for these phantom children she'd never know.

'I want two, and Chaz will no doubt marry some earthy thing who wants half a dozen.'

'Make sure you only tell them the good things.'

'That's all there is; good things.'

'I'm delighted you feel that way.' She put the letters in a neat stack. 'I'm feeling rather energetic today. Let's walk Patch into town and buy a scrapbook.'

'Getting tired?'

'A little, but it feels good to be out and about for a change.' Liz knelt down and picked a stick up from the ground. She tossed it to the dog and laughed as he arced into the air to catch it. 'Do you realize you haven't mentioned Oliver since you've been back? That's not like you.' They were picking their way slowly along the path between the shops and their home.

'I suppose I'm afraid to say too much, afraid of pulling down the attention of the evil eye or something.'

'The evil eye?'

'Or something. We got off to a bit of a rocky start before things started making sense between us.'

'And then you came home.'

'Thank God I came home when I did. Oliver and I needed a little space to figure out what's going on between us.'

'Worked anything out?'

'I'm really nuts about him. I'm not sure if it's enough, though. I've been nuts about lots of men, as you know.'

'I recall a few.'

'A few? Well, whatever. I suppose it's hard for you to relate since you fell in with Daddy when you were so young. I think I envy you that.'

'He wasn't my first relationship, you know.'

'He was the first serious one, and that's the same as.'

'Actually, I was quite mad about a young man before your

father.' The faces in her memory blurred for a moment and she picked up another stick for the dog while she decided who to talk about. 'His name was Jim Wolters.'

Clifford, California, May 1966

Lizzy was surprised at how nice his lips felt. Jim looked to be all angles and crisp lines, but his lips were soft and tasted almost sweet. He would run his thumb along her jaw line and bury his fingers in her hair. Sometimes he would move his fingers across the outline of her bra, stopping when he felt her stiffen under his touch.

She took another look at the forbidden library shelf and the books made more sense now. She went into the university library and found a current best-seller that promised to explain the whole subject in two hundred and twelve pages. She read the book in one afternoon while she crossed and uncrossed her legs. Certain it was obvious what she was reading, she kept her hands cupped around the book, away from prying eyes. She watched the boys walking past her table in their tight jeans with new interest.

She took him to the river one night. The moon on the other side of the world hid its light from her body as she quickly removed her clothes and walked into the river.

'Where are you, Liz?' She could hear his feet against the riverbank's pebbles.

'In the water.' She dropped her hands to her sides and took a deep breath. The book had said it was supposed to be playful and fun, which was why she'd chosen the river. She'd played there for years. More her home than Laura's little house. 'Come in.'

'Why didn't you tell me we were going swimming?'

'I wanted to make sure you didn't bring swimming trunks.'

Grateful for the dark, she felt the colour and heat in her cheeks.

'What are you playing at, Liz?' His voice sounded harsh in her ears.

'I'm not playing at anything.' She walked out of the water and stood next to him on the bank. She stood so close she could feel his warmth, but didn't touch him. Finally she took his hand and put it on her wet breast.

He dropped his hand and stepped away. 'What do you think you're doing?'

'I think it's time. I want to know what it's like.'

'Why now? You've always frozen if I tried to do anything but kiss you.'

'I've been afraid, but I'm not afraid any more.'

'What's different? I need to know what's changed.'

'Hold me, please.' The books talked about the warmth, but even in the eighty-five-degree night, she felt cold.

He pulled her towards his chest, carefully wrapping his arms across her back. 'Tell me what's going on,' he whispered into her ear.

'I've been afraid of this since I was twelve. I knew I had to do it someday, but I've been so afraid of what might happen.'

'Do you mean getting pregnant?'

'No, well, partly. I remember what happened with my sister. She lost herself after she did it. I know it's supposed to change you and I don't want to be different than I am right now.'

'What do you think is going to be different?'

'I don't know. I just know I'll feel different. I'll understand more about how the world works once I've done it.' She'd belong. Be a part of something new.

'It won't change anything, Liz. You'll still be you and I'll still be me. I want you to be sure, I want you to be safe.'

'I know I'll be safe with you.'

'You're going to be safe with me because you're going to put your clothes back on and I'm taking you home.' He released her and stepped away.

'Oh, God.' She put her hand to her mouth as though he had struck her. 'I'm sorry.'

'You don't understand, Liz.'

'I understand completely. Just let me get dressed. No. You go ahead. I can walk home. I know the way.'

'Listen to me. It's not that I don't want you, believe me. I want you more than I've ever wanted anything in my whole life.'

'Would you just leave?' Her hands were shaking and she couldn't find her jeans in the dark.

'No, you have to hear me out.'

'I can't find my clothes.'

'Here.' He pressed a cigarette lighter in to her hand. 'I'll turn around and you can find them.'

She grabbed the lighter and found her clothes by its dim flicker. For a moment she watched the light dance across his still back. She dressed quickly, the lighter clenched in her hand.

'Thanks. Can we go now? She handed the lighter back to him.

'Not until you understand something.'

'I think I understand plenty.'

'If we had sex right now it would be for all the wrong reasons and I don't want that. I want you to be with me because you love me. I don't want it to be because I'm safe, or I'm convenient. I know it sounds corny and old-fashioned, but I want to have sex because I love you. I love you with all my heart and I want you to feel the same way about me.'

'You love me?'

'I love you. I think I will always love you and it scares the shit out of me because I don't think you feel the same way about me.'

'What do you think this was all about? I threw myself at you tonight because I hated you?'

'You mean you . . .'

'I love you. I don't know what the hell that's supposed to mean, but I love you. And for what its worth, I'm scared too.'

She felt sickened by her revelation, appalled she had handed him so much. She thought of Ellie and her Steve and hoped this was different.

'Can we start over?'

'Do you have any idea how long it took me to get the nerve to do what I did tonight? I planned this for over a week.' She took his hand and put it inside her shirt. Newly brave, she wanted confirmation, a sealing to the pact.

He pulled his hand from where she'd placed it, but put his hands on either side of her face. 'I want you to know I will never hurt you if I can help it.'

'The book said the first time hurt.'

'I wasn't talking about sex, Liz.'

'I think I knew that, Jim.'

'Are you going to wait for me?' Jim lifted his head from her stomach and looked at her. They were sprawled across his bed in the room he shared with his brother. His mother and brother weren't due home for another three hours.

'Wait for you to what?' She ran one finger across his arm. The night at the river had left them replete, yet always hungry for more. A Chinese banquet of flesh and fluid. Wanting more an hour later. She touched the end of his penis where a tiny drop of damp hung, shimmering in the light.

'Liz, I'm serious.' He took her hand and held it against his chest. 'Are you going to wait for me?'

'I'll be here when you get back.'

'That's not what I mean.'

'I know, but it's the best answer I can give you.'

'Why?'

'Because I can't be sure who's coming back.' She pulled her hand away from his. They were coming back after a year of duty. They were coming back strangers. Long-haired, vacant-eyed strangers in battle jackets. Drunken and stoned, angry and tearful, on the news, in the streets.

'I'm coming back. The same me will be coming back.'

'Neither of us knows that, Jim. Events change people. God only knows what you're going to be when you come back.' The campus police had taken another one away this week. He'd wandered into the student union and simply started screaming in a high keen. She'd heard he'd been a sophomore when he'd lost his student deferment and found himself drafted into the infantry. Local boy, played basketball in high school.

'I'll still be me. I'll still be the same person who loves you.'

'Will you? You'll be ordering boys to kill people and you'll come home the same person?'

'I have to go and I'll do what I have to do. I'm going to be leading men and doing whatever needs to be done. You know that and you've always known that.'

'Guys are going to Canada. Guys are going to jail. You don't have to go, Jim. I'll go to Canada with you. I've been reading about it. We could apply for landed immigrant status in only three years. You've got your degree and I can finish mine up there.' She was quiet for less than ten seconds. 'I read that they're still giving a few family deferments. Get me pregnant and marry me.' Anything to keep him near. She could barely sleep at night now. A year without him loomed ahead, a black space threatening to engulf her whole world.

'I'm not going to Canada and our babies deserve more than being draft deferments. I made a deal a long time ago, Lizzy. They paid for me to go to school and now I serve my time.'

'You've made a deal with the Devil, if you ask me.' A year without him.

'I'm not asking you. You started this conversation, which we've had way too many times. I'm merely telling you, again, what I'm doing and why.'

'But that's just the point. You are asking me. You're asking me to wait for you. You're asking me to keep a light in the window and send you brownies twice a month. You're asking me to keep everything the same for you while you go off and kill innocent people.' A year of waking up and wondering if he'd died while she slept.

'I'm not going to be killing innocent people, Liz. I'm going to be protecting the Vietnamese from the Vietcong.'

'The Vietcong are the Vietnamese.' Small people in black pyjamas who sent second lieutenants back in boxes.

'Haven't we been through all this about a thousand times?' Jim sat up and started to dress. 'You have such tunnel vision about this whole thing. You're the one who's supposed to be so smart, but you've bought the whole leftist programme, hook, line and sinker. There are two sides to this conflict, just like there are the two of us.'

'The war is wrong and you know it!' Fierce and protective, she wanted to hurt him so he would have to stay, so they wouldn't want him. Blind an eye, crush a bone, take a finger, let him live.

'I don't know it! I have to believe that the greatest political and military minds in this country know what they're doing. I have to believe they know a hell of a lot more than those characters who think it's a political statement to drive a VW bus with flowers painted on the side.'

'Who are these great minds? Nixon, McNamara, Johnson? Not enough brains between them to fill a tea cup.'

'And you would know?'

'I know what I read. Unlike you, I don't just read the local newspaper which is controlled by a family that practically handed Nixon California in the last election.'

'That's right, I forgot. You are Liz Sinclair, girl genius. Not quite seventeen, but already one of the leading thinkers of our time. What is it now: three or four pieces in the student newspaper?'

'You know it's five, and at least I don't have my head stuck in the sand.' Head in Vietnam, she watched the news and noted the body count. Half hoping if the count got high enough they wouldn't need to add his number to the nightly news.

'I don't have my head stuck in the sand and in a few weeks I'm going to have my ass on the line! Maybe then you'll give my opinions some credence.'

'Pax.' She put her palms in the air. 'I don't want to fight about this. I don't want to fight with you about anything.'

'Could have fooled me.'

'I just don't want you to go. I don't want to lose you.'

'I have to go, but you aren't going to lose me unless you want me to get lost.'

'I'm going to be a year older and so are you.' Liz sat up and hugged her knees. 'Neither of us will ever be the same again. Look how we fight now. What are we going to be like after a year apart?'

'Isn't that what's supposed to happen? Isn't that the whole point? We are supposed to keep growing and changing.' He'd pulled on his briefs, but held his jeans in his hand. 'Let's figure out what happens in a year, in a year. Nobody's got a crystal ball.'

'It's never going to be the same as it is right now.'

'That's right. It's never going to be the same, but maybe it's going to be better. Did you ever think of that, Liz? Did you ever think we might be the happiest people in the world if we gave ourselves a chance?'

Liz released her knees and slowly lowered them to the bed. She smiled and reached for his jeans. 'We've got three more hours to test your happiness theory.' Sex could drive away demons. There were more and more demons as the day of his leaving approached.

'I want to talk about this, Liz.'

'You want to argue about it, Jim. You also have an erection and I find it terribly distracting to have that little blind eye bobbing at my face.' Small comfort, but the rhythms and the spasms helped. The smell and feel of him stopped the clock and tore the calendar.

'You have to expect me to have an erection when you sit on my bed with your knees spread.'

'I expect you to do something with what appears to be a perfectly serviceable erection.' She watched his face relax as he came back to her side.

He sat on the bed and kissed the curly yellow hair mounded between her thighs. 'Will you come to the Presidio? Will you see me off?'

'I'll be there. I'm also coming to see you in Hawaii when you have R and R.' She'd saved this. Oil to pour over the angry waters of his leaving.

'How are you going to manage that?' He played with the curls before touching the shiny pink flesh of her cleft.

'Oh, that feels good.' She pressed herself against his hand. 'I've sold two articles to a magazine.'

'About what?' He flicked his tongue across her nipples.

'About the girls the soldiers leave back home.'

'Which magazine?' He licked her navel.

'*Pacific.*'

'You're kidding? *Pacific*?' He looked up and grinned. 'THE *Pacific*?'

'The one and only. They're planning a special issue on the war. Just dumb luck, but one of my teachers is a friend of one of the editors. She suggested I submit something. They bought the piece I wrote and asked for a second one. Impressed?'

'Completely. What's the second piece on?'

'I haven't written it yet. I still have to do some research.'

'What's it on?'

'The widows. I'm calling it "Little Widows".'

Cotherstone, West Sussex, June 4th

Dear 0,

I'm very excited by your news. Pant, pant, actually. I can't believe you'll be back in three months. Now all I have to do is find something in London (preferably a job) and things will be just about perfect.

I've thought what you said about the two of us sharing a flat. First of all, I did tell Amanda I would share with her, and secondly, I'm not sure we're ready for cohabitation. I could say something flip about it taking the romance out of things, but it's really a great deal more than that.

I don't want you to think for a second that I don't love being with you, because I do. I miss you so much I could scream. The problem I have with living together is it seems like an enormous amount of work and sacrifice if it's going to be done well. I don't think I'd be willing to put in what's needed unless I knew there was complete commitment on both ends.

This isn't a marriage proposal, nor is it a hint that I want one from you. I'm just letting you know how I feel. Living together is too much work unless it's a lifetime commitment. We'll spend lots of nights in each other's bed, but let's not live together.

Things are a bit better around here, relatively speaking, of course. Mum seems to have found somewhere in her head where she's no longer angry. She's started telling me about her life,

*pre-Randall once again. Right now we're going through the
Vietnam years and her first romance.*

*My gran is being a shade dotty, but I suppose that's to be
expected. Yesterday she gave me these wonderful earrings which
she bought for me because she sold her car. They're chunky gold,
baroque pearls and small amethysts. They make me look like a
pagan. Gorgeous, gorgeous, but Gran had her nose out of joint last
week because I hadn't thanked her for them. I didn't know what
was wrong and finally she told me why she was angry and then I
had to tell her that she hadn't given me anything. We had a hug
and a laugh and then she gave me the earrings. I took her out for
tea as a thank you, so we're chums again.*

My brother is a useless human being.

My father is marginally better.

My period starts in three days.

*Apart from the above items and the fact that my mother is
dying, things are peachy.*

*I finally heard from Karen. I can't believe she's actually
sleeping with Lance. Judas, how can you sleep with someone called
Lance and not laugh every time you see it? Do you suppose he has
a brother called Willie?*

*I'd better close. This afternoon I'm supposed to call someone my
father went to school with whose sister is a curator or some such
thing. She probably runs a doll museum in Bognor Regis.*

I love you and I miss you AND I miss your lance.

Love

Mary

PS American girls are such twits. Thank God you've got me.

CHAPTER TWENTY-ONE

'His name was Jim Wolters. I met him at university. He was in
ROTC, Reserved Officer's Training Corps. The government
helped to finance his education and he was indentured to them
for two or three years of service after graduation. Vietnam was
getting worse every day and most of the ROTCees ended up
being second lieutenants in Vietnam. A very dangerous job,
that was.' She fluffed the cushion behind her before easing into
it. She glanced at her watch and was relieved to see she only had
an hour before she could take another pill and have two and a
half hours of relief.

'Were you in love with him?'

'Oh yes. Very much so. Before he went to war he was very
sweet and very patient with me. Very much the officer and the
gentleman. The sixties were just beginning to swing and it
wasn't considered cool for girls to keep their knees together. I
don't think most blokes would have had the patience Jim did
with my fears about men and sex. He let me take the initiative,
which was wonderful. He gave me control rather than taking it
away. He was really, really lovely.'

'Did he die in the war?'

'Yes, in more ways than one.' Liz closed her eyes for a
moment.

Are you all right, Mum?'

'I'm fine. I just got this visual impression. Awful thing, a
memory like mine.'

'What did you mean, "more ways than one"?'

'The war was horrible for him. He changed so much before
he died.'

'What did he look like?'

'He looked like a Randall, strangely enough. He looked a lot like your uncle did when he was a young man.'

'Bit of a dish?'

'The full monte. He was handsome, good posture, smelled nice, clean-cut, the whole thing.'

'That does sound like my uncle.'

'Doesn't it just?'

Honolulu, November 1966

'I told you I wouldn't die. Sometimes I think I've stayed alive just so I could prove you wrong.' He finished the beer in his hand and dropped the can on the floor of the balcony. They were on the twelfth storey of one of the hotels that enjoyed a booming trade from catering to men on R and R. The servicemen and their girls had replaced the sunburned Midwestern tourists since the escalation of the war.

'You romantic fool. You know just the things a girl wants to hear.' She tried to purr like a Southern belle in hopes of making him smile, make him relax. Together less than twenty minutes, he'd kissed her once and smoked two cigarettes.

'Sorry, babe. I've been in that shithole for six months with people who'd yank the eyes out of you if they thought it would be worth ten minutes of fun.'

'I refuse to believe the Vietnamese are anything like that Jim. Before this war started they were regarded as fine, gentle people.' Her convictions had grown. Twice a week she joined the silent vigils. Her two article assignment with the magazine had been expanded to four, each more anti-war than the last.

'I'm not talking about the slants, Liz. I'm talking about the Americans.' The corners of his mouth twitched, but he didn't smile.

'What do you mean?'

'I mean you take a bunch of guys and send them to hell. What the fuck do you think is going to happen to them? It's not like those Second World War flicks where everybody is so fucking noble and cheerful. We're over there getting our asses shot off for all of you who think we're a bunch of baby-killers. Most of the grunts are stoned half the time just so they don't shit their pants every time they see another slant.'

'Jim . . .'

'And you should see the guys they send. They empty out the damn ghettos and try to make them soldiers. Or they get these guys out of the hills who are the result of two hundred years of inbreeding. They hand them to us and tell us to win their damn war for them. But don't kill any civilians. No, don't kill any civilians. 'Course, they don't bother to tell you how you're supposed to know who's a civ. They all wear the same damn black pyjamas.' His words bunched together as his voice rose.

'Jim, listen to me. We've got ten days together. Let's take it easy and try to get to know each other again.' She smoothed the short hair above his dark forehead. Thinner than before, his cheekbones seemed ready to push through his browned skin.

'Yeah, I suppose you're right. It may take you ten days to make me fit for civilized company.' He put his arms around her and kissed the top of her head.

'If you're not fit for civilization we may have to spend the whole ten days in the room.'

'Ten days in a room with a beautiful girl. Might get bored.'

'Maybe I could read to you from the Gideon Bible.'

'Maybe.' He pulled down the straps of her sundress.

'Maybe I could turn on the television for you.'

'Maybe.' He turned her around and slowly lowered the zipper on her dress.

'Maybe I could learn the hula for you.' She backed against him and gently swayed her hips against his.

'Maybe.' He put his hands on her breasts as he pressed closer to her.

'Maybe we could forget everything outside this door.'

'Now you're talking.' He scooped her into his arms and carried her to the bed.

'Wake up. Wake up, Jim.' She patted his face to awaken him. She'd lain in the dark listening to thrashing and muttering for several minutes before putting an end to his dream.

'What? What?' He awoke with a jerk, sitting up in bed.

'You were having a dream.' She sat up on her knees and put her arms around him. 'You were talking in your sleep.'

'What did I say?'

'You kept talking about bins or something. You sounded angry.'

'Binh Gia.'

'What's that?'

'Just a village.'

'Let's try to get some sleep.' She kissed his forehead.

'I think I'll get up and go for a walk. I need to get some air.'

'Do you want me to go with you?'

'No, babe. I like knowing you'll be here when I get back.' He kissed her arm, just below the shoulder, and climbed out of bed.

Liz leaned against the bathroom door jamb, watching him. 'Where did you go last night?' He hadn't come back to the room until dawn. She'd been awakened by his noisy stumbling in the bathroom.

'I walked around for a while. Stopped in a bar and talked to some other guys from 'Nam.' He stood naked at the bathroom sink, shaving with a hand that seemed unsteady.

'Do you miss it?'

'What kind of question is that?' He looked at her with red, puffy eyes.

'I was just wondering if you miss it. The excitement, the rush.'

'You think it's exciting?' He looked at her as he wiped away the foam with a towel.

'I don't think it's exciting, but I thought maybe you did.'

'Why?' The air in the bathroom was thick with the smells of bourbon and cigarettes.

'Because men keep fighting wars. Little boys like to play at war and men keep going off to war. It must have some kind of pull.'

'Yeah, the excitement of having one of your men's brains blown across your face.'

'Jim, I'm sorry.'

'Is that the best you can do: you're sorry? I've killed more people than I can remember and you are sorry?' He leaned forward, his face less than six inches from hers.

'I'm on your side, Jim.' Lizzy started to back out of the small room, frightened by his words and the tensing of his long body.

'Bullshit! You think I'm a fool for being there. You think I should have gone to Canada with the other pussies and shit-heads.'

'You're scaring me.' She put her hands in front of her. 'Stop it or I'm leaving.'

'I wish it was that easy. I wish I could have left.' His breath was coming in rasping gasps. His dark skin looked grey in the bathroom's light.

'Jim?' She listened to his laboured breathing and reached out to touch him.

He pushed her hand away. 'Do you want to know about Binh Gia?'

'Do you want to tell me?'

'If I don't talk about it I'm going to burst.'

'Then talk about it, I'll listen.'

'You have to promise me you won't tell anybody else.'

'I promise, Jim.'

'No matter what I say, you won't tell?'

'If that's what you want.'

'Sit down over there.' She perched on the chair he'd pointed to and watched as he tied a towel around his waist and sat on the small sofa in the corner. In the dim light she could barely see his face.

'Let me open the drapes.' She stood and began to reach for the cord.

'No. I want it to be dark.'

'Whatever you say.' She sat back down and pulled the collar of her robe to her throat.

'It was about a month ago. I had twelve men with me. We came into a village during the middle of the day. It wasn't the village we were looking for. That village was another mile or so up the road. I don't know what happened. One of the guys saw something inside one of the huts. He fired a round and then all these people started screaming and running around.

'Somebody else panicked and started shooting. Pretty soon we were all shooting, again and again and again. We were killing everything that moved. Babies, dogs. Didn't matter. If something was already dead, we'd keep shooting till we tore it apart.' She could see his hands shaking as he held them in front of his face.

'It was like we were in a trance. Like we didn't know they were people. We killed them all. One of the guys started cutting off their ears for souvenirs. Somebody else wanted to cut the vaginas off the women, but I stopped them both.'

'Jesus.' Lizzy ran her hands down her face and listened to the blood pounding in her head. She thought she might throw up, and shut her eyes tight, trying to block the bloody picture he'd painted for her.

'They don't know it's my guys. I don't think the brass really give a fuck who did it, anyway. Probably goes on all the time.' He pushed his fingers through his short hair.

'Nobody knows so that makes it all right?' After forcing the words out, she swallowed down the burning at the back of her throat.

'Of course it doesn't make it all right. I told you because I wanted you to know what it's like. I want you to understand what I've had to do.' His words swam above the whisky and the tears. 'Can you understand?' He sniffed and ran his arm under his nose.

'I'm trying. I just can't see you doing anything like that.' Liz got up and pushed the curtains open and stared into the thin morning sunlight. 'It was your men. It wasn't you.' She turned to him and shook her head. 'I know it wasn't you!'

'It was me, that's what I'm telling you. I could have stopped them, stopped myself. I knew it was wrong, but I didn't stop it. I know I can't do anything now, but I had to talk to you. I had to talk to you, to somebody.' He leaned forward and cradled his head in his arms like a tired child.

'I'm not the one to tell. I'm not the one you need to talk to. You need to let someone know. If this could happen to you it could happen to anyone. It probably already has. How many times has this gone on over there?'

He lifted his head and looked at her. 'Do you have any idea what would happen to me? Any idea at all? I'd be court-martialled. I'd be thrown in prison and so would my men.'

'Maybe you would go to jail, but maybe you would stop it from happening again. Perhaps you could put an end to this kind of thing. It might even end the war sooner.' She walked over and knelt beside him. 'You could make something good come out of this.'

'How?'

'If people knew what was going on they'd put a stop to it.'

'Liz, you don't know what you're talking about. You still believe in fairy tales. If enough people don't like something it will go away. If something is bad, it will end. The war would end tomorrow if all the good people living their good lives knew what was going on. Bullshit! War is money. As long as enough people are making money we will be fighting the 'Cong.'

'Don't go back. We could fly to Canada tonight.' Liz watched him shake his head before she'd finished speaking.

'Out of the question. I've put six months into that hellhole. If I left I could be jailed as a deserter. I'm not going to jail over this, no way. Besides, they probably all would have died sooner or later anyway. Everybody is dying over there. We just speeded things up for them.'

'Don't talk like that. I know you don't really believe that.'

'It's the only way I can feel. It's the only thing I can believe.'

'That's not so. I think you . . .'

'I thought you'd try to understand, but you don't. I'll be lucky if you don't sell it to some fucking magazine.

'It's tempting.' The bile in her throat threatened again.

'If I thought for a minute you'd really do that I wouldn't let you leave this room.' He rose and stood behind her, putting his hands gently around the back of her neck. 'I could snap your neck and you'd never feel a thing.'

'I know you'd never hurt me.' A mere statement of fact.

'Why not? What makes you special?'

'You love me.'

'Yeah, there's always that.' He dropped his hands. 'It makes it better. You, just by being here, remind me of what I can be when it's all over. Sometimes I think about the house I'll build for you. I think about how many kids we'll have.'

'How does that help?'

'You're my anchor, Liz. I don't know what I'd do without you.'

'I'm still here, Jim. I'm still here, but I'm not someone who is going to stare adoringly at you and tell you that what happened wasn't horrible.'

'But you're going to stay?'

She looked at him for several moments before speaking. 'I'm staying. I don't understand what happened, but I know it wasn't you, it wasn't your fault.'

'Good. I couldn't take it if you saw me as some kind of monster.'

'I could never think you were a monster. The monsters are in the White House and the Pentagon.'

'Liz, I'm not a monster, but it's inside of me. The monster is inside all of us.'

'I don't believe that.'

'I hope you never have to.'

Cotherstone, West Sussex, June 15th

Dearest O,

For the first time since I got back, I'm starting to feel at home. Mum's illness made everything seem so weird, but now even that has slotted into normality. Just goes to show that you can get used to anything.

I think part of the problem has been having Gran in residence. She's the sort that people who don't have grandmothers think they want to have as grandmothers. (All white hair, pink skin, Jaeger knits, and the ability to spout clichés that sound terribly wise, unless they're examined.) Chaz and I reckon she discovered this niche about ten years ago and has been sort of a professional old lady ever since. Gran sees herself as the Queen Mum with attitude. Every chance she gets she throws in her thoughts on 'how we did things when I was a girl' and that ever-popular favourite, 'that's about the time things started to go wrong in this country'.

Great old gal and all that rot, but this isn't the best time to throw another strong personality into the pot. I adore her in small doses, but I'm not in the mood to see her at breakfast every bloody morning. Bitch, bitch, whine, whine. Oh, I'm glad I got that out of my system!

Anyway, as I said, I'm starting to feel at home again. Although things aren't exactly Alton Towers around here, we all seem a lot more relaxed. My father and brother are no longer walking around as though on eggshells, and Mum seems to have found her smile again. She feels progressively worse, but she's resigned to it now and seems to be genuinely committed to making the most of whatever time she has left.

I envy you in SF, bopping around and doing whatever. It seems like a year since I just jumped in the car and took myself off. I know it's only been a few weeks, but it seems like much longer.

I'm going to close now. Gran has gone up for an afternoon nap, so I'm going to grab Mum for a good old one-to-one.

I love you and miss you.

Mary

CHAPTER TWENTY-TWO

'They really are lovely on you. They make your eyes look terribly blue.' Liz reached over and touched the earrings her daughter wore.

'It was so sweet of Gran to think of doing this. I teased her and asked her if she wanted the earrings back if she decided to get another car.' Mary glanced at her image in the mirror over the fireplace.

'What did she say to that?'

'She said it was better not to drive because it brought out the courtly instincts in her gentlemen callers. Actually I wasn't aware she had any.'

'She hasn't. She chucked them all a year ago. It seems that these blokes have kept pace with the changing mores while your gran is still keeping the barbarian at the gate. Apparently crinkly gents like a little something to get them through the cold nights.'

'What a pity she doesn't feel the same way. I intend to die in my bed at the age of ninety-five the morning after I've thoroughly exhausted a twenty-seven-year-old professional windsurfer.'

'Poor chap. What a blow to find your aged inamorata all blue and stiff the next morning.'

'He'll recover. All kidding aside, I think Gran is closing herself off to an awful lot of what's going on. How boring to spend all your time with the family and the "girls".'

'I suppose I understand how she feels. She and your grandfather were a real love match. She feels she's had the best and doesn't mind knowing that part of her life is over. I think it's quite healthy. She has her friends and her family. She has loads of interests. The main thing is she has the life she's chosen. I suppose one can't ask for more than that.'

'I still think she could enjoy a bit of the old rumpy-pumpy on occasion. I doubt if you're going to close up shop just because you get a bit crinkly.' Mary looked at her mother and covered her mouth. 'Oh, Mummy. Oh, Mummy, I am so very sorry. I just forgot. I wasn't thinking.'

'Relax, darling.' She patted her daughter on the hand. 'I forget myself sometimes. Not for long, mind you, but sometimes.' All too true. All too painful when the truth returned and shoved aside normality and hope. Faith and future. 'It's quite extraordinary to imagine a world that doesn't include oneself. I think all of us are infants to a certain extent; we don't really believe the world existed before we did and can't imagine it without us.'

'I think you're being amazing.'

'I'm trying to be pragmatic and realistic. Since I can't change the outcome, none of us can, I can at least influence the process that takes me to the outcome.'

'Aren't you frightened? I'd be terrified. I'm absolutely terrified of death.'

'As you should be. You are young and healthy. Every bit of

your body wants to live and procreate. It would really be quite
odd if you weren't terrified by the thought.'

'But you're not old. You'll be dying much too soon.'

'Only by today's standards. Mid-forties was a relatively ripe
old age, even a hundred years ago.'

'But this isn't a hundred years ago. You should be living to
over eighty like Gran is.'

'I'm afraid I agree, but there's really no one I can complain
to. What's happened has happened and we all have to accept it.'

'I don't really understand why you're not frightened.'

'I don't really understand it myself. I'm not particularly religious, but I do feel somehow, some way, something goes on.'
Ellie had sat by her bed every night until the aunts found her,
after all. Something didn't die, not all the way. 'Besides, I feel
I've had a wonderful life, for the most part, and I've made my
bit of the world slightly better. Along with your father I've created a lovely family and my work has given enjoyment and
hopefully some food for thought to people. I've been a good
friend to some and I was recycling before it was fashionable.'

'I don't know if I should admire you or resent you.'

'You don't need to admire me, but why would you resent
me?'

'This is hard to explain. It's as though you've joined some
club I can't join. You've become a different species, not just
another person. It almost seems like you've started to leave
already. Your hand is on the doorknob and I'm still sitting in
the far corner of the room.'

'I'm sorry that's your perception of things. I don't feel that
I'm withdrawing, but perhaps if you feel that way, I am.'

'It's not really a withdrawal. That's the wrong word. It's
more as though you have become a Buddhist nun or something.
It's as though you now know things the rest of us don't. You're
in a different place and I can't follow you there.'

'I don't know anything more than I ever did, darling. Is it
possible, just possible, that you are drawing away from me? I

don't feel it, but maybe this is easier for you if you draw away from me, and one way to do that is to feel that I'm the one who is doing the pulling away. If anything I think I'm trying to hold on to everything I can. I feel as though I'm looking at everything with new eyes in many ways.'

'I think I'm really afraid of you and what's happening to you. I'm so bloody afraid that I will die before my time. What if the same thing is in me and I'm never meant to grow old either? I am so scared.' Mary put her hands to her face and began to sob.

Liz put her arms around the girl and rocked her back and forth while she hummed softly. She hummed a nursery song about long-legged rabbits and dogs with pocket watches. They fell into a swaying rhythm, and soon Mary began to hum the tune as well.

'I'm sorry about earlier. I shouldn't have let that happen.' Mary poured water from the filtering jug into the kettle.

'Don't be sorry. I want you to be able to talk about what you are feeling. If you can't say what you feel, neither can I. The worst thing you could have done is to not have told me how you feel.'

'Have you always been so wise?' Mary laughed as she rubbed at her reddened eyes.

'Am I wise? What a wonderful thing to be. I've always wanted to be wise.' Liz's hands made a fluffing motion above her head. 'Do I have a glow of wisdom around my head like the saints in an old prayer book?'

'Now you're just fishing for compliments.'

'No. Honest to God, I've always wanted to be wise. Ever since I can remember, even when I was a little kid, I knew there must be "things", profound "things" that would give me wisdom. I've been chasing wisdom forever. How fine that someone thinks I've found it.'

'How do you define wisdom? Now that we are feeling so cosmic and philosophical I think we should be on the same page.'

'I can't really define it, but I know it when it hits me in the face. I know if a person is wise or not.'

'Then who is wise?'

'Your gran is wise. I know you think she's a bit dotty and stuffy, but she's wise, nevertheless. I've seen so many things happen to her over the years and she never loses her perspective. She has a wonderful sense of grace about her.'

'I think I know what you mean, but I'm more inclined to see it as passivity. Taking what the Lord, in His own good time, presents.'

'We're all products of our time, and India is certainly no exception. She came from a time and place where she was given a very clear picture of who she was and how she fitted into the rest of the world. Be that as it may, she's created something very satisfying within the perimeters she was given. She's lived her life with style and grace. She was a wonderful wife and raised a family of solid, fairly well-adjusted people.'

'Fair enough. I'll concede Gran is wise. Who else?' Mary measured twisted dark leaves into the teapot.

'I don't think you can say whether someone is wise or not unless you know them awfully well. One would assume a Nobel Peace Prize winner is wise, but they may be the biggest git in the world. Because of that I'd have to say my Aunt Beryl was wise. Maybe Mrs Harper, but definitely Aunt Beryl.'

'Why Beryl?'

'Because she always knew what was important. She would seem very flighty and girlie, but she was wise, nonetheless.'

'Let's see: we have you, Gran and Beryl. Don't we have any men on the list?'

'I'm not sure it's really fair to put any of them on it.'

'Why not?' Mary poured milk into a jug.

'If this is my list I get to set the criteria, and the kind of wisdom I appreciate doesn't come easily to men. This had nothing to do with material success, degrees earned or any kind of record of achievements. This kind of wisdom is the sort that helps people live, die and get through the night.'

'And men can't do that?'

'Men don't want to do that. Men like to measure things and then they like to fix them. Talk to a wise man about a problem and nine times out of ten he'll tell you how to fix it. Talk to a wise woman and she'll listen to you talk until you've decided for yourself what's best.'

'You just might have something.'

'I'm glad you see my point. My kind of wisdom also demands agreement from anyone who will listen.' She grinned at her daughter and took a tin from the shelf. 'Fancy a biscuit?'

'If my choice is a bicky or more wisdom, I'll take the bicky.'

'Good choice. I'm tired of being profound.'

Clifford, California, December 1966

'It wasn't how I thought it would be.' Liz twisted the gold band with the three pearls on her left hand. Jim had asked her to wear it as a token, a promise of their future. She hadn't been able to pull it off, although she knew the years stretched ahead for her without him.

'I was wondering when you'd want to talk about it. You've been home almost a week.' Beryl carefully rolled meat and rice into a damp grape leaf, adding the finished roll to a growing pile on the kitchen table. Two and a half weeks from Christmas, Rose and Beryl's annual open house was to be held the next afternoon. Beryl, who liked themes, had decided on a Middle Eastern Christmas party. She'd been marinating lamb for two days, making the whole house reek of onions and red wine. The kitchen floor was sticky with honey and rosewater from the trays of homemade pastries.

'Jim told me about some of the things that have happened over there. I wake up in the middle of the night thinking about the things he told me. I dreamed about him last night and he was covered with blood. He was shooting this pile of bodies and screaming my name.' She stopped talking, not wanting to tell the rest of the dream. She'd been there too. The bodies were on the riverbank, by the grave. She'd tried to run away, but her clothes fell off and she stumbled. Jim picked her up and kissed her and then put his mouth to her breast. He pulled away and she could see blood, her blood, dripping from the side of his mouth. She looked down and saw blood arcing from her breasts. Jim swallowed her blood, turned grey, then melted into the dark soil of her mother's grave. She hadn't been able to sleep after that.

'Do you want to talk about what he told you?'

'I don't know if I should.' She thought of his brown hands on her neck. 'I promised him I wouldn't tell anyone. Of course, that was before I knew what he was going to tell me.'

'Whatever you tell me will go no further.' She wiped her hands on a dishcloth. 'If you don't talk about it I'm afraid it will be like dry rot: very difficult to get rid of.'

'You won't tell anyone? No matter what I say to you?'

'Lizzy, I didn't tell Rose that you went on the pill, did I? I didn't tell her you were staying in Jim's room in Hawaii, did I?' Liz and Beryl had agreed early on that Rose was best left in the dark on all matters sexual. 'If you can't trust me, who can you trust?'

'This isn't anything like that.' She looked at Beryl and tried to come to a decision. 'Jim's done some things. He's done some horrible things and I don't know if that's just what happens during war or not.'

'What kind of things, Liz?'

'I promised I wouldn't tell.'

'That's fine and that's admirable, but I've known ever since you got back that something was tearing you apart. I think you need to talk to somebody, if not me, about this.'

Liz took a deep breath and smoothed her hair off her face. 'He and his men wiped out an entire village. They killed everything that moved, even the children, tiny babies, everyone.' Liz laid her head in her arms. 'How could they have done it? How could someone like Jim do something like that? How is this possible?'

Beryl sighed and shook her head. 'I suppose everyone has read the rumours, but I've been hoping all those stories were just anti-war propaganda.'

'They're not. I'm sure Jim and his men aren't the only ones. He gave me the impression it happens all the time. He says the brass know all about it and don't care.'

'How do you feel about Jim now?'

'Part of me feels the same. I keep telling myself he's the same guy. He was always so gentle and kind with me. I tell myself when he's back, when he's home, he'll be himself again.'

'That's how part of you feels. What about the other part?'

'The other part knows he must have lost his mind. I don't see how he could have done it otherwise. I don't understand how he could even hear the rumours and not report them if he was sane. I know the rules are different during war, but this isn't even human. This is something a mad dog would have done.'

'What are you going to do?'

'What can I do?'

'You know there are a lot of things you can do. You can pretend that you never heard anything about it. You can go public with it. You can send him a "Dear John" letter and try to forget him and his story. You can stay in his life or you can leave it, the choice is yours.'

'I don't even know how I feel about him any more. Can you just stop loving someone? Could you stop loving Aunt Rose?'

'I would stop loving her if she stopped being Aunt Rose.'

'What do you mean?'

'If she did something truly, truly horrible she would cease to be Rose. She would be someone else, because we are the sum total of our actions.'

'And you would give her up?' Liz couldn't imagine the women without each other.

'Only if she, by her actions, stopped being the person I loved. I can't imagine her doing anything that horrible, but yes, I would stop loving her, at least the person she'd become. Love is not unconditional; it has limits, like everything else.'

'Do you think Jim has done that? Do you think what he did changed him that much?' She could almost smell the bourbon and cigarettes over the onions and red wine. Odours of the new Jim.

'Only you can decide that, Liz.'

'That's not what I need to hear. I want to know what you think.'

'What I think doesn't matter in the least. I'm fond of Jim, but I'm not in love with him. I'm not indifferent about him, because of the profound effect he can have on my one and only child.' She smiled at this. 'I'm quite aware that among our circle there are men who saw combat during the Second World War as well as in Korea. I have to assume some of the things they did were cruel, even horrible. War is horrible. That being said, most soldiers come home and live out their lives in a reasonable fashion.'

'Being a soldier doesn't give anyone the right to kill civilians. It doesn't give anyone the right to murder infants and old people.'

'Of course it doesn't, Lizzy. I'm not suggesting for a moment it does; however, from everything I've read and heard, the lines seem to be blurred between who is exactly who over there.'

'Are you making excuses for him?'

'No, darling, I'm not making excuses for Jim. I am making excuses for you, however.'

'For me?'

'Yes, for you. In case you still love him.'

Cotherstone, West Sussex, June 21st

Dearest O,

Just a short note today. Big excitement around here on two counts. First of all, Mother's new curtains are coming today. As if that wasn't enough, she also ordered new soft furnishings! Yes, I am a wee bit bored. Bless her cotton socks, but she has been going on about whether she chose the right colour or not since I got home. I'm so glad they are finally arriving so we can all tell her they're wonderful.

The second count is actually rather interesting. My uncle is coming to visit. He's my father's brother and a bit of a black sheep, at least according to Daddy. They had a falling-out before I was born. Nobody ever says what the problem was, so it was probably one of those stupid family things that wasn't a problem at all. My uncle is gay, or maybe bi, but my father doesn't seem to be a homophobe, so I don't think that's the problem. I've seen him a number of times through the years when he visited Gran, and I've always found him really lovely.

Anyway, he's coming for dinner. Gran has her knickers in a twist, afraid the 'boys' may not get along, but Mum seems quite relaxed about the whole thing. I'm supposedly cooking dinner, but in truth it's going to be a Marks & Sparks sort of evening.

*Well, lamby, I'm going to close and go admire the sitting room.
I love you and miss you.*

Love

Mary

*PS Can you imagine being concerned about curtains when you
are dying? She's always been rather house-proud, but this does
take the cake.*

Chapter Twenty-Three

'I like it. I like it very much.' Mary stood in the doorway,
admiring the new curtains and soft covers. 'I think it will take
me a while to get used to all the yellow.'

'It is a bit bright, isn't it?' Liz reached over and plumped a
cushion on the settee where she sat. 'I feel a bit as if I'm sitting
inside a daffodil. I just hope the colour doesn't reflect off our
skin. We could all end up looking as though we suffer from
jaundice.'

'We won't look jaundiced, we will just glow. Actually, the
colour suits you nicely. How do you feel today?'

'Tired, but if I took to my bed every time I felt tired, my feet
would never touch the ground.'

'I just don't want you to push yourself.'

'Afraid I'll get run down and take ill?' She adjusted the reading glasses on her nose and peered over the rims at her
daughter.

'You and your gallows humour. I worry about you.'

'And well you might.' Liz patted the spot next to her. 'Sit

down and chat with me while I work on this.' She held up a piece of *petit point*. 'If I don't have someone to talk to I'll be tempted to turn on one of those awful American chat shows. That truly trashy one is on this afternoon.'

'Which one is that?'

'I can never remember her name. Skinny, dark hair. She always has lots of in-bred people who live in trailer parks and have tattoos.'

'Joni Clarke.'

'That's the one. Horrible stuff. I love it.'

'I know what you mean. Do you suppose people make that kind of thing up so they can have their fifteen minutes on the tube?'

'Unfortunately, no. Some of it reminds me of my own background. There but by fortune go I.'

'I can't imagine you bearing your soul on the Joni Clarke show.'

'Neither can I. Actually, I'd like to go on it just so I could tell them all to get over it and get a life. I get so annoyed with the people she parades in front of the camera. It's nothing but a modern-day freak show. Frankly, it was more honest when people paid their money to stare at the Fat Lady and JoJo the Dog-faced Boy.'

'But you still watch the show?'

'Every chance I get. Can't stop myself, it's like watching snakes.' She grinned at Mary and tossed her needlework on the table. 'Want to see it today?'

'Sure. What channel?'

'I don't know, you'd better check the paper.'

'Now, you're certain you want to watch this?' Mary picked the newspaper off the table.

'Why not? We can have a good time taking the piss out of everyone on the show.'

'Aren't you the one who's always told us that now was the most important time in our lives?'

'Of course that's what I told you when you were a child. That was my job.'

'But?'

'But sometimes I lied. Personally, I think there's a great deal to be said for the banal pleasures. Something almost spiritual about wasting a bit of time. We're not ants or bees, after all.'

'Now you tell me.' Mary picked up the remote and turned the television on.

'I had to wait until you finished university. If I'd told you sooner you might have spent the whole time watching *Neighbours*.'

'That was singularly unsatisfying. What a waste of trash telly.' Liz picked up the remote control and turned off the set.

'Only in America would they hold a contest for the sexiest firefighter.' Mary stretched her arms above her head and yawned.

'Don't be so smug. You Brits with your Blackpools and Page Three Girls! Maybe you've impressed the rest of the world with your art and institutions, but I've lived here long enough to know the tawdry truth.'

'Oh, poo and piffle. You are English in everything but birth. You're no more American than Daddy any more.'

'I'd like to disagree, but you may have a point there. When I left I was so eager to start afresh I didn't try very hard to hang on to my "heritage". Not that much of it was worth hanging on to.'

'I don't think I could ever do what you did. It was enough of a wrench for me to be gone for six months, and I'm several years older than you were at the time.'

'Mary, you have to understand I wasn't really an eighteen-year-old by then. I had stopped being a child years before. Apart from the aunts and Mrs Harper, I had no ties whatsoever.'

'That's my point exactly. The only personal connections you had were in California.'

'They were my only connections, but they were connections to a life I didn't want to live any more. Of course I still loved the women dearly, but I felt I had to "get out of Dodge". I desperately wanted to leave the country. The war changed everything for so many of us.'

'Was it just the war?'

'For me, at least, it started with the war. I remember when I was much younger, one of my anchors was the government. The presidents were my father figures to a certain extent. I couldn't trust my mother, but I could trust Eisenhower, and later Kennedy. These were people I believed to be concerned with my welfare. They cared about me and my generation. I know that sounds terribly naïve, but that's how I and, I think, many young people felt. We grew up proud to be Americans.'

'What was it about the war that changed all of that?'

'I can only tell you how I felt. To me, the war was clearly a tribal conflict we had no part in. I watched it become an American war every night on television. The government seemed oblivious to the fact that our young men were dying for a cause that the American people didn't support. It flew in the face of everything I'd been taught about the way my country was supposed to function. Of course the last straw was what happened to Jim. After that I jumped at the chance to leave the country.'

'I can certainly understand being angry about government policy. I'm mad every time I pick up *The Times*, but I don't think I'd ever be so upset that I would pack up and leave my home. When you left, did you think it was forever?'

'No. I didn't realize that until I looked into your father's eyes.' Liz put the back of her hand to her forehead in a mock swoon.

'Bollocks!'

'Of course it is, but it's what he likes to think.'

'I'm surprised you didn't make straight for Uncle Tarquin. He's certainly better looking than Daddy.'

'He's also gay.'

'He's bi.'

'Trust me, he's a lot more gay than bi.'

'I take it he's discussed this with you?'

She nodded. 'In spite of the schism between the brothers, Tarquin and I have remained friends.' In spite of everything, she was tempted to add.

Clifford, California, April 1967

Not surprisingly, the editor had been receptive. She half hoped he wouldn't like the idea, but her first articles had been very well received. He'd even hinted at a more permanent arrangement after graduation. 'A fresh voice' he'd called her.

It had taken less than twenty-four hours to write. She sat down at the typewriter at seven on Saturday morning and put it aside on Sunday morning at four. She ate a sandwich and went to bed. She awoke on Monday morning with a headache and a stiff neck. Without getting out of bed, she reached for the article and reread it for the third time. After climbing out of bed, she rummaged in her desk for an envelope which she quickly addressed and sealed.

'It lives. I told you she was alive, Beryl.' Aunt Rose sat at the kitchen table with the morning paper and a cup of coffee. Beryl was frying eggs at the stove. She read the paper later at the library because she knew how much Rose liked to start the day with a hearty breakfast.

'Morning. Thanks for letting me sleep. I didn't get to bed until almost dawn on Sunday.' She filled a mug with hot coffee and took a quick sip of the steamy liquid.

'We knew that you had your senior thesis to work on, so we've tried to stay out of your way.' Beryl smiled at her. 'Bacon and eggs, dear?'

'Not this morning, Aunt Beryl. I'm not really hungry.' Not hungry, but aware of her hip bone pressing into the kitchen counter as she leaned against it. The emptiness felt good and right.

'You should really eat something, Liz. Breakfast is the most important meal of the day.' Beryl held up the carton of eggs as though Liz might find the cardboard an inducement to eat.

'Leave the girl alone, Beryl. She can always get something to eat before class.' Rose looked towards Liz. 'When is your first class? I thought you had an early class on Monday.'

'I do, but I'm going to skip it this morning.'

'Aren't you feeling well, dear?' Beryl put the eggs down on the counter.

'I have to go to the post office and mail something off to *Pacific*. I promised them I would have it in the mail by today.'

'I can run it by on my lunch hour if you like. No need for you to skip class.' Rose put the paper aside.

'Thanks, Aunt Rose, but I want to walk to the post office with this. It's hard to explain, but I want to be sure I'm doing the right thing. If I walk to the post office it will give me time to think about it.' She'd thought of little else for over four months, but still absolute assurance stayed just out of reach.

'Think about what?' Rose looked at Beryl and shrugged her shoulders.

'I've written an article. It's about Jim and the things he's seen and the things he's done. I've changed the names to protect him, but I'm still not sure I should send it.' She put her cup down. 'That's a lie. I know I shouldn't send it. I promised him I'd keep quiet. Changing names doesn't change anything.'

'What are you talking about, Liz?' Rose turned to Beryl. 'Hon, do you know what she's talking about?'

'Aunt Rose, Jim and his men did something horrible. I promised him I wouldn't tell anyone the things he told me.'

'So that's what you were doing this weekend?' Beryl moved the pan off the stove as she glanced at Rose.

'I wrote down everything he told me. I wrote it just the way he told me and then I wrote how I feel about him now. I wrote about this stupid little pearl ring and how he still sits around thinking about names for our children. I wrote about the house he thinks he's going to build for me and how he thinks I'll be able to forget what he's become.' Liz rubbed at her temples. 'I wrote it all down because I couldn't think of anything else to do. I don't know what's going to happen if they publish it just the way I wrote it.

'Liz, if you don't want it published, just write it in your own journal. You don't have to publish it.' Rose lit her first cigarette of the day.

'I do. I do have to publish it. There are lots of girls who feel the way I do. Everybody seems to have forgotten about us. Those boys go off and they come back with horrible stories and horrible scars and they still expect us to love them. The whole society expects us to love them. There's supposed to be something sacred about your feelings for a soldier. All I know is I fell in love with this nice guy and now I'm expected to keep loving him, no matter what he's done, no matter how much he's changed. I can't do that. I can't love someone who could do that to another human being.'

'I don't know what Jim has done, but let's for a moment assume it's as bad as you think it is.' Rose pulled out the chair next to her and motioned Liz towards the seat.

'It is that bad, and then some.'

'OK, he did something horrible. What good is it going to do to publish it?'

'The American public has a right to know what's happening to the men who are going over there. The American people need to know what is happening to all those men. They need to start thinking about what's going to happen when those men come home.'

'Terrible things happen in every war, Liz. War is terrible and soldiers do terrible things. Did you think Jim was going over there to help little old ladies across the street? He is an army officer. His job is to win the war. I know it's not a popular war, but he is doing the job he's been assigned. Soldiers do not have much choice when it comes to war.'

'He's been butchering people. He and his men went into a village and shot up everything that moved. Old people, babies, everyone.'

Rose sat back in her chair and sighed. 'Back to my original question: why publish it? What is going to be helped by this thing being published?'

'If I keep a secret it stays on my conscience, and I don't think I can live with that. I've lived with it for months and it's making me nuts. I can't keep it in any longer.'

'And Jim? What about him? Are you willing to betray him so you can get it off your chest?'

'I don't think he's really faced what he's done. He's been over there for months and things like this seem normal to him. If he sees it in black and white maybe he'll understand that he can't cover this up any longer. He'll see that he has to admit to what he's done.'

'And even if he doesn't, at the very least you'll feel better?'

'What would be so bad about that? Would it be so awful if for once I could get rid of some of the junk that's been dumped on me? I'm tired of being the keeper of everybody's secrets.

'First it was my mother: I couldn't let anybody know she was a drunk and a whore. Then it was the two of you. Outside this house I have to pretend that you two are just good chums. And now, just to top things off, I have to pretend that Jim is some kind of war hero instead of a mass murderer. I'm sick of it. Where is it written that I can't be honest, that I can't tell the truth about what I know?' She watched as Beryl turned towards the sink and Rose stubbed out her cigarette.

'I'm sorry our relationship has been a problem for you.' Rose poured more coffee into her cup and looked at Liz.

'I'm sorry, I didn't really mean that. You know I love you both.'

'But?'

'But it's been another secret. Before everything happened I always felt that worrying was my job. My mother never seemed concerned enough about us to worry and I decided it was my job. When I came here I realized I might be sent away if anybody knew, if anybody found out . . .'

'That we are lesbians, dykes, queers?'

'Rose!' Beryl turned towards the pair, but Rose signalled her to silence.

'I guess that's what I meant.'

'Has our relationship compromised you in any way' Rose lit another cigarette, her hand shaking slightly.

'No. I've worried about your being found out, but it hasn't had an effect on me otherwise.'

'Then it's none of your affair, is it?'

'No, I suppose it isn't.' Liz rose to leave the table.

'Sit down. I'm not done with you yet.'

'I said I was sorry.'

'Apology accepted. I don't think you've understood what I'm getting at.'

'Which is?' Embarrassed, Liz hoped the linoleum would open up and suck her out of the bright kitchen.

'You can walk away from the two of us. We share a secret that you agree has not compromised you. You have no right to betray us because we haven't hurt you.' She took a deep drag at her cigarette and blew the smoke out through her nose. 'Are you with me so far?'

'Yes.'

'Jim told you a secret. You agreed to keep it a secret. Tell me what right you have to betray him.'

'What he did was wrong. Horribly wrong. If it's kept a secret it's more likely to happen again. If I ignore what I know then I'm as guilty as he is.'

'Do you want to know what I think?'

'Yes, Aunt Rose, I do.' She held on to the back of her chair, braced for the woman's anger.

'I think you need to get going because the post office opens in ten minutes. You should still have time to make your second class if you hurry.'

Cotherstone, West Sussex, June 29th

Dearest Oliver,

Received the photos and they made me so anxious to see you. I found myself following a ginger-haired man down the street yesterday because he reminded me of you. Don't worry, I didn't follow him very far.

You'll be thrilled to know that Mum's curtains are a huge success. I frankly don't know how much longer she'll be able to enjoy them. She's been in a lot of pain this week and is spending more and more time in bed. Their bedroom is at the top of a flight of narrow stairs and those are difficult to navigate too. I think we'll move a hospital bed into the conservatory for her. That way she can still feel as if she's in the middle of things. I haven't quite got up the courage to discuss it with her, but I would certainly prefer that to having her tucked up in a bedroom away from everyone else.

Dinner with my uncle was rather bizarre. Funny, we're not the sort of family that usually does bizarre. Strictly roast and three veg for dinner, that's us. Clearly bones were being gnawed that evening, but they weren't the ones on the M & S roast chicken. Daddy and Uncle were saying terribly polite things to each other, but it was like watching one of those old Italian movies about Hercules that have been dubbed into English. The words were somehow out of sync. The smiles were in all the wrong places.

Gran was a nervous wreck and kept chattering like a magpie. Uncle kept looking at Mum and then over to me. Every time I'd look up he would be staring at me while pretending he wasn't. After dinner we all had coffee in the garden and he got real matey with Chaz and started kicking the old ball around. We three fems kept surreptitiously looking at Daddy to see if all that athletic muscularity was offensive, but he didn't seem to mind.

Mother was warm and gracious, but she looked like hell and I insisted on making it an early evening because of her. Nobody objected, even though Mum suggested Uncle stay the night in spite of her need to go upstairs.

I couldn't put my finger on what was wrong, I just know something was. Oh well, at least now we can say that the black sheep is back in the fold. Sort of. Gran is pretending it was a great night and the rest of us just smile at her.

I've decided normality is one of the most underrated things on this green earth. Oh, the joy of having some idea as to what tomorrow will bring! I'm not sure I'll ever trust or believe in normality again, but I'm looking forward to giving it a try.

I love you and miss you. I like the boring way you dress. You are so normal.

Love

Mary

CHAPTER TWENTY-FOUR

'Since Daddy's going to be in France tonight, shall we rent a video?' Mary came into the room carrying the morning's mail.

'You can certainly rent one if you like, but your father has cancelled his trip.' Liz put her hand out for the letters. 'Anything interesting in the post?'

'Just the usual. Why did he cancel his trip? Just last week he was saying that we were low on plonk and it was a good thing he was scheduled to go over this week.'

'We talked about it last night and he's decided not to do any travelling for a while.' Liz tossed the small pile of mail on to the table.

Mary slowly sat in the chair facing her mother. 'Is there anything I don't know?'

'We just decided it would be a good idea for him to be around.' She looked at her daughter for a moment before lowering her eyes. 'I'd like to have all of you around me as much as I can. I'm going to miss you all so much.' She put her hand over her eyes. 'Oh, shit, shit, shit. I didn't want to do this, not to you. I was doing this last night to your poor father.' She wiped at her cheeks with her hands. 'I just don't want to leave. I want to grow old and be a grandmother. I'd like to be a great-grandmother. I want to get wrinkly skin and have bosoms that hang down around my waist. I haven't even had a chance to get any white hair.'

'Is there anything, anything at all I can do?'

'Just stay as close to me as you can. God, that sounds so needy. I keep thinking about my mother and how she died alone. Almost unmourned, for that matter. I think I'm terrified of being alone.'

'You won't be alone.'

'I've been trying so hard to keep my wits about me, but this morning I feel as if I'm standing on the edge of a cliff. I feel as if there's a black hole waiting to suck me down, and once it does, I'll be gone. I will never know what happens to any of you, and that's the worst part of all.' Liz leaned back against the cushions. 'The party isn't nearly over, but I'm being kicked out of the gate.'

'We're all pretty sturdy, you made sure of that. We're never going to stop missing you, but we're going to be fine.' Mary's voice caught and she licked the tears off her upper lip. 'Does that help at all?'

Liz nodded. 'I hate to leave things unfinished, and there are still so many things I need to do as a mother. Promise me that you'll remember my voice if you need me. Maybe it's just vanity, but I want to be remembered. I don't want to disappear like my mother and sister.'

'I promise you'll be remembered.'

'Try not to remember me like this.'

'What do you mean?'

'I want you to always think of me in my prime. I want you to think about me when I was still strong and pretty. I don't want you to remember me being the way I am now. Not emaciated and weepy.'

'You're still beautiful and I think you're very strong.' She gathered her mother in her arms.

Clifford, California, May 1967

'Liz! Telephone for you!' Mrs Harper yelled for the girl out of the screen door. The old woman had grown increasingly hard of hearing and hated to wear a hearing aid. To compensate she'd taken to shouting whenever she spoke.

'Coming.' Liz raised her voice to just short of a shout in hope the woman would hear.

She hurried into the house, smacking the cat with the door as she entered. 'Sorry, cat.' She picked up the handset. 'Hello.'

'Elizabeth Sinclair?' The voice was young and male.

'Speaking.' Liz assumed as soon as she heard the voice that it was another military recruiter. They had the lists of everyone graduating this spring. The draft took care of the grunts, but they were always trawling the campuses for officer material. Sending the young male officers to Vietnam had created vacancies stateside which the recruiters were hoping to fill with young women. She'd told the last two recruiters who called that she was a lesbian. It annoyed Rose and Beryl, but it got the recruiters off the line.

'Liz, my name is Mike Halford. I'm with the *Chronicle* and I know you've done some very good articles for *Pacific*. I've been reading your stuff and it gets stronger all the time.'

'Thank you. I really appreciate hearing that.' Liz tried to keep the excitement out of her voice, and instead rose on the balls of her feet and did a little dance. She'd submitted a piece to the *Chronicle* just the week before for their weekend magazine. She'd heard that phone calls were almost always good news for writers.

'I'm especially interested in this article you've done for them about the massacre. A friend of mine gave me an advance copy and it's very powerful stuff. I wanted to be the first to congratulate you.'

'I didn't write anything about a massacre. The last piece I did for them was about "Another Mother For Peace". It was in the May issue.' The editor had assured her of anonymity.

'Elizabeth Sinclair? You've had five articles published by them?'

'That's right, but only the five.'

'Nothing to be ashamed of kiddo. The sixth is your best one. As I said, you keep getting better and better. You should be especially proud of this last one.'

'Since I don't know what you're talking about, I can't be very proud of it, can I?' Liz leaned against the wall. One hundred per cent anonymity. The bastard had promised. Said he'd be the only one in the organization to know. 'I'm sorry, I don't think I caught your name a minute ago.' She'd caught it, but wanted some time to think.

'Mike, Mike Halford.'

'Mr Halford, I'm really glad you called. I can't tell you how much it means that you like my work. I wish I could help you,

I really do, but I didn't write anything about a massacre. I know it sounds like I'm trying to get rid of you, but I've got finals coming up in two weeks and I've got a million things to do right now.' She heard her voice beginning to rise, beginning to sound shrill.

'I keep forgetting you're still a student. Makes your stuff even more impressive, I know what those last few weeks are like. I graduated just a few years ago myself. Listen Liz, just tell me how I can get to talk to this girl in the article. I need to talk to the girl you quote. I want to talk to her directly and confirm the things she told you. We've been hearing these rumours for months, but up until now, I've been chasing air on this one.'

'I'm sorry to disappoint you Mr Halford, but you're still chasing air on this one. I don't know anything about a girl or a massacre. I didn't write the piece and I can't help you.'

'It was a funny thing. I started talking to my buddy at *Pacific* and he mentioned that you actually have a boyfriend in 'Nam. Second lieutenant, I think he said. In fact, he said you went over to Hawaii for his R and R. I still haven't been to Hawaii. Did you have a good time when you were there?'

'Listen, I don't know where you get off or who . . .'

'Liz, I've done my homework. It was actually pretty easy to put two and two together and figure out you were the girl. Besides, you have a fairly distinctive style. That's a good thing, by the way. Serve you well if you want to make a career in this business.'

'I'm hanging up now.' Liz began to pull her ear away from the receiver.

'I'm coming to Clifford this afternoon. Talk to me half an hour and I'll never bother you with this again.'

'You'll never bother me again, but you'll give my name out? I'm supposed to trust this, trust you?'

'Cooperate with me and your name stays out of it. You can trust me. The only reason I got your name out of *Pacific* was because my friend knew I could be trusted.'

'Honour among thieves?'

'Come on, Liz. You're one of the club. You know we have to stick together to get the stories out.'

'I'm not a member of your club.'

'Good as. You've got the talent and I could help you expand your contacts.'

'The next thing I write is going to be fiction. Seems safer.' As the words were spoken she realized she'd confirmed his suspicions.

'Listen, I should be in Clifford in about three, three and a half hours. I'll give you a call and you can decide where we meet.'

'Right.' She decided she'd be in the university's library in three hours.

'Oh, one other thing.'

'What's that?'

'This story is my story whether you talk to me or not. I just want to make that clear from the get-go. If you want to keep your name out of this, if you want to keep his name out of this, if you want any control at all, you'll meet me today. Understand?'

'Perfectly.' She slammed the receiver down and banged the back door against the side of the house as she went out.

She slipped off her leather sandals and pulled on a pair of worn sneakers. After a quick wave to Mrs Harper, she went to the front of the house and began to run along the road towards the river.

She'd left a stone every time she'd visited. Some of the pebbles and stones would always get moved, but enough would be left for her to find the grave amongst the rutted tracks and exposed tree roots on the riverbank. She scoured the bank until she found a piece of quartz studded with pyrite. The fool's gold that had disappointed so many. Liz placed it on top of what she hoped was the mason jar and sat next to the quartz, her arms hugging her knees.

It started softly at the back of her throat. She closed her eyes and hummed the tune a little louder. The shrimp boats were a-coming with their cargo of ghosts and shattered lives. Their sails were in sight. She smiled to herself as she gently rocked herself back and forth. Ellie was dancing now. Dancing at the water's edge and kicking tiny drops of water into the air towards Laura.

Laura stood at the riverbank, slight and dainty in a beautiful green dress which she held away from the silver drops of water. She tossed her head, shaking the long dark hair as she laughed that quicksilver laugh of hers. Her slim face was bright with the pleasure of being with her daughters on a sunlit day in May.

Liz hummed, then whispered the words until her throat burned and her temples throbbed. She opened her eyes reluctantly, knowing they would leave as soon as the song was over. They always did.

'I'm glad you decided to meet me, Liz. Appreciate what you're doing and I want you to know you can trust me completely.' Mike Halford leaned across the formica table at the Koffee King and gave Liz a smile that reminded her of a dentist who was about to drill a tooth.

'"Said the spider to the fly." I don't think I can trust you or anyone else about this. You got me here by threatening me. Maybe it's just me, but I don't think things have gotten off to a terribly good start.'

'Threaten you? How did I threaten you? I just said the story gets written. I'm doing you a favour by giving you a chance to tell your side now.' He had the smooth, pink face of a prepubescent boy, but his fine brown hair was already being combed across his scalp to disguise a large bald patch.

'I don't want my name in this. I don't want his name in this. I want to finish my degree and go to sleep for three months. I don't want any part of this and I don't want to talk to you.'

'Then let's agree to make it as painless as possible. You answer my questions and we both go home. Now, when does your second louie come home?'

'His tour ends in August.'

'Then what?'

'He's got three more years of his commitment after that.'

'No, I mean what happens to the two of you? I'm looking for the human angle on this.' He turned away from her and signalled for the waitress. 'Do you want coffee?'

'Yeah, thanks.'

'Miss? Miss! We need two coffees over here, please.' The waitress, her hands filled with plates, tucked her chin and glared at him.

'Great. You did real well there. Now we'll be lucky if we get served in the next twenty minutes.'

'What? What did I do?' He held his hands palms up and looked around him.

'I don't know how they do things in San Francisco, but in this place you don't yell at the waitresses. They know we're here, they saw us come in and sit down. They'll get to us as soon as they can. Look around you. It's only Vera and her daughter, for God's sake. Ever since Phil had his heart attack they haven't been able to hang on to a cook for more than a month. A little common courtesy goes a long way. You should try it sometime.' It felt good to gnaw on his bones and watch him wince. She thought about kicking him in the shins, just for good measure.

'How was I supposed to know about Vera and Phil? All I wanted was a lousy cup of coffee.'

'Vera said hello to us when we came in. You should have been able to figure out from that that she was fully aware of our presence. I think you just like throwing your weight around with the hicks. God's gift to journalism.' She paused for breath. 'And for what it's worth, you don't get a lousy cup of coffee here. Their coffee is very good and they are quite proud of it.'

'OK, OK. Now just listen to me.'

'I'm listening. You've got ten minutes and not a second more.' Liz glanced at her wrist and hoped he wouldn't notice that she wasn't wearing a watch.

'You wrote an article. You wrote a good article. As I told you on the phone, I've been hearing rumours about this kind of thing for over a year. I just wanted to talk to you about what you've been told.'

'What I know is in the article.'

'Not quite. You don't mention any names, of people or places. I need to know some specifics. I need some details.'

'I don't have any details. You've read the article and that's it.'

'You can't just walk away from this. You have an obligation. You have information about war crimes committed by American servicemen.'

'I'd be willing to bet a lot of people have the same information. You know that's true because you told me yourself you've been hearing rumours for over a year.'

'I told you over the phone I was going to use this, with or without your cooperation. Just listen to me for a minute. This is big stuff you're sitting on. And I'm not talking about some article in the *Chronicle*. That's just the start. Things like this win Pulitzers, for Christ's sake. We might be talking about collaboration on a book. With what you know, I think we could get a book deal that would keep both of us in the chips for a few years. Wouldn't you like to graduate next month with a nice publishing contract under your cap and gown?'

'No, I don't think I want that at all. At least not this way. I never should have written that piece. I betrayed someone who loves and trusts me because it made me feel important. It made me feel important to think I could have a hand in changing the war. I kept telling myself I had no right to keep this kind of secret and I kept telling myself it might help end the war.' She slid out of the booth and stood up. 'It's not going to change a thing. The only thing that's changed is me. I used to be a better person.'

'Sit down and we'll talk about this.'

'I'm not going to talk to you or anyone else. You go chase your story and sell your newspapers. You go ahead and make everything cut and dried and forget about decent people. Forget about decent people who have been put in terrible situations that are beyond their control. I'm going to go back home and write a letter to the "second louie" and tell him what I've done. It's too late to change anything, but at least he'll hear it from me and not have to read about it.'

'Liz, sit down.'

'No. There is nothing, I repeat nothing, for us to talk about. Articles. Mine, yours, anybody's, nothing but stupid words that don't change anything.'

'I suspect you've forgotten what a little pond you're swimming in.' He lit a cigarette and looked up at her.

'What do you mean?'

'I mean it's a small world. I have friends at *Pacific*, *Time*, *Life*, you name it. This is a tight little industry, you might even say it's incestuous. I can help you. The *Chronicle* can help you.'

'What are you talking about?'

'I can get you on at the *Chronicle*. If you don't like the idea of being tied down, I can put you on to enough editors to keep you in freelance work for the next five years.'

'I don't need your help. I've done just fine without it.'

'Don't be so sure about that. As I said, this is a tight little group. You get a reputation as somebody who uses iffy sources, somebody who writes things that can't be substantiated, and pretty . . .'

'And I'll never work in this town again? What crap. I may be from a small town, but I don't buy that for a second. You are nothing but a hack and we both know it.'

'Listen . . .'

'No, you listen to me. I am so glad you came down today because you made me see just exactly what I could become if I join your "tight little group" of vermin. I could end up not giving a damn about anything but seeing my name in print. I could learn to chew people up and spit them out to sell a crummy piece of paper that is nothing but damned fish wrap the next day.'

'Don't ever say I didn't warn you. Don't say I didn't give you a chance to change your mind.'

'I deserve whatever happens to me.' She turned to Vera who was bringing two cups of coffee to the table. 'Don't give him anything, Vera. He's been sitting here the whole time making cracks about the way you spell "koffee".'

Cotherstone, West Sussex, July 11th

Dear Oliver,

I loved hearing your voice the other night. I loved it and hated it. I so wanted to drop everything and get the first flight out of here. Bad daughter. I am so tired of all this. It only gets worse. Things get worse every bloody day and the horrible thing is, I know I'll look back on this as the good part in a few days or weeks.

I'm feeling quite down this morning. My mother's beautiful conservatory has been turned into a hospital room. We've installed one of those mechanical beds as well as all that other ugly stuff that goes with it. She has one of those tray tables and in the garage we have stowed a commode chair. I can't bear the thought of her needing to use that.

Four days ago she started needing morphine. Daddy and I give her the injections. I thought I would vomit the first time, and now it's just another bit of housekeeping. Amazing what one can get used to.

I know this is a lousy letter. My world has become almost as small as hers. I've started watching Neighbours *again, twice a day. I'm watching Australian soaps because things like* Coronation Street *and* EastEnders *are a little too true to life and I've got enough reality in my life right now.*

*I love you and miss you. I wish you were here and I'm glad
you're not. I'm losing my mind.*

Love

Mary

CHAPTER TWENTY-FIVE

'You have to try. Everything here is soft and easy to swallow.'
Mary put the plate on the tray table and made a minute adjustment to the bed's position.

'Thank you, darling, but everything tastes like cardboard. I'm
sure it's all fine, but my taste buds aren't working today.' She
absent-mindedly petted the cat, who had taken up residence on
her bed. Patch rarely left the doorway leading into the room.

'How about something to drink? I've got some of those sup-
plemental drinks in the fridge.'

'I'm fine, really. Why don't you just sit and keep me company?'

'Are you sure that's all I can do for you?' Mary removed the
tray and set it on the bedside table.

'That's why I want you to sit; there is something I want to
talk to you about. There's a project I want you to do, but I'm
not sure you'll want to do it.'

'There's only one way to find out.'

'I'm not going to be able to finish this book and I'd like your
help with it. I want you to write the last third for me.'

'That's a wonderful idea. You dictate and I'll do the inputting
for you.'

'That's not really what I had in mind. I'm afraid I can't

concentrate enough to dictate much of anything. What with the drugs and all I simply can't cope with the work any more. I'd like you to actually write it. I've got the outline, so it shouldn't be too hard.

'Mum, I'm not a writer.'

'Only because you've never tried. The hard part is already done. Since it's a sequel, the main characters are already established and the thing is already plotted.' Almost plotted. She hadn't decided on an ending.

'Won't that be awkward, to change "voice" in midstream?'

'That's why I'd like you to try. We are so much alike, I know you could do it, and very well, at that.'

'Is it that important, to have it finished? You said yourself it wasn't the kind of thing you really wanted to write.'

'It's not the kind of thing I wanted to write, but it is the kind of thing I do, or did, write. It's not the great, transcendent novel I always wanted to write, but I suppose that was never a realistic aim for me anyway. I always joked about wanting to win the Booker, but the truth is, it wasn't a joke. I would have loved a Booker, but I'm not that good, never was. I'm a storyteller, not an artist.'

'I've always loved your stories.'

'I'm glad you've enjoyed them and I hope they stay in print for a while. I want you to make sure to get lots of copies so all my grandchildren and great-grandchildren can read them. If I can't know them, at least they can know a little something about me through my work.' She chuckled slightly. 'I never realized how terribly vain I was until this happened. I've become obsessed about being remembered.'

'Mum, you're going to feel a little stronger. The weather is improving and that always cheers you up. I bet by the end of the week you'll feel like dictating the book yourself. Let's just not worry about it for a few days.'

'Mary, it's going to take more than a few sunny days to make me feel better. I'm dying and I'm not going to be around much longer. I feel weaker and smaller every day. I have become so self-centred it takes all my effort to think about anything beyond this rotting body of mine. It's a supreme effort to remember to enquire after anything other than when the sister is coming to bath me.'

'I'll try to finish the book. I can't make any promises, but I'll try.'

'Good. Thank you. I'm glad I don't have to worry about it any more.'

'Now, how about something to drink?'

'Later, darling. I think I should sleep now. If I sleep I can be alert when your father comes home. I know he worries about the way I nod off.'

'Ring if you need anything,' She placed a small silver bell next to her mother's bed and kissed the top of her head.

Clifford, California, June 1967

Liz ran to the mailbox before the car had a chance to stop. 'Hi, Ken.' She waved and stuck her hand out for the mail.

'Hey, Lizzy. Waiting for something special?' He winked in mock flirtation. Ken, a grandfather of five, was retiring next year.

'Yeah, I'm waiting for a "Dear Jane" letter.' She smiled at the old man as she looked eagerly at the mail in his hand.

'Then I'm going to have to disappoint you, sweetheart.' He handed her the pile of magazines and advertisements. 'Nothing from that young man of yours today, Liz. I'll bet he's too excited about coming home to write about it. What's he got, just a month? The day I got home from the Philippines and saw Thursa standing at the dock was the happiest day of my life.'

'Thanks, Ken. See you tomorrow.' She waved him off and turned and walked towards the house, muttering under her breath, 'Bet Thursa didn't write an article with enough crap in it to get you court-martialled ten times over.'

'Mail's here.' She tossed the stack on the hall table.

'Hear anything from Jim yet?' Rose picked up the mail and began to thumb through it.

'Not a word. I wish he'd get it over with. I'll feel a lot better after he's told me what a terrible person I am and how much he hates me. The suspense is killing me. I hate waiting for the other shoe to drop.' She clawed her hair into a rough braid at the back of her neck.

'Maybe he'll understand. After all, he wanted to talk about it, too.'

'He needed to talk about it, he didn't need to spread it across the pages of a magazine like I did.'

'Lizzy, regret is the most useless emotion in the world. What's done is done. Concentrate on your finals. That's something you can do something about.'

'I suppose you're right. I'll try to put it out of my mind, but until I hear from Jim I think I'm going to be a basket case.'

'Things tend to end with a whimper rather than a bang. He'll probably never even answer your letter. Even though the *Chronicle* wrote about it, they didn't mention names, and I doubt if the powers that be care enough about a bunch of Vietnamese villagers to do anything about it.'

'You might be right. I keep expecting a knock on the door from the military, but that hasn't happened, at least not yet. I guess I'll just have to wait and see about everything.' Liz pulled aside the curtains at the sound of gravel in the driveway. 'Who do we know who drives a white Lincoln?'

Rose glanced out of the window. 'Looks like something a pimp would drive.' A tall man untangled his legs and climbed out of the car.

'He looks familiar. Oh God, it's Honest Jack, Jim's dad.'

'You said you were waiting for the other shoe to drop.'

'I thought he would send me hate mail. I never expected him

to send his father to beat me up.'

'Don't be ridiculous. Besides, I could take him.'

Liz glanced at Rose to see if she was kidding, but she looked deadly serious as she clenched her fists. 'I think I'd better let him in.'

'Do you want me to stay in the room with you? Just in case you're right and he tries something crazy?'

'No, don't stay in the room.' She bit her lip as she watched the man approaching the house with his head down. 'Why don't you wait in the kitchen, with the door open. I know it's silly, but I think I'd feel better if I knew you were there.'

'You've got it, girlie.' Rose walked into the kitchen, leaving herself a view of the front of the house.

Liz opened the front door and watched as the man climbed the half-dozen steps to the porch. He wore black trousers and a white Western-cut shirt with a bolo tie. On television he always wore a cowboy hat, but now his head was uncovered. Honest Jack had thick silver hair that matched the silver thunderbird on his bolo tie.

'Miss Sinclair?' He made a motion of tipping his hat, which he seemed to have forgotten he wasn't wearing. His voice cut the air with the twang distinctive to the Central Valley.

'That's right, and you're Jack Wolters.' She was aware of the lack of twang in her own voice. Mrs Harper had made certain that she didn't use the Okie vowels she'd heard from her mother.

'May I come in, ma'am?'

'Of course, please.' She moved aside and motioned him into the front room. 'Have a seat. Would you like some coffee, or maybe something cold?'

'No, but thank you.' He sat on the edge of the chair. A surprisingly dainty gesture for such a tall, angular man. 'This is a nice place.'

'Thank you. It's nice to finally meet you.' Liz sat in a chair several feet away. 'Of course, I feel like I've known you for years, from seeing you on the television, that is.' She stifled a nervous giggle.

'Can I call you Liz?' He looked at her, and she noticed the dark smudges under his eyes. 'Last time I saw Jim, he told me all about you. You were about the only thing he could talk about. Sort of feel like I know you already.'

'Of course you can call me Liz.' She waited for him to say something, but he kept looking around the room. 'Mr Wolters, if this is about that article I wrote, I want you to . . .'

He cleared his throat and looked towards the corner of the room, away from Liz. 'My ex-wife called me yesterday. Jim's gone. He was killed two days ago.'

'No.' Liz wrapped her arms around herself and leaned forward. 'No, I think there's been a mistake. This isn't real.' She looked at the man and shook her head slowly. 'This isn't real and neither are you. This is some kind of dream and I'm going to wake up. I'm going to wake up and you'll be gone.'

'It's real. They say he died in friendly fire. Something went wrong and one of his own men killed him.'

'No.' She looked towards the kitchen, remembering Rose. 'Aunt Rose, tell him he's wrong. Rose! Tell him he's wrong!' She stood and screamed for the woman. 'Rose!'

'I'm here, Liz. I'm here, baby.' She grabbed the girl and held her tight.

'You tell him, Rose. He'll listen to you. He'll believe you. He thinks Jim is dead, but that's not right. You need to call someone and tell them there's been a mistake.' Her teeth began to chatter and her hands were shaking. 'I need to talk to Jim. He can't be dead because he hasn't had a chance to tell me he hates me. He needs to tell me that!'

Rose held her tighter and spoke over her shoulder to the man. 'Mr Wolters, I'm Rose Harper, Lizzy's aunt. I am so sorry for your loss.' She led Liz to the sofa and gently sat her down before settling next to her and pulling her into her arms. 'Just take some deep breaths, angel.'

The man cleared his throat. 'Virginia, that's Jim's mother, and I thought it would be better to tell her in person.' He stared at the floor.

'We appreciate that, Mr Wolters. It was the right thing to do.' Rose smoothed Liz's hair. 'If there's anything we can do for you or your family, I hope you will let us know.'

'Thank you, ma'am. Right now I think I'd better get back to Virginia's house and see to things.' He rose and stepped towards the door before turning back. 'I'll call once we have the details of the funeral decided.' He once again reached to the imaginary hat. 'Liz, Miss Harper.' He closed the door quietly behind him.

'He was killed by one of his own men, Aunt Rose. He killed all those people and then one of his own men killed him. It doesn't make any sense.' She wiped at her face. 'Does anything make sense, anything at all?'

'I don't think so, baby, I don't think so.' Rose pulled the girl towards her and kissed her hair. 'At least not on days like this.'

Cotherstone, West Sussex, July 27th

Dearest Oliver,

Having a wonderful time, wish you were here. No, it's true. Mum decided she couldn't finish her book and asked me to take it over. Now I see why she loved to spend hours at a keyboard. Granted, I've only been doing this for three days, but it is a wonderful change from the sickroom. Now that I've thought about it, it wouldn't shock me if she has me writing to give me a diversion. Knowing Mum, it's probably one of her two-birds-with-one-stone things.

This cancer is a strange beast. She'll have a day or two, sometimes three, of misery. I'll think she's going to be dead by morning, but then she rallies and seems so much like her old self.

This morning she was more like someone who was recovering from the flu than someone who was dying of cancer. I almost forgot that the disease was still there, spreading through her vitals and our lives.

Baby brother is off from school now. Poor kid. He's gone very quiet. Normally he's a can of worms, but not now. He doesn't bring his friends around and he doesn't seem interested in leaving the house. I feel like there's a tall, gangly ghost in the house. We sat out in the garden last night, just the two of us. I was hoping

*we could have a good talk, but we both ended up crying. Maybe I
should sit him down at a keyboard. It's helped me, God knows.*

   *I'm going to ask Daddy to fax this and I'll call you on
Sunday. I love you and miss you.*

   Love

   Mary

Chapter Twenty-Six

'I think this is quite good actually.' Liz handed the pen and the
stack of papers back to her daughter.

   'But?' Mary sat sprawled in a chair next to her mother's bed.

   'But what?' For almost a week she'd been able to cut back on
her pain medication. Knowing it was nothing more than a short
reprieve, she'd had her bedside table piled with the tasks she
planned to finish while she still could.

   'I know you too well, Mum. "But" hangs heavy in the air.'

   '"But" does not hang heavy in the air, darling. I think it's
quite good. I do think Andrew needs to be more clearly defined.
You've made him a bit too nice and that takes tension away
from the story. Don't be afraid to be a little vicious. I think it
was Oscar Wilde who said, "Don't be afraid to kill your darlings". Make things a bit tougher for everybody.' She smiled,
pleased she'd avoided the use of 'but'.

   'I think I've become too attached to his lot.' Mary laughed
and put her foot on her mother's bed. 'I want to go easy on
them.'

   'That happens. It's easy to forget what's real and what isn't
when you stare into that green screen long enough. It's one of

the nicest things about fiction, writing it and reading it. Even now I can go anywhere I want.'

'I think I know what you mean. I've had times when I'm a bit fuzzy on where my "alternative reality" ends and where the real world begins. I'm starting to understand why you seemed so bizarre sometimes when you were working.'

'Bizarre? Me?'

'Distracted is probably a better word. I realize now how hard it is to shift from one reality to the next. It's kind of the ultimate escape, isn't it?

'When things are really cooking, it can be. I think you may have caught the midnight disease.'

'What's the midnight disease?'

'The curse of the writer. The incurable virus that pulls you out of a warm bed because you just figured out what a character really wants. It can cause you to leave parties early because the conversations in your head are so much better than anything you're hearing via your ears. In my case it was responsible for piles of dirty laundry, and my family eating a hell of a lot of cold suppers. I suppose it's a bit like being an alcoholic, except there isn't a twelve-step programme for it.'

'Oliver says one can't write fiction until the age of thirty.'

'Nonsense. Utter crap. He's just saying that because he's a technical writer who probably wants to be a novelist.'

'I don't think he does. He's terribly down to earth. I can't imagine him spinning yarns in his head.'

'Good. I'm glad to hear it. I think you need to have personalities that balance each other in a relationship. If you had two people who spent a good part of their lives in fantasy worlds I think it could get awfully sticky. There needs to be someone who's good at reading maps.'

'Reading maps?'

'It's one example of what I mean. Your father reads maps and we get to places in a fairly reliable fashion. I, on the other hand, tend to head in the general direction and enjoy the ride. Some of the nicest things have happened to me when I got lost.'

'I suppose I should be grateful I've reached this age without any major mishaps or injuries, what with having a mother who spent a lot of time God knows where, literally and figuratively.'

'I suppose that's the main reason I didn't start writing again until your brother was eight. Being a mother required all my concentration and creativity when you two were younger.'

'Any regrets? Do you wish you'd spent more time on your work?'

'Oh, God, no. Once I figured things out, I wanted a family more than anything.'

'What things did you figure out?'

'After Ellie and my mother died, I thought nobody could get close to me. Nobody but the aunts and Mrs Harper, that is.'

'Then you met Jim?'

'I met Jim, but I didn't get involved with him right away. I'd convinced myself that I couldn't stand another loss, another death. Bad luck, but the one guy interested in me, that I was interested in back then, was headed for Vietnam. From the minute I met him, I agonized over what would happen if he died. Then Jim died and I survived. After that I slowly came to realize that loss is inevitable, all kinds of loss. Jim's death freed me to take chances with myself and everyone else.'

'Eat, drink and be merry, for tomorrow we die? That doesn't sound like my mother.'

'That's because it isn't what I'm talking about. When Jim died it made me realize that nothing is permanent. Everything is going to be lost eventually. Everything, the good as well as the bad. The bad has to be accepted and dealt with, but the good is there to be treasured and enjoyed. The only way to live is to live without looking ahead and worrying about what's just around the corner. Whatever is around the corner is not going to change just because you worry about it.'

'Do you still feel that way?'

'More than ever. This crap that's taking over my body simply confirms my belief. If I thought too much about my death, I'd forget about what's left of my life.' She adjusted her reading glasses. 'Let's take another look at this. I think I have an idea about what you can do to make Andrew a little rougher.'

Fresno, California, June 1967

The Prayer Tabernacle was wedged between a motel and a Mexican restaurant, across the street from a supermarket. The sign in front of it assured all who might enter that it was dedicated to the true word of the Risen Lord. It also promised to be the church for the whole family and illustrated that with a badly drawn family smiling as though they'd just won a three-day trip to Disneyland and Knotts Berry Farm.

Liz stood on the front steps, the sun hot on her black linen sheath dress. The service wasn't due to start for another thirty minutes, but she'd promised Virginia Wolters an early arrival to help greet the mourners. It had taken almost two weeks for Jim's body to arrive from Vietnam. Jim's father had suggested a memorial service to be held right away, but his mother had insisted on waiting for the arrival of the body. Apparently the members of the Prayer Tabernacle didn't approve of services that didn't include the earthly remains, even if ex-husbands did want to get back to their used car lots and television commercials.

'Morning, Liz.' Jack Wolters stepped out of the church into the white sunlight. He wore a black Western-cut suit with white trim. His boots were polished lizardskin with silver points on the toes.

'Morning.' She thought he looked like Death dressed up to play cowboys. 'Is Virginia inside?'

'Yeah, that's why I'm outside.' He lit a cigarette and exhaled through his nose. 'Sure not hard to remember why I divorced that woman.'

'I don't suppose this has been easy for anybody.' Virginia and Jack avoided being in the same room with each other. When they spoke it was with a cold formality which chilled anyone who heard them.

'How are you doing? Virginia said you finished your finals yesterday.'

'That's right. As of next week I'll be a graduate.'

'Good girl. I'm real proud of you, but I'm surprised you were able to keep going like that. I haven't been into the office since I got the call. Just can't seem to think straight.' He rubbed his jaw and yawned. 'My wife said it wouldn't look right either. Doing those commercials before the funeral. Guess she's right, but she's going to be the first one to squawk if the sales are down.'

Liz wasn't sure if he was critical or envious that she'd gotten away from the house of mourning, at least for a few hours. 'You do what you have to do. I knew the material so it wasn't a big deal.' She shrugged, feeling guilty about how she had looked forward to taking the tests to avoid being around Jack and Virginia. Jack and Virginia and the shrine Virginia had erected on her pine mantelpiece. Jim's smiling face looked out between two American flags and a straight parade of sympathy cards. Tucked behind the sympathy cards were his baby bootees, diplomas and two swimming trophies. The bookends of his life, blue bootees and the flag.

'I know that's what Jim would have wanted you to do. He was a great one for doing the right thing.' Jack flicked his half-smoked cigarette towards the picture of the festive family. 'He couldn't stand me because I didn't live up to his ideals.'

'I don't think that's true. Jim loved you.' She didn't think a lie would matter at this point. No real reason why Jim's distaste for the man couldn't be buried along with his sharp cheekbones and the newly acquired pieces of shrapnel.

'He thought I was dirt and you know it, Liz. I think he went into the ROTC so he could learn to be a man, whatever the hell that means. He wanted to be a man, but he didn't want to be a man like me. He told me in not uncertain terms he didn't want to be anything like me.'

'He told me he went into ROTC to pay for his tuition.' At least it had been part of the reason. Surely half-truths counted for something?

'That was just an excuse. Bet he didn't tell you he never asked me for help with college. I would have given him the money if he'd asked, but Jim wouldn't ask, would he? He wanted to be an officer and a gentleman. See, Liz, an officer and a gentleman doesn't sell used cars. An officer and a gentleman stays with his first wife even if she's the biggest ball-buster in the damn country.'

'I guess we'll never know why he did anything now.' She pointed down the street. 'Here comes the hearse.'

'Yeah.' Jack let out a long sigh. 'Before this gets started, I feel like I should thank you.'

'For what?'

'You've been a big help to us the last two weeks. I've felt better knowing my boy had such good taste in girls.' He stared at the hearse as it approached the kerb. 'You were good for him. I know Virginia feels the same way. I'm glad he loved you.'

'It didn't change anything, though, did it?' She watched the two young men in black open the back door and slide the casket out before turning to Jack. 'When I was with Jim, I thought love was the one thing that made any sense. I thought it was the one thing that could make a difference.' The gurney under the casket snapped open and they slammed the doors of the hearse shut. 'Turned out to be just smoke and mirrors.'

'Smoke and mirrors. I like that. I'll see if I can work that into a conversation with Virginia.' He belched softly into his fist and put his arm around her waist. 'I guess we'd better be going in now.'

'Jack, before we go in, there's something I've been wanting to ask you.' She pulled away slightly from his damp touch and faced him.

'Sure, what is it, Liz?'

'Have you been sent, has Virginia been sent, Jim's things, his personal effects yet?' For two weeks she'd been expecting their fury. She'd imagined walking in the door and hearing their curses as they waved her last letter in her face.

'His stuff came two days ago.' He looked away from her and appeared to study the Mexican restaurant next door.

'I'd sent him a letter and I just wondered if he saw it. It was a particular letter and I expected a reply.'

'Was it important?'

'It would have been to him.'

'There weren't any letters from you, none at all. I told Virginia I thought that was strange. I thought he probably would have saved your letters and reread them. That's what men in the movies always seem to do.'

'I guess he didn't want to keep them.'

'Did you send him a "Dear John"? Is that what happened?'

'No, it wasn't like that.'

'Well, I guess he was pissed at you about something, but like I said, he loved you, he would have gotten over it. You don't stop getting over things until you've been married for a few years.'

'Jack, I think I should tell you what was in that letter. I wrote to him because I'd . . .'

He leaned down and kissed her, softly and quickly, on the lips. 'Sugar, I'm going to bury my oldest son way before his time. Nothing you could tell me could make me feel any better or any worse than I feel right now. Whatever you wrote to my boy was just between the two of you. Nothing to do with me. That goes for Virginia, by the way. I guess I owe her that much, for old times' sake if nothing else. Whatever is on your mind is going to have to stay there. Do you know what I'm saying?'

'I understand and thank you. I didn't want to tell you, but I just thought I should.'

'Don't thank me, sugar. You're the one who has to live with it.' He put his hand around her waist again. 'Let's get this over with.'

Cotherstone, West Sussex, August 3rd

Oliver,

What planet are you living on? I call you on the phone and tell you I've just broken a needle in my dying mother's arm and you mumble something appropriate then launch into how empty your bed is. What an asshole!!

Do you have any idea of what I'm going through here? Any idea whatsoever? Did you think I came home early to help seed the lawn?

I wake up in the middle of the night with panic attacks. I keep hearing Mum call for me, even when she's asleep. I sometimes get freaked out during the day and have trouble catching my breath. I'm afraid to walk into the conservatory because I'm afraid I'll find her dead. Other times I'm afraid to walk in the room because I'm afraid she'll still be alive. I'm going crazy, I know that.

Everyone is looking to me to do all the things she's always done for them. My brother and father seem to think my tits are homing devices and are forever asking me where they've left their fucking socks or their bloody keys. Gran thinks I'm fascinated to hear anew each morning that a glass of prune juice is her secret to long life and lovely skin. Did you know she takes twenty-two pills each day? She tells me every damn morning. The housekeeper is so anal-retentive she can't think for herself because she's too frigging busy cleaning the bathtubs until you can see your face in them.

My mother is dying and you've got a stiffy. Yes, you're right:
I should drop everything to listen to you whinge about how blue
your balls are! Did I mention that I have lost a stone in weight
and bitten my fingernails down to the quick? I could really use
some emotional support, ASSHOLE!!!

I had a wonderful dream last night. I was somewhere I didn't
want to be and all I wanted to do was get home to my mother. I
knew I'd be fine if I could get home. When I woke up I went in
and gave her a shot. My dream came true. I'm going to avoid
dreams in the future.

The only pleasure I have right now is the writing. Pleasure
may not be the right word. Yesterday I cut one of the character's
hands off because I hated her whingeing. Consider yourself
warned.

If you understand the reason I wrote this letter, I love you. If
you don't understand why I wrote this letter, go fuck yourself!

Mary

Chapter Twenty-Seven

'I've never seen this before. Is it yours?' Mary held up a gold
ring set with small pearls.

'Where in heaven's name did you find that?' Liz took the ring
and rubbed her finger across the pearls.

'I was trying to find your garnet cuff. It wasn't in your jewellery box so I started ratting around in your bureau drawer. It
was inside a little silk pouch which had been tucked into a bon-
bon tin. It's very sweet; is it yours?'

'Did you find the cuff?' The pearls felt almost warm, almost
alive to her touch.

'Finally. You shoved it inside your make-up tray. I had to clean the gunk off it with a brush.' She shook her finger at her mother. 'You should take better care of your nice things, young lady!'

'Fine talk for someone who used to shove leftover sandwiches in her desk drawer. From the smell of things I thought you were the first twelve-year-old schoolgirl to become a mass murderer. I could only assume you were hiding the victims' bodies in your room.'

'You're one to talk. I always thought you were so neat, but your drawers look like a dog's dinner. Another myth exploded.'

'Oh, piffle. I've always been just about as neat as I needed to be. Besides, I've actually cleaned my things out, you should have seen the drawer before. The important thing is you found the cuff. Why did you want it?'

'Why are you changing the subject?'

'Am I?' Liz smiled sheepishly at being caught out.

'You are and you know it. You palmed that ring as fast as you could and started nattering on about sandwiches.'

'It's just a little pearl ring, nothing special.' The ring seemed to jump in her hand, protesting her denial.

'Mum, we are too much alike for me not to be able to read your mind. Isn't that what you've said to me since I was a kid?'

'We are alike, aren't we? It was wonderful for me, I always knew when you were up to something.'

'That door swings both ways, mother of mine. I can read you like a large-print book. And don't try to change the subject again. I want to know about the ring.'

'You're not going to let this drop, are you?'

'I'm just getting awfully curious. It's not like you to be secretive.'

'It's not a secret, it's just something I couldn't wear and I couldn't bring myself to get rid of, either.' She slipped the ring on to her right hand, surprised at how loosely it hung on her finger.

'Where did you get it?'

'Jim; I told you about him. He had it made for me in Hawaii. During the war men were given some time off halfway into their year's tour of duty, for R and R: rest and relaxation. I met Jim in Hawaii for his R and R.'

'That shows how much I know. You never even told me you'd been to Hawaii.'

'It was very pretty. We were in Honolulu most of the time. Honolulu was pretty tacky, but some of the outlying areas were gorgeous. I can't remember the name of the place where we had the ring set, but it wasn't Honolulu.'

'Sounds terribly romantic, having rings made of Hawaiian pearls.'

'Technically I suppose they're Japanese pearls. Some Japanese company had these stands around the islands where you could pick your own oyster out of the tank. It was rather fun, watching the oyster being opened and finding out what was inside.' The sign had guaranteed that each oyster would contain a pearl. Liz had insisted on opening three to test the claim.

'I've seen those places in San Francisco. Personally I thought they were a bit touristy.'

'Well, they are touristy, but we were tourists. Don't forget, we were small-town Valley kids. Nobody had taken us to Venice and Rome before we could walk, like some people I could mention. Before Hawaii I don't believe I'd ever been more than two hundred miles from home.'

'Is that why you were always dragging us across the map?'

'Partly. I wanted you to see as much as possible and be the least provincial you could be, living down here, that is.'

'You still haven't told me why you hung on to the ring. I've never known you to wear or even have any rings other than your wedding and engagement bands.'

'I suppose I had to keep it. I couldn't wear it because Jim had thought of it as a promise ring, the next step before engagement. He saw this bright rosy future for us, although even when I put it on my hand for the first time, I knew we wouldn't be together, not really together after Hawaii.'

'You mean you had a premonition of his death?'

'No, nothing that dramatic. As a matter of fact, I'd stopped worrying about him being killed. After those days in Hawaii it never occurred to me that he might not come home. I recall the day I found out he was dead. My first thought was that there had been some sort of mistake. I thought it was some kind of bureaucratic screw-up. There was such a sense of unreality about the whole thing. I couldn't believe it.'

'What happened in Hawaii? Did you just not fancy him any more?'

'Jim and his men had wiped out an entire village. All civilians. There was no real provocation, they just started shooting and didn't stop until every person, every animal, was dead.'

'Oh, God. How sickening. How did you find out what happened?'

'He told me. It was eating him up and he trusted me enough to tell me. I promised him I would keep it a secret and he believed me. Big mistake, trusting me.'

'I couldn't have kept something like that a secret. I don't think anybody could.'

'Jim wasn't the only one involved and I doubt if I was the only person outside the squad who knew about it. I was the one, however, who didn't keep the secret.'

'Who did you tell?'

'I wrote an article about it for a large magazine called *Pacific*. It's been out of print for years. I'd done some other pieces for them in my senior year at university. Anyway, I changed the names, but somebody from a newspaper tracked me down and an investigation was started. By the time the investigation was complete Jim had been dead for several months. I don't know if it changed anything, but at least it got the whole thing out in the open. I was already living here, but the massacre was a big deal in the American press for a few weeks.'

'Jinkies, my mum, the hard-hitting girl reporter.'

'Hardly, I was just a kid who couldn't be trusted.'

'But you did the right thing. You couldn't keep something like that a secret.'

'At the time I wrote the article, obviously I felt the same way. It didn't take long for me to start looking at the other side of the coin. I'd betrayed someone who loved and trusted me. Jim wasn't much more than a kid himself. He was in a horrible situation that he was ill-prepared for. He was dead and couldn't defend himself, so he became a scapegoat. Now he's a footnote in the history books. Jim Wolters, aka "Butcher of Binh Gia". I did that to him and he deserved better. All the boys did.'

'What else could you have done?'

'At the very least, I could have told him to stop talking. I could have put my fingers in my ears and started humming "The Star-Spangled Banner". I knew he was going to tell me something awful and I listened.'

'It doesn't really sound like you had much choice. If that butt-head mouth-breathing Oliver wanted to tell me something, I'd listen.'

'Butt-headed mouth-breather?'

'Isn't that what you used to say?'

'Booger-eating mouth-breather, get it right. What's Oliver done, by the way.'

'He's being a total penis and expects me to drop everything because he wants my undivided attention.'

'I feel awful. You could still be with him if it wasn't for all this nonsense.'

'Frankly Mum, if he's a booger-eating mouth-breather I'd rather know now. I've put him on warning, so I'll see if he straightens up.'

'I'm sure he will. You're much too good to let go, and even a booger-eating mouth-breather would be able to see that.'

'Thanks for the vote of confidence.'

'You're welcome.'

'I still don't think you had any real choice in the matter of Jim.'

'You might be right. I've been thinking about it all these years and I still can't decide if I did the right thing or not. I just wish I could have listened to his story without really listening or feeling like I had to act on what I'd been told. He needed a shoulder to cry on, and I just couldn't be that shoulder. At the time I recall feeling that I really had no choice but to tell what I knew. I hung on to it for several months and the feeling kept getting stronger.'

'Why did you feel so strongly?'

'I don't know if it was the time or my age. Of course, it was the late sixties and there was all that hype about the dawning of a new age and the youth revolution. Back then we really believed we were going to change the world. I think we pretty much thought we could do it without breaking into a sweat. For the first time in history all the cameras were focused on a bunch of teenagers. We thought love, peace and honesty could change the world. It was fed to us daily like a dose of cod liver oil.'

'Must have been nice. My generation just assumes we will be facing a lifetime of financial and emotional insecurity, at least according to the *Sunday Times*.'

'It was nice until everyone realized that the world wasn't getting better. Love and peace seemed to be just another advertising slogan. Sometimes I think the sixties were nothing but an adman's inspiration.'

Clifford, California, June 1967

She gently pushed the tiny squares of orange carrot against the creamy white of the potatoes. She kept the bright green peas off to the side for a later gathering. She planned to snake them up the side of the starchy mountain, one at a time. Carefully she cut a short gully for the butter to melt, a shiny stream slipping into the red pool of beef juices waiting at the bottom.

'Liz?'

'Huh?' She looked up, surprised to see the three women staring at her. 'I'm sorry, did you say something?' Her address was general, she didn't know which of them had spoken.

Beryl leaned towards the girl, scraping her black sleeve through the leavings on her own plate. 'Sweetheart, I don't think you've said three words since we left the cemetery.'

'I'm sorry.' She took her fork and began to blend the stream of butter into the bloody pool. 'I can't think of anything to say.'

'Elizabeth, look at me.' Rose put her palms on the top of the table.

Liz put her fork down and looked up, her pale eyes underscored with purply smudges.

'Lizzy, this is the day where you leave it all behind.' Mrs Harper reached for the girl's hand. 'The funeral is over and now you get back to the business of living. We need to make plans for your graduation. You need to look forward. There's nothing more you can do for Jim.'

'I asked Jack about my letter. There were no letters from me at all. Do you know what that means? Do any of you know what that means?' She pulled at the neck of the dress she'd worn to the service. 'He got my letter. He got the letter and threw all my other letters away. I tried to tell Jack, but he said I'd have to live with whatever had happened. That's all he said.'

'Darling, that means it's over.' Beryl dabbed at her sleeve with a dampened napkin.

'It just means Jim knew what I did before he died. It means his father doesn't want to know about it. That's what it means. It would have been easier if they'd gotten really mad at me. I was dreading it, but it would have been better. I feel like I've gotten away with a crime.'

'Clearly you haven't gotten away with anything. Look at you.' Rose lit a cigarette. 'You look horrible. I don't think you've eaten anything in days. It doesn't even look like you've washed your hair in over a week. If I knew where to buy sack-cloth and ashes I'd get the giant economy size.'

'Rose!' Beryl put her hand over her heart.

'Shut up, hon.' Rose placed her hand over Beryl's and gave it a squeeze as she smiled at her. The smile left her face when she turned towards Liz. 'Liz, this isn't mourning, this is guilt. Now we can sit here for the next ten years and talk about whether or not you've got anything to feel guilty about, but in the meantime we'd let ten years of our lives slip away. Jim is dead and we can't change that, but I'll be damned if I'm going to let you drag around like something the undertaker forgot to throw in the casket before he nailed it down.'

'I know I haven't been easy to live with, but . . .'

'You've been hell to live with since you came back from Hawaii, but that's not the point. We're family and we put up with each other, no matter how rotten a patch we're going through. Besides, in the next two years or so, Beryl and I will probably be going through the change at the same time and we'll make this blue funk of yours look like a course in positive thinking.'

'Then what is the point?' Liz pulled her hair back, realizing it did feel less than clean.

'The point is we have to pull you out of the hole you've dug for yourself. When I was a kid we had an old cat who just gave up and dug herself a hole under the house. It took her almost another year to die, but before she did, she just spent most of her time lying in her shallow little grave, day in and day out. I'm giving you notice right now: you are not going to be allowed to lie in your shallow grave until you finally stop breathing.'

'I have no intention of lying in a shallow grave and you know it.' Liz smiled at the woman. 'Besides, I know for a fact you never even had a cat. You brother was allergic to cats and dogs. You read that in some novel.'

'Stop splitting hairs, Liz. You get my point.'

'I get your point.' She held her hands up in a gesture of surrender.

'We were going to save this for your graduation, but I'm afraid if we don't tell you about it now, you'll never wash your hair.'

'It's not that dirty.' She knew it was. Since Rose had mentioned it her head had started to itch.

'Two more days and it's going to start looking for some other girl to grow on. But enough about your hygiene. Who wants to start this thing?' Rose looked at the two other women.

'Oh, Rose, go ahead. You know you want to anyway.' Mrs Harper waved her hand in her daughter's direction.

'We all thought the best thing might be for you to get away for a while. Last week Mother got an invitation that got us all thinking.' She reached behind her and took an envelope out of a drawer of the breakfront. 'This is from all of us.' She handed the envelope to Liz. 'Happy graduation. We're all very proud of you.'

Liz opened the envelope as her eyes went from face to face. 'Airline tickets and a passport application?' She opened the ticket folder. 'London? You're sending me to London?' Her mouth started to tremble.

'You want to go, don't you?' Beryl watched Liz's face anxiously.

'I don't believe this. I can't believe you're doing this. It's so wonderful.'

'I'll be joining you for the trip over,' said Mrs Harper. 'My cousin India's youngest daughter is getting married at the end of July, so we'll be there for the wedding. Everyone is so anxious to meet you. Of course, they've been hearing about you for years. I'll come home after three weeks, but India says you can stay for several months if you like. There will be lots of young people for you to meet, and India is lovely. She has a big house down on the south coast and she always has lots of people coming and going.'

'You're all the most wonderful family.' Liz felt tears slide down her cheeks. 'I'm sorry, I didn't mean to start crying again.'

'That's all right, Liz. You can have one more good cry.' Rose laughed and stubbed her cigarette out.

'I think I'll go have my last good cry in the shower while I wash my hair.' She smiled at the women, certain they all knew it wouldn't be the last of the tears.

Cotherstone, West Sussex, August 13th

Dear Oliver,

I have thought about it, at some length I might add, and I don't want you joining me. You and I have a lot of work to do and I've got enough going on right now. I don't have the time or the energy for you. I know that sounds harsh and it no doubt is, but you are not what I need right now. For that matter, I'm not what you need.

A crisis is not the best time to get to know someone. That's why all those wartime marriages fell apart. Well, some of them fell apart. I also must tell you, I resent your offering me a marriage proposal as a balm for my shattered nerves. I take marriage very seriously and I'm not sure that you do if you're offering me a proposal like a trinket or a packet of sweets.

I know you meant it lovingly, but it's clear to me that you really don't understand what's going on here. I suggest you talk to your mother and others who may have had a similar experience to the one I'm having now. Perhaps they can give you some insight that I can't seem to.

I care about you deeply. You know that, and for now it has to be enough. If it's not enough then I free you of any obligation you may feel. Enough said.

Believe it or not, I'm starting to see some good in all this. My mother is telling me so many things I never knew. I wish I had known these things earlier. When I was a young teenager I used to think she was such a lightweight, what with her puffy little novels, her silly dog and her twin sets. Through the years I've caught glimpses of the other side of her, but now it's all out there, what's left of it anyway. I'm afraid she might have burned a little too bright, my mum. God, that sounds awful and maudlin. She'd hate it, but I'm not going to change it. It's how I feel.

Gran is leaving to visit my odious aunt in two days. I almost get the feeling she's trying to get out of the house so she won't be around when Mum dies. Gran has buried two husbands and one of her own children, so maybe she just can't bear to do one more. Whatever, I for one will be glad to have her out of the house for even a few days. I've become very jealous of Mum and want to keep her for the three of us.

My Uncle Tarquin calls almost daily and says he wants to come down and see us, but something always 'comes up'. Given his reputation I force myself not to giggle about what in his life has 'come up'.

I do think you're a lovely man and I know you love me. Give me some time and space. Patience is supposed to be one of the virtues, after all.

Love

Mary

CHAPTER TWENTY-EIGHT

'What time did you get your gran on the train?' Liz trailed a piece of string just out of the cat's reach. Mugs, lazy in the sunny room, merely watched with interest.

'Just after ten. She was so excited you'd think she was going to Mecca instead of Bristol.' Mary busied herself with plucking the dead blooms from a bank of geraniums.

'The lure of Clairey. India has always thought Clairey was the most fascinating creature on earth.'

'I think the only interesting thing about Aunt Clairey is the fact that she can't go more than thirty seconds without discussing herself.'

'You find that interesting?'

'I find "it" interesting. I don't find her interesting. I think she's a complete and utter bore.'

'You just think she's boring because you aren't interested in the breeding of King Charles spaniels or the many uses of beads in decorative embroidery.' Clairey found both to be fascinating.

'And you are?'

'Of course not. I think she's duller than shit and always has been, but she's India's favourite in spite of her limited spheres of interest.'

'Well, I can't imagine why anyone would find her interesting. Daddy and Uncle are both much more interesting. They're more presentable as well. Clairey looks like an unmade bed on her good days.'

'Meow! Sounds like you haven't had your saucer of milk today.'

'It's true and you know it. She looks worse every time I see her and I can't imagine where it comes from. Gran is always so neat and crisp-looking, even at her age.'

'Clairey just doesn't give a damn, I suppose. She used to be quite attractive until she got so heavily into the doggie thing.' Her sister-in-law had started breeding dogs shortly after her third husband had left. 'I suppose the dogs are some kind of child substitute, although I can't imagine what she would have done with children. She's never seemed the maternal sort at all. I imagine it's difficult to keep up one's appearance with those nasty little things always slobbering and reproducing.' She could hear the cat in her own voice.

'I don't know how Gran can stand to stay there for two or three weeks at a time. She barely tolerates Patch, and God knows he's better behaved than those little messes Clairey keeps around.'

'I suppose it's the mother-daughter thing. I think once Jane died, all that daughter hunger went into Clairey. Actually, I feel a little sorry for Clairey. I think even now India is still trying to turn Clairey into Jane. She told me she was planning to take her shopping for her winter wardrobe. India made it sound as though Clairey wore something other than men's trousers, plaid shirts and a brown cardigan with the elbows out.'

'Good luck to Gran. I can see them now; Gran will be sorting through the frocks and chatting to the shop assistant while Clairey stands outside smoking.'

'I'm sure you're right. Not that India will be discouraged for a minute. She'll come back and tell us about the lovely time they had shopping and lunching. Obviously she sees Clairey through kinder eyes than we possess.' Liz looked at her daughter and squinted slightly.

'Do your eyes bother you today?'

'Not at all, darling.' She tossed the string on to the now sleeping cat. 'I was just trying to see you without "mother's eyes". I was trying to be completely objective, but I can't. You will always be the most glorious young woman in the world to me.'

'You mean everyone doesn't think I'm the most glorious creature on earth? Quick, a potato peeler. I'm going to kill myself.'

'Actually, you are the most glorious girl in the world, but some other mothers may feel the same way about their offspring. Silly cows will probably never know the truth. That aside, I think India still sees Clairey as the lovely young thing she was over twenty years ago. She was India's baby then, and she is India's baby now.'

'I don't recall her being quite so enamoured of Jane. Of

course, I was only twelve when Jane died, and she'd been living abroad all my life. I really only remember her from the Christmases she'd spend with us.'

'Jane was terrific. I was never around her that much, but I felt like I knew her so well. I adored her, I think everyone did, especially India. She was very clever, very witty, and so chic, with lots of wonderful silks and exotic jewellery. In spite of that, she was the family outsider. Not only did she choose to live on the other side of the world, but when the rest of the family would close ranks and put on blinkers, Jane was the one who revelled in mentioning the truth. Not always the way to make friends.'

'I wish her kids would occasionally come back and see us. I envy people with tons of cousins living close by. Even after, what, ten years, Christmas still seems strange without them.'

'I wish you had seen more of them too. I think their father didn't want to come here and didn't feel comfortable sending them by themselves from Singapore. They were certainly invited enough.'

'I think it's because Gran never approved of Jane's marriage.'

'What makes you say that?' Although her mother-in-law had referred to Jane's husband as a 'wog' on numerous occasions, she'd assured Liz she never used the term in front of Jane or the children.

'Whenever Barbara or Ward were around she would make a fuss about my hair. She would go on and on about the colour. I think she must have used fifty different words for "blonde". Golden, wheaten, flaxen, you name it. She never missed a chance to mention that my eyes were the exact same shade as her dear departed Edgar's. Of course, all the time my drop-dead gorgeous Eurasian cousins are sitting there with their blue-black curly hair and eyes so dark you could carve them into chromatic piano keys.'

'I never knew. I wish you'd told me, I would have tried to put a stop to it.' Liz still had to remind her mother-in-law, child of the Empire that she was, that 'darky' was not the term for anyone with hair darker than medium brown.

'Everything seems normal when you're a kid. Besides, I probably lapped up the attention. Everybody likes to be the favourite, even if it's at someone else's expense.'

'I understand, and she probably wouldn't have listened to me anyway. She doesn't consider herself to be a racist after all, because she loves a good curry and doesn't mind Chinese food.'

'Oh, God!'

'India is who she is. She was born in India and lived there until she was five or so, like an English princess looking down her little white nose at the "natives". She's a product of her time and culture, like all of us. We can't expect her to be politically correct because it makes us more comfortable. I think she really does try, in her own way.'

'"Her own way" is right. Don't forget the time she sat at the same dinner table with the bishop from Guyana. "Perfect manners, the man had perfectly elegant manners."' Mary imitated her grandmother's trill.

'That's right. "Lovely man even if he was as black as the ace of spades. Charming wife as well. Dressed in one of those native costumes, but quite pleasant nonetheless."' Liz spoke in the plummiest tone she could muster.

'You have certainly been more tolerant of her than I've been. I don't know how you can stand to hear the same stories twenty or thirty times.'

'In most respects she's an absolutely terrific old gal. She can be narrow-minded, bigoted and pig-headed, but at the end of the day she's been very good to me.' Liz wondered if her daughter should be told just how good to her the old woman had been. India had never blamed her for what happened.

'I think it's more a case of you being good to her.'

'Let's just say we have both created some good karma with this relationship. India could have made life very difficult for me those first few months, but she didn't.'

London, July 1967

'Tarquin, over here, Tarquin!' Mrs Harper waved her arms at a young man leaning against a partition in the arrival terminal. He waved back and rushed towards Liz and the older woman.

'Auntie Lou, welcome home. You look as gorgeous as ever.' He leaned down and kissed the woman on her powdered cheek. He turned to Liz and his eyes widened. 'And you must be my little cousin Lizzy.' He grinned and shook her hand. Liz almost said his name. Almost said it because he looked so like him. His hair was longer and a little darker. He was maybe an inch shorter, but he looked like Jim. Could have been twins.

'Liz, this is my cousin India's son, Tarquin Randall. According to his mother he's responsible for most of her grey hair.' Mrs Harper put her arms around the young man and gave him a brief hug. 'Oh, it's so nice to be home again.'

'Still home after more than fifty years?' Tarquin laughed as he began to push their luggage trolley.

'This will always be home, at least Foreshore will be. I can't tell you how excited I am to be seeing everyone. And a wedding! I can't wait. I've been coaching Liz and I think she's got most of the names straight, don't you, Liz?' She glanced back at Liz as they manoeuvred their way through the crowded airport.

'I hope I've got it straight.' For weeks Mrs Harper had been briefing her on facts about her extended family. The women, India Randall and Louise Harper, were first cousins. India was a number of years younger and had lived in what had been her grandmother's house, Foreshore, since her family's return from India when she was five.

Louise's home had been London, but she and her mother had spent every summer with her grandmother at Foreshore. Louise's father had died the year India came home, and the older girl found a welcome respite from mourning in the pretty little girl. In spite of the age difference, they became, and stayed, fast friends.

Within two years of her husband's death, Louise's mother had remarried, to an American professor who was doing research at the British Museum. When his project ended, he returned to Palo Alto in California, where he taught at Stanford University, bringing his new wife with him. Louise was allowed to stay a few years longer in England to finish her education. A school was chosen which was less than two miles from Foreshore.

On an extended visit to her mother and stepfather she met Mearle Harper, a young dentist. She married, taught, had children and put aside enough money to return to Foreshore every two or three years.

Her cousin India had married twice. Her first husband had died in a swimming accident when he was in his thirties. India, then forty, married Edgar Randall. To her own amazement the marriage quickly produced David and Tarquin. Five years later Jane arrived, and to the older children's embarrassment, Clairey was born the year India turned fifty. Edgar had died five years ago, leaving India widowed, and David in charge of the family business, a manufacturing concern on the south coast.

'Mother sends her apologies for not picking you up herself. Today the females are all at the dressmakers for the final fittings. Mother said to be sure and tell you this wasn't the original schedule, but something about the wrong colour of something throwing everything into turmoil. I don't know what all the fuss is about, but I suspect less planning went into D-Day than has gone into Clairey's wedding. It's frightening to think what it takes to get just one fairly average girl married off.' He stopped and turned to speak to Mrs Harper.

Liz, distracted by a group of women in brilliantly coloured silk saris, walked into Tarquin, stepping on his feet and almost knocking him to the ground. 'Oh, shit. I'm sorry, I mean I'm sorry I said that, and I'm sorry I ran into you.' She felt her face redden as the words tumbled out.

'No harm done.' He brushed a strand of hair off her face. 'I'll just have to learn to stay out of your way.' He grinned and turned back to Mrs Harper. 'We were having a bit of a debate over breakfast this morning. How long has it been since your last visit?'

Liz followed behind, half listening to their conversation, careful not to take her eyes off Tarquin. He even walked like Jim.

Foreshore, West Sussex

Tarquin started to climb out of the car to open the wide wooden gate.

'No, please, Tarquin, let me.' Mrs Harper climbed out of the car with surprising speed and swung the gate open. She slid back in and turned to Liz in the back seat. 'It was always my job to open the gate whenever we came down for a holiday when I was a little girl. Silly how these things stick in one's memory. I think I've spent the happiest times of my life right here at Foreshore. Did I tell you that my grandfather built this house for his new bride in eighteen sixty-five?' Mrs Harper leaned forward in the seat, her head craned for her first glimpse of her grandfather's wedding gift.

'You've told her twice just since we got in the car, Auntie Lou.' Tarquin laughed and patted the woman on the knee. 'Welcome home, stranger.' He rounded the corner and the house appeared, framed by the sea behind and the garden all around.

'There it is. Lizzy, look, that's Foreshore. Oh, Tarquin, it looks just the same.' Built of pink stucco and topped with thatch, it rose above the smooth green lawn of the garden, an improbable mushroom of a house. Trimmed with freshly painted white woodwork and hung with flowering baskets, it reminded Liz of the cover of one of Mrs Harper's biscuit boxes.

'Please don't tell Mother it looks just the same. She's spent a fortune the last few months getting the house and garden ready for the next few days.' He pulled into the circular drive. Cutting the motor, he stepped out of the car and opened Liz's door. 'Welcome home, cous.'

'Mother said to put you in here with Jane. Jane's only here for another week and then you'll have the room all to yourself.' Tarquin put her cases on the floor next to a canopied bed covered with a faded floral spread. He shook his dark brown hair off his face with a snap of his head. 'Jane's not in Mother's good graces right now, so you might want to ignore most of what she says about us.'

'I can't remember; Jane is your younger or your older sister?' She wanted to keep him talking. The voices weren't the same, but words did the same things to the faces. The tip of his nose moved slightly when he talked, just like Jim's.

'Jane's younger, but not youngest. Clairey, our blushing bride, is the baby, then Jane, then yours truly, and finally David, the old man of the bunch.'

'I think I can keep that straight.'

'Don't worry if you can't. Just call everyone "dear" and you won't have a thing to worry about. Mother's been doing it for years.' He smiled, the skin pulling tight across his high cheekbones.

'I can definitely remember one word.' She glanced around the room, noting several doors. 'I don't suppose one of these leads to a bathroom?' She was suddenly aware of a full bladder and teeth coated with airline food plaque.

'As a matter of fact . . .' He opened a door with a flourish. 'Sorry, I'm not much of a bellboy. On the other hand I don't expect a tip.'

'Thanks.' Liz looked at Tarquin, who made no move to leave. 'Maybe I could meet you downstairs in a few minutes?'

'Right, right. Fancy a walk on the beach? Best thing after a long flight or a long night.'

'That sounds fine, but I'd better check on Mrs Harper.'

'No need. She told me she was going to snatch a kip until Mother and the others came in.'

'Snatch a what?'

'A kip, a nap.' He made a cradle of his hands and rested his head in it. 'A short sleep. Stop me when you understand.'

'Stop.' She found herself giggling at his antics.

'By the way, that bathroom thing is going to cause some confusion in certain circles. Call it a loo, maybe a WC, and you'll have more consistent luck.'

'Thanks for the tip.'

'I live to serve.'

'I bet.' Tarquin Randall didn't seem the least bit servile.

'A hint of sarcasm? Good. We'll get on just fine. Meet you downstairs in the kitchen in about ten minutes.' He nodded his head once and walked out of the door.

She washed her face and ran a comb through her hair. While replacing her toothbrush in the vanity case, her hand slipped and the case fell to the floor, spilling its contents across the black and white tiles. She gathered up the mess into the case and started to leave the room when something on the floor caught her eye. She scooped up Jim's ring and looked at it for a moment before slipping it on to the third finger of her right hand. She hurried downstairs, trying to remember when she'd put the ring in the case.

Cotherstone, West Sussex, August 21st

Dear Oliver,

Your mother called this morning. She's so sweet. She told me she was cooking dinner for us for the next three nights and I started crying. I was so touched.

I do that a lot these days. People have been so kind and I usually respond with tears and blubbering. An old chap who lives across the road comes by twice a day to walk Patch. He told me he knew other people in the family could do it, but he wanted to do something for Liz. Oh, shit. I'm crying again.

The vicar has become almost a daily visitor. Mother has always been strictly a Christmas Eve and Easter-morning kind of churchgoer, but bless him, that doesn't seem to matter. Mum doesn't mind because she said the C of E doesn't take itself too seriously anyway. She's always liked this vicar since they share an interest in UFOs. They've swapped books and articles for years.

I've been getting things in order for Mum's burial. Unbeknownst to any of us, she applied to the council weeks ago for permission to bury her in the back garden. Apparently it's quite legal as long as it can be established that it doesn't interfere with water sources. I'm seeing to the coffin this morning.

Funny, strange, but the burial, thinking about the burial, doesn't make me cry. Your mother cooking our meals and the neighbour walking the dog make me sob.

Thank you for talking to your mother. Thank you for trying to

*understand. Thank you for the flowers. Thank you for the lovely
letter you sent to my mother. Thank you for you.*

All my love

Mary

CHAPTER TWENTY-NINE

The plastic pitcher fell, splattering ice and water across the terracotta floor of the conservatory. 'Perfect.' Mary kicked the pitcher into the potted palm and threw a towel on top of the spreading damp. 'This has all the hallmarks of being one of those days.'

'Mary, sit down.' Liz turned herself slightly by holding on to the side bars of the bed.

'I can't sit down, Mother. I've got to clean this up and then I have to take Chaz into Worthing for his uniform.'

'I don't care about the floor, and your father can take care of Chaz and his uniform. For that matter, Chaz can take care of his own uniform.'

'You don't realize how much I have to do. Even with Connie here, there are still so many things involved with running the house and taking care of everything.' She shrugged her shoulders and turned away from her mother's gaze.

'I know how much there is to do. If you need more help, just bring it in. There's no reason to wear yourself out.'

'It's not just the work.' She picked up the soaked towel and tossed it into a wicker hamper behind Liz's bed.

'Sit down and talk to me.'

'Uncle called this morning.'

'He's back, then. How is he?' Liz rubbed her fingernails against the soft cotton throw across her body. An old habit, it made her nails glow like small pink shells. She held her hand close to her face and examined her nails, surprised that a part of her could still be pink and healthy-looking.

'He didn't know how sick you are. I had to tell him. I'm so angry at Daddy for not telling him.' She sat heavily in the bed-side chair. 'Didn't it occur to him that if he didn't tell him, I'd have to do it?'

'I thought he was finally making some kind of adjustment.' She blinked, trying to clear her thoughts. She wasn't sure which brother should have made the adjustment.

'He's not, not at all. Uncle isn't the only one I've had to tell. Daddy likes to tell people you're going through a rough spot.'

'Does seem to be a bit of an understatement, that.' She closed her eyes. 'Not like him to be so inaccurate.'

'I don't understand why he's acting this way. Doesn't he see what it's doing to me, to all of us?'

'He can't face it, Mary, he simply can't face it.'

'He faces everything else. He runs his business, he fusses over Gran and Aunt Clairey. A few days ago he was on the phone with somebody about doing some kind of fund-raising for something or other. He handles everything, everything but this. Somehow he seems to think if he pretends this isn't happening it will all reverse itself. I think he expects to walk in the door one of these days and see you sitting at your desk or dividing plants in the garden.'

'I told you weeks ago that he wouldn't be able to deal with this.'

'Why the hell not?' Mary threw one leg over the other.

'I'm his life. I've been the focus of his life for over twenty years. He feels that his whole way of life is dying, and I suppose in some ways it is.' She tried to take a deep breath, but found something inside her blocking the expanse of her lungs. She imagined she was dying in neat little segments, the way an orchid plant does.

'That's happening for all of us. He's not thinking of us at all. If he can't handle it I don't know why he assumes I can.'

'You're my daughter so he knows what you're made of. He knows you'll manage.'

'What if I don't manage, then what happens?'

Liz opened her eyes and looked at her daughter. 'You don't have any idea of how strong you are and how strong you can be.' Always felt so fierce about this child. Wanted her no matter what. 'It's a bit watered down by the Randall side, but deep down you're still a ditch-bank Okie Viking.'

'That's supposed to help?' She smiled ruefully at her mother's assurance.

'I know it will.' Liz closed her eyes again and thought about the shrimp boats sailing on a sea of opiate-induced blue clouds. Sailing towards a riverbank in a dusty farm town.

Foreshore, West Sussex , July 1967

'Let's see if we can find a pair of wellies that fit.' Tarquin had led her to a room off the kitchen that was hung with dozens of coat-hooks holding an assortment of jackets, sweaters and hats. The floor was strewn with rubber boots and canvas shoes.

'What's a wellie?' She'd changed into jeans and a loose white cotton shirt. At Beryl's insistence she'd abandoned the costume of unremitting black she'd adopted for university. Her suitcase seemed like someone else's, with its whites and colours neatly stacked by Beryl's hands.

'This is a wellie.' He indicated a green boot with the toe of his stockinged foot. 'Necessity for where I'm taking you.' He looked at her shirt. 'We'd better find a jumper for you as well. This isn't California, but you knew that, didn't you?' He handed her a worn blue cardigan from one of the hooks. 'This looks as though it will probably fit.'

'Thanks.' She pulled the cardigan on and pushed the sleeves up to her elbows.

'It's low tide so I'm going to show you your first real piece of English history. Isn't that what you read at university?'

'It was my minor.' She was surprised he knew that much about her. 'But we say "studied" instead of "read".'

'Between loo, study and kip, we're doing pretty well talking at all.' He handed her a pair of boots. 'Try these, they look about right. I checked the tide tables and St Mary's should be showing up just about now.'

'What's St Mary's?' She leaned against the wall to pull the boots on.

'It's an old parish church. Went underwater sometime in the seventeenth century, but you can still scramble around the ruins when the tide is low.' He watched her for a moment. 'How are those?'

'They fit like socks on a rooster.' Liz put her booted foot in the air, shaking it back and forth.

'Certainly conjures an image. Do many barnyard animals wear clothes in America?' He dropped to the floor, looking for a smaller pair.

'Only the modest ones.' She slid the boots off, balancing on one foot.

Tarquin put his hand on her calf and worked her foot into the smaller boot. 'How's this?'

'Better, thanks.'

He patted her thigh, just above the knee. 'All part of the service. Now the trick will be to find the mate.' He pawed through a pile of seemingly identical boots. 'Doesn't make the job any easier, the fact that Mother can't bear to throw away anything that might have five minutes of use left in it. Here we go, Cinderella. Let's have the other leg.' He held her foot for a moment before guiding it into the rubber.

'Thanks.' Liz took a tentative step. 'Is this really necessary? I feel like a duck.'

'Rooster, ducks; you're a basic, earthy sort, aren't you?'

'I suppose when you grow up with the smell of fruit-packing plants and cow shit, it has some effect.' She looked at his face for signs of a reaction, regretting the use of 'shit'. He'd probably never spewed a vulgarity or even acknowledged the by-products of a colon, man's or animal's.

'Well, basic or not, you look charming. Not the least duck-like.' He tossed the compliment over his shoulder.

'Are we ready?' Liz felt the colour rise in her cheeks again. She suspected the comment was given freely because it had no value to him.

'Follow me.'

The receding tide left a quarter of a mile of sand and rock exposed on the other side of Foreshore's sea gate. A motley assortment of children and dogs chased after a flock of seagulls basking in the bright afternoon sun. In spite of the sun, a cool wind blew across the water, making the air at the shore sharp and bringing the salty smell in to the land.

'There, the black rocks just to the left.' He leaned close to her back, his chin almost touching her shoulder. 'Can you see it?'

'I see the rocks, but it doesn't look like much of anything.' She slipped her hair, warm from his breath, behind her ear. She stepped away from him, not comfortable being so close to another person. A person who wasn't an aunt, or Jim.

'I don't imagine you'd look like much of anything either if you'd just spent three hundred years in the English Channel.'

'I don't suppose I would, but then I'm not made of rock, am I?' She winced at her attempted coquetry. She knew such things were skills for which she'd shown little aptitude. Ellie had been born with the talent, but died before she could train her sister. Liz had never regretted the lack of tuition until now. She should be witty and saucy, she should leave him wanting to know more about her. She knew she should toss her hair, perhaps flick an imaginary piece of something from his jacket. The best she had done was to remind him that she wasn't a rock. The afternoon opened before her; hours of stuttering denials of mineral content.

'Is the water always this calm?' Maybe if they couldn't talk about the water she could quiz him about his family, anything so that there wasn't a deadly silence.

'It's low tide now, but when the tide comes in the waves will as well. Certainly not the sort of thing you get on the Pacific coast. I'm afraid this stretch is terribly calm compared to what you're used to in California.'

'I've only been to the beach twice in California. We live about one hundred and fifty miles from the water and Rose and Beryl aren't really water people. Also, Beryl gets car sick, so she's not too excited about the idea of a long car ride. I was in Hawaii in the winter, though, and the waves were enormous there.' She bit her lip, knowing she was rattling on like a pan of boiling water.

'Hawaii?' He pulled her away from a mass of dark green vegetation lying on the sand. 'Watch your step, the seaweed is awfully slippery. What were you doing in Hawaii?'

'I was visiting my friend, my boyfriend, who was on leave from a tour in Vietnam.' She wondered how the 'friend' had slipped out. Wondered why she'd reduced Jim to a casual acquaintance.

'Mother said something about that; died, didn't he?'

'In June. Just a month ago.'

'I can't imagine what that must be like. We lost our father, but he was ancient. It must have been hell for everyone, him being so young and all.'

'It was horrible.'

'Is that why you're here?' He put his hand to his forehead and slapped it. 'Oh, fuck, that sounds bad. It sounds as though you're not welcome and you are. I just wondered if your coming here now has something to do with him.'

'It didn't sound bad, I knew what you meant.' She smiled at

him before looking towards the remains of the church. 'The aunts, your cousin and Beryl, thought I needed to get away for a while.'

'I bet you did.' He picked up a stone and threw it towards the water. 'I'm not doing much of a diversionary nature, talking about him, am I?'

'It's all right.'

'No, from now on I will be nothing but diversionary. I will be your tour guide and primary source of amusement, at least until Monday when I go back to London.'

'You don't live down here?'

'No, thank God for small favours. Sleepy old Sussex is great for weekends and selling postcards, but I couldn't live here. I have a flat with a couple of chaps I've known forever.'

'What do you do?'

'You mean for a job, work?'

'That's right.'

'I work in a gallery, but I'm also a painter. I haven't sold much, but I've got my fingers crossed because I'm being exhibited next month in a new gallery.'

'Not the one you work in?'

'No such luck. You have to be dead or famous to be hung where I work.'

'Chin up, you're bound to be dead someday.' She put her hand over her mouth. 'Oh, shit, I didn't mean to say that.'

'Why, I thought it was great. Black humour is very British, actually. Besides, now that we've each said something boorish, we can relax and get on with the tour.' He lifted his arm and pointed towards the ruins. 'See, right here you have the north side of the foundations.'

'Here?' She pointed to a line of stones off to the left.

'No, over here.' He stood behind her and moved her head gently to the right. 'Straight ahead. Can you see the space where the doorway was?'

'Yes, I can. Was it sudden, the church going under?' She

imagined a tidal wave submerging it on a Sunday morning.

He took his hands from her head and put them on her shoulders. 'Oh, not at all. They had years of warning. In fact, they had time to build another church about a mile inland. It's still the parish church. About ten generations of my family have been married and buried out of the new church, but this one is still my favourite.'

'Why?'

'Partly because I don't have to sit through sermons out here.'

'What's the other part?'

'I kissed my first girl right out there by the old doorway.'

'The poor girl must have gotten wet.'

'We both got soaked to the skin.' He folded his arms across his chest as he stepped away from her. 'It seemed terribly romantic at the age of fifteen.'

'Sounds wet and cold to me.'

'Not a romantic, Liz?'

'No, not a bit.'

'That makes two of us. What say we go back and get something warm to drink? You look cold.'

Cotherstone, West Sussex, September 1st

Dearest Oliver,

Gran is back, but pretty much staying in her room. I think I might have offended her by being less than interested in Aunt Clairey, but that's life. She can sit and pout in her room as much as she likes.

Chaz came home, drunk as a lord last night. Poor kid. I found him crying and vomiting in our bathroom. He clung to me like a five-year-old and then we both cried for the longest time. I don't know what to do for him.

I tried talking to my father, but he just spluttered and focused on the under-age drinking. At least last night he spent most of the night in the conservatory with her. That's the first time he's done that. Maybe even he finally realized we're coming to the end.

The phone is ringing off the hook, but I let the housekeeper take all the calls. She hands me little pieces of paper with messages, but I don't have the energy to sit on the phone chatting about this.

I think I'm going to have Mum's book finished by next week. I'm going to read it to her. I doubt if she'll hear or understand much, but it's still something I want to do. I love you and miss you.

All my love

Mary

CHAPTER THIRTY

'Tell him he can't come. I won't see anyone but the three of you and India.' It had been almost a quarter of an hour since her last injection and she could feel it finally taking effect. She always felt it first in her mouth. Her tongue would start to grow and soften. It made it hard to speak, but she had little left to say. The only real things of interest were in the syringes and her dreams.

'He's already on his way, Mum. I just tried to reach him, but it was too late.' Her uncle had insisted on seeing his sister-in-law one more time.

'Send him away. I won't see him.' Liz closed her eyes and felt herself relaxing as Ellie walked towards her. Ellie came every day now. She looked wonderful, happy and well. She said she'd bring Laura soon. It would be just the three of them again.

Foreshore, West Sussex, July 1967

'Lock the door and don't let anyone in here,' the short, brown-haired girl whispered, and put her finger to her lips.

'Why not?' Liz whispered back at her.

The girl put her hands on her hips and raised her voice. 'Because this is a goddamned madhouse! If I have to look at one more wedding present I'm going to scream!' She turned to Liz with a beatific smile on her round face and extended her hand. 'I'm Jane Chang, and you must be Liz.'

'That's right.' Liz took her hand and laughed. 'It's nice to meet you, I think.'

'Nice to meet you too. Sorry about my tantrum. I don't think my mother has used a sentence that didn't include the word "wedding" since I got here.'

'Wasn't it like this when you got married?'

'Good grief, no. Mother was so appalled about my marrying a "native" she didn't even come to the register office.'

'What a shame. You must have been terribly hurt.'

'I was thrilled, actually. My older brother was there, and tons of friends. We all went to a pub afterwards and got absolutely pissed. After we went home to Singapore Hugh's parents gave us a traditional wedding, but the first was my favourite.'

'Is that your husband?' Liz glanced at a large photograph Jane had left on the bedside table. It showed a bare-chested young Chinese man on the deck of a wooden sail boat.

'Yes, isn't he gorgeous? That was taken the first day we met. I took one look at him and knew I'd have to get used to the weather in Singapore.' She picked the photograph up and gave it a kiss.

'How did you meet?'

'A friend of mine from school has parents who live out there. I went out for two weeks with her and turned my ticket in on day fourteen. It was love at first sight.'

'Really? I never thought that was possible. Lust at first sight I can understand.' She really couldn't but wanted to. Falling fast and hard, not thinking about it.

'Lust, love, it's all the same in the first few weeks, isn't it?' Jane laughed and unzipped her dress. 'All that aside, I did feel an immediate sense of connection with Hugh. I felt like he was the person I'd been looking for all my life, and frankly I didn't even know I was looking at that point.' She stepped out of her dress, leaving a pool of dark blue silk on the floor.

'That sounds wonderful.' Liz thought it sounded childish and moronic. She wondered if Jane had been drinking, testing the wedding champagne a day early.

'You're a lousy liar. I like that in a person.' Jane grinned at her and pulled on a red silk dressing gown with an embroidered dragon across the back. With her soft brown hair and wide blue eyes she looked like a missionary who'd wandered into a Chinese brothel.

'Pardon?'

'You don't think it sounds wonderful at all. You can say what you want with me, you know. I realize how crazy it sounds. Maybe it is crazy, but I know how I feel.' She looked at Liz for a moment. 'It's really not much crazier than you coming here because of what happened to that poor boy.'

'I don't think . . .'

'Don't worry about it. I know the whole story. Auntie Lou wrote to Mother and Mother told me.' She picked up a silver-backed hairbrush and started brushing her hair. 'You did the right thing, coming here. A change of scene is the best tonic. That's one of the things I love most about Singapore; of course it's one of the things Mother simply hates. She's livid that I've chosen a life that's different from hers.'

'Maybe all mothers feel that way.' Liz shrugged, having little current information about mothers and how they felt.

'I think it's worse for me. You see, I'm the one who's most like Mother. I'm loud and bossy and I like to have things my own way, just like her. Clairey will do what anyone tells her to do as long as they leave her alone. Mother's been trying to push her to get a response since the day she was born. It's like fighting with marshmallows and Mother finds it all awfully frustrating. She loves me around because we really get into it and have big, gorgeous rows.'

'If you're like your mother I'd think she'd understand what you've done.' The machinations of the Randall clan sounded exhausting.

'I went a bit far beyond what Mother considers an acceptable range. I could have done anything I wanted as long as I stayed in Sussex. Ever since our father died she's been like a brood hen fluffing her feathers over her chicks. She wants to keep us all under her wing.'

'Your brother Tarquin got away to London.'

She made a dismissive gesture with her hand. 'Tar gets away with murder because he's the artiste in the bunch. Mother loves all that crap and thinks it gives us a certain sheen. Actually most of what Tar does looks like a pile of old poo. He's lovely, but his work isn't.'

'What about your other brother? I haven't met him yet.'

'You probably won't meet him until tomorrow. He's the workhorse and runs the family business. Mother stays out of his hair because she needs the dough he brings in to support her in the fashion she thinks she deserves. He's something of a monk as well.' Jane plopped on the bed and made little circles in the air with her right foot. 'This is supposed to give you nice ankles. I wonder if it really works.'

'That's awfully sad.'

'They're plump, but they're not really sad.' She grinned at Liz.

'You know I don't mean your ankles, I mean your brother.'

'That's the way David is, always has been. He had polio before I was born and I think that had an enormous effect on him; I know it did, actually. He's spent his whole life inside his head. His brain tries to compensate for what his body lacks. He's fine with business, but not terribly comfortable in strictly social situations. Promise me you won't be offended if he ignores you completely?'

'I won't be offended. I don't mind being ignored, I rather enjoy it. I used to love it when I was a kid. You learn so much when nobody knows you're around.'

'I hate being ignored. I like being in the middle of everything. Mother says I was the noisiest baby she'd ever heard. She could only put me to bed if there were other people around. I've always hated being alone.'

'David and Clairey are the introverts, you're an extrovert, and what about Tarquin?'

Jane sat up quickly. 'Tar is . . .' She put her hand over her mouth. 'Shit.' She stumbled into the bathroom.

'Are you all right? Can I get you anything?' Liz called through the bathroom door once the sound of Jane's retching stopped.

Jane opened the door, holding a wet flannel to her face. 'Don't tell Mother.' She dragged past Liz and threw herself on the bed. 'I feel like I've been ridden hard and put away wet. Actually, I suppose I have.' She giggled, and then groaned with the effort.

'What's wrong with you?'

'In seven months I will present my mother with her first grandchild.'

'That's wonderful, congratulations.'

'Thank you. We're very excited, but I meant what I said: don't mention this to anyone. You're the only one here I've told.'

'Why?'

'Because you saw me sicking up.'

'That's not what I mean, Jane. Why haven't you told your family?'

'My mother is not going to be happy about having a half-Chinese grandchild. She can't admit she's a racist, so instead she will pretend that she's terribly concerned about my health, which is utter nonsense, by the way. I was a bit poorly as a child and she's implied ever since that I won't be able to "carry" as she so delicately puts it. When she first met Hugh she told him so. He misunderstood and assured her he would do any carrying that was necessary. When I explained what she really meant he laughed, which she really hated.'

'Maybe she'll surprise you. She seems like the type of woman who would be interested in her family's expansion.'

'She wants the family to be expanded along the appropriate lines. She wants all of her grandchildren to be proper little Brits with the right accent and the right parents. She wants them all to have blue eyes and soft wavy hair.' Jane glanced over at Liz. 'You'd do nicely, in spite of being American. American would be just a little exotic. Certainly within the acceptable range.'

'Is she really that much of a plotter?'

'I think the potential is there. I've seen her checking over my friends and I think she's probably looking for someone appropriate for Tar, or even David, for that matter.'

'So when are you going to tell her about the baby? Are you waiting until the wedding is over?'

'I'm waiting to get on the plane. I'm leaving a note on her bed which she will find after she takes me to the airport. I'm telling her not to contact me until she's ready to be happy for me. She can't play games with me if I'm not on the pitch.'

'Families are so strange. Sometimes I think it's best not to have one.'

'Really? I wouldn't trade mine for anything. I know Mother can be awful sometimes, but I still love being a part of all of it. I think we all do.'

'Why? You can't even tell your own mother that you're pregnant.'

'It's like a dance, Liz. It's a dance and we all know our parts. I'm the rebellious one, David is the saint, Tar is the wild one, and Clairey is whatever everyone else wants her to be. I think we all quite enjoy it, really.'

'Why is Tar the wild one?' She tried to sound casual, unconcerned with his role in the family.

'You don't fancy Tar, do you?' Jane looked closely at Liz. 'You do, don't you? Yes, you're blushing. Damn, she was right again.'

'Who was right?'

'Mother. After she met you this evening she said you would be perfect for Tar.'

'What crap. Would she like to see my teeth, check my hooves?'

'What's the big problem? You like him, don't you?'

'I don't know if I do or not. I only met him this afternoon and talked to him for less than half an hour.'

'I can see that you're attracted to him.'

'Jane, he reminds me of someone, that's it.'

'Auntie Lou said she thought he looked a little like your friend who died.'

'Well, "Auntie Lou" is right. They could almost be twins. I'll admit that I do feel an attraction, but that's because of the resemblance, which is purely physical, by the way. Apart from looks, they seem very different.'

'Listen, Liz.' Jane sat on the bed next to her. 'Forget I said anything. I was really just fooling around. Relax and have some fun. Once you learn the dance, it's terrific.'

'I'm not sure I'm much of a dancer.'

'Give yourself a chance.'

Cotherstone, West Sussex, September 8th

Dearest O,

Do you believe in ghosts, in saints? We've never discussed religion. A strange omission for people who claim to want to know everything they can about the other.

We have ghosts. I'm not allowed to see them, but she assures me they come. Ellie comes after every jab of morphine. Before she was a ghost she was my mother's older sister. She and her unborn child died when she was fourteen. Sometimes Laura stops by for a visit. She was my grandmother. She was a drunk and a whore, but she named her daughters after queens.

We have other ghosts, I'm told. My Aunt Jane came by just yesterday. Jane was married to a solicitor in Singapore and died of heart failure about ten years ago. Mother always said that Jane had too much heart, in a ditzy sort of way.

Only one of the aunts has come by, as far as I know. Beryl has been here twice. My mother supposes that Rose is waiting for her in the car.

Edgar dropped in two days ago. He was a visitor I didn't expect, neither did Mum. She had to ask him who he was because she didn't recognize him. Edgar was my grandfather. I have his eyes. He was several years dead before my mother came to the family. Funny, but he still seemed to care about her. Another one who wants to hurry her along.

I've started thinking about the lot of them as the Elizabeth

Sinclair Randall Hagiography. These are the saints that matter to her. Much better than praying to St Jude if you think about it. They've started to matter to me.

I was baptized, but I wasn't confirmed. I never could understand the Trinity, but I do understand the ESR Hagiography. I've started praying to them, or with them. Quick prayer for luck when I think they might be listening.

Ellie is the easiest. She's an uncomplicated saint. She's earthy, basic and without guile. A Madonna with eyeliner, our Ellie. Remember the Dylan song, 'Forever Young'? That's Ellie.

Laura is complicated. She's the Magdalene of the ESR Hagiography. So stained, so soiled, and yet so pure. Soiled by semen, booze and lousy decisions. Yet so pure of intention, so pure of purpose. Some think that Christ was married to Mary Magdalene. I hope he was. I could support a man who liked a bit of rough. A man who could reconcile purity of purpose with lousy decisions. Laura always wears green and her hands are very important. I don't pretend to understand why.

Jane is an easy saint to like. She wants some lively company to while away the eternity that stretches before her. She wants to giggle about the mother-in-law and brag about her children to someone who loves them. She wants to try on the latest wings and eat heavenly manna with a girlfriend.

Beryl is deeply concerned about all the pain. She wants to make things better, whispers encouragement and promises relief. Overwhelmed with love for her only child, she sometimes cries, sometimes grabs the blankets and mounds them on the floor.

Edgar is a mystery. I almost wrote 'bit of a mystery', then realized that all mysteries are vast, at least when they involve saints and ghosts. I don't know if Edgar is a saint. I think he might be only a ghost. He upsets my mother. He's a bit confused over which of his sons is my father. Truth be told: my mother, aided by her shots of morphine, doesn't seem too clear about which brother is my father.

Saints and ghosts and questions of paternity. This has been my

*week. Amidst the bedpans, the jabs, the schedules, the tears, I have
begun to wonder who I really am.*

*Time is running short. Her breathing becomes worse with each
new spirit. Her colour seems to fade with every plea to join them.*

All my love

Mary

CHAPTER THIRTY-ONE

'Ellie was here again, did I tell you? I can't remember who I've
told.'

'You told me, Mum. She always comes after you get a jab.'
Mary adjusted the covers over her mother's feet. The books all
warned about not keeping any pressure on the feet.

'That's right. I hope I don't need jabs any more. Ellie said I
won't.' She tried to lick her lips, but her tongue couldn't reach
that far.

'Are you thirsty? Would you like to try a little water?'

'No, just dry.' She'd heard this part. They thought she was
asleep, but she'd heard them. Dehydration, the doctor said. It
was better than pneumonia. A swirl of dry leaves, she'd be. Dry
and curled, then gone.

Mary sprayed a little water into her mother's parted lips and
rubbed white cream on the cracked skin. 'Did anyone else come
to see you?'

'Maybe Beryl, but not Rose. Rose is busy with something.'

'I'll let you sleep now.'

'Wait.' She paused and tried to raise her hand. 'I want a mirror. Ellie said I looked bad.'

'First you rest.'

'How do I look?' Grey skin was pulled tighter across her fine bones as she attempted a smile.

'You look fine, Mum. I think Ellie's just trying to wind you up.'

'We like to tease each other.' Her eyes were closed as she slurred the words.

'I know, darling. You're just a couple of wild and crazy girls.' She whispered the words and ran her hand lightly across her mother's hair.

Foreshore, West Sussex, July 1967

'What do you think?' Jane turned around in front of Liz. She was wearing a bright yellow silk dress cut in a Chinese style. She'd pinned her hair back and festooned it with yellow and red flowers. On her ears were the biggest diamond earrings Liz had ever seen. 'Do I look terribly exotic?'

'You look darling.'

'But do I look exotic?'

'Do you want the truth?' Liz was adjusting a pink linen suit that Beryl had fallen in love with.

'Of course. I wouldn't ask if I didn't want the truth.' She adjusted a flower that had slipped its position in her hair.

'You look wonderful, but you remind me of a Caucasian waitress in a Chinese restaurant. Remember: you wanted an honest opinion.' She smiled to soften her words.

'Perfect.' Jane laughed as she slipped yellow stilettos on her feet. 'Mother has spent the last year pretending to ignore my marriage, and this will serve her right.'

'How's she going to react?' Liz felt like a mixed-breed spaniel next to a champion Pekinese as she adjusted Beryl's prized cameo on her suit.

'She's not going to react at all, not on the outside at least. I wouldn't do it if I thought she might pitch a fit and ruin Clairey's wedding. It will, however, make her see that I'm not going to pretend that Hugh and my life in Singapore don't exist. I've already told her I intend to come here every year for Christmas with Hugh and whatever children we've managed to produce. She's going to have to get used to seeing black eyes and hair around the table.' She tugged at the front of her dress. 'My breasts are killing me.' She turned sideways to the mirror and put her hands to her stomach. 'Can you see anything? I've gained just shy of a stone, but it feels it's all inside my bra.'

'I can't tell if you look any different, Jane. I just met you yesterday.'

'That's right, isn't it? Whenever I like someone I feel that I've known them forever. Of course, Auntie Lou has been keeping us up on you for the last few years, so I suppose I have known you for a long time.' She relaxed her stomach muscles and watched her belly swell the yellow silk. 'This is going to be so much fun. I can hardly wait to get really big. Do you want children someday?'

'I haven't really thought about it.' Jim was the one who had wanted children, and a house with two cars in the garage.

'I want lots of them. I want to be an old lady with two hundred descendants. I want there always to be a baby or two crawling along the floor.'

'Sounds awfully complicated.'

'I know, that's what I like about it. Hugh's great-great-grandmother is just like that. She's never alone and she's always surrounded by people who adore her.'

'There must be an easier way to be the centre of attention.'

'Maybe, but I love the idea of being the mother to generations of Changs. Have you seen Eurasians? They are the most beautiful people on earth and I'm going to have a dozen of them.' She reeled her belly back in and patted herself.

'Better you than me. I love to be alone and I think I'd go crazy if I was surrounded by people all the time.' Liz thought of the hospitals and the group meetings. The screams and the smells. She blinked quickly and looked at the clock. 'Aren't we supposed to be someplace in about three minutes?' India had instructed everyone that they were to be at the church no later than ten. It was now three minutes to the hour.

'Oh, fuck. Well, she won't even notice the time once she sees my dress.'

'You look wonderful. You don't even walk like a duck today.' Tarquin came up to where she stood, just outside the marquee. He smiled and handed her a glass filled with pale bubbling liquid. 'I thought you looked thirsty.'

'Thanks.' She took a sip and smiled. 'This tastes wonderful. I've never had it before.' She took a larger sip, almost finishing the glass.

'Really? Don't you drink your way through university in America? Most of us over here graduate with enlarged livers.'

'One of the drawbacks to starting early, I suppose. I graduated just before I turned eighteen and you can't even walk into a bar in California until you're twenty-one.' She took another swallow and looked at her now empty glass. 'This is really great stuff.'

'What an uncivilized country.'

'Which one?'

'Yours, my dear girl. What kind of place doesn't give pretty young girls champagne at an early age?'

'Is this a trick question?' Flirting wasn't all that hard once you got the hang of it. She tried putting her head to one side as she'd seen other girls do, but the motion, along with the wine, made her feel strange. 'It's the home of the brave and the land of the free and it was founded by English Puritans who didn't approve of this stuff or pretty girls.' Her skin felt warm under the bright sun. 'It's hot out here. I think I need another drink.' She took a glass from a tray as a waiter passed by.

'You'll want to pace yourself with that a bit. It can go to your head if you're not used to drinking.' He took another glass for himself.

'I want to have a wonderful time. I want to have the best time I've ever had. Do you know this is the first wedding I've ever been to?' She tapped her finger on his tie to drive her point home.

'Don't people get married in America?' He slipped her arm through his and walked her towards the white marquee.

'Sure, but I've never seen it happen. I'm not what you'd call a social butterfly.' She lowered her voice to a whisper, as though she were divulging a state secret. 'I was a goddamn nun until not that long ago.'

'Why were you a "goddamn nun"?' He leaned over and whispered in her ear.

'What?' She'd heard him the first time, but she liked the way his warm, moist breath felt on her ear.

'Why were you a "goddamn nun"?' He leaned closer this time, his mouth almost touching her ear.

'It seemed like a good idea at the time.' She stopped walking and turned to him. 'I'm not a nun any more.'

'Good for you. I, for one, am glad to hear it.'

They entered the marquee and Liz turned around slowly. 'This is really beautiful.' The tables were decorated with white and pink flowers planted in moss baskets. Garlands of blooms were hung about the place and even the napkins were wrapped in twists of ivy and jasmine.

'Mother wanted it to be perfect, since she's only getting to marry one daughter off properly.' He glanced at the seating chart near the door. 'We're right over there.' He took her elbow and steered her through the crowded tent, pausing several times to greet guests and introduce Liz.

'I think Mother got her wish; everything seems perfect.' Tarquin passed Liz a basket of rolls.

'Is your mother pleased with Clairey's choice of husband?'

Wonderful stuff in those glasses. She felt as charming and social as a sorority girl. She thought she probably looked a lot like Grace Kelly in *High Society*. The food was wonderful, and he looked so much like Jim.

'Yes, Evan is quite suitable. Boring and dull, but very suitable. You can dress Evan up and stand him in the best corners. Actually, I hear he comes from a long line of bores. Splendid chap. He and Clairey are the perfect match. It's wonderful that they found each other, because they could each drive any normal person to kill himself out of the sheer boredom of being in the same room.' He poured red wine into her glass.

'They couldn't be that bad.' She took a sip from her glass and felt the liquid warm her throat.

'They're worse. I pity the poor bloke who's his best man. He has to stand up there and make a humorous speech about Evan and his wedding night with Clairey. The man is so boring I'm sure his hand falls asleep when he's masturbating.' He whispered the last, leaning close to her.

'You're terrible!' She giggled and crossed her legs.

'Actually, I'm apparently quite good.' He widened his eyes and laughed. 'Sorry, the champers and all have made me a little cheeky. Forget I said that.'

'Tar?' The man stood behind Liz's chair, leaning heavily on two black silver-topped sticks.

'David! You did a damn fine job of giving Clairey away. You have my undying gratitude.' Tarquin grasped his brother by the elbow and laughed.

'Yes, I thought it went rather well. I manfully kept my tears to myself.' He chuckled and twisted himself towards Liz. 'You must be Lizzy.'

'Sorry, didn't realize that you two hadn't met. Liz, this is my big brother David.'

'It's wonderful to meet you. I was delighted when I heard you'd be spending some time with us.' He slipped the cane to his wrist and offered his hand. 'Are you enjoying yourself?'

'Yes, I'm having a wonderful time.' She took his hand and felt hers disappear inside it. His head and body seemed enormous in comparison with his almost childishly narrow hips.

'I've been giving Liz a crash course in champagne and wine.' Tarquin lifted his glass to Liz in salute.

'You'll have to excuse me, Liz. Duty calls, but my table is just over there and we'll have a chance to talk later today.' He smiled at her and then, leaning over, whispered something in his brother's ear which she couldn't hear.

Tarquin poured them each some more wine and took a deep swallow of his before he spoke. 'I'm surprised he didn't check to see if I'd washed my hands before lunch.'

'Is something wrong?' She watched as David made his way back to his table.

'No, I'd say things are just about perfect.' He leaned over and kissed her lightly on the lips.

'Good news, Liz. We've been invited down the road to the Browns'. They're having a little "after the party party".' He put his hand on her shoulder and she covered it with her own.

'Shouldn't I ask somebody something?' She was having a hard time getting her thoughts to move in a straight line.

'Shouldn't you what?'

'Is it all right to leave?' The bride and groom were gone, but the band was still playing. Some of the garlands had been pulled down to accessorize a conga line, but the waiters were still serving drinks. Liz was drinking her second Pimm's.

'Of course it's all right. Come on, chop-chop.' He put his arm around her waist and pulled her out of her chair.

She turned towards him and put her finger on the tip of his nose. 'Did I tell you that you look just like Jim?'

'More than once, Liz.'

'Really? Are you sure? I'd remember something like that because I just thought of it. Just now.' She put her hands on his shoulders to steady herself.

'Congratulations. You are in the middle of your first piss-up.'
'What?'
'You're drunk.'

'Just pull the smoke in, like this.' He sucked on the little ciga-rette and handed it to her.

'I've never had this before.' They sat in the summerhouse, lanterns swinging above their heads in a light breeze.

He exhaled and laughed. 'Didn't drink, didn't smoke. I always thought California was the place to be.'

'Not Clifford.' She took the narrow stick and made a tenta-tive pull on it. It reminded her of burning leaves in November.

'Harder. Get a lungful.' He took it from her and demon-strated, his chest rising, his shoulders pulled back as he sucked the acrid smoke down. 'See?' His teeth were clenched with the effort to keep the smoke in his lungs.

She took it from him and did as he'd instructed. She exhaled slowly and burrowed her head into his shoulder. 'I think you'd better take me back while I can still walk.' Closing her eyes for a moment, she slid through time, slid through space. She felt his hand move up her thigh as he pressed his mouth into her neck. 'Jim?' He was back from wherever he'd gone and she put her mouth on his, relieved that he had forgiven her.

Cotherstone, West Sussex, September 15th

Dearest O,

Everything takes so long. I keep thinking I'll walk into the room and she'll be gone, but there she is. Smaller, greyer, but there.

They're all here now; the whole ESR Hagiography has moved in. A cocktail party of the departed. Clearly they're more real to her than anything else now.

I almost helped her die last night. If I'd filled the syringe twice as full it would be over now. I would put away my apron, throw away the drugs and be myself again.

I didn't do it. I don't know why I didn't, but I didn't. Maybe the ESR Hagiography has work they need to do before she can die.

I'm not losing my mind. This would be much easier if I did lose my mind. Don't think I haven't tried.

I love you and miss you. May the ESR Hagiography make their light shine on you.

All my love

Mary

CHAPTER THIRTY-TWO

'Look.' Liz lifted her chin slightly and stared at the corner from her bed.

'What is it, Mum?' Mary watched her mother's mouth struggle to form words.

'See?' She watched them, watched them all. Ellie was the most impatient. For days she'd been trying to pull her from the bed.

'Darling, I can't see them. I know they're there, but I can't see them.' Mary felt the tears streaming down her face as she watched her mother smiling into the corner.

Foreshore, West Sussex, July 1967

'Liz, Lizzy.' A hand on her shoulder shook her and started the waves of nausea. She tried to swallow, but gagged instead.

'Just lie still and take it easy. It's David.'

'David.' The word echoed through her ears and she winced. 'Where am I?' A tiny belch raised noxious fumes to her mouth and she vomited on to the floor.

'You're in the summerhouse. Do you know how you got here?'

She wiped at her mouth. 'Tarquin. Where's Tarquin?'

'Never mind about him now. I'll take care of him later. Can you tell me how much you had to drink?'

'What time is it?' She was aware of a handkerchief wiping her face. Her eyeballs felt as though they had been rubbed with hot sand.

'It's about six in the morning. I've been looking for you for the last hour. Tar showed up and couldn't remember where he left you.'

'I'm going to be sick again.' She closed her eyes and took shallow breaths.

'Here. Take this and just be as still as you can. I'll be right back. I'm going to get you a doctor.'

She put her hand to her chest and found she was naked under a thin blanket. 'My clothes? Where are my clothes?'

'I don't know, but I'll find out.'

'God, I feel like such a fool.' It was six in the evening and she could finally sit up in bed. 'I can just imagine what your family thinks.'

'Oh, I wouldn't worry too much about that. Mother and Auntie Lou didn't even get out of bed until after two this afternoon. I think the only people who stayed anything close to sober yesterday were David and me. Frankly, if it weren't for this damned morning sickness, that lasts all day, I would be in pretty bad shape myself. That's what weddings are for, among other things.' Jane carefully painted her toenails with a dark vermilion polish, making her toes appear to be the victims of a bloody attack.

'I still can't believe your brother found me without my clothes on.' Liz turned on her side and pulled the covers up to her chin.

'I told David I'd find out about that. What do you remember?'

'Drinking is what I remember. Drinking and smoking one of Tarquin's hand-rolled cigarettes.'

'Did you have sex with Tar?' She stuck her foot out to get a better look at her toes. 'Don't be embarrassed. I'm not a prude. I certainly wasn't a virgin on my wedding night.'

'I don't want to talk about it, Jane. I really want to be left alone.' She'd had sex with someone. She thought it had been Jim; at least, last night he was Jim.

'It's not really that important, Liz. David is furious, but he's mad at Tar, not at you. He's already sent Tar back to London.'

'Jane, would you mind if I just slept?' The other girl's voice made her head pound.

'Not a problem. I'm going to go for a walk. Dinner is in an hour if you're hungry.'

'I'm never eating or drinking again.'

'That's what they all say.' She left the room, closing the door behind her.

Liz pulled her knees up to her chest, forming the tightest ball she could. Sent back to London. She closed her eyes, shutting away his face, and Jim's.

'I hope you like it. The Swan is one of the oldest pubs on the south coast.' He held the door open for her using one of his sticks.

'It's beautiful.' They walked into a small dining room with painted panels on the walls.

'This has always been a popular area for artists. The story is that the artists would trade their paintings for a meal and the paintings were later incorporated into the panelling. You'll see the work of some of these artists in museums all over the world.' He eased himself into a chair.

'This is how I thought a pub would look.'

'It's how a pub should look, but most of them aren't quite this attractive. This is one of the best.' He looked at her and smiled. 'I thought you deserved a treat after what happened with my brother.'

'I feel so stupid about that. If it's all right with you, I'd rather not discuss it.' It had been three days since the wedding.

'I feel that you're owed an explanation.'

'You don't owe me anything, David.'

'I owe you an explanation and an apology.' He held up his hand as she began to protest. 'I'm the head of the family and you are a guest in my family's home. I insist that you hear me out.'

'All right.' She looked down at her lap.

'First of all, Liz, the apology. I never should have allowed Tarquin to take you off like that. I know Tarquin's habits and, frankly, I assumed because of that I could trust him with you. I knew you weren't used to drink and I should have been monitoring what he was giving you. My only excuse is that I was busy trying be a host. It doesn't seem like much of an excuse in light of what happened to you.'

'Tarquin's habits? Does he make a habit of getting girls dead drunk and sleeping with them?'

'I thought you knew about Tarquin.'

'What about him?'

'Liz.' He leaned towards her slightly. 'Tarquin is not generally interested in women. He's a homosexual.'

'He's what?'

'He's a homosexual, at least for the most part.'

'Then what was that that happened with me?'

'I've spoken to him about it and he was also very drunk. No excuse on his part, certainly, but there you are.' He shrugged and looked away. 'I'm sorry, and I take full responsibility for what happened.'

'He was so drunk he thought I was another man? And I thought, well, never mind what I thought.' She thought it was because she looked like Grace Kelly, at least for one night. 'Why didn't Jane tell me? Why didn't *he* tell me?'

'He's quite open, quite himself in London, but he's very concerned about our mother's reaction. I'm the only one in the family he's confided in.'

'Incredible.' She wondered if all men looked and felt like Jim if you drank enough.

'I know what a damper this has put on things for you. I'd like to make it up to you.' He spoke quickly and put his hand up when she once again tried to interrupt him. 'I'm taking the next five days away from the office. I'd like you and Louise to be my guests on an insider's tour of England. I want this trip to be memorable, for the right reasons.'

'You don't have to do this.'

'Liz, I want to do it. I've already spoken to Louise and she's terribly excited about the whole idea. We don't want to disappoint her, do we?'

'No, I don't want to disappoint anyone.'

'Splendid. Now, let's order some lunch, shall we?'

'Fine. What would you recommend?' She studied the menu rather than allow herself to think about how much she wanted to get home to Beryl.

Foreshore, West Sussex, August 1967

'I wish you'd stay longer.' They sat on lawn chairs in the back garden.

'It's tempting, I've had a wonderful time.' The five days had been extended to sixteen.

'Then stay. You've only seen a small portion of what there is. I'd like to take you over to see a bit of France.'

'You need to get back to work, you said so yourself.'

'I could do some long weekends. I'll find the time.'

'Save the time until I return. I'm coming back as soon as I've got enough money set aside to see all of Europe. I've got a long list of ideas for articles I think I can sell.'

'So I have your solemn word that you'll be back?'

'You have my solemn word. I feel so at home here.' She looked around her at the house and grounds, already missing them.

'I hope you know the door is always open for you.'

'Thank you, David. That means a lot.' After a moment's hesitation, she leaned over and kissed his cheek. He turned his head and brushed his lips against hers.

Cotherstone, West Sussex, September 18th

Dearest O,

I'm having the housekeeper fax this to you and I'll call you tonight when it's all over. This late in the process is very predictable, according to the doctor.

   None of us really knows what to do or how to act. We just look at each, deer in headlights.

   I love you and I wish you were here, right now. Stay by the phone.

   All my love

   Mary

CHAPTER THIRTY-THREE

'I wanted you to know that I figured it out. It doesn't matter, it really doesn't. You picked the right man to raise me and he'll always be my father.

'I don't know what's going to happen after this, but I know we're going to be fine. Somehow we'll be fine. I know what you mean now about being a ditch-bank Okie Viking. I *am* made of strong stuff. I haven't done as well with your dying as I would have liked, but I've done better than I thought I could. Tomorrow, after you're gone, Chaz and I are going to write the obituary to put in the jar. I talked to him about it and we thought you'd like that.' She put her fist in her mouth, but it didn't stop the flow of tears.

Clifford, California, October 1967

'So, now you know the whole story.' She'd sat the three women down together. It seemed like the best way to deliver the news.

'How long have you known?' Beryl put her hand over Liz's and gave it a soft squeeze.

'I just got the test results this morning, but I've suspected for about three weeks.'

'I'd like to kill him. I can't believe my own cousin could do something like this.' Rose kept staring at the table in front of her.

'I got drunk, Aunt Rose. I have to take some responsibility for this too.'

'Who is going to be responsible for the baby, Liz? Have you thought about that?' She finally looked up as her voice got louder. 'Have you thought about what's going to happen if you go through with this?'

'Rose, keep your voice down! Can't you see the girl is upset?' Mrs Harper put her hand on her daughter's arm.

Liz pushed her hair back and crossed her arms across her lap, shielding its contents. 'Aunt Rose, I've thought of little else. I've got enough freelance work lined up to keep me busy for the next seven months. I've got enough money saved for first and last months' rent on an apartment. If you don't want me to stay, I won't. I'll understand if you prefer me to go. I'll understand, but I won't get rid of this and I won't give it away. This, what

I'm carrying, is my family, my blood, and I've already lost everyone else.' She leaned forward and sobbed into her knees. 'I won't get rid of it, no matter what you say.'

'Oh, Lizzy, don't listen to Rose. You know how she can be.' Beryl glared at the other woman. 'You are staying here and so is your baby.'

'Beryl, I just . . .' Rose held her hands up in supplication.

'Rose, get over here right now and give our daughter a hug and tell her you're sorry. We're going to be grandmothers and you're acting like a sorry old cow.'

Rose walked around the table and gathered the girl in her arms. 'It's going to be all right, hon. It's going to be all right.' She glared at Beryl over Liz's shoulder.

'Liz? Liz, there's someone here to see you' Mrs Harper called from the front room. Liz put aside the laundry she was folding and walked towards the voice.

'David!' She hurried towards him and kissed him briefly on the cheek. 'What are you doing here?'

'Auntie Lou called me.' He indicated the sofa with one of his sticks as Mrs Harper left the room. 'Can we sit down?'

'Sure. I can't believe you're here.'

'She told me about what's happened and I'm here to help.'

'That's very kind of you, it really is, but I'm fine. I've got some work lined up and I've got a home.' She bit her lip and looked away. 'It's not a good situation, but I'm going to be fine, so is my baby.'

'Liz . . .'

'Stop right now, David. It's taking everything I've got not to start bawling. I do that a lot.' Again the tears started and she accepted his handkerchief.

'I called Tarquin and told him.'

'I don't want to hear this.'

'He's willing to marry you. He would like to do the right thing and feels that the two of you could be good friends.'

'I think my baby deserves more than a sham marriage.'

'I agree. I've already told Tarquin that if you are going to marry anyone it is going to be me.'

'What? Didn't you hear what I just said?'

'I'm not suggesting a sham marriage, Liz. At least not on my part. I want to marry you and be a father to your child. I would like to have more children, but that will be up to you.'

'You want my child. You want to take me back so that India can have her grandchild.'

'I want to take you back with me because I love you. I know you don't love me, probably never will, but I think I can live with that. I only ask that you be discreet.'

'Discreet? You assume that if I marry you I'll sleep around? How dare you?' She grabbed one of his sticks and threw it across the room. 'How dare you come all this way and tell me you love me and in the same breath tell me that you expect me to cheat on you? How can you think I could ever treat you that way?

'I don't know what kind of love you need to make a marriage, but I know I wouldn't have anything to be discreet about.' She watched him and tried to see what life with him would be like. She walked around the room slowly, touching the familiar objects that would be so far away. She thought she felt her baby stir, but she knew that wouldn't happen for another six weeks. She thought about Ellie, and Laura, the poverty and the shame. She sat down beside him, staring straight ahead.

'Forgive me. I only wanted you to know that I want you in my life on any terms you find acceptable. I have loved you from the first moment I saw you, Liz. I denied it, especially to myself. I wanted to kill my brother, I really did. I didn't know I was capable of that sort of passion.

'You're a beautiful young girl and I'm a cripple who's much too old for you. You will no doubt outlive me and be a young widow living in a country that isn't your own. My physical limitations will always be a burden to you. On the plus side I can offer you a comfortable life with stability for you and your child. Don't say no right away. Take some time to think about it.'

'I wouldn't want the child to be told about Tarquin.' She glanced in his direction.

'Nor I. I think we should agree never to mention it again.'

'If we go to Nevada we can get married tonight.'

'You'll never regret this.'

'No, I don't think I will.' She took his face in her hands and kissed him.

CHAPTER THIRTY-FOUR

Cotherstone, West Sussex, September 18th

'Daddy?' Mary could see him sitting in the moonlight.

'Come in, dear. I was just keeping her company. Did I frighten you?'

'Not really. She's talked so much about Ellie and the others, I just thought . . . never mind.' Mary pulled a chair over and sat by her father.

'I was just telling her it was time for her to leave us.' He put his head in his hands and groaned.

'I'm glad you told her. I think she's been waiting for that.' She put her arms across her father's shoulders, felt the shaking. She held him until the shaking stopped.

'I wish I could have given her more. There's so much she missed because of me.'

'She doesn't feel that way, she's never felt that way.'

'I hope you're right. Your Uncle Tarquin told me the same thing earlier today.'

'He loved her too, didn't he?'

'Still does, I suppose, in his own way. If things had been a little different it could have been him sitting here now.' He rubbed at his temples for a moment. 'And I would have missed the most wonderful things in life.'

'Would you like me to stay up with you?'

'No, darling, you get some rest. I'll see her through. Maybe we'll even make it through to morning. Lizzy loves the morning.'

'You'll call us? You'll call us at the end?' She leaned over and kissed the top of her father's head.

'I'll call for you. Try to get some rest now.' After she left he leaned on his silver-tipped sticks and stood slowly. He bent down and kissed his wife's lips and the palm of each of her hands. 'I think your shrimp boats are finally here, Lizzy.'

CAREFUL MISTAKES

Joyce Mandeville

Where is Oprah when you need her?

So demands the long-widowed Jilly, a 40-something American facing a barrage of crises: she has a mother-in-law from hell, and a loving but terminally ill father, a retired bishop. Then on the day that she rushes off for the homecoming of college-age Chloe, her pride and joy of a daughter, the bishop dies and – bang – Chloe reveals she's pregnant.

Too much at once for some, but Jilly is a fighter and knows, too, that she is surrounded by people she loves – including best friend Sue, wayward Chloe and the good and sexy Elliott, Jilly's partner in lust and life. Love conquers all, but sometimes it takes over and suddenly, Jilly feels the time has come to take stock and create a future of her own . . .

'A witty and satisfying debut novel'
Home & Country

☐	Careful Mistakes	Joyce Mandeville	£5.99
☐	Stoats and Weasels	Kitty Ray	£6.99
☐	A Fine Restoration	Kitty Ray	£5.99
☐	The Oldest Obsession	Annette Motley	£5.99
☐	The Windfall	Prue Carmichael	£5.99

WARNER BOOKS

WARNER BOOKS
Cash Sales Department, P.O. Box 11, Falmouth, Cornwall, TR10 9EN
Tel: +44 (0) 1326 372400, Fax: +44 (0) 1326 374888
Email: books@barni.avel.co.uk

POST AND PACKING:
Payments can be made as follows: cheque, postal order (payable to Warner Books) or by credit cards. Do not send cash or currency.

All U.K. Orders	**FREE OF CHARGE**
E.E.C. & Overseas	25% of order value

Name (Block letters) . . . .

Address . . . .

. . . .

Post/zip code: . . . .

☐ Please keep me in touch with future Warner publications

☐ I enclose my remittance £ . . . .

☐ I wish to pay by Visa/Access/Mastercard/Eurocard

Card Expiry Date